DEAR BOSS:
THE HUNT FOR THE NEW YORK RIPPER

DEAR BOSS:
THE HUNT FOR THE NEW YORK RIPPER

LAWRENCE A. DE GRAW

Copyright © 2023 by Lawrence A. De Graw

Library of Congress Control Number: 2023900111
ISBN: Hardcover   978-1-6698-5652-8
              Softcover   978-1-6698-5651-1
              eBook   978-1-6698-5650-4

All rights reserved. No part of this book may be reproduced or transmitted in any form or by any means, electronic or mechanical, including photocopying, recording, or by any information storage and retrieval system, without permission in writing from the copyright owner.

This is a work of fiction. Names, characters, places and incidents either are the product of the author's imagination or are used fictitiously, and any resemblance to any actual persons, living or dead, events, or locales is entirely coincidental.

Any people depicted in stock imagery provided by Getty Images are models, and such images are being used for illustrative purposes only.
Certain stock imagery © Getty Images.

Print information available on the last page.

Rev. date: 01/20/2023

To order additional copies of this book, contact:
Xlibris
844-714-8691
www.Xlibris.com
Orders@Xlibris.com
848039

TABLE OF CONTENTS

An Opening Gambit: Tabram and Tabor on Commerce Street 1
   Walking Barrow 2
   A Killer Among Us 5
   Danger Close 7
   A Walk on the Wet Side 9
A View to a Kill: Novaks 11
   Pomeroy and Robles: The Tiger and the Bull 13
   A Captain's Mandate 20
   Pimleur's Way 23
   Ellen Macklin, Cub Reporter 28
   Skip Trace on Kettle: Who Was That Man? 33
   Macklin Meets Pomeroy on Grove Street 35
   Skip Trace on Kettle: Where Did He Go? 38
   Pimleur Reaches Out 41
   Pomeroy Meets Macklin: Setting the Rules 45
   The Grove Street Findings 47
   Pimleur's Worry: Macklin at the Coroner's Inquest 51
   Action9News: 1st Broadcast 58
Murder Most Foul: Chapel 60
   Dr. Richard Pimleur (Chapel) 65
   It All Comes Back to the Numbers 68
   The Captain's Progress Report I 70
   By the Numbers: Numerology or Algebra (Prysock) 75
   Action9News: 2nd Broadcast 77
   Volstad Plans His Third Kill 79
Berserker: The Double Event: Strunk 81
   Dr. Richard Pimleur (Strunk) 83
   The Captain's Progress Report II 86
   An Update for Prysock (I) 88
   Action9News: 3rd Broadcast 91
   The S Progress Report III 94
   Bogdan Volstad: A Killer's Profile 97
Berserker: The Double Event: Enders 98
   Volstad on Bedford 99
   Dr. Richard Pimleur (Enders) 102
   A Look at the Initials: The Big Reveal (I) 103
   Robles Catches a Break 104

- An Update for Prysock (II) 108
- The Big Powwow 110
- Action9News: 4th Broadcast 116
- In the House of Butchery and Contempt: Kirwin 119
  - Action9News: 4th Broadcast 122
  - Dr. Richard Pimleur 122
  - Action9News: 4th Broadcast 135
  - Pimleur Findings on Kirwin 135
  - Action9News: 4th Broadcast 136
  - A Roundtable Case Review: The Big Reveal (I) 136
  - Action9News: 4th Broadcast 146
  - The Ripper: Scourge of the News 146
  - A Roundtable Case Review: The Big Reveal (II) 150
  - Action9News: 4th Broadcast 150
- Bogdan Volstad: Revenge Tactic 157
  - An Evening Out for Two 159
  - Nights of Stalk and Prowl 165
  - A Ripperologist's Insight 167
  - Shots Ring Out in the Night 173
  - A Moment of Terror 175
  - Volstad Bolts: Beating a Hasty Retreat 178
  - The Captain Responds 180
  - A Profile Emerges 185
  - Follow Our Best Lead 190
- Brown and Bruner: Catherine and Water Street 195
  - Volstad the Butcher Meets Bruner 197
  - In the Course of Pursuit 201
  - Volstad Revealed 203
  - A Sluggish Recovery: Alhambra Nights 205
  - Volstad Returns 210
  - Finding the Long Way Home 213
  - Evil Stalks the Night 215
  - A Truth Told 215
- Tender Moments Dispirited 219
  - The Grinding of Teeth 223
  - Rounding a Corner 224
  - The Hell Out of Dodge 226
  - The Captain's Inquiry 227
  - Fear Goes for a Ride 229
  - Riding Shotgun 230
- A Persecution Most Real 232

- Pedal to the Metal: The Quickest Way Out 233
- Night Flight 235
- Out of the Line of Fire 236
- The Next Move Is Yours 240
- A Captain on the Edge 241

Parlor Games 243
- Stomping in the Mosh Pit 244
- Follow the Blood Trail 246
- Picking Up the Scent 247
- Any Port in a Storm 248

Terror Stalks the Night 251
- A Gnashing of Teeth 251
- Inner Sanctums 253
- A Stitch in Time 255
- The Long, Long Hall 257
- Two or More Blades 259
- Steeped in Blood 260
- Where the Trail Leads 260
- Closing in for the Kill 261
- Guns Down, Safeties Off 264
- A Deadly Ruse 266

The Knight-Errant 268
- Stay Put 270
- A Turn to the West 272
- 20-David Sergeant 274
- A Parting Shot 277
- Ears Up! 279
- In the Blink of an Eye 280
- Two Shots and a Quick Flight 281

The Captain Throws Down 282
- In the Turning of a Corner 282
- Loaded for Bear 283
- Run, Duck, and Shoot 283
- "Suspect is Down!" 285
- Blessed Are the Vested 285
- The Takedown 286
- Gun, Gun, Gun! 286
- Slow to Rise, Quick to Recover 288
- Officer Down 290

Endgame: A Dead Reckoning 293

A Prosecutor's Delight	295
"Justice Delayed Is Justice Denied"	297
A Tale of the Dragić	298
Pinca, Kielbasa, and Istrian Stew	300
Throw the Book At	301
The Last Escape	304
Epilogue: A Delicious Evil	307

TABRAM AND TABOR

"Jack the Ripper Under a Lamppost" is used courtesy of, and permission by, the Jack the Ripper Museum at: https://www.jacktherippermuseum.com/.

AN OPENING GAMBIT: TABRAM AND TABOR ON COMMERCE STREET

7 AUGUST—PRESENT DAY

Historically, much had happened on the date of August 7, as indeed somewhere in the world it would mark the birth of the infamous courtesan and failed spy Mata Hari in the Netherlands in 1847. In World War II, it would mark the bloody beginnings of the Allied invasion landings at Guadalcanal in 1942, as Tulagi and Henderson Field soon went up in flames in advance of the amphibious assault on the beach. In 1944, a young IBM Corporation much on the rise would find its footing in a brand-new data-processing industry by unveiling its rollout of a prototypical ASCC automated calculator that would be called the "Harvard Mark 1." And in a series of seedy dark-shadowed alleys and backstreets of old London town, a fleshed and bloodied Jack the Ripper would indulge his lustful and savage urges as he ran wild and terrorized the citizens of Whitechapel in late 1888.

And on at least one of those London fog evenings, it was even then that a tipsy Martha Tabram would stagger about her seedy underworld and sit down with "Pearly Poll" and two soldiers at a tavern called the *Angel and the Crown*, just off George Yard, to savor a pint of ale with friends. Much would still need to be done to even "finalize" the very payment terms of their nightly trysts, and the two men must pay up first before they could even indulge their lustful urges.

Carnal pleasures were the note of the day, and soon enough monies would change hands to seal the agreement, and the two ladies of the evening would split up and walk off into the London mist with their respective clients. But it would also be the last time Tabram would ever be seen alive, soon enough to be found at the place of her final undoing on a step landing in a dark hallway of a George Yard tenement.

Jack would have taken his first victim that night—*perhaps*. Or perhaps it was just the studied speculation of the many present-day "Ripperologists" who only now might hint that he had even done so. Of the five lost women that old "Saucy Jack" was alleged to have slain in steeped blood in his time, had it been only Polly Nichols, from the list of the ACCEPTED canonical five that would most matter as his "first" on August 31? Or had it indeed been otherwise? Might it indeed have been the debaucherous Tabram herself on a far earlier date of August 7?

The debate would rage on for more than a century—a century of dark uncertainty and years of piecing together the many puzzle parts left behind by the slasher himself. Only now had it become more and more likely and almost accepted as truth. Could Martha Tabram have been Jack's own *first*, with others following in suit with their own foul deeds? Perhaps it had truly been so, much as it would be all these years later ...

☙☙☙

Padding the dark and deeply shadowed lanes just at the end of Barrow Street in New York City's own West Greenwich Village, old Martin Tabor stumbled along with a halting gait, head down and collar turned up against the trespass of cool pelting rain. Heavy with sorrow by the burdening news he'd just received earlier in the day, the ailing seventy-nine-year-old veteran had just been given a virtual death sentence with a chilling diagnosis of a stage-4 renal cell carcinoma that was even now slowly eating away at his kidneys with an immeasurable decay. Indeed, for the better part of his life, in fact, it was a condition he didn't even know he had, but one with which he'd now have to cope as best he could.

And thus the old man ambled on in silent solitude with coupled misery, much as distracting visions of a life gone by flashed through his head like a series of daguerreotype stills that seemed ever in motion. They were stills of a lifelong past and a life well-lived, snapshots of a time fraught with high adventure and daring exploit, of a life lived voraciously and without regret, always pushing the envelope with seemingly slight regard.

Born in late 1945, old Martin Tabor had been too young to be a conscript in any of the service branches in World War II and had instead found that his niche and time could only come much later during the early years of the Vietnam conflict itself. And when indeed it was his turn to volunteer, he had decidedly gone "naval aviation" all the way since, in his estimation, what else was there?

An Opening Gambit: Tabram and Tabor on Commerce Street

The old soul continued walking, now sauntering past a recessed, low-walled courtyard, a dark niche that was heavily foliated and nestled between two red-brick buildings just at the very end of the narrow lane that was itself Commerce Street. It was an open gate to a rarely seen city garden that was at once dark and forbidding—frightening both for its eeriness and the very absence of light. And strolling along with stark memories, a saddened heart, and waning health, old Tabor could not have known just what might await him only steps away.

But returning on the moment to his dated reflections instead, he could almost too easily recall his aviation days—days of speed and high jinx in aerial combat—remembering all as if it had been only yesterday. And from the outset, he'd been drawn to the finest aircraft of the day, the all-weather A-4E *Skyhawk*—the Grumman-built attack plane. "A pilot's choice," they'd called it, the one with the fat, stubby wings and a heavy-duty undercarriage that could carry a full shitload of ordinance and deliver it on target any place, anywhere, anytime.

Old Tabor could only dream on further in his stroll down memory lane, as he continued walking the dark backstreets of west Greenwich Village. And almost at the instant was the old man carried back to a distant past, much as if it had been only yesterday, and he was right back home in his *Skyhawk* cockpit.

"Foxtrot 7," the midnight call had begun as he punched in on his radio comm. "Foxtrot 7 attack force leader calling feet dry at 2347," he remembered reporting just as he flew on with his first toehold over dry land. The aircraft, part of the battling VA-164 Air Group itself, had just entered contested airspace over South Vietnam after jumping off the deck of the *Essex*-class carrier USS *Oriskany* (CV-34) with a full complement of attack planes and a payload of deliverable armament.

The flight commander's target package had that night been tasked as an intensely troublesome cluster of missile hardstands and SAM sites just near Biên Hòa, the enemy's in-country seat of virtually all North Vietnamese surface-to-air-missile launch sites. In fact, it was well known that these very sites were already taking a big toll on American aviators overflying the area.

"The sites must be neutralized," he remembered being told by the squadron commanders, and now it was simply his turn to go in and lead the charge to eliminate the enemy threat in full.

Then, moments held in deep suspense as the very worst of the worst seemed to unfold, as the flight leader tickled the comm button and relayed his discovery to his wingmen, even as miles away the Air Boss himself listened in from the bridge of the carrier.

"*Oriskany*, I've got missile tone, missile tone. Negative, I've got full lock at this time," came the harried, long-distance cry from the lead pilot of the probing naval attack force, himself now quickly "punching the chaff" of decoying aluminum strips from his fast-moving jet while initiating evasive maneuvers.

Only then would come the interminable lapse of time and a freeze of action, followed closely by the even more menacing call that none might ever wish to hear: "Foxtrot-4 is hit—say again, Foxtrot-4 has been hit—no chute, no chute, no chute," the voice had said as it trailed off into the night.

The impactful words still rattled around emptily inside the old man's head, even now all these years later—and perhaps especially now—just as he walked the late-night paths of old Greenwich Village in late July. And even at the moment the elder Tabor was already fast approaching the Commerce Street "elbow" at its most western end, just as it emptied into the crooked meeting place and the odd confluence with Barrow itself.

And thus the old vet labored on with halting gait, soon tripping past the area's best version of a scaled-down off-Broadway venue touted as the Cherry Lane Theater now just across the way from him, with its nightly troupe of stage actors and off-center plays.

Now the old soul sauntered past a recessed, low-walled courtyard, a dark niche that was heavily foliated and nestled between two red-brick buildings just at the end of the narrow lane. It was a gated opening to a rarely seen city garden that was at once dark and forbidding—frightening both for its quiet eeriness and the very absence of light. The aged man continued strolling along and nursing his dark memories, much with a saddened heart and waning health, and old Tabor could not at all have known just what might await him only steps away.

For all the world might the shadowy stalker have most resembled a swarthy Slav, one perhaps hailing from some distant Baltic state just at the northern edge of the Adriatic Sea somewhere, but he was not. Instead, he was simply a nameless man of nameless origin—a sheep of never and a man from nowhere. A revenant whose favorite thought embraced the idea, "If you don't know where you're going, then you're probably already there." How strange indeed. He was an enigma enshrouded in mystery and a man who most thrived in dead of night, one who shuffled with stealth and hot swiftness through his dark underworld, always stalking shadows, much as he had proposed to do this very night. As well indeed he might already have his mark.

Now the shadow man held tight the breath and knitted the brow, clenched the teeth, and made ready the keen-edged knife for the bloody work he now so cruelly intended. All this even as old Tabor ambled into view lost in deep thought, oblivious to all and carrying his bushel of woes. And thus the cunning attacker pressed himself hard against the shadows of the walls of the building next to which he stood, just inside the small but leafy courtyard just at the end of a curving and intersecting Commerce Street in west Greenwich Village.

The old man was only steps away from the open-gated courtyard entrance, much the better for the evil stalker. It would be quick work indeed to strike out and pull the old man back ever deeper into the shadows of the small city garden.

The area had already been carefully selected by the slasher and was ideal for feeding the intent of his foul deeds. He had taken special care in selecting both his target and the kill-site alike, and knew the attack itself would be sudden, vicious and decidedly not random at all—he had already found his intended target.

The hidden figure listened carefully for old Tabor's footfalls even as the man approached nearer, nearer to his place of crouching. Then he lunged forward, in an instant clapping a large hand over the old man's mouth and stifling all sound before its very pronouncement. Now with a grunt and a tug of brute force did he strong-arm the elder victim back, back, back into the leafy overhang of the shadowy garden courtyard, quickly placing the long and slender blade just at the man's throat, and without hesitation swiping left to right—once-twice. And in seconds had the fiendish deed been done.

> Dear Boss:
>
> I ripped this goat for sport and folly;
> Expect another just for jolly.
> A feast of carnage with each man,
> Look to catch me if you can.
>
> Signed, Red Jack

The frail mass of the old man's form had already begun slumping to the ground heavily, slipping like a dead weight that the killer now simply let fall almost where it had stood, and all without sound, without resistance or note of interest by any nearby, and much of it without remorse.

"DEAR BOSS," the blood-thirsty rogue muttered to himself, much with an evil contentment that spoke volumes unto itself, this as he coolly reveled in the raw effusion of blood, almost savoring the man's faltering last breaths. Then he set about the gruesome task of laying out the scene, stepping carefully through the several ritualistic labors that he had set out for himself. All of which he seemed to now so richly enjoy, even in his plaguing sickness: the horrid tasks of lavishly abusing the corpse, staging the kill scene, and adding his own "signature" placements—all of it a macabre collection of tricks and hallmark rituals that would only later allow him to relive each crime in full much at his leisure.

Quick and quiet then did the Butcher now go about the dark, unsavory business of carefully organizing the calling-card "trinkets" about the slain man's form—much of which he would soon come to be known for himself: a single red Jack playing card and the phrase "Redrum" scrawled hastily across the forehead in the victim's blood. Found also would be the grisly and taunting note folded neatly and tucked just inside the victim's mouth.

Pulling himself slowly upright, the villain wiped clean the felon's blade as he slipped out of the courtyard with a swiveling view to both his left and right. Pulling fast the light trench coat about him, the slippery eel of a killer took a moment to secret the bloodied knife in its under-jacket sheath, then simply melted off into a drizzle of spotty rain and headed east across an otherwise unpeopled street in dead of night. And in an instant, he was gone.

The frightful Village Slasher had dared both circumstance and discovery to the teeth and had delighted in his first kill. Now might he only wish to have more, since indeed there was much work yet to be done. And in but a tick of the clock had old Martin Tabor quickly become Red Jack's own Martha Tabram. But the ruthless slasher knew this victim would only be the first of many yet to come ...

Old Martin Tabor had continued plodding along, ever disfavoring the right leg with an annoying imbalance that had always kept him slightly off-kilter and constantly re-correcting his carriage and standing, much like a drunken man sauntering unsteadily from a Third Avenue bar. Inevitably, it was always about gait and balance—unfailingly and much to his detriment—and he knew he might be faltering on both counts.

A battery of savvy doctors had told him long before that it was a rare condition called BPPV, a kind of benign vertigo that only too often had him staggering about with mild dizziness and disorientation that for all the world left him careening about and forever plagued with labored walking.

So he pulled tight the collar of the light jacket around his neck as if to snugly stay the rain, but cursed himself for not having worn a hat. He was getting wet and did not like it.

Still much in the moment and still quite in his head, however, he simply cycled back to the studied remembrances he'd enjoyed but only moments earlier, and was right back over the darkened skies of Biên Hòa in war-torn Vietnam.

DEAR BOSS: The Hunt for the New York Ripper

"Foxtrot 7-Foxtrot 7, we've got missile tone—negative, negative—missile lock!" was all he managed to get out to his wingman, breaking radio silence just before he got hit. And now, however hard he might try, his mind kept calling back the haunting words of more than four decades past. "Foxtrot 7—danger close, danger close!"

In his present state, as he sauntered along the dimly lit Commerce Street, Tabor could only feel his legs hurting—throbbing like the very devil itself—still with a block to go before the real comfort of his home. So he bravely pushed on under a pelt of rain that dampened both his form and spirit, seemingly without relent.

The old refurbished "pre-war" building he'd called home for so many years was now just around the corner from the Commerce Street bend, just at the end of Barrow, near Hudson, and in his mind, he could only relish a warm bath and a hot meal once there. He comforted himself with thoughts of an evening at home in his rent-controlled flat, dry and fattened by a plate of hot food, after which he might simply languish in his favorite armchair and indulge his fancy of watching some old cops-and-robber film—preferably in a classic black-and-white format. Or perhaps just some old "bang-bang-shoot-'em-up" Western instead, he mused to himself with a mild chuckle. Or who knew, perhaps even *both* were he so inclined.

All this the ailing old vet considered with a half smile and warm anticipation, just as he approached the open gate that led to the courtyard garden couched between the two red buildings just at the corner of Commerce opposite the cozy backstreet playhouse. Ah, how utterly convenient all of it must have been for the murderous lurker hidden just in the shadows nearby.

Seemingly unable to contain his native curiosity, old Tabor casually turned to look at the theater offering, struggling with aging eyes at a squint to read the title of the stage play that emblazoned its playbill across the night street and bannered its name over the small theater marquee, but he could not.

What did that infernal sign say anyway? the old man could not help but wonder. And why can't I even read the damn thing from here? he almost muttered out loud. He was a man suffering with insufferable pain, and a man angry at that very suffering, often cursing his dysfunctional legs, his eyes—his very age.

And then he felt the snatch and cruel embrace from directly behind him, the pull and throttling choke as he was hurtled backward into the shadowy gateway. The massive arm and brutish strength seemed to only drag him in further, further, further, back into the dark of the small and leafy courtyard, soon enough to meet the sharp of the killer's blade that now sat poised at his throat, the biting edge striking brutishly once-twice, then all went dark.

Old Tabor was slowly fading out now, locked in the last of his death throes, and the old man could only struggle feebly, effusing blood with a muted gurgle and slumping gracelessly to the ground, recalling one thing above all else: "Danger close—danger close," and then he slipped away and died a death that was itself only ironically profane.

☙☙☙

It had decidedly not escaped the view of many that much of the metropolitan New York area had already experienced an unseasonably wet month for August, at least for this year, now at the end of an already record-hot summer. Temps had soared insufferably, scorching through much of June and July, only to cool off significantly by mid-August. Unusual for this time of year, temperatures had flown much in the face of the calendar itself, obeying nothing, and were indeed quite uncommon for the season, just now at the lag end of summer.

A fairly wet autumnal wave had ushered in an early nip in the air as well—much to the surprise of all—and a spate of rain seemed to kick off almost nightly without fail or relent. For trees, plants, and a slimy assortment of mud-caked frogs, it was probably a welcome drench. For New Yorkers across all five boroughs, however, it was probably just a pain in the ass. All was soak and saturation, and to most people, it was simply a source of mild irritation and much inconvenience. And even now a light swirl of drizzle was already dropping a curtain of mist that seemed to suspend itself with dreary hanging.

This then would be the climatic backdrop against which a spate of the city's most horrific murders would begin to unfold, each homicide unprecedented and unspeakable in its very degree of butchery and barbarity. And soon the city would itself be quite on guard, walking a razor's edge, with many afraid to venture out into the night. But even that would be surpassed by the terrifying and seemingly *specific* demographic within the city's population: elderly men were being targeted, and veterans of foreign wars were now being savaged and pulled into evil focus. But why—and perhaps even more importantly—*who* might be responsible for the series of unspeakable crimes themselves?

And thus the locals of New York City's own west Greenwich Village could only hold their collective breaths and loosely ponder the answer to those very concerns. Might the citizens themselves be afraid to even learn the answers to those same questions, or even solve the mystery of the killings that would soon plague that very community? None could have known that the killings of the old men might already have begun …

A VIEW TO A KILL: NOVAKS

31 AUGUST—PRESENT DAY

Only the steady tap-tap-tap of the old man's cane could be heard in soft cadence to the shuffling footsteps that scuffed along the sidewalk on Grove Street, just at Seventh Avenue South in New York's famed west Greenwich Village. For now, it was an unusually cool and rainy August night in one of the city's liveliest nightspots, with the smells of good food wafting out from the several pricey, upscale restaurants in the neighborhood, and the sounds of sweet jazz thumping out onto the sidewalks from places like the Village Vanguard, Sweet Basil, and the cross-street hipster hangout the Garage.

It had long been known that the street lighting along this easternmost edge of Grove Street, at least here at its nexus with Seventh Avenue South, was at its best poor—at its worst, almost non-existent. Much as it was this night, even as the old codger hobbled along with studied deliberation, his slowed footfalls echoed lightly off the façades of the old buildings that fronted either side of the street, such that amplified their every sound.

For now, the eighty-year-old Paul Novaks picked his way slowly along, carefully eyeing his footing and dodging any potential slippery spots that may have puddled up as a result of the steadied drizzle that continued to fall. The old man was himself but an aging veteran who seemed of late to be constantly nursing an old injury left over from the Korean War during the early 1950s. He'd taken a hip full of lead and shrapnel from an incoming mortar round that had landed a skosh too close for comfort during the landings at Inchon, and he'd paid the price in pain and lifelong suffering.

And when he had returned home from the fires of war, he had carried with him the stench of death, the tears of great loss, and the anger of a hundred dead men. And what a living hell it had been too, he recalled, even all these years later, his face almost contorting into a wince that he could only hope to smother from outside view. And for now, at least he wished to only get home, and soon enough indeed to be back in his modest flat on Cornelia Street, where he might enjoy perhaps some respite and food before retiring for the evening.

And so he mused on, fixed on a time long past and laboring along the broad end of an isosceles triangle of a block that was itself Grove Street, bordered on one short side by Bleecker and on the other by Seventh Avenue South, only to finally end and merge a half block down. His head cocked down to carefully survey the very passage of his way, the old man was otherwise unmindful of much else occurring around him. Now he paused midstride, turning his head ever slightly ... there'd been a sound—an odd sound—much like the hiss of a snake or the tinkling of tin metal, such that had caught his aged ears and piqued his struggling interest. And thus had he never once seen the shady, hooded figure that held back in the shadows, lurking suspiciously in an unlit recessed doorway in the middle of the dark and shortened street.

Sadly, it would also prove to be his very last mistake, even as the slippery shadow emerged from its seat of darkness, the gloved hand shooting forward from behind, almost embracing the neck and immediately exposing the throat. Then would come the ripper blade and slice of death. Then would he feel the biting edge of the knife cutting deep—once-twice—slicing cruelly with a left-to-right swipe from a practiced hand, followed by a horrid outpouring of blood. And yet few saw a thing and none saw all.

Now staying his very retreat from the scene, the killer lingered just long enough to crudely pen in bold print across the brow of the old man a simple word, "REDRUM," and carefully placed on the victim's chest a single playing card—a red Jack, to be certain—now also with a neatly folded note carefully placed just inside the slain man's mouth. And etched across its very face was the cryptic and all-too-familiar "DEAR BOSS—catch me if you can" scrawl, both taunting and evil. And emblazoned across its open page was a cryptic series of numbers that were rendered only as 515200 00605. But what indeed might be said of any of it, and what might any of it even mean?

His very life flashing before his eyes, even as he saw less and less of the light and slowly passed on, the old veteran could not help but think that as a younger man, he might indeed have been able to grapple with (and perhaps even best) his man in battle, but he was not. He was but an old man, now but flaccidly enfeebled by his very age. And so he could not at all resist the brute-force attack that had now so fiercely been thrust upon him. And for now, might he only succumb to the slashing assault, recalling only the bright lights and passing cars that could still be seen but a few steps away on Seventh Avenue South.

And yet no one person ever heard a sound or saw a thing, and only the night's shuttling darkness pressed down upon him as it swallowed up the victim's mute cries and masked his very killing. And in an instant, close upon the heels of the killer's final ritual of the "placement of the objects"—on and about the body itself—the contemptible cutthroat had already turned his corner and sped quickly off into the press of the crowd. And for all intents and purposes, the man was simply gone.

"Make mine black, Robles—couple of sugars maybe. Hell, just bring me TWO cups already—one for each eye," said the senior man with a comic wink. "Something tells me I'll probably need a running start today!"

The wry comment had come from the seasoned homicide detective Sergeant Joe Pomeroy and had been directed at his junior partner of five years, Detective Damien Robles. But to most in the precinct house who knew them, the two couldn't have been more of a Mutt and Jeff pair if ever there were one. Pomeroy was a cop of great stature and standing about 6'3". Robles, on the other hand, was far more squat and strapping as the 5'8" bull of a man he was, well-built enough to fully offset his size and stature. It was Robles himself who had once said that his physique was simply the result of a "poor man's" workout—a hot, pump-it-up regimen of energy bursts done entirely on the cheap. No gyms or fancy exercise salons for him, he'd once told his boss Pomeroy, just hard double-tap, bare-knuckled push-ups on the floor, and even that at an astonishing interval of twenty push-ups every twenty minutes. Ah, the very insanity of it! The two men had continued to work quite well together though, a weird kind of yin-and-yang, and both seemed to love cajoling each other, much as they were precisely on the moment.

"Well, we better make that coffee to go, boss. The cap is calling us into the bullpen for a consult—and she didn't look very happy either. Anyway, she said her office now, Joe," said Robles, referring to their immediate supervisor, the highly decorated head of one of the city's most active Major Crimes Unit herself, Captain Angie Fuller.

Aw hell, opined the senior man uneasily to himself, a call to the "bullpen" could only mean one of two things: either he'd screwed up on a case, or they were about to dump a new one on him—something, of course, that would land right in his lap. He'd been on the job for some ten years now, and in that time had learned to quickly read the writing on the wall, and to stay as far away from the politics of the job as he could.

Here, above all else was a "cop's cop"—an investigator and a closer who could easily boast of a near impeccable service record, numerous valor awards, and more felony collars than most in the stationhouse could ever hope to shake a stick at, and to a person he was simply "good police." It's not that he was a fast-tracker per se—hell, he never sought the fame. He was just good at what he did, and reward and advancement had come quickly, based more on merit and not at all owing to favor or even whom he knew. Fame had come only on the heels of his many successes, following along behind him like a puppy dog he didn't quite want but would not necessarily turn his back on.

"You know you're going to be impossible to live with today, don't you? All that coffee's going to give you the jitters, and I'm the one who gets to ride with you all day. Gee, thanks," Robles ribbed his partner with a half-smile and a poke of an elbow as they headed for the door.

"Okay, wise guy, how about just giving me my joe and maybe put a cork in it. C'mon, let's just go see the boss already," said Pomeroy as he took off at a clip, now with Robles in quick tow as both men headed in the direction of the Captain's office forthwith.

All about the two detectives as they strolled purposely across the squad room floor was a milieu that might itself have been a page torn from a book that was typical of a New York City police precinct in any of the five boroughs. Old gray Steelcraft desks, rolling bulletin boards, coffee urns, and an assortment of glass-partitioned cubicles that all seemed to dot the building's landscape, accented by an otherwise drab interior that simply had to be depressing, both to those working the "house" and to those few unfortunates just "passing through." Those few being booked, that is, before being shipped off to yet other holding facilities at other even less-glamorous locations like those called the MCC, Riker's, and the "Tombs." And everywhere came the sound of phones ringing and a general clamor of noise that probably went up to the rafters. Added to this was a general hustle-and-bustle of movement and activity, such that seemed to permeate the very air like a static crackle coursing through a beehive.

"Pomeroy, Robles, get your butts in here—chop-chop," said Captain Fuller with a squint of an eye and an impatient tone after spotting the two approaching her office. Never a good sign when it's your boss calling you in, whatever the reason. Fuller, a sharp-eyed intuitive leader with an abundance of field experience already under her belt, was a fifteen-year veteran of the force who'd only recently been bumped up to a new command as the head of one of the city's Major Crimes Units, in one of lower Manhattan's busier districts, that being much of the downtown area and Greenwich Village itself. But she was also known to be a bit of a disciplinarian and a hard-ass—when the need served her—and was often seen as a somewhat humorless sort, perhaps even one to entirely avoid at all costs, if at all possible. But avoiding her today was not a working option for either of her subordinate detectives.

Pomeroy took Fuller's sharp directive order in stride, now waiting an obligatory five seconds to digest what was happening and to see just whose head was on the block if any. But the seasoned detective only stared intently out the captain's office window instead, surveying the grime and rain streaks on the outside pane. He could see across the street from the 6th Precinct window itself, and couldn't help but take in the refurbished façades of the several older pre-war buildings that lined the narrow street, most of which could have pre-dated the 1950s. And all of them sat in a neighborhood that was itself being slowly gentrified, revitalized, and reclaimed by an influx of upscale Wall Street millennials.

Perhaps wanting to be just a little closer to the high-life action, without having to live over in any of the outlying boroughs, it was far better to not have to pay outrageous sums for a small one-bedroom condo on the Upper East Side. Or even try to ante up on an even steeper price tag for a "studio" on an even more inaccessible Central Park West.

And for at least a few select downtowners—the "new-money" up-and-comers that made up a whole new class of nouveau riche—clearly there'd be no "bridges or tunnels" in their immediate future. They'd just simply live right here in old Greenwich Village, now a neighborhood but newly defined. It was a semiformal lifestyle with a kicked-back look and feel that was just shy of being a little too much of a little too posh—if that were even a thing.

Zooming back in, Pomeroy in time completed his dusty virtual tour of the world just outside the boss's window but had still kept one ear cocked lest he missed any tidbit of relevant information. And at length, he turned his gaze back to his immediate superior and waited for the other shoe to drop. Quickly he found he need not wait too long.

Perhaps one of Manhattan's most preeminent medical examiners, the good Dr. Richard Pimleur's studied view of the murder scene at this point as he continued squatting low and examining the body of the slain elder man who lay sprawled in a growing pool of blood across the Grove Street sidewalk—was that none of this could be classified as "accidental" in any way, or by any rational standard. Most of it stank of premeditation—pure and simple—a well-orchestrated and rancid act of violence, such that was not often seen, even here in the odd end of New York City.

There could be no question about it, the M. E. thought to himself soberly. The very mention of the whole thing might already summon up the dark and dreadful images of late 1888, when a certain bloodthirsty butcher named Jack the Ripper roamed the alleys and backstreets of Whitechapel, London.

Only this was New York, almost two decades into the new millennium. So what in hell was this, questioned a puzzled Pimleur, just as an unmarked vehicle appeared on the near horizon. He was just about to cover up the body from public viewing when the black unmarked Crown Imperial carrying Pomeroy and Robles rolled up on the scene and ground to a screeching halt.

"Okay, so here's the plan going in, Junior. So listen up, and don't go jumping off the deep end of the pool," the senior detective said before they had even exited the vehicle. "Forget about Pimleur. I need you to just concentrate on the crime scene—I mean really look at the crime scene—even better, simply *walk* the scene—always make certain to walk the scene.

"Understand what you're looking at, Robles, listen carefully to what it's telling you and understand what clues it's trying to give up. We'll gather as much hard data as we can, get all of it bagged and tagged and back to the lab, then we'll take it from there, savvy?" Pomeroy concluded as he wrapped up his Homicide 101 lesson plan for the moment.

His junior man was still a little new to the job and just green enough to still have a touch of wetness behind the ears, and every tidbit of instruction was all very much a part of the man's training cycle to make him a good (or certainly a *better*) Major Crimes investigator. Then the two opened the doors of the car and sauntered over to the crowd of police that was already huddled around the crime scene itself.

"Well, well—lookie here what the cat dragged in," said Pimleur, wasting no time and already starting in with his ribs and jabs at the younger Robles fairly immediately, almost before his feet even hit the ground. Himself a stocky, bearded man in his midforties with thick glasses and a receding hairline, the man was already known in his field to be a forensic genius, albeit one with a discernible attitude. He was an irascible sort with a grin and a biting joke around every corner. Highly competent but annoying to a fault.

"If it's not Pomeroy and Robles. Well, it's about damn time. What happened, you guys just get sidetracked by some doughnut factory somewhere?" he said as he needled the two detectives with the sly smile of a neighborly heckler. "I've been here for the better part of fifteen minutes already waiting for you guys to traipse in. 'Smatter with you guys anyway?"

God, how I hate this guy, was all Robles could think to himself as he walked his way over from the vehicle and began sizing up the scene and the situation. Pomeroy, instinctively sensing his partner's intense dislike for the fat, smarmy forensics guy, placed a restraining hand on the junior man's arm to perhaps calm him down and maintain some semblance of good civility in their joint investigation. After all, the senior detective reasoned rightly, they did all have to work together— however infrequently—and would probably have to do so in the foreseeable future as well. Better to keep a cap on the hostility now than to have to quell the raging fires later on. And there perhaps an end.

"Okay, how about you two just cool it" was all Pomeroy said, somewhat affecting a tone of authority, perhaps his best attempt at trying to defuse the friction between the two before it even flared up.

"What can I tell you, Pimleur, the captain had us both tied up at the station on a predispatch briefing when the call first came in. Have to tell you, from everything I'm hearing, if this is NOT a crisis, it'll certainly do until another one comes along. Anyway, that said, what exactly do we have here?"

"Male, Caucasian, age somewhere between seventy-five and eighty years old, estimating about 5'9", 150 pounds—maybe wet. Full lividity has not quite set in yet, and cause of death is probable as being 'massive exsanguination' from these double slash marks across the throat," said the good ME as Robles fought back a retching urge. "And even that nearly ear-to-ear.

"It's a pretty bad one, men—and your guy must have bled out in minutes, I suspect. Everything I see here tells me we have only medium-velocity cast-off and spatter all around. Look here," he said, pointing directly at an ugly red splotch on the wall. "And here—and here," he said, tracing a finger along the brick wall.

The three investigators paused quietly at the moment, swiveling their heads about as if in a full survey of the area, each man undoubtedly put off by the very gruesomeness of the scene itself. Emergency vehicles had all but shut down the short-blocked Grove Street location itself, and everywhere first responders of every order had already descended upon the area, almost en masse, in response to the call that had gone out over the open channels.

The veil of the street's normally darkened appearance had now been lifted and pulled back almost in full, as high-wattage stanchion-mounted lamps now illuminated the area in total to help investigators on the scene move forward in their studied collection of every found clue and a shred of evidence. And all in compass did their level best to avoid the ebb and flow of blood that had spewed so freely from the Novaks killing, and which by now had cascaded in a long crimson trickle that eddied its way slowly out to the very gutter.

Now only adding to the seeming ordered chaos of the moment, a small throng of crime scene techs had also just arrived at the location as well, each working well apart from Pomeroy, Robles, and the others as they each saw to their time-sensitive investigative matters. Each in their own way.

The CSI team stood quietly conferring among themselves and analyzing anything of seeming good interest in a studied and efficient manner, seeking to shelter much of what they were doing from public view under a makeshift canopy that had only hastily been put up by the investigating authorities.

"I can tell you this much, gentlemen, the cuts were sharp and penetrating, the wounds all left to right and coming from a single angle, undoubtedly quite deliberate. The cuts were carved deeply into the neck and throat, almost to the bone—once, twice—like so," Pimleur offered, demonstrating with a gesture to a somewhat astonished audience of two.

With a stubby finger slicing neck-high through the air—once-twice from left to right—Pimleur's graphic reenactment was most like one dragging a long-bladed knife across one's own throat. An already unnerving gesture in itself, it was at once both macabre and eerily suggestive.

"It's pretty much the damnedest thing I've seen in a long while—certainly the most gruesome of its kind," said the coroner, having to fairly raise his voice to a bellowing pitch just to be heard over the din. And even that but a shout above the background noise of cars and people but a half block up on the still heavily trafficked Seventh Avenue South.

"God Almighty, Doc," said the young Robles, a little green in the gills and thrown off by the whole scene. "This shit couldn't get any more grisly than it already is here. This is about as bad as it gets. Jesus Christ! Even with five years on the job, I can tell you I've never seen anything like—"

"Aw, man up, Robles—for God's sake—and stop your caterwauling. Maybe let me finish my work already. I'm trying my best to get out of this drenching rain here and you're making this whole thing take a helluva lot longer than it ought to."

Now a certain fire shot from Robles's eyes as he tried to formulate an appropriate hot response for his aggravating nemesis, but having none, he was left only with a sour grimace and a certain gnashing of teeth as he forced himself to look away, perhaps choosing to disengage from the fray and ignore the comment entirely. It sure as hell beat smacking the guy upside the head and would probably result in *far* less trouble for him if he didn't. Dammit all to hell.

"Can we maybe pick this pissing match up some other time? Maybe we can actually get back to the business at hand here?" chided the senior sergeant with a snort. The upbraiding remark had also been accompanied by an irksome frown that was aimed at both men, as Pomeroy soon found himself tiring of the incessant bickering and back-and-forth sniping that seemed to always happen whenever these two crossed paths and whenever they were forced to work together. Much like oil and water.

છેંછેંછેં

"Looks like we've got us a bad one here, men—I mean a *bad* one. Apparent homicide over on Grove Street just off Seventh—an old guy was found dead with his throat cut. The hell of it is that all of it must have happened almost in plain sight," said the captain as she paused at the moment and looked up, almost as if to ponder her very words and swipe at an unruly wisp of hair. Then she slammed a soft palm down hard on the desk in front of her. Somehow the drama suited her just fine. "A stone's throw from Seventh Avenue South, for God's sake. And the thing of it is, this time of night there had to be dozens of people down there strolling the whole area—but seems no one saw a thing—again. Of course. Hell, the whole thing just sticks in my craw!

"That's why I'm sending you guys out on the call forthwith. I need you two to get down there ASAP—maybe nose around the crime scene itself and see what you can find. We need to know what we're dealing with here and exactly what happened."

"'Bitch of a night to even be out there, Cap—cold, rain, and fog—some pretty soupy stuff," he said out loud, then checked himself and thought a moment, perhaps harboring a moment of doubt.

"Crime scene's probably shot to hell by now and already 100% contaminated I'd wager," a still-aggravated Pomeroy observed dryly, maybe just a tad disgruntled about having to even venture out in this muck. He cast a last casual look outside the office window, shooting a knowing look at his partner, a still-quiet Robles. Now he queried the boss and asked the question everyone was hoping to avoid, "So we can assume that the ME is already on-scene then, right?"

"Sure is. Sorry, boys, Murder never sleeps—especially in this city. You two of all people should know that I should think. What we have here trumps a little rain and a mild nip in the air. You'll live.

"Besides," the captain resumed, "It might actually be good to shake you two up every once in a while and get you out of your cushy little seats for a change," a canny Captain Fuller said with only a hint of a smirk. "Maybe get out there and take in some of that crisp evening air. And to your question—yes, Pimleur's already at the location and has managed to somehow beat you two to the scene—again."

The head of Major Crimes absently rubbed the eraser end of a pencil against the temple of her brow, perhaps subconsciously trying to even rub away the minor thump-thump that she was experiencing just over the brow, a rapid pulsing that just would not go away, then continued with her briefing.

"Sergeant, you and Robles pull together whatever resources you need to work this case. And you keep me up to date on anything you need for this case—funding, assets, and warm bodies—and I'll see that you get it. This has priority—coming down from upstairs!

"Look at the evidence, motive, and means—all around. Round up any potential suspects you uncover and get 'em in here. We'll have us a little meet and later weed out whatever's not relevant to the case."

"Boss?" asked Pomeroy, perhaps his way of prodding her on.

"Have some of your people look through the files—see if there are any newly released repeat offenders who might fit the bill. Follow the MO, gentlemen—you know the drill. Anyone with a past record for precisely this kind of thing who maybe got caught.

"Also, take a closer look for any alleged 'anniversary killers' as well, those who might be seeking some kind of name recognition or retribution, whatever. Those few who might be most capable of even perpetuating this kind of horrific crime.

"Anyway, just see Pimleur when you get there—and make sure you keep me fully apprised of any new developments. Sooner or later this one's bound to get some pretty good visibility—probably BAD visibility, actually—so maybe handle all of it with kid gloves, savvy? But be thorough. Process everything you find—nothing through the cracks. Oh, and did I mention see ME Pimleur when you get down there?"

"Pimleur? Geez, not Pimleur for Chrissake," chimed in Robles with at least an honest scowl. "The guy gives me the heebie-jeebies already. He just rubs me the wrong way."

The junior cop seemed to already have his hackles up and was immediately irritated at the very prospect of having to even see the guy again, then realized his misstep and backed off directly in the face of the captain and his sergeant's studied scowls.

"Oh, can the complaints already, you guys," ordered Captain Fuller with just a flash of anger. "It's always bitch, gripe, and moan with you two—so maybe cool it. Don't WORRY about Pimleur. He's all bark and no bite."

"Sure he is," growled Robles to no one in particular. "He's a pit bull with a temperament that pretty much goes along with exactly that. No, sir, don't like the guy and not a big fan."

"Anyway, I need you two to get to the location like *yesterday*, so maybe just find a way to work with the man and get over it already. No one expects you to always see eye-to-eye with the man, Robles. Just find a way to bury the hatchet once and for all, is all I'm saying. Let's keep our focus here, people. Maybe get on with the business of actually investigating the crime itself. In full, gentlemen—in FULL."

"Copy that, Captain," replied Pomeroy. "I'll have him knock it off. We're rolling on it," said the wiser and more compliant of the two men as he shot a mild but reprimanding look at his junior. Then both detectives turned and headed for the door, only to be stopped by a single final postscript from the wag-finger captain.

"You two better listen up. You keep your heads on a swivel—and be SAFE out there," Fuller said, her comment now far more an instruction than a request. Then the two investigators slipped quietly out of the office and prepared themselves to venture out into the drenching Greenwich Village night.

Once outside the precinct, both men sloshed over in shoe-deep rainwater to their aging unmarked *Crown Victoria* unit, opened the doors, and entered, shaking off as they got in. The wet-booted pair shaking off like two wet spaniels, then Pomeroy picked up the comm handset and punched in on his radio mike.

"Dispatch, this is 20-David Sergeant on the move. Show us rolling on the 'man-down' call and proceeding to the Grove Street location. Show us with the medical examiner at the scene. 20-David is out."

Then he gunned the engine and punched it, jolting the car out into light traffic.

જાજાજા

"I'm good, I'm good," assured the still-focused ME, pulling an already wet rain cap even farther down over his eyes. "Well, right to the matter at hand then," he said as he shuffled heavily over to the other side of the body. "As I was saying, a double horizontal slash in a left to right motion, I'd say—which could already tell us that our offender might at least be right-handed," Pimleur noted as he paused just long enough to run a web of stubby fingers through a tuft of coarse and graying hair, then resumed his considered observations.

"Both wounds were deep, cutting almost directly through the hyoid bone of the neck and nearly crushing the old man's larynx. Geez, both of these are some pretty nasty cuts."

"Hyoid bone?" queried a seemingly baffled Robles of the learned ME, trying his best to avoid any view of the scoring of the victim's neck."

"Yeah, hyoid bone, a U-shaped bone located under the tongue itself, just near the front of the neck. Between the lower jaw and the cartilage of the larynx—in layman's terms, a voice box. See—look here," Pimleur said, pointing a thick unmanicured finger at the victim's neck. "You can see the disarticulation here ... and again here."

"So what's your thinking here, Doc?" queried an overly eager Sergeant Pomeroy. "Would you care to go out on a limb and maybe give us your best guess? Something—anything?"

"Well, first off, you're looking for a weapon that'd have to be a long, serrated, and probably single-bladed knife. Something with a sharp saw-tooth edge—a filleting knife of some sort—or even a butcher's blade perhaps. But I'd expect I'll have a lot more on that for you later."

Pimleur seemed to slow his roll for a moment, perhaps to gauge each man's reaction, or simply ensure they were all still on the same page and following along, then he shook his head from side to side almost woefully and stood in front of both men with arms akimbo.

"It is unspeakable, really, gentlemen. Simply unspeakable, if you ask me," concluded the podgy ME with a mournful tip of the head. "And a shame too. Who even does this kind of thing, Joe? Without apparent motive? And so far with this case, I can tell you that we have none—nothing at all.

"But fear not," assured a still-optimistic Pimleur, "I should have a more definitive finding for you once I get the body back to the lab for a full workup and a more thorough forensic examination."

"So we got any ID on this guy yet or what, Doc? Anything?" asked a hopeful Robles, still recovering from the stinging darts that had been hurled at him only moments ago, and even more than a little repulsed by the sight of the mutilated form on the sidewalk in front of him, at least in its current state.

Now, on the moment, one of the several uniformed officers stepped forward from a sea of blue and quietly injected himself into the conversation. "Excuse me, Sarge. My partner and I were first on the scene, but we had to wait until the ME had wrapped up his preliminary examination before we could even check the body more closely—then we found this at least," Officer Reid offered, handing over an old, tattered wallet."There wasn't much else to be found though—no watch, no jewelry, no real cash to speak of. Plus we even found money still on the body in a pocket here. Best we could tell anyway, Sarge."

"You mentioned a wallet? Well, there's a piece of good luck—finally. What do you say we have ourselves a little look-see at whatever we can find? Anything that might help us develop a lead or two? Lord knows we need a place to start. But a nice catch anyway, Reid," postured the Major Crimes detective as he gladly received the only bit of evidence they'd found so far. Then he gingerly opened the billfold itself for a quick walkthrough of the slain man's wallet in full.

By now the rain had increased twofold, coming down almost in a diagonal slant, soaking all. Directly across the narrow street, a line of faces seemed to adorn the windows of the nouveau-cuisine Italian restaurant as the dry onlookers inside peered out. Most were curious to a fault, undoubtedly, and straining for a better view and any workable explanation for all of the stepped-up activity happening just outside their window, such that had now taken over the entire street.

Outside the patrons could see the pulsing red and white strobe lights from the emergency vehicles that had already arrived, and the yellow crime scene tape that was already being put up to cordon off an entire stretch of street that might otherwise have been near or around the discovered corpse. And all of them left to only wonder what exactly was going on.

Now Robles huddled under the light cover of a single umbrella that barely sheltered him and Pomeroy from the rain. Both men were little more than a soggy duo, now only trying to shake off the wet as they hunched over the body and took a mindful tour of the slain man's wallet with good scrutiny.

Standing again, Pomeroy huffed loudly and continued riffling through the several compartments of the man's flimsy wallet, looking for a clue—any clue. A lead perhaps—a name, an address, or anything that might even tell them who he was. Then the man found exactly what he'd been looking for—a name on a card tucked away with good care.

"Novaks, Paul J. White, male elder, born 1940. That'd make the old guy somewhere around eighty or so—maybe more! No active driver's license looks like, but we do seem to have some sort of a VA card here that says 'SGM—U.S. Army, Retired.' So what the hell's that? What's an SGM?"

Oddly, it was Patrol Officer Reid who would step at this time to fill in the gaps as he approached the clutch of investigators, seeming to know the answer right off the bat. The junior cop was eager to share his information, or perhaps just wanted to help out, but far and away, he more likely wished to simply impress his colleagues and maybe rack up a few brownie points in the process.

"I was in the Army, sir. That SGM is a military rank abbreviation, I believe, stands for 'sergeant major.' It's a pretty big deal in military circles, and the Army's highest enlisted grade—'least ways from a private's point of view. It's pretty much the top of the enlisted man's food chain if I remember correctly. Of course, on a noncommissioned officer level only."

"Nice catch, Reid—hopefully it'll tell us something we don't already know. Looks like this ID card says the old guy lived somewhere right over on Cornelia Street, boss," added Robles, anxious to maybe get back in the conversation however he might. "So what the heck is he doing all the way over here, I wonder?"

"Well, no mystery there, whiz kid," snickered Pimleur, the city ME, never one to miss out on an opportunity to stick it to the newbie detective, and to somehow always manage to stretch out their ongoing feud and "mutual defamation league" dance, that for all the world seemed to go on between the two like an ill-blowing wind itself.

"Hey, that's only three blocks from here. It's not unlikely that the old guy could have made it this far."

"It is if you're eighty, cabron," steamed Robles, getting hotter under the collar by the moment and more than just a little annoyed by the snotty chucklehead he essentially had no use for.

The needling by the ME was having its best effect and was only continuing to piss off the younger cop, much as expected. And once again, it was Pomeroy who had to step in to officiate and quell the mounting fires. And with these two, only "distraction," itself seemed to always work best.

"Okay, so how about us a TOD at least—you have anything on a time of death? A ballpark figure."

"You know the drill, Pomeroy. You know how we work here: collect, process, and analyze," said Pimleur with a half smile that was aimed only at the senior investigator.

"I don't like second-guessing my findings any more than you do, and never before I've completed my own series of tests. That said, I think I can go out on a limb and say two to three hours tops on your TOD. From what I can see here, rigor hasn't even set in yet—the poor guy."

"Well, that pretty much jives with our timeline as well," answered Detective Sergeant Pomeroy observantly. "The first cops to arrive on-scene had to be out of the 6th Precinct right there on Tenth Street. Those guys must've been here in minutes."

Anxious to maybe still be an integral part of the conversation perhaps, even in the face of his wounded pride, Robles now beckoned to the two uniformed policemen, Paxton and Reid, asking them both over to perhaps get an even more detailed report on their initial findings.

"You two find anything else significant on-scene here when you first arrived, other than the wallet? A weapon maybe, a blood trail? Any other forensics at all that might have been left behind? Just maybe we got lucky with something?"

"Negative, Detective. We were both on foot patrol up on Seventh when the call went out over the radio. We responded within minutes of each other and upon arriving, found things pretty much the way they are right now. I did a quick forensic sweep of the whole area for a weapon or anything that might have been discarded or left behind, but in the end, we both came up empty."

"Anybody else see anything? At all? Anybody have eyes on what actually went down here?" asked a hopeful but impatient Pomeroy, tightly scrunching his face into a knot of disbelief and dark frustration.

"We canvassed the entire area for witnesses, Sarge—any witnesses to be sure—but apparently no one heard or saw a thing," reported Officer Reid, the junior of the two beat cops, now also pointing to a restaurant location just across from them on the same narrow side street. "Including all those faces craning their necks over there in that restaurant window."

"And you got nothing, from no one?" asked the forensics expert Pimleur with a deadpan face, perhaps to satisfy his curiosity, even though he was always more than content to leave the really hard grunt work to the actual police detectives themselves.

"Well, there was that one homeless guy," said Paxton, with hand on hip and scratching his head, as if recalling some lost tidbit of information that might already have been carefully tucked away somewhere in the back of his mind.

Then he watched as the eyebrows of the senior investigators arched in disbelief, then he waited for the probing questions that he knew might soon be coming his way. He found he needed not to wait too long for the other shoe to drop.

૪૭૯૭૯૭

"Hey, Cubby, pop in for a sec. We should probably have ourselves a little chat," called the gruff senior station manager of the *Action9News* telecasting outlet, Jim Prysock, to his editorial assistant and sometime cub coanchor, reporter Ellen Macklin. Prysock was in charge of the night desk at the busy downtown TV network service, and even now as he seemed to enjoy a good stretch and a yawn, he knew it was probably going to be a slow news cycle. Indeed, very little of substance had even crossed his desk this night, and the network already had fewer back-page "fillers" creeping in that might be considered newsworthy, or even hold a borderline interest for its viewers. Clearly, it was just one of those nights.

Jim Prysock was a man of diminutive stature, nervous and fidgety, a man of "mickle might" and middle age, with a penchant for scruffy shirts, bland suits, and mute-colored ties. No slave to fashion, the senior editor might never be expected to adorn the pages of GQ, but what he did have was a nose for news and a keen eye for a good story and headline, however small it might start out. And right now, he was already juggling a full load of second-rate stories and rearranging priorities like puzzle pieces on a board—all of it based simply on a principle of "What was hot and what was not"—at least for the moment only.

So far, there'd been only a minor lead on a story about a rash of burglaries in the Soho district of lower Manhattan, a clutch of small animals that had escaped from a local zoo, and a new extension ramp going up on a short stretch of the Major Deegan Expressway way up in the north Bronx.

And all of it was already being juggled with a global warming feature, and an even more contentious column on a follow-up revisit to a particularly thorny piece of legislation that was focused on the commissioning of a new class of nuclear "Boomer" submarines and fast-attack boats for the navy that had only recently been introduced on the floor of the House Armed Services Committee just the previous morning. And much of it was either all yawn or all fluff, thought Prysock since indeed Friday itself was almost always a "news-dump" day.

As such, it was probably that one day of the week when a fuzzy cornucopia of far less important stories would be released to flood the news reporting cycles as "fillers" almost always done to beef up each day's broadcast and network standing.

And today was no different, save for the fact that he knew the suits upstairs would probably be breathing down his neck to dig up something more substantial, something far more significant that they could sink their teeth into—complete with blaring headlines—come morning. And it was perhaps only then that a particular story crossed the senior editor's desk, having just come straight off the wires from the dusty ledgers of the police blotter itself, one that might just need to be followed up on. This might just be the very story he'd been looking for all night: a bizarre and brutal attack on an elderly citizen … and a decorated veteran no less. Why?

"Cubby," the senior editor said, pressing a speaker button on his inter-office phone for yet a second time. "Get in here—pronto. We've got us a live one here, but we'll need to move on it fast!"

Ellen Macklin quick-stepped her way obligingly into the man's office, gracing the room with her charm and quiet good looks. She was herself a highly competent up-and-comer who'd happily aced her way through Columbia University's School of Journalism and had even made *magna cum laude* look easy.

She had passed with distinction and flying colors and was even now working her way in from the ground up, stuck with a come-from-behind TV network and locked on the "night beat," maybe going nowhere—but always with nowhere to go but up from where she was right now. And if paying her dues now might later pave the way for her getting promoted up and out of a "graveyard-shift" cycle of news, then she would gladly do so without misgiving or complaint.

And it was precisely what everyone around her seemed to like most about her. Now a young woman in her early thirties and perpetually—almost annoyingly—cheerful, Ellen was quietly attractive with a dimpled smile and a warm *zäftig* form that was more than pleasing to the casual eye. Now a pert cascade of auburn hair was tousled up and pulled back in a loose bun behind her head that ever seemed to bounce back and forth as even now she strolled on through the corridors of the newsroom on her way to her boss's office.

But far and away the thing Ellen loved most of all was the great working relationship she enjoyed with her boss and mentor of three years. And she deeply appreciated the fact that he'd been kind enough to even take her under his wing imprimis. And so she walked into the senior network editor's office with a confident and upbeat stride, eager to tackle whatever new assignment might be coming her way.

"From what you said on the phone, it sounds pretty pressing—and intriguing, boss. I have to admit you've piqued my interest. So what exactly do we have?"

"The wires have been burning up with a number of reports of a savage and particularly grisly slaying. Some kind of ritualistic murder—not exactly sure what yet. Just something downtown. Word is the victim was some old guy with his throat cut in a rather bizarre manner."

"My God, you make it sound so cloak-and-dagger, Jim—like something right out of some old London case file. Some Jack-the-Ripper story or something. Sounds like some pretty gruesome stuff, boss, maybe ripped right from some old turn-of-the-century London headline."

"Could be, Ellen, could very well be. Police are pretty tight-lipped about the whole affair, of course. They've essentially slapped a news blackout on the story, but a few choice details might still have been leaked about the killing," said Prysock, leaning back comfortably in his chair and eyeing his top-performing apprentice.

"So, is this your way of maybe dropping a hint on me, boss?" probed the alert newsie assistant, maybe hoping for a big break, a new trail, or even a new assignment. And only the latter would best serve her investigative purposes and meet with her unbridled ambitions.

The inside of the senior editor's busied office seemed to be nothing else than an untidy mosh pit of activity, with tripod-mounted storyline easels, grease boards, empty water bottles, and a meeting-room table for him and his people to huddle around whenever in deadline crisis mode.

The very walls themselves were plastered with posters and sticky-note reminders that must have been set for only himself, and almost everywhere lay a high stack of proofs and papers, books and magazines, and a slew of showcased celebrity photographs in which he was featured prominently with any number of dignitaries and Hollywood celebrities, all of which he must have been particularly proud.

Behind him, a keen-eyed Ellen Macklin could see with a measure of great curiosity—perhaps for the first time even—a number of dusty old Journalism awards of the highest order that the man had received, and a collection of letters of appreciation from "named" individuals mounted virtually everywhere on the walls around him. He was good at what he did and had been frequently recognized for such by his peers. He was a driven man, and now much of it seemed to already be rubbing off on her as well, for which she was eternally grateful.

Now the attractive young woman's eyes shifted away from her own "trophy" daydream and swung back to the little Lou Grant—looking character that was seated in front of her who was also her boss.

"No hints needed, Macklin. I just need a quick follow-up on a new lead that is. Ruskin and Baker and all of the other news teams are presently off on other assignments, so for the time being at least, you're IT. But I do have to warn you, you probably won't like what you find. Word is it's a pretty gruesome scene, so you might want to brace yourself for the worst," advised the senior editor, a little reluctant perhaps to even put his most junior reporter on a news item of such magnitude in the first place.

But she'd insisted on being thrown into the deep end, and so he'd indeed obliged her with a number of tough assignments in the past, but this one—this particular one—he just didn't know. And thought the lead newsman to himself, if history were to repeat itself as it had in the past, these assignments always had a way of somehow mushrooming completely out of control—often starting as one thing, however minor, then becoming something far, far worse. A thing perhaps most monstrous and most foul. Would it be any different this time, and was he even sure that she'd be ready to go out on a call like this?

"I'll take it!" said Ellen with an unbridled eagerness, pouncing on the proffered opportunity like a lion after its prey on a Serengeti plain, even if she only got the assignment by a quirky default.

"I can pull Dirk Fenton out of the press pool and have him grab his camera gear, then we'll head out," she said, more to herself than anyone else, turning on her heels at the moment as she headed for the door. Then Prysock pulled her up short for a final time.

"Cubby," he said with a heightened caution, "you be careful out there, please—and I'm serious about that. There's just something a little spooky about this one that makes the hairs on the back of my neck stand up, so you be sure to watch your back out there—you hear?"

"Copy that, chief, copy that," she assured him as she swiped a cautious wave to her boss and left the office with a discernible spring and bounce in her step that hadn't been there only moments before. She might be getting her shot, finally, and perhaps even her best chance at the story of a lifetime. Was she even up to the task? Macklin was still smiling quietly to herself even as Prysock brought himself to utter one final advisory.

"And Ellen, you listen good too. No heroics out there. I don't want you taking any unnecessary chances!" the gruff editor advised, now almost a kind of fatherly advice offered to a daunting, daring daughter. "Just get the story and get back home here—copy? Don't get brave on me. I need you to be okay, and I'd never quite forgive myself if something were to happen to you. This promises to be a tough one, Cubby, so ears up and eyes open."

☙☙☙

"Wait, so now you're telling me that you and Reid found some homeless guy who might have been in the vicinity of our crime scene?" queried an incredulous Pomeroy, grasping at straws and hoping against hope that it might still pan out to be an actionable lead. "You mean, someone who might have had an eyeball on the killing itself? What the hell?" said Pomeroy with a measure of exasperation. "And he just walked away? So just who is he and where's he at now?"

"We had nothing on the guy, Sarge, and no reason to detain. We're not even sure he saw anything, plus the guy looked to be a somewhat unreliable sort, either drunk or disoriented—maybe both, and frankly we couldn't tell which he was. Hell, we couldn't even understand most of what he was saying. We might have caught every third word or so of whatever he was talking about. Kept repeating some crazy 'Red Jack, Red Jack' mantra over and over, but what he might have meant by it is anyone's guess, Sarge. In the end, we simply sent the old guy packing and he went off on his way."

"So let me see if I've got this straight," said the senior homicide detective, rapidly losing patience with the two lax patrolmen. "You let a potential witness—maybe our *only* potential eyewitness to the crime—simply walk away from our scene without getting a name, a statement, or a description of the perp? So what kind of rookie mistake is that?" demanded Pomeroy, now almost visibly shaking with anger. "Christ, you two!"

The two junior officers, Paxton and Reid, were sharply stung by the senior detective's rebuke and visibly taken aback by the man's words and harsh tone, but said nothing, having maybe screwed up in the first place by even letting their man get away. *And now there might be hell to pay—clearly*, thought a gloomy Reid to himself, knowing only too well that his ass might be the second one on the line, right after Paxton himself.

And Paxton too must clearly have known they'd both be found at fault as well—probably, and that the sarge was right, it had been "a rookie mistake" indeed. And yes, even a serious breach of perimeter security protocols, but thankfully it could also be a mistake he might be able to remedy. He and Reid could probably get back in the game if they could only chase this guy down and get lucky enough to find their potential witness and bring him back over for questioning—a feat that might itself perhaps go a long way to redeeming themselves in the eyes of Pomeroy and Robles.

"On it, Sarge, we'll track him and find him," an obliging Reid chimed in, hoping to make some quick amends for their earlier fluff-up. "The guy couldn't have gotten that far—hell, it wasn't more than ten minutes ago. Last we saw he was shuffling along behind some old shopping cart thing headed straight across Grove Street—he's probably just on the other side of Bleecker by now.

"'Leastways at the pace he was moving," the patrolman concluded, just as Paxton nudged him with an elbow that urged him to look up on the moment. What the two saw was nothing short of sheer blind luck itself: the old man still rummaging through a selection of trash bins just on the corner of the next block.

"Well, here's a spot of luck," said Paxton with a hopeful glimmer and a finger that even pointed the way, each man straining to see through the steady sheet of rain. "That sure looks like our guy right there, Sarge—just on the corner of the next block."

"Then get on it. Nab him! And get it right this time! Bring his ass back here so we can have ourselves a little chat with the gentleman. He might have seen something out of the ordinary, for all we know, and right now we need to know what he saw."

"Copy that," said a compliant Paxton, the senior of the two uniformed cops, as both men dutifully stepped off at a hurried clip in pursuit of the elusive homeless man who either may or may not have even seen anything at all. But in more ways than one, both men already knew it was probably their best shot at a quick redemption.

☙☙☙

"Can we maybe hustle it up, Fenton? You always do this," Macklin observed, trying to speed up the photographer's always slow and methodical process of taking a full inventory of each and every item in his camera "go-bag."

And so he sat like clockwork, still shuffling and paddling his way through the bag, making sure he'd have everything he might need to get just the right shot at just the right moment. And in almost every event, the shutterbug was usually 100 percent right. The extra time spent now could well be worth the picture-perfect shot he might just be able to get later on.

"Fenton, are you even hearing me? Can you maybe step it up a little? Hop-sing already. Time's a'wasting and we're losing precious briefing time—and daylight. We still have to get down to Grove Street and the 6th Precinct and meet up with a Detective Pomeroy to get access to the scene. He'll be our immediate liaison for the duration of the assignment. C'mon, light a fire under it and let's get a move on!"

"Okay, okay, I'm ready—let's go, let's go!" advised photographer Dirk Fenton, a dusty-haired millennial in his midtwenties and clad in a loose-hanging Bermuda waist-shirt. At long last wrapping up all of his rummage-and-stow activities—checking and rechecking his rucksack bag—he slung the whole shebang over his shoulder and made for the door, shadowing Macklin close behind.

It was only sometime later that they arrived at the Grove Street crime scene itself, the two almost immediately spying on the two police detectives still bogged down in close discussion with the medical examiner on the merits and anomalies of the case. The small news van had arrived on the scene with little fanfare, the *Action9News* channel name and trademark logo emblazoned brightly on the side of the vehicle itself. And that fast had the reporter Macklin and her photo sidekick Fenton already arrived with what looked like a busload of cameras, recording equipment, and what might only be an "all-access pass" attitude that must have already opened quite a few doors for both.

At first sight, it might have already been clear on the surface that neither one really liked the other—Macklin or Pomeroy. *Hmph, this Sergeant Pomeroy guy here must surely think he's God's gift to women,* the young reporter mused. *Probably just another hairy alpha male. First impressions counted,* she thought to herself, sizing the man up in her mind in just the first moments alone.

Sure, that had to be it. Perhaps he just seemed a little too full of himself to even be at all likable. Odd then that he might at the same time be mildly appealing to her best first view as well—or so it did at least appear to her. Ah, the irony of both attraction and a feigned repugnance that really wasn't there, to begin with.

To Pomeroy, however, the whole affair had the potential to be little more than a nerve-wracking nuisance, and this newsie was already a bit too pushy for him, promising to perhaps only get under his skin—*rapido,* as Robles would say. And from what he'd seen even offhand on the tube, she was already annoyingly perky and bordering on bubbly—perhaps even too much so for a still-active crime scene like his at any rate.

And in his own experience, he already knew the type—up front all "bubble, bubble." Days later, all "toil and trouble," and there an end.

In fact, Pomeroy could already sense that she was going to be a major distraction, both to him and his investigative team. In other words, they were like two trains pulling into the same station with both going in opposite directions and neither one showing any signs of slowing down. Or maybe just him. *Hey,* he thought quietly, almost saying the words out loud as he harshly reprimanded himself in his silence, *Just stay focused and be professional, Joe—maybe just do your job!*

But it was also clear that the young reporter could just have her agenda as well. After all, Macklin had already reasoned, this was her lead and her story to develop as she saw fit. And not even this guy with his easy manner and rugged good looks would put her off her course or stand in the way of this story—or even take it away from her.

She'd paid her dues quietly and with good patience, now with a calm understanding that had her dutifully waiting her turn in line for her next bump up. And now indeed might be her best shot, and best moment in time, to move up a rung or two on the ladder. For her at least, it was a fast pony that she was prepared to ride into the ground if she had to, but tacitly she had also hoped for a little assist from this Pomeroy guy. But she couldn't help feeling that her chances were still somewhere in a 50-50 range with the man's perceived arrogance and innate stubbornness.

"The name's Macklin, Detective," she said, "Ellen Macklin—from the *Action9News* network night desk. My boss spoke with your captain earlier?" Macklin said, almost posing the remark as a question while reminding him of his mandate with a tonal inflection that clearly went up in pitch.

She had done her best to be amiable, hoping to at least forge some kind of good working relationship with her NYPD liaison officer for the tag-along, but now she was already beginning to think that even that might actually be next to impossible. *This guy's a cowboy and a character* was all she could manage to say to herself. She knew the type.

"Detective Sergeant Joe Pomeroy, NYPD Homicide Division, working out of the Major Crimes Unit, 6th Precinct" was the most the senior cop could manage before actually looking up. But when he finally did, he was simply stunned into a discernible silence.

She was 5'9", immediately attractive and well-toned, with sparkling hazel eyes and a bouncy flow of auburn hair, aromatic scents, and an ebullience that could simply not be ignored in any room. And for at least the seasoned Pomeroy, she was a vision quite to behold, and now his case's most immediate distraction, starting right now, since God only knew she was certainly drop-dead gorgeous and seemed to command almost all of his attention. Dammit to hell.

"So it looks like we'll be riding together—I mean, with you and your partner, that is. At least for duration of the current investigative assignment at any rate," Macklin said, uncharacteristically stammering away, which was so unlike herself, trying to be polite while at the same time seeking to keenly stand her ground should she ever need to. Like right now.

In other words, she was one tough cookie, which then led quickly to her next follow-up question, one that caught everyone off guard and almost immediately ushered her right into the doghouse.

"So any chance my camera guy could get a shot of the body? You know, maybe pan out across the full crime scene itself to get a few establishing shots for our initial on-scene report?" she asked with a naive half smile that bordered on a studied coyness.

Pomeroy stood transfixed, almost completely taken off guard—both by the person and by the question itself—much amazed at the nerve and very naïveté of the request imprimis. *Unbelievable*, he thought to himself as he struggled to recompose himself enough to even speak once again, the only word finding its way out of his mouth now being, "WHAT—?"

෩෩෩

Officers Paxton and Reid knew instinctively that their asses might indeed be on the hot seat for their slip-up with the potential witness who had gotten away and slipped their grasp. Now both officers bolted off toward the corner with quick-time running, and soon enough came upon the scruffy vagabond who was still busily rifling through an assortment of garbage cans just across the corner of Bleecker and Grove.

At first glance, he was both an eyesore and an amalgam of dirt and grime—musk-ox nausea to the nose that immediately attacked the senses—and the two cops thought it odd that the rag-picker never really looked up even once until their most immediate approach, just as Paxton himself was poised to speak.

"Excuse me, sir," the senior beat cop said, expecting maybe a quick and compliant response from the derelict, but truly never receiving one.

"Good sir, I wish not to be harassed," mumbled the ratty vagabond with a strong and curious British accent that seemed to be at once both intelligent and oddly quite out of place for his otherwise seedy look. "I have committed no crimes and I've broken no laws, sir," the disheveled old guy repeated, perhaps even annoyed at the very prospect of being rousted by the cops, perhaps for yet another time.

"But indeed, if you insist, I shall gladly find myself moving along now," he said, pronouncing his words crisply and with near-perfect diction that had to be wholly uncharacteristic for one in such dire straits, then made to step away from the immediate area.

Only in New York, thought Paxton as he chuckled lightly to himself—only in New York might we find such a curious "Jeeves the Butler" type so down on his luck but still gracing the streets with his very own brand of seedy pomp and circumstance—then held up a quiet hand.

"Hold on, old-timer, just hold on now. We just need a minute of your time—and no, we're not here to hassle you. We only want to ask a few questions, maybe have a little chat is all. Come on over here," Paxton instructed.

Now toting a full load of soiled bags and ratty clothes that were all draped over some old supermarket cart that he always seemed to hold close at hand, the old hobo ambled cautiously over in the direction of the two uniformed officers.

"Here—here, Constables," the odd man said. "My name is Howard Kettle sir, and I can assure you there is no villainy afoot here. I am no cad, sir," the old man said in perfect pitch in his English dialect, much like a man being accused of something and believing himself entirely innocent, much as he stood right now with hands on his hips as a gesture of both innocence and only mild defiance.

"And I've nothing to do with any of that hubbub going on down there on the next block. Indeed, gentlemen, I could only find myself getting out of there as quickly as I could. And I can tell you these old eyes saw nothing, sir, nothing out of the ordinary at all," said the quirky derelict with an odd, unplaceable accent.

"Okay, slow down, slow down. We just had a couple of questions for you, old-timer—no hassles, so come along now. Maybe just help us understand what you were doing down there—maybe just what you saw," offered the senior Paxton, still hopeful for a lead—ANY lead that might help them take their investigation in a new direction.

"Minding my own business I was, gentlemen, I can assure you, and bothering no one at all. And to satisfy your inquiry, I was only dining out and foraging for a few discarded scraps of food from that fancy eatery there on the other end of Grove Street. And—and I did not mean to watch—anything, I can assure you."

"So maybe you did see something then, yes?"

The old man frowned at the thought as he considered hard and long about just what had been said: just how far did he wish to go to even implicate himself in the whole affair imprimis? Better to perhaps just let them think he'd seen nothing. "Well, maybe I did, sirs, and maybe I didn't," replied the stubble-chinned vagrant with a seemingly defiant sniff. "Who can tell, gentlemen, who indeed can tell? Our position was indefensible by land, sir. Indefensible by land!"

Paxton and Reid only chuckled and cast each other a curious look, perhaps deciding to take the high road rather than confront the old man directly in any negative way.

"Easy there, old-timer, easy. What's your name anyway? And when was the last time you had a bite to eat—I mean real food?"

"Aye, sir," the old man said almost comically, even offering the two policemen a mock salute as he stood unsteadily with hand to brow seeming to almost snap to attention with a muffled click of heels.

"The name, sir, is Kettle, sir—Howard Kettle, liberator extraordinaire of trash and knight-errant of both alley and street. At your humble service, Constables," the old guy concluded with a slight doff of cap and a quiet half smile. "As for when last I might have dined, sirs—why, just what day is it now?"

The two cops might otherwise have been mildly amused by the vagrant's chatty antics were it not for the far more pressing business each had at hand for the moment—namely the Novaks murder itself that was still under investigation but a block away. For the time being, they were simply playing a hunch but thought it also possible that the tatty scrounger right here might indeed have heard something—perhaps even *seen* something—but the old guy was not inclined to speak without some further incentive.

"Say no more, sir. Tell you what, if your information is good, we'll be glad to spring for a meal—maybe get a little solid food in you. How'd that be?" queried Reid, always a soft touch and one who would probably get the guy a meal anyway, whether he had anything to report or not.

"Splendid, sirs, simply splendid. Perhaps then I did just see something, perhaps something indeed that I cannot ever UNsee, gentlemen—ever," he repeated, almost stammering as his very look changed on the instant and a dark shadow swept over the man's face. His voice cracked under the very burden of recollection, then the old gent began to unfold perhaps one of the most bizarre tales either policeman had ever heard in their collective short careers.

ಶಿಶಿಶಿ

Dr. Richard Pimleur, the medical examiner for much of Manhattan south, returned each of the probing instruments he'd been using back to his surgical table after cleaning them, having fully examined the distressed body of Novaks, then removed his protective gloves and washed his hands in a nearby scrub basin. The still-tired ME now ran wet fingers across the top of his brow as he swiped at a wild lock of hair and exhaled deeply, then reached for his desk phone to put in the call he knew he had to make. The phone on the other end of the line would ring a full four times before finally being answered by the police precinct desk sergeant.

"6th Precinct, Sergeant Romano," came the almost immediate reply.

"Sergeant Romano, ME Pimleur here," said the medical examiner to the sitting desk sergeant at Pomeroy's stationhouse.

"Ah, Pimleur, my favorite ME—to what do we owe the honor today? You maybe having a slow day at the morgue or something?" cajoled Romano as if to an old acquaintance, which indeed he may have been.

"Still up to your old antics, I see? I guess some things never change," Pimleur said, reminding himself that he'd have to someday actually get a direct-dial number for Pomeroy, perhaps to avoid just such a consequence of calling on the main line and continuing to deal with this often-ribald jokester.

"Put me through to Pomeroy, posthaste, Romano. I need to speak to the man ASAP—he in or what?" queried Pimleur, not entirely tickled by the man's usual pointless banter in the face of the even graver matters he had at hand, and was about to say so when the line clicked back on and the voice itself changed to a smooth and authoritative baritone that he knew to be Pomeroy himself.

"Detective Sergeant Pomeroy—your dime," came the seemingly tired voice on the other side of the line.

"Pomeroy? Pimleur here. Just wanted to check in with you and maybe bring you up to speed on some new details I've been able to confirm in the case. Once I had a chance to further examine Mr. Novaks, I came across some pretty unusual findings for you."

"Oh?" said the detective, for the moment checking his enthusiasm, his natural curiosity almost immediately drawn to the man's very remark. "Enlighten me, Doc—just what did you find?"

"It's this Novaks case, Joe, kind of weighing heavy on my mind. A pretty nasty piece of work that's not exactly the kind of thing we see every day. You come up with any new developments on your end?" asked Pimleur of his work associate.

"We're still running down a few workable leads right now, Pimleur. But that said, truth is, this whole affair's pretty much got all of us stumped. At this point, we don't know *what* we've got. We're still working on motive and developing a working list of possible suspects."

The sergeant leaned back in his chair, blew air out of billowed cheeks, then continued. There had been a slight lull on the line, then Pomeroy resumed his almost one-sided conversation with the ME.

"Helluva thing it was too, Doc—it kind of reminds me of a fat kettle of old fish—the whole thing stinks."

"Well, what have you got so far?" asked a distracted Pimleur, cupping the phone mouthpiece under his chin as he continued probing his shards of evidence back in the lab.

"Right now, frankly? Bupkes, zero, nada—nothing. I'm only now beginning to get a handle on some of the clues we encountered at each of the scenes. But hey, I can't even be sure about that—if any of it's even believable, I mean. Or was it all deliberately staged to only mislead us, maybe send us off on a false trail?"

"My thought exactly, Joe. How about you maybe pop by the lab when you get a chance? Can't really talk too much in detail about any of it over the phone. I'm sure you understand. The good news is, I might have stumbled across a few items of note, some of which might be of good interest to you. Say, in a half hour or so?"

"Copy that, I'll be there in a jiff—but..." replied a cautious Pomeroy into his end of the line.

"But?" echoed a perplexed ME back over the phone. *What else might there be to ask*, Pimleur mused. There were no buts in any of this.

"But as in we might have us a small problem, my friend. Our captain here has caved and slapped a bit of a tail on us—saddling some nosy reporter and her tag-along photo guy—both liaising with our department to cover the story. Imagine that Pimleur—on a case like this!"

"You're shitting me, Joe?" scoffed the disbelieving ME, commiserating with his phone host. "Well, I'm sure you've heard the old saying 'ours is not to reason why.' That's just where we are. But that said, how about you figure out a way to ditch the tail? What I've got for you should be for your ears only—at least for the time being. I'm sure I don't need to tell you that we don't want any of this getting out to the press—not yet, at any rate. This one could get messy," the ME concluded.

The strapping NYPD homicide detective drummed his fingers roughly on the desktop, perhaps waiting now for the other shoe to drop, but instead found himself simply adding, "I don't know what to tell you. My hands are tied here—like I have a choice.

"Anyway, what's so all-fired important that you're calling me at the crack of dawn here? Can't a guy get a little me time?" the cop asked with a hearty chuckle.

"Hell, it's all of it really, Joe—all of it. The DEAR BOSS notes, the numbers, the playing cards—everything we've found on each victim's body. All of it in spades. Also, the manner of death and the timing of each event still pretty much eludes me as well."

"Pimleur, it sounds like you're trying to tell me something, but you can't quite find the words. C'mon, spill the beans, Doc, out with it."

Now there came a studied pause on each end of the line as the forensic pathologist struggled to find just the right words. "I'm fairly convinced the numbers might mean something more than they're made out to be, Joe, but I'll be damned if I can wrap my head around any of it."

"Funny you should mention that," the police detective said, dovetailing nicely with the ME's observation. "We were pretty much arriving at the same conclusion as well. There's got to be some significance to the presentation of the digits. Maybe they're a part of some greater numerical sequence perhaps, placed one after the other as they are for a reason, but just what any of it might mean is still up for grabs. You care to hazard a guess?"

"Negative, not at this time, Sergeant Pomeroy—and certainly nothing on the record—but at this point, we can't be 100 percent sure of anything. All of these are just my preliminary considerations, of course. Call it a coroner's hunch—a professional stab in the dark as it were," said Pimleur with an audible huff, knowing that he'd already looked at each series of numbers over and over and from every angle.

"Point is, we could be looking at some kind of code or something ... some kind of numerical sequencing. Hell, all of it's just a little too odd, to say the least."

"Kind of sounds like an old case I had a while back," offered Pomeroy with a quiet snicker. "Some old mobbed-up hitter who'd been canceled out when we found him in an alley just off Eighth Avenue. Apparently, he'd died of lead poisoning..."

"Lead poisoning?" queried Pimleur with a kind of mild fascination.

"Yeah, three bullets center mass—lead poisoning," said Pomeroy said with a manly titter as he savored his dark humor, then added, "Give me fifteen and I'll be right over."

"Copy that," said Pimleur, then he hung up and the line went dead.

❧❧❧

Detectives Pomeroy and Robles had both been put off by reporter Ellen Macklin's request and her seeming insensitivity about filming at a live and active crime scene, as much by her apparently singular focus on simply getting her story whatever the cost. But she seemed to know next to nothing about crime scenes—or how they must be processed. Perhaps the cub reporter just didn't mind whose toes she stepped on in pursuit of a given story, and that in itself was enough to almost throw a monkey wrench in the works, and *him* off his game. But even that might itself have been tempered by the woman's quiet charm and startling good looks that might have tripped him up as well ... so perhaps no real surprises there either.

"Photos of the victim and the crime scene? Obviously not, Macklin—*Macklin*, is it?" he asked, perhaps purposely pretending not to remember her name just for good effect. "You serious? You must know we can't have you taking pics of anything here or poking around the body now, can we? Not until the area's been processed and the crime scene techs have completed a full workup of the murder site. We can't have you contaminating the area and traipsing all about an active investigation scene here now, can we?" the lead detective asked as he wiped away at a splash of rain on his forehead. He was fairly convinced that she was up to something, having perhaps some kind of hidden agenda, but who knew what.

Now almost immediately, however, he found himself regretting the harsh remark, feeling as if his words might have been spoken in haste and a bit too harshly, and immediately felt apologetic for his very gruffness. But what he didn't admit, even to himself, was that he might also be enjoying the cat-and-mouse game that was already apparent between the two so far. Had the others noticed as well?

"I'm sorry to get off on the wrong foot, Sergeant Pomeroy, but not on your life. We've been cleared straight through, and don't try to keep me off the story either—it won't work. Your captain said we'd be granted unlimited access—at least on a one-time basis—for the duration of the ride-along itself," Ellen responded as if to almost sternly remind him of his new marching orders. But she also found herself having to rein in her own emotions, now understanding that her response might have been a little too hotly delivered as well.

"Sorry. What I meant to say is that it's my understanding from your captain that we've already been cleared for unrestricted coverage of the crime scene and the follow-up investigation itself. I would have expected that she'd already spoken to you about it."

"Yeah, I got the memo this morning," countered Pomeroy, with just a smidge of reservation. "But that doesn't mean I have to like it. And frankly, I find all of it's still a little over the top. And I won't have you tramping all over my crime scene. Just so we understand each other," Pomeroy said sternly.

"I understand completely," said a far more contrite Macklin as she found herself waving off the senior cop's scowl.

"I have to say I can't help but wonder just who you know. And what's with all the interest in this specific case anyway? The whole thing might be nothing more than just another random murder. Probably just another robbery gone bad maybe."

"But—" Macklin began to protest before being once again politely interrupted by the homicide detective himself.

"And anyway I can't imagine your viewers would even be interested in this kind of stuff. I'd expect all of this might only be perhaps a little too ghastly for most tastes—and pretty much all of your readership for that matter." Now Pomeroy paused in midsentence, the features of his chiseled face softening just enough to bespeak perhaps a slight yielding of position, then he resumed his cautioning conversation.

"But if it'll make you feel better, you can have your camera guy pan across the crime scene area itself ... but *only* the crime scene area. That means no close-ups of the victim's body. No tight-in shots of the extent of injury either. I won't have any of this being posted on social media or used to simply boost network viewership and ratings.

"And I can tell you right now the NYPD will take a very dim view of the whole affair if any of this is leaked out and seen on TV—or splashed across the headlines of tomorrow's newspaper. Savvy?" said the detective in a short conclusion.

"I understand perfectly, Sergeant ... I mean, roger that," said Macklin almost demurely, perhaps doing her best to adopt his police lingo and looking back at him with just the right amount of flirt and a wry half smile that must have hidden something.

Then the two newsies stepped off to the side to quietly consult among themselves on optimum camera angles and just what to capture—and what NOT to record—per the senior detective's stringent orders. *God, it's going to be a bear working with this guy*, thought the newsie to herself in near resignation but also knew she was still up to the challenge.

And it was only then that Pomeroy could feel free to get back to work, even as the two investigators now settled back into another consultative huddle with the Manhattan medical examiner.

ىھىھىھ

Detective Sergeant Pomeroy was still in animated consultation with Pimleur and Robles just near the covered body of Novaks on Grove Street when Officers Paxton, Reid, and a scruffy old man approached from the east from just across Bleecker Street.

Almost immediately there was a certain fustiness and rank odor that assaulted the nostrils and permeated the air about the man's very being—itself almost a musk ox nausea to the nose. But Pomeroy had wisely decided to simply take the high road and had opted to instead not notice at all, perhaps to not offend the old soul, but again to also hear just what the vagabond might have seen, however bizarre the tale might be.

"This is a Mr. Howard Kettle," reported Reid. "We caught up with him about a block up on Grove. I think you might be interested in hearing what the old guy has to say, Sarge," the junior man said, seemingly pleased to have had the chance to at least redeem himself and his partner by finding their "slipped" witness. Pomeroy and Robles sized up the old trooper then introduced themselves and began a line of soft but pointed questioning. If the old codger had something to say or had even seen anything related to this grisly homicide at all, they might damn well want to know about it as soon as possible.

"Mr. Kettle, what can you tell us about what happened here earlier this evening?" the police sergeant asked quietly in a way of an overture, and to also slowly break the ice without being overly intimidating. "So what exactly did you see, old man?"

The dotard seemingly paused far longer than he needed to then inhaled deeply and spoke, "The devil, sir. I can tell you—a very ousel, sir," began the tattered Howard Kettle, almost shivering in the drizzle of rain that carried with it an odd chill from the unusually damp August night. "A wretched devil, sir, with a soul as black as night is what I saw, Constable."

Now the old cuss seemed to pause in his breathing, perhaps uneasy at the moment and loathe to readily trust cops after consistently being rousted by them and told to move along—as oft indeed he was. Hmm, move along to where indeed, he had often wondered.

"Just take your time, sir," coached a patient Pomeroy, showing a measure of compassion to the elderly gent while also trying to drill down to the depths of the man's sketchy truths.

"He was a devil, I say, sir, a very devil," the shoddy trash-picker repeated for a second time, almost shrinking back in terror and looking around in survey of the bloodbath scene that was still only yards away from where he stood on the very eastern edge of Grove Street with a full gathering of investigators. Not at all a comfortable place for him.

Police barriers had already been hastily erected, and the area had been cordoned off in full behind a spider's web of streaming yellow crime scene tape that had been stretched and anchored here and there almost corner to corner from Bleecker to Seventh Avenue South.

"Indeed, he was a very villain, sirs," Kettle continued with a stammer, almost blurting out the terrifying words with good clarity. "With a black hood and eyes black as coal is what I saw, and I'm ashamed to say I found myself turning away in fear. I could not watch, and almost did not wish to see, but much to my horror I did," said the shuffling old vagrant. "But by then I had already shuttled off and I got away as quickly as I could."

"And just where were you when you saw this—this figure?" asked Robles, elbowing his way into the soft interrogation that was still pushing to get to the dark underlying truths of whatever it was the old man either may or may not have seen.

"Well, I was just there by the trash bins," said Kettle, pointing to a row of garbage cans just across the street from the crime scene itself, just adjacent to the dimly lit upscale restaurant right there on Grove. Kettle was relaxing a bit, perhaps, now becoming far less animated as he cast a sullen look down on the ground.

"I tell you, gentlemen, he looked like some demon giant—a big guy— eyes dark as night and cloaked all in black with some hoodie thing," he said repeating himself yet again. "A devil, sir, a very devil, I tell you."

"Okay, just calm down and take your time, sir," Pomeroy urged calmly, slowly walking the man away from the bloody mess of a scene. The man was hunched and sunken-eyed with seeming fear then moved on to resume his terrifying tale.

"I remember he was wearing one of those sweatshirt things that the kids wear nowadays—his face pulled back deep inside the hood. I saw him—yes, I did, sirs—and the old man struggling right here," Kettle noted as he pointed directly at the covered form that lay coldly on the ground still waiting to be carted off to Pimleur's morgue. The old cuss seemed thankful to no end that the body had at least been covered and not entirely left open to view.

"And just what time was this, would you say, Mr. Kettle," inquired a now-bolstered Robles, the smarting wounds of Pimleur's earlier barbs now seemingly healed over in full.

"Stale baguettes and soggy pasta," said the cloudy wanderer, seemingly to no one in particular.

"Pardon, what was that? What did you say?" responded a curious Robles, now glancing at his boss with a near chuckle as he scratched the back of his head with an assured lack of any true understanding.

"Stale baguettes and soggy pasta, I say. So it had to be somewhere between 10:30 to 11 PM or so. The restaurant there always dumps out its day-olds right about that time, Constable, and believe me, I always know where to find a meal, and exactly when to be there—rain or shine! And that's when I saw it."

Pimleur and the two detectives shot each other a dubious expectant look, with Pomeroy picking up the tab of the questioning. "Saw what, Mr. Kettle—what did you see? Did you at all get a look at the man's face?"

"He was a brute, sir—a very fiend of a devil," he repeated now for yet a third time, as if still holding on to some horrid mental image or tangible clue that might be of good use to the police. Either that or he'd been completely scared out of his wits.

"A tall man he was, with eyes etched in coal with a darkened glimmer and a sharp beak of a nose—a very imp of hell with a dull glint of a blade that slashed that poor man's throat before my very eyes. And much, sir, much to my shame, sir, I admit freely that I just ran for my life hoping I'd never see that kind of thing again. I may never be able to get the very terrible image of it out of my mind!"

"Yes, yes, we understand that, but could you identify this man if you saw him again?" asked Pomeroy with more than just a passing interest.

"I should not wish to see this man again, Guv'nor, but yes, I think I could recognize him—if I were to ever see him again, that is," responded Kettle, trying his best to be as clear as he could under the current circumstance of his delirium tremors and still-shaky inebriation.

"Joe," Detective Robles said in quiet confidence to his sergeant, "this guy's three sheets to the wind already—clearly—and anyone can see he's pretty snockered as it is," concluded Robles as he caught Pomeroy's eye and coarsely whispered his observation to him, far less convinced than the boss that the old guy had seen anything, or that he was even credible.

"I mean, your call, boss, but just how much of this can we even believe from a source as shaky as this guy here?"

"Well, let's get him downtown anyway—perhaps have a bit more of a chat and maybe get a little food in him to sober him up, even if it's just for an hour or two. Hopefully, we can get some kind of composite sketch out of the guy—maybe even get a first look at what our offender might look like."

The junior investigator carefully weighed what Pomeroy had proposed and saw the validity of it all, and so began shuffling the old vagrant back to the police vehicle, when Kettle abruptly pulled up short with a single final outburst.

"Constable, you must get this man. He must not be allowed to remain at large. He will do this again—surely—he will do this again. He is a very barbarian and a black heart with a sick and torturing bloodlust, as I could see. And worse, sirs, he cannot help but kill again."

❦❦❦

Pomeroy hesitated for a heartbeat before actually putting the call through to reporter Ellen Macklin's network office at the *Action9News* network studio.

"Macklin?" he asked, maybe reluctant to even make the overture but also glad to hear the woman's voice, now for a second time over. "Detective Sergeant Pomeroy here. Just thought you'd like to know, I'm just back from a quick powwow with my captain, and for some reason, I've yet to understand, she seems to have confirmed giving both you and your shutterbug friend the green light for the ride-along. I don't know who you know, or how you did it, but you've been given a go-ahead to come with us down to the crime scene and the medical examiner's office for a look at his follow-up report. But I don't know … I just hope I don't live to regret her decision."

"Splendid, I'm looking forward to it—and no, you won't regret it. I'll make sure my team understands clearly to stay out of the way," said Ellen, glad to have an opportunity to continue chasing her story and to also follow up with Pomeroy on some additional details centered on the homicide case itself.

Plus, she thought quietly to herself, it probably also wouldn't hurt to see the detective once again to both mend fences and maybe patch up any differences the two might have had from their first meeting, such that had itself been a little stilted and off to a somewhat rocky start.

"Oh, and one last thing, Macklin—and please make sure you hear me on this. You cannot release any information on anything you see," he continued, almost as if reading from a laundry list of absolute no-nos.

"There can be no leaks, no observational notes, nothing said about any of the victims, the crime scene locations, wound patterning, or extent of the injury.

"Our investigative team will need to keep all of this under tight wraps until such time as it's appropriate to release. You understand what I'm saying?" he asked cautiously in summation of his taut advisory.

"I understand perfectly—and may I say I'm glad to be able to team up with you again, Sergeant. Maybe it might be beneficial to actually get an extra pair of investigative eyes on any new leads that might crop up later. In fact, it is my greater hope that we can work even more effectively together as a team."

"Well, thank you, but I already have Robles and a team of others for that, Macklin—plus we're not really a team, per se," the senior cop advised, maybe still a little irked and put off by the pushy assumption itself imprimis. "You should probably understand that right off."

Macklin took in what the police sergeant had just said but also could not help but feel a little stung by the man's seemingly incisive remark. Nonetheless, she still found herself nodding with mute compliance at the comment itself.

"And please know that you're only being allowed on the ride-along at all with the following aviso: You keep quiet, record nothing, and don't pester us with too many questions.

"But most of all, you must stay out of ME Pimleur's way," instructed the NYPD detective, maybe still a little ruffled over the whole affair and puzzling over Captain Fuller's charge that he even take her along in the first place on his visit to the forensic pathologist's lab.

Lord knows, he'd fought tooth and nail with the boss to wrangle his way out of having to even be burdened with the tagalong newsie and her click-click—however fetching she might actually be—or even found by him to be.

"My team and I need to move quickly and stay fluid, Captain—you know that more than anyone else," Pomeroy had argued unsuccessfully as he gently admonished his immediate superior. He'd made the remark with due diplomacy for what he felt was an ill-advised decision and a clear capitulation to the news media, whatever favor had been called in to finagle any of this. He found himself bristling slightly as he thought angrily about both the circumstance and the consequence of Fuller's seemingly erratic decision.

"I mean, c'mon, Cap, you know as well as I these paparazzi people will slow us down and only hinder our investigation," Pomeroy had told Fuller, not entirely masking his annoyance and no longer willing to walk on eggshells to simply placate his boss. He never had and wouldn't start now.

"Well, orders are orders, Detective" was all the captain had said. "And I can tell you this much, this is coming straight from the top—definitely. Hell, for all I know somebody upstairs could have owed someone a pretty big favor. Obviously a favor that must have been called in just for this."

Then her look had darkened, and her brow furrowed as she concluded with a final advisory to her lead detective. "Just make sure you keep them both on a short leash, understand?" Then she added as an afterthought, "And as for you two, you guys watch each other's backs and make sure you keep your heads on a swivel—are we clear?"

In the end Pomeroy had found that he'd simply have to capitulate, and so reluctantly received his walking papers and agreed to the news team tag-along, whether he wanted it or not. In reality, he already had mixed feelings about the entire buddy-up assignment, and even from their first meeting, he could already see that she was far more than just quietly alluring and appealing, but also suspected she might be nothing less than trouble underfoot.

But orders were orders, the captain had told him, and he'd now been saddled with both newshounds whether or not he would. What was the word—willy-nilly? the senior homicide detective asked as he chewed pensively on his lower lip. In the end, he'd decided to simply go with the flow and hope for the best of all options, however distasteful, while also vowing to keep close tabs on both of the embedded reporters.

Now arriving at Pimleur's forensic lab, Pomeroy, Robles, Macklin, and her cameraman Fenton all stood within view of the medical examiner's table, but only Pomeroy got the most glowering look of all from Pimleur himself.

Now beckoning the senior cop aside with a subtle gesture, Pimleur leaned in close in quiet consultation with the detective, such that was probably not meant to be heard by the others as he whispered, "I thought you told me you were going to ditch the tail and duck out on these people.

"You know I can't have these press people nosing around my work area here. After all, this is still an active police investigation and I need to get on with my work."

"I know, I know," said Pomeroy, deftly parrying the man's next remark, almost fully anticipating what was coming. "Believe me, Pimleur, I tried. I pled my case with the boss and all I got for my trouble was my ass handed to me and my heels clicked together—and so much for that, thank you very much. And so here we are."

"Gotta say I'm not a happy camper having these people running amok in my lab here. I don't need the sensationalism *or* the reckless, half-baked headlines that this thing is sure to generate. And I don't want to see my name or the results of any of my inquest findings splashed across the banner page of tomorrow's newspaper!"

"I understand, Pimleur, 100 percent—believe me, I do," said the NYPD detective sergeant with a sad measure of "same-boat" commiseration. "Hey, this is not exactly my idea of a good time either, trust me. Frankly, I'm still a little surprised the captain even authorized their being here—and gave 'em damn near full access—don't ask me why."

"Well, I don't like it" was all the ME said with feigned indignation as if he'd in some way been slighted.

"But you can rest assured I've had a few choice words with them already," continued Pomeroy almost loudly enough to be heard by all.

"And I've made sure they know to hang back and not film any of the actual scenes themselves. You just go about your normal routine as if they're not here. They won't be rolling any film on any of your activities—I can vouch for it—so maybe just go about your business and try to ignore them."

Turns out "hanging back" was not at all a problem for either Macklin or Fenton, who were both already removing themselves to the back of the room of their own accord, maybe repulsed by the very image of the coroner's presentation of the Novaks body on his examination table, or simply by the very fullness of the whole morbid affair itself. Maybe they weren't as ready for things as they had initially let in.

But all of that notwithstanding, the two simply waited for the ME's detailed autopsy report without at all advancing forward. WHO, after all, they each must have thought, who'd really even want to look at such a mutilated human form in the first place?

"If you say so, Joe—but I'm expecting you to keep them in line. That said then, let's have us a look over here," the irritated M.E. said, as he now did his best to rein in his justifiable anger.

Hovering quietly in the background, the news team was a bit taken aback but now found themselves inching back forward, seemingly at the invitation of the ME.

"So looking at the body then of our Mr. Novaks here, we can see almost immediately that the incisions were sharp and penetrating, indeed more than two inches deep from point of incision, nearly decapitating the man's head," the forensic pathologist said as he began his report, now even with a twinge of melancholy that almost made his voice waver and vibrate.

"Clearly the killer must have surprised his victim from behind, I expect, then grappled with the victim, then cut across the throat—once-twice, thus. The cuts came from right to left—Jesus—nearly severing both the hyoid bone and much of the thyroid cartilage itself. I'm afraid this has all of the hallmark traits of both an ambush attack and a brutal take-down that ended violently with the results you see here."

Pimleur looked up for a moment, pushing the spectacles on his nose further up with a pudgy finger, and met Pomeroy's gaze in full, giving the detective a knowing glance. Then he swung his view over to Robles and Macklin who had both opted to hang back, away from any full view of the table. Fenton, Macklin's able sidekick and photographer, was now doing his level best just to suppress his hurls as he continued to only quietly gag with dry heaves in the corner.

Perched in the corner where he had somehow continued to roll frame after frame of a film without notice—unknown to the already-suspicious medical examiner. He had done so under the cover of a shoulder bag that he'd held surreptitiously close to the body tucked under his arm, even as he still battled a serious urge to turn a certain shade of nauseous green. Then Pimleur returned to the cadaver on the table and resumed his monotonic discourse over the slain man's body.

"With what appears to be a double incision starting on the left side of the neck, about an inch below the jawline. The cut itself was approximately eight inches in length, running from a point immediately below the left ear with a semicircular cut terminating at a point about two to three inches below the right jaw.

"In other words," the somber coroner continued, only pausing midsentence for good emphasis while flashing a deadpan look. "So basically cut from ear to ear it would seem."

"Jesus Christ, Pimleur!" muttered Robles as he made a quick sign-of-the-cross gesture north, south, east, and west across the front of his body. The poor man now found himself increasingly more repulsed by the body, the blood, *and* the brutalized chest that had itself been laid open—essentially the whole messy affair.

"You still with us, Junior?" Pimleur chuckled as he winked at Robles on the moment, seemingly back on the heckle and perhaps never really a fan of the younger cop, to begin with. "Man up or step off, Robles—and don't go all weak in the knees on me either. Not in my lab again—you know, like you did last time.

"I was up half the night cleaning up behind the radiators!" he snickered to himself with just a pepper sprinkle of sarcasm. And even a quick slide of eyes told him that Pomeroy seemed to also enjoy the joke as well.

"I'm okay, Pimleur, I'm okay—just get on with it already" was all Robles could muster for the moment. It might even seem that the man had already been fully "insulted out" and had nothing left with which to counter, so he'd decided to do the only other thing he could do: take another step back from the table itself, fight an urge to gag, and try his best to just blend into the background.

The forensic examiner seemed pleased with his coy jibes at the thin-skinned junior cop, then swung back to the work at hand and resumed his analytical discourse, almost oblivious to distraction.

"The two incisions I found, appear to have severed the tissue almost completely to the vertebrae, as was the case with many of the other larger vessels of the neck, which were themselves almost cut in full. The cuts themselves were fluid with a surprising degree of facility and continuity, not at all jerky or sporadic, which might itself indicate that the killer was not at all tentative or hesitant in his attack. Instead, it is clear the man was determined and knew exactly what he was doing."

"And the weapon itself?" asked a hopeful Pomeroy, perhaps himself grasping at an elusive straw.

"Yes, yes, of course. I was just getting to that. The series of incisions themselves were probably caused by what could only have been a sharp, long-bladed knife with a deeply serrated edge, which clearly must have been used with great force. This was nothing less than a premeditated act of violence, Sergeant, and it's very probable that your victim must have bled out in only minutes."

"This is not good—at all," observed Robles, probably most known for stating the obvious and fairly expecting to be slammed yet again by the contentious ME who seemed to simply have it in for him. But indeed he was almost pleasantly surprised to find this time that he was not at all being attacked when Pimleur simply looked up at both men and whispered his own ominous words.

"You two have simply got to get this guy and stop him—you understand me? Stop him. Anybody who'd do this is already a tortured soul who's already got a special place in hell. In fact, it is my considered opinion—and frankly my greatest fear—this guy's not going to stop any time soon.

"I mean, I know it's your case and all, but I think our killer's just getting started. And if I had to hazard a guess at all, I might even venture to say that we could easily be looking at more victims here, Detectives ... many more victims," the portly medical examiner concluded as a wave of stark fear seemed to wash over his face. "This man *will* kill again, gentlemen—you mark my words."

෴෴෴

"Okay, people, let's get this show on the road—we're going live in thirty seconds," said the harried stage director to his three-angle camera crews, much like a conductor orchestrating musicians in a pit. The news set was hot and brilliantly lit, buzzing with all manner of busied activity.

"First we'll need an establishing shot, panning out from here to here," a busied set boss ordered with a wide sweep of his arms. "With a capture of the entire set from down-angle, then pan right, zoom wide left, and end with a full-body shot telescoping tight onto Macklin.

"Camera 2, you can roll in slowly for a medium close-up then tighten in for a full frontal, then a close-in face shot of Macklin. Everybody good now? OK, so everyone in their places—please."

Then the stage director wagged a tentative finger in the air above his head and silently began his trademark countdown ticking backward. "And in 5-4-3—" he said in a hushed underbreath tone that swallowed the last two numbers. Then an entire citywide viewing audience watched on as a contributing newscaster turned coanchor named Ellen Macklin abruptly came to life at precisely the same moment as the camera's red light flashed on.

"Good evening New York, I'm, your news desk co-anchor Ellen Macklin, and here are some highlights from your seven o'clock nightly news.

"Tonight, in our ongoing coverage of the recent spate of lower Manhattan killings right here in New York, *Action9News* has received confirmation from unnamed police sources about a series of heinous crimes being committed in several locations throughout the historic Greenwich Village area of lower New York.

"In an unusually tight-lipped interview with informed spokespersons at Manhattan's 6th Precinct, *Action9News* has just learned that there are a number of new leads in the case. However, those same sources stopped just short of providing any further details about the investigation itself, which they noted is ongoing.

"In a brief statement to our on-the-scene reporter, a department spokesperson told us that every effort is being made to follow up on all aspects of the case that might lead to the arrest of a suspect, or suspects—but also indicated that the police have identified at least one person of interest in the unprecedented string of killings. *Action9* will of course continue to bring you updates on this breaking news event as new information is made available to our news team.

"In other news, extended road repairs are expected to continue on an upper Manhattan stretch of the West Side Highway just at the approach to the George Washington Bridge. Driving commuters are urged to expect ramp and lane closures, as well as heavier-than-usual delays and traffic snarls throughout most of the morning rush hour until the work is wrapped up.

"The BQE is also experiencing a greater than usual backup, with a three-car pile-up just near mile marker 22 by the Gowanus just at the split to the Belt Parkway.

"Your *Action9News* weather moment is next, with more expected low cloud cover, strong upper-air steering winds, and—sad to say—only more rain. Coming up, we'll take an even closer look at your *Accu-Forecast* from our meteorology desk's own Brian Mulroney right after this commercial message ..."

MURDER MOST FOUL: CHAPEL

8 SEPTEMBER—PRESENT DAY

Now it was the darkened evening of the third day, just beyond the initial slaying, and the same soggy deep-weather storm front had stalled right where it hung, its winds and cloudy overhang now virtually at a standstill, blowing only lightly and moving nothing.

Overhead, a confluence of burly cumulus clouds had all grumbled and bunched their way together, now crowding about and colliding oafishly like drunkards on a barroom dance floor. It was the very same system that had spawned the nor'easter that had already tormented much of the New England area since the previous weekend. And still, a cold damp curtain hung luxuriously all about with a pesky on-and-off drizzle that was coming down far more frequently than most would have liked. Now more than three days' worth of nonstop rain was finally beginning to be more than enough, taking its toll on a collective public psyche and infusing many with a clouded depression that caused them to ask only one thing: when would this spate of bad weather end? And yet it had just rained again, now for the fourth day in a row.

It was therefore exactly the kind of dismal, fog-enshrouded night that might itself have been spawned in hell for precisely the kind of handiwork it would soon witness. And everywhere the soaking rain seemed to only pick up in intensity, now coming down in buckets and cascades, permeating all and leaving nothing untouched, nothing undrenched. And even navigating the soakage of the city streets was now itself a chore, especially if you were indeed Anton Chapel—a little slow and infirm of health—of late perhaps even a little unsteady afoot. But hell, he was eighty, he thought to himself with just a stain of melancholy—perhaps much of what he was experiencing now might simply be the dark expectation of his age at this very juncture of his life.

The location was only blocks from the first Novaks killing itself. This as the old man trudged slowly along and approached the corner of Washington Square Park North and Fifth Avenue.

Now he passed just beneath the famed landmark of the Washington Square Arch itself, such that stood like the city's own Colossus of

Rhodes, squatting firmly on bulbous haunches and perpetually facing north while guarding its uptown purview against its posh perch. The monument sat just at the lower end of the Fifth Avenue boulevard as it started on its long rolling journey north to its uppermost parts.

The rain had graduated steadily from a slow drizzle to now a heavy downpour that pelted almost noisily on the sidewalk, pooling up in concentric rain rings on the many windows fronting the square, even as the old gent carefully picked his way along and stepped off the curb to cross the narrow street just at the end of Fifth and Washington Square Park North itself. It was already 10:45 at night, and most of the streets had emptied in the face of the teeming rain, with much of the area now but a bleak unpeopled landscape with few if any night strollers in sight, most folks having already been forced back into their homes by the black inclement weather. And such then was the setting for yet another of the night's most horrid events: the killing of Anton Chapel himself.

Historically, the great Washington Square Park had itself been around for more than a century, a green oasis of a park in a curious canyon of city buildings that had been built sometime in 1871, spreading out in all directions to the north, east, south, and west.

It was complete with sprawling greenways and meandering paths that eventually all led out to any number of secondary side streets and even larger avenues.

And always in its very center had sat the park's landmark fountain itself, which was precisely where the old man was walking as he skirted around the western edge of the ornate font on his late-night shortcut through the park.

In most areas of the small green space had there always been ample lighting the way made by the park's many halogen lamps, but it was equally well-known that there were still several darkened blind spots as well. The almost entirely blacked-out kiddie Jungle Jim climbing area for one, just north and east of the concrete "chess tables" just at the park's most populous entrance, at MacDougal and Fourth, which by now was precisely where the old man was.

The good Anton Chapel was himself a man of good stock and good orientation, whose ancestors had emigrated from a small Bavarian region in southern Germany, but whose family had originally hailed from some other low-country area in the south of France. But it was only much later as a young child then, that he had even traveled west to the United States, with both parents and grandparents, as early as the 1930s. His family had tried to make a go of a homesteading venture somewhere in central Nebraska, eking out a rugged "pioneering" life as they devoted their hand to tilling the land, growing crops, and raising livestock.

Only it had not quite panned out for the family, and after an unsuccessful bid at making a go of their agrarian venture, the clan had simply pulled up stakes and moved back east to a far more habitable New York City, and there an end to the rough wilderness life for the Chapels forever.

And so only slowly now did old Anton Chapel amble on through the dark and slanting rain, busily contemplating all of these events: his grandparents and the move west. His parents and a hastened return back east to New York—and all of their combined histories together almost as one. But far and away, his life had mostly been shaped by the dark days of his service to his country as an army infantryman during the bloody dealings of the Korean War. He'd been a belt-feeder on a .30 caliber machine gun crew in a ground pounder infantry unit of rank-and-file grunts. And he'd done his best to stand proud with his Eighth Cavalry combat unit and had indeed helped to hold the line more than once on some Sino-Korean border in late 1950 even when all hell had broken loose.

Pitted against the very best of the PVA Thirty-ninth Army—China's feared People's Volunteer Army during the First and Second Chinese Offensives in October and November of that same 1950—the terrifying words of that time still rang in his ears even all these years later: "Position overrun—overrun! Hold the line, hold the line!" one sergeant had yelled over and again to his fighting band of soldiers.

And oh, the bitterness and the anger they'd felt—the very ignominy of the American lines being breached, a piercing dishonor that still stuck in his craw and burned his ass even to this day. If only we'd done this, or if only we'd done that—he'd often thought to himself during his moments of solitude, thus always second-guessing both his men and his very commanders of the time. And so indeed he'd stood his ground well—and found himself even charging up from his secure position to save several injured men who had fallen in a free-fire zone that was already known as "Murder Meadow," a place where men came to be mowed down en masse.

Old Chapel had forged ahead that day and saved five men—in as many trips into the very kill zone itself—sadly all of whom would later perish and succumb to their wounds that same torrid day in 1950. But one would survive the day and live, and that was enough for him. And for his heroic efforts, he'd been accorded the nation's highest award: the Medal of Honor itself for his selfless acts, a coveted medal that was envied by all and only awarded a few.

Odd then—that like so many others before him who'd received that same award—he had come away from the whole experience believing only that he was not at all worthy of the auspicious honor, since only he and one other remained alive, of all his platoon. Yet later that next morning around him would be found some twenty-six enemy combatants that then lay dead at his feet, but he could recall only very little of it as having even happened.

But indeed he'd somehow held the line against the advancing ChiCom wave, and he'd done so bravely and with good commendation. The Americans had ultimately fought to a stalemated truce, and even strengthened its nearly lost foothold in the region. It had even restored most of its critical "real estate" losses across the Korean peninsula, but on at least that one occasion, his unit had finally been compelled to quit their standing and withdraw to points farther south. "Position overrun" they had called it, as much a yielding of position as a strategic withdrawal. And such then were the very thoughts that had wracked his mind and tortured his soul, even as he paced along unevenly in the present day, oblivious to all around him as he passed through his late-night Washington Square Park.

Now the hour was fast upon 11:00 p.m. and steeping, steadied rain had only continued to pelt the streets and very pathways that meandered through the city-locked village green. And thus it was that a pensive and deeply distracted Anton Chapel now fully kept his gaze low and head pulled in close against the very elements, and saw not the dark shadow lurking just nearby. But the old man's passage had not gone unnoticed by the sly stalker who only now looked for his best moment to strike.

And only now would come the strong and grappling chokehold around the neck and sinking chest. Only now would come the lunge and glint of blade. Only now the biting edge across the sharp crease of neck as the Ripper's knife cut deeply into an area just above the man's collar—once-twice—now all a sound of throaty gurgling and a ruddy purge of blood.

It was only after the dastardly deed had been done that the killer had hastily scrawled across the fallen man's forehead—in his finger-dipped blood—the single word "Redrum." Rendered poorly in some terrible creep show font, the smudgy tag had been placed on the victim's brow and jotted in the penmanship of blood. And on the victim's chest placed a single playing card—a red Jack of Diamonds to be sure.

But even far more sinister, for investigating authorities later looking into the case, would also be a similar hand-scribbled note—a "DEAR BOSS" note to be certain—crammed deeply in the man's throat, almost defying logic. The ominous words themselves formed a kind of ghoulish, iambic rhythm that read in full

Dear Boss:
I ripped this goat for sport and folly;
Expect another just for jolly.
A feast of carnage with each man
Look to catch me if you can.
Signed, Red Jack

All followed once again by a seemingly illogical series of numbers that were presented as **51311335-042120**. What could it mean? And thus the stalker's second kill, in the person of old Anton Chapel, would now itself become a grotesque twin to that of his first victim, the ill-started, ill-fated Paul Novaks himself. Whoever was killing these men was following a trail of macabre and matching initials, but who knew WHO, or HOW, or even more importantly, WHY?

"What we have here, gentlemen? Appears to be an almost identical crime—and almost identical crime *scene*—as the one we had at the earlier Grove Street location just at the end of August."

"Sorry, Pimleur, maybe beat the drum a little slower here—back up—what exactly are you saying? What do you mean by *almost identical*?" asked Robles, now with a far more sobered tone, but still also recovering from the barbs he'd had hurled at him the last time he and Pimleur had crossed paths. "How so?"

"Sure, I forgot—you're a little slow, so I'll take it down a notch until you catch up," answered the ME, almost hurtfully as he watched Robles flush redly and almost wince. "What I'm saying is that we're seeing virtually the same findings from the current homicide as we had at the first Novaks killing over there near Seventh Avenue South and Grove—coming back to you now?" taunted Pimleur almost meanly. Almost as if he was going out of his way to do so.

"And not just the same findings either, but the same weapon used, the same attack profile, same kill scene staging, and even the same presentation of the victim in its post-mortem posturing. Gotta say, it's one of the damnedest things I've seen in a while," Pimleur said as he smacked his lips audibly and looked mournfully over at the two detectives.

"My opinion, gentlemen? None of this is a coincidence—at all. And our offender's nothing if not shrewd, methodical, and dangerous to a fault. But that said, I'll probably know a lot more once I can get the body back to the lab."

Having now at least wrapped up a cursory examination of Anton Chapel, Pimleur held back the crime scene techs that were still momentarily cooling their heels off on the sidelines, then ushered Pomeroy and Robles in for their look-see of the man's partially covered body as well.

"So just what do we have here?" asked Pomeroy as he carefully began going through the pockets of the fallen victim on Minetta Street. Methodically he searched each pouch and pocket until he found exactly what he might be looking for—a wallet, a card, an ID badge—or *anything* that might tell him just who he was, and then he found it.

Fingering a card that he carefully extracted from the man's billfold, he studied it for a long moment then spoke out to the others.

"Okay, okay. So our vic's name here appears to be one Elon Strunk," noted a tired and already-overworked Detective Sergeant Pomeroy to Robles and the onlooking ME. "Born January 1938, with an apparent address somewhere over on Sullivan Street. And judging from this street number here, I'd say this can't be more than a few blocks away."

Now it was Robles who spoke up, this time with a measure of gravity and good sincerity, addressing his question to Pimleur directly. "So what's your take on the condition of our victim—you got any other preliminary thoughts on what might have happened here or what?"

"That's the troubling part, I find no evidence of strangulation—no ligature discolorations, and only a rough grouping of contusions across the upper torso—just like our previous killing. This might indicate that the victim may again have been tackled from behind, pulled close, then violently assaulted and slashed across the throat—here again with the same signature double cut that we'd seen in the earlier attacks."

"And you found no drag marks at all—with either victim?" asked Robles pointedly, maybe trying to test the ME's prevailing theory as presented so far. "I mean, nothing to indicate that the crime could have happened somewhere else, someplace other than at the actual locations where the bodies were found? No blunt-force trauma, no ligature markings—nothing?"

"Can't really say there was, Robles. We found no clear evidence of such—not at the first crime scene or at the second—and no evidence of blunt-force trauma or ligature constriction either, such that might indicate any kind of choking attack. This was not asphyxial, gentlemen. This guy's not a strangler. He's a slicer and a gutter.

"And the only drag marks ever found, in either case, were those found near the doorway entry points where the old men themselves must have been dragged back to complete the siege cycle at the time of each attack."

"Interesting take," concluded Pomeroy with a subtle but absent-minded scritch on the tip of his nose. This one was a real poser, and he'd need time to figure it all out.

"I don't know quite what to tell you, gents, but this is pretty much all I have for you—for the time being, at least. I'd hope to have more once I can walk through a more thorough exam and get some forensics back from the lab. And of course, I'll be cataloging any evidentiary material we might find as a result of those exams as well. I've got all of my people working double-time on all of it."

"Hell, how'd you rate the preferential treatment, I wonder? And I'm still waiting to hear back from these people on Oswald and Kennedy. You must've called in a favor or something—or maybe just lit a fire under someone's ass," a humorous Pomeroy poked at Pimleur with a discernible chuckle. "Cough it up already."

The three seemed to share a quick tension-breaking laugh, then Pomeroy pushed on to the real business at hand. "Of course, you'll make all of that available to our investigative team when you're done, yes? It's kind of important to the case, Doc. You find anything unusual, you let us know. We desperately need to find a way to maybe get ahead of this guy—before he can strike again."

"Hey, for you guys it'll be hot off the presses," Pimleur said with a grin and taking little time in his response. "I'll get all of it to you by Pony Express if I have to—ASAP." Then he packed up his coroner's satchel, nodded once at Robles, and began heading back to his van dodging raindrops.

"Oh and, Pimleur," reminded Pomeroy, still a little stiff-lipped as he stopped the ME almost cold in his tracks, "Let's also get a check on fibers, biometrics, and prints as well—whatever other forensics you can fish up, okay?"

"Copy that, Joe, not a problem. You'll have it," Pimleur answered dutifully as he opened the door to his official van and plopped down into the driver's seat.

Then the senior detective turned his attention back to his own partner saying, "The boss wants us wall-to-wall on this one, Robles, so you'd better get your game face on. We need to pull as many surveillance tapes as we can find from this whole area here as well—savvy? Somebody somewhere had to have had an eye on this street. One of these cameras around here had to have caught something on video. Find something, Robles—find me something."

Then the senior homicide detective simply stepped off in the direction of the bevy of police vehicles and first responders just near the brilliantly lit arches of Washington Square Park to brief the on-scene watch commander, and in a moment was gone.

※ ※ ※

"It all comes back to the numbers, Detective Pomeroy, these same infernal numbers. In this case, **51311335 042120**." *Aw hell*, thought the police sergeant smugly to himself with a jeer and an accompanying sniff. Leave it to this one to go away and come back with this same numbers crap again.

"On the surface at least, they only *look* like a ragtag sequence of integers that otherwise seem to defy interpretation, but I'm fairly convinced they're somehow tied into all of this—but just HOW precisely, we just don't know. In fact, for at least the time being, we have no idea what any of it means, but we're still working up to our own Charlie Epps[1] moment. And we could probably use one right about now."

Pomeroy and Robles were still centered on the ME's inquest and studied presentation, carefully mulling over whatever small clues they'd just been given to maybe help them further along their stumped case. There'd already been the single red playing card, this from a full deck of fifty-two such cards—a single red Jack to be sure. And the cryptic "DEAR BOSS" note found on each victim post-mortem, the scribbled phrase "Redrum" scrawled on each man's forehead in their own blood, and all of it consistent with the first killing on Grove Street. But could they even find a link between the two crimes themselves?

---

[1] The character Charles Epps, of course, is the noted mathematics professor and FBI consultant, who is also the brother of the FBI Team Leader Don Epps himself, in the blockbuster TV series *Numbers*. In fact, one of his more memorable theorems was the curious advancement of his "Axiom of Coherent States."

"Ah, well to your point, Detective, I might have an idea on those numbers—if I may," Ellen said softly but with some seeming good authority. "It's probably just a long shot, but perhaps it could work out—maybe even provide us with some viable clue or two.

"I'd like to continue working this numbers angle and see what I can drum up," she offered, perhaps holding back a little and still overwhelmed from having entirely been thrown into the deep end of the pool—sink or swim—by her own senior editor Prysock. "What they might mean, that is," she concluded.

"Could be a step in the right direction," responded Pomeroy, surprising her for the moment by not biting her head off, as she might otherwise have expected. "Or it could more likely be a step over the edge in another direction completely. But you should probably keep looking, I suppose. Continue working that angle, Macklin—hell, we never know—we could just catch a break in a case that's got us all stumped."

Now Ellen looked up with impeccable timing just in time to catch the man watching her as well. *Oh, how awkward*, she thought shyly to herself, then cast a fleeting glance herself at the striking Pomeroy. She had to admit that she was pleased as well with her first working contribution to the team, however small. And the promise she'd made to herself to truly ferret out a truth or two in the process;, and to also find her defining headline, much like the one she had in front of her right now.

"By the way, you don't have to keep calling me Macklin all the time either. You can just call me Ellen, you know—I promise I won't bite. After all, we are going to be working together for a couple of days, so maybe we can find a way to bury the hatchet and simply start anew," she offered with a certain twinkle in her eye that could not have been faked, and that was probably not at all lost on the senior police detective.

In front of the two sat an open portfolio with a fresh copy of the team's most up-to-date collection of crime data, case photos, fact sheets, leads—both tangible and dead-ended—and even a few profile mock-ups. The updated case file lay on the table, all neatly collated in a tabbed folder within reach of both Pomeroy and Macklin just to their front. And it was only when reaching for the same document at the same time then that their hands even had a kind of the first touch, however inadvertently, if even for a static moment only.

However unintended, and however fleeting the contact might have been, a spark now ran through both, the crackling touch itself maybe inspiring more than just a brief but undeniable surge of energy between both of them, if even for a second only. And both had felt it at pretty much the same time, like a minor carpet shock that spoke volumes and maybe told them everything they might otherwise wish to know.

"I'm sorry" was Ellen's first response option as she turned a quiet shade of crimson with a near-schoolgirl blush that made her feel like a curtain had been drawn somewhere, and some great secret had perhaps been revealed. But first things first, she opined, she'd already proven her worth to the team with her first major finding, and it bolstered her spirits just to be a part of a very real investigative effort. And as of right now, at least things were finally looking up indeed.

"Okay, so bring me up to speed, Pomeroy—what've you got for me here? You guys able to pick up on any noticeable patterning yet—anything we can trace, I mean?" asked a troubled and still-harried Captain Fuller of her two key investigators. This was her peeking in for a quick midweek check on her team, and an impromptu off-the-cuff spot check on the ongoing case, such as it was.

"Captain, our people are working around the clock on the case, and I can tell you this thing's got a way of taking us in directions we never imagined—basically all at once. We've made sure to clear the decks so we can now pursue any leads in real time, almost as they come in. But since you mention it, Cap, we *could* probably use a few more uniforms to help out around here—maybe get a few more feet on the ground. The case is beginning to take on a life of its own," concluded Pomeroy with a slight corroborating nod of assent from Robles.

"I understand perfectly well, Detective—even if our resources are stretched a bit thin right now—but you'll get them, you'll get what you need. But for now at least, how about we just concentrate on piecing together a working profile of this offender, based on what we have so far that is.

"And we'd better get as far ahead of this thing as we can before an alarmed public gets wind of any of it and decides to go off the deep end on us. We don't want to know what that might be like."

Oddly, it was Robles who would be first to speak this time, spilling his bad news like a carton of broken eggs on a sidewalk. "Captain, we keep coming up empty on all of our database searches on this guy, and nothing pops. Plus no hits on facial rec either, obviously," said the junior cop as he referred to the facial recognition software they used to both interpret, and later build upon, the scant visuals that might just help them with their case.

"This guy has to be some kind of ghost," added Pomeroy, responding to both Robles and Fuller. "And he's probably already living off the grid somewhere. Or more likely living the 'quiet life' like some Johnny Good Citizen in Scarsdale with no priors and adored by his neighbors. Ironic as hell, I grant you, but something we've seen only too many times before."

"And?" prompted Captain Fuller, now being her turn to add to the conversation. Plus, she felt it imperative to hear more from two of her best-performing subordinates in all of the MCU.

"Well, the bad news is we've still got jack, Captain, and we keep coming up with the same fat goose egg—up to now, that is. The good news is, it's still early on in the investigation."

"Still, none of it makes me feel any better gentlemen—it's simply NOT ENOUGH," observed Fuller, furrowing an angry brow at both men as she set down her coffee cup on the table and skillfully began twirling her pen over the fingers of one hand, much like the cinematic "Iceman" in the mission briefing room in *Top Gun*. The very manual dexterity of it was pretty cool to watch, for the deft theatrics of it all, but it was also a little unnerving to Pomeroy and Robles, who were both just a little more unsure of their footing now than they had been just earlier.

The captain continued to glare intently in Pomeroy's direction—as the senior of the two investigators met her gaze unflinchingly—then continued with her invective and hot dressing down. "You guys have had this for what, a couple, three weeks now maybe—and nothing? You two had better start working this case a little harder and drum up some leads—and I mean some real and tangible leads—if you're hearing what I'm saying. Something that can bring this case to a good close."

"Understood, Captain" was all the sergeant could manage, being unaccustomed as he was to being made to stand on the carpet and getting his ass chewed out by his boss.

"I mean, you have to know I've also got people breathing down my neck as well—some pretty high-powered people with pay grades that are probably two or three times above mine," said a still-hackled Captain Fuller as she paused just long enough to stab a finger at the middle of the odd Ben Franklin–style glasses that dressed her face and pushed them further back onto the bridge of her nose. Then she turned back to her two A-team homicide investigators puffing air out of billowed cheeks.

"Gentlemen, our task here is simple and threefold: First, unmask the killer. Find out just who's behind all of this and why he's pursuing this vendetta in the first place—if that's even what this is. Maybe determine what his weapon of choice might be, and why he's chosen this method of killing.

"Second, find out what exactly is driving this guy: *Why* is he targeting only older men and people in their late seventies to eighties? And thirdly, what is this guy's statement: What's he trying to say to us, and what's his endgame? After all, who even does this kind of thing anyway, for God's sake, without a compelling motive?"

The room now had a certain pin-drop silence to it as Fuller shifted in place and set a teepee of fingers in front of her face, then ventured on to her next remark. "It's also my understanding that we don't have any biometrics on this guy—still. No prints, no forensics, no eyewitnesses, and nothing on AFIS,[2]" the captain observed dryly as she continued to pursue her point in search of a more viable lead or explanation.

---

[2] AFIS—**A**utomated **F**ingerprint **I**dentification **S**ystem.

"Captain, we have what we have here, Ma'am—I'm sorry," said Pomeroy. "'Best we can figure it, this guy's either a boy scout or a recluse living in the boondocks somewhere. Or worse, someone simply hiding in plain sight. Only we can't see him due to the very nature of his otherwise persona of normal behavior, boss—i.e., his ability to blend in, like the kind old gent living quietly next door and all that."

"And what about our guy, Pimleur? We have anything preliminary from the ME as yet?"

"All of our people are staying right on top of everything, Captain, but Pimleur still doesn't have comprehensive for us to go with yet—or so he's telling me. But hey, we know him to be a good man, Cap, and the right man for the job at hand. Plus he's been with us every step of the way for each of the killings—at all of our scenes. He knows the case as well as any of the rest of us."

The captain thought about that for a minute then responded with, "Clock's still ticking and we need to stop this guy before he strikes again. That, gentleman, is what we should be more focusing on."

"Captain, we're expecting to hear something back from the ME almost momentarily. Same with the crime scene boys as well, but CSI's still a little backed up sifting through a mound of evidence on their own. They're looking for any clues they can round up that they say they'll then expedite for us if anything's found," advised the square-jawed Pomeroy to his boss. "But everything they've cataloged so far is material we've pretty much seen already. Essentially it's ground we've probably already covered."

Even the most cursory look around the room might have told anyone looking that the captain's office was nothing if not drab and severe, much as one might have expected. It was a dreary admixture of wood and *Steelcraft* desks, with dusty bookcases and a disheveled stack of file folders that complemented a collection of discarded paper coffee cups that dotted the entire room.

The air was still, and the room was rank with a smell that came off much like an odor of lemons and stale perfume. There were also two windows facing into the office, but even these seemed to be caked with a year-old streak of grime and grease, almost preventing any real view. Now Fuller studied her two-star performers and waited patiently for the follow-up response she hoped only Pomeroy could provide.

"The best we have is a prelim and baseline report from Pimleur on the Grove Street homicide, which we now all agree must have been the stalker's first kill," noted Pomeroy, "such that seems to indicate a COD[3] that was directly related to the obvious slashing itself.

To substantiate this, Pims found two deep ridging cuts across the throat, both left to right. And for this guy by now almost a trademark of sorts—along with bruising across the chest—as if taken close from behind, tightly pulled in, then quickly dispatched.

"Well, that dovetails nicely with our theory and ties right to the suspect profile we have so far," said Fuller to the small team gathered around her.

"Our best estimate from the ME seems to tell us the old man probably bled out in minutes, pretty much right there on the sidewalk where we found the body," Robles added.

"All in all a pretty grim business and a macabre scene, boss—for the most part. Much unlike anything any of us might have seen in all our years."

"So what else have you got?" prodded Fuller, not willing to hamper the continuity and flow of the team's progress report.

"Well, there was also the matter of the series of cryptic notes that each scene presented, and the playing card thing as well, which in every event was always a red Jack of Diamonds to be sure," Pomeroy said as he continued with his updating report, then decided that he was probably covering old ground.

"And we can't overlook the consistency of the scrawling on the victims' foreheads either—the odd word 'Redrum' written each time in blood or some kind of black grease pencil. The lab is just now starting to look at all of this stuff we found, and we still don't have a clue what he might turn up with any of it yet."

---

[3] COD—Cause of Death.

"Well, I can probably solve at least one of those riddles myself," responded Captain Fuller after a long and distracted look. "I've seen it before actually—this REDRUM imprint thing. It's simply the word MURDER itself spelled backward. Some spooky Hollywood thing perhaps. But just how much any of it means is anybody's guess, in terms of solving this case."

"Hey, look at the bright side, Cap. Today we know at least a little more than we did yesterday," said Pomeroy. "Who knows what we'll find out tomorrow? That in itself might be a good enough start for the time being."

"Okay, I'll bite. So how about we all just get back to work and maybe find a way to pick up this guy's trail" was all she said in the face of Pomeroy and Robles's protests.

"But Captain, we can't..." the junior man was about to say, only to be rudely brought up short by the head of the MCU herself.

"Robles, read what it says on this badge," she said holding her shield up just over her head. "Well, what does it say?"

"It says Captain, ma'am."

"Good, now read between the lines and get your asses out on the street and make the case, Detectives, just make the case. Lean on your CIs[4]—hell, talk to the trees for all I care. Just find this guy already and bring this city some well-deserved relief. Now you are dismissed, gentlemen!"

ಶಿಶಿಶಿ

"Jim, I think what we should be looking at more here are the numbers themselves, I mean, if my hunch is right, that is. Or maybe I'm just going around in circles here."

"Well, don't sell yourself short here Macklin," prompted her sage editor. "You've proven yourself right enough times before. You've earned your questions now."

---

[4] **CI**—**C**onfidential **I**nformant(s).

"It's just these numbers, Jim—somehow it always seems to keep coming back to the numbers—and specifically these very numeric *sequences* we keep running into, to be sure. I'm convinced they mean something Jim, in every event, each time. So bear with me for a minute—and maybe just hear me out," offered Ellen Macklin to the small group, now back at her desk in the news station's bullpen rehearsal room as she sat in a short conference with her senior editor, Jim Prysock.

Only once he'd been read in and fully brought up to speed could reporter Macklin even expect to draw her boss into the greater confidences of the case, so for now the two still sat in animated conversation over the day's events and tomorrow's lead line, with both of them kicking around a flurry of scenarios and hypotheses like sand pebbles on a beach.

Could it be *this*—or could it be *that*—or could it be some other thing completely?' they'd asked, but always seemed to arrive back at the same point: the fact that all they'd ever really had was at *best* but presumptive evidence with no viable conclusion. And more questions than answers.

Having scanned the conclusions and each of the number series, she and her team had already looked at numerology sequences, algebraic integers, and even plain rational numbers. They'd walked themselves through everything from birthdays to telephone numbers—postal codes and even area codes—but all with no appreciable results.

"You need to stop beating yourself up over this, Ellen," offered Prysock to his excitable up-and-coming reporter, who seemed to be on a roll. "Maybe you're going down the wrong road completely. And what's the deal with the numbers?"

"They're the key to the whole thing, I tell you, Jim—somehow. I'm convinced of it," Ellen had said, thinking more out loud than anything else as she stood in front of the newsroom storyboard with one hand on her hip. "But as to how any of it ties together with any kind of meaningful interpretation, who knows?"

And so the two journalists had sat in silence, carefully mulling over their thoughts for a moment longer, then found themselves lapsing into even other reasoned sidebar discussions that had so far already continued for most of the morning and well into the afternoon. And still they were both stumped.

Then Ellen had her "light-bulb" moment, her eyes going wide and her mouth forming a small *o* as she stepped lightly through the next portal of sheer enlightenment.

"Then there's only one thing left," she offered as she leaned over her desk and looked at her senior editor with pinprick focus. "Probably something neither one of us may have even considered earlier: What if it's latitude and longitude?"

And even on the moment everything froze on the spot and fell into a kind of deep silence that lent the favor of an immediate focus on all things—a small view that brought with it a momentary illumination—even as every eyebrow in the room went up in mute surprise. Could it be as simple as that?

ชชช

The large rolling studio cam panned slowly across a full panorama of backdrop graphics in the newsroom set then swung back and settled squarely on the comely, fine-featured face of the news desk anchor herself. In her hands, the woman gripped a sheaf of cheat sheet notes and color-coded reminders that had been only loosely scripted and bundled together, and which she tapped neatly on the desk in front of her over and again. The off-camera stage manager was set to cue her shortly, then spoke into his headset mouthpiece in a whisper as he counted down the time and wagged a cadenced finger just in the air over his head.

"And we're live in five, four, three..." he said, trailing off into silence while only mouthing the last two digits in full. The anchorwoman glanced over in the direction of her dapper co-host once, then straightened up and focused hawkishly back on the camera with the glowing red light.

"Good evening, New York, I'm your coanchor Ellen Macklin with a wrap-up of the news stories that are making the rounds today. Tonight, in an exclusive *Action9News* report, our community news team has learned from reliable police sources that there has been yet another tragic killing in the metropolitan area—that again of an elderly man in the Greenwich Village area of New York City.

"Our *Action9* team has learned on good authority from confidential sources that the body of an eighty-year-old man—whose identity has not yet been released to the press—was found earlier this morning in the vicinity of MacDougal Street in the city's West Village district itself.

"An inside spokesperson close to the investigation has now indicated that the attack now marks the second such area killing, all of which victims appear to have been slain in like fashion, in what can only be described as being a manner most horrid.

"In a later follow-up report with our news desk, a police department representative has indicated that the attacks could be the work of a single attacker, one whom the media has already dubbed 'The Village Ripper,' further noting that the investigation into the unprecedented string of murders is still ongoing at this time.

"The City of New York remains on a much higher alert footing, with many people still quite on edge. Citizens are urged to not attempt to take action themselves and are urged to instead immediately report any suspicious activity they might see or hear to the proper authorities. Your police are here to help and will respond immediately.

"This is your *Action9News* co-anchor, Ellen Macklin. Please stay tuned for further updates on this story as we receive them on the hunt for the Village Ripper," concluded the incisive news anchor as she wrapped up the still-developing story.

Then the camera-friendly newscaster deftly passed the news baton back to her co-host with the ease and grace of a dead-sprint lane-runner in a relay race handing off. "Now here's a look at your sports, with a report on last night's major upset. Bob?"

"Thank you, Kathy—a great report as always—and we'll certainly need to keep a close eye on that story," the animated sportscaster said, almost pretending to be out of breath, then he switched gears to re-enter the world he knew best of all. The bounce and dunk of sports.

"In other news tonight, we go right to our nightly sports recap with a roundup of scores. The diamond was hot last night when the New York Mets finally snapped a three-game losing streak with a 5-to-4 extra-innings win over a stunned St. Louis Cardinals team.

"The New York Yankees also won their game last night as well, struggling in a back-and-forth battle of pitchers that was marked by injury and several key errors in the fourth and fifth innings. The team, however, was still able to capitalize on a number of boggled-ball plays and pulled out a last-minute win in the final minutes of the game.

"The win now also allows the team to move up in the league standings and can only improve their chances for a playoff berth later on in the season.

"And finally, for a quick look at your *Accu-Forecast* weather, we go straight to Mark Roland on our chief meteorologist's desk."

"Thanks, Bob—gotta love the boys in pinstripes. Now if they could only keep up the streak and grab a few more wins. I guess only time will tell.

"But as to our current weather outlook, our local forecast still shows much of the metropolitan New York area experiencing a slight shift in weather, and a cooling front that is expected to move in later tonight. There will also be an unusual early-season chill developing late morning, topped off with a confluence of strong upper-air steering winds and a 40 percent chance of rain coming late in the evening. A light breeze is expected out of the SSW at about 13 miles an hour with temps thought to steady out in the low-60s..."

Volstad was angry and stank of a grievous hunger that would grant him no ease of mind, and no peace for either soul or body. For much of his life, he'd been a brute and a bully given to fisticuffs, barroom brawls, and a fondness for kidney punches as much as his even subtler forms of quick persuasion using his long knife. He had squelched his violent inclinations and had managed to curb his growing bloodlust for some time now without prey, battling his restless demons and fighting off a pressing urge to once again kill.

But now even that was quickly eroding itself, and the killer was fast losing his battle of patience. He might soon indeed succumb to his baser instincts. It had now been some three weeks since the second Anton Chapel killing of 8 September in Washington Square Park, and the grimacing Volstad was almost beside himself with a steeped appetite and a ghastly urge to feed his need. He knew he must act soon since the date itself was simply far too important, at least to him—September 30—and so he sat quietly in his dingy apartment in dim light and deep cover, skillfully whetting his long blade on a flat stone and planning his next kill. Perhaps already a man in search of his next victim.

"DEAR BOSS," the villain could be heard muttering to himself with a menacing growl as he took a long and sloppy swig of warm leftover beer and lit another stale cigarette, then turned back to the work at hand with a self-satisfied leer and a hiss.

"Just for jollies," he muttered to himself. "And CATCH me if you can." Then he continued with a careful honing of the cutting edge of his ripper's blade, relishing the sharp prospect of a future kill. And thus again would he don his workable disguise and make for the hovel door. His time to stalk and roam the streets was once again at hand, and he knew he would find his next victim and strike well before the first light of dawn.

BERSERKER: THE DOUBLE EVENT: STRUNK
30 SEPTEMBER—PRESENT DAY

Old Minetta Street in Greenwich Village, New York, was a small and sequestered side street with an unquestioned "old world" charm that somehow magically worked to transform its alley-like purview into something far more alluring and upscale. In its entirety, the street probably ran in full for only a block or two on a long and curvy track up from Houston Street on its southern end, to Minetta Lane on its northernmost leg, just off the famed MacDougal Street itself.

A landmark venue that might have dated back to some pre-Revolutionary War time, and even later during the post-slavery years of the late nineteenth century as a somewhat downtrodden neighborhood of free African Americans, the crooked geometry of Minetta Street itself was like a page right out of some historical chronicle, rife with a violent past of mayhem, and near-nightly murders. It was also a virtually isolated street that had almost always been poorly lit and quietly underpopulated, as even now the area itself was both obscured and unpeopled, perhaps even an almost ideal setting for precisely what the Ripper had in mind, even as his next victim approached now slowly afoot.

The aged Elon Strunk had always been a navy man and was a retired master chief of the service, a petty officer of the highest order in his own time. An avowed submariner by preference, he'd served proudly aboard the second incarnation of the famed USS *Tang* (SS-563) right after her very commissioning in late 1951. Back then his call of duty—along with the rest of his submariner crew—had been all about ASW, Anti-Submarine Warfare, operating within the **SUBRON1**[5] command out of Pearl in the Hawaiian Islands.

He'd done well and had been advanced in grade accordingly, based on merit and his outstanding time in service. He'd quietly entered service at seventeen and had made a full twenty-seven years of it, staying the course and retiring only in 1978 as an **MCPO**[6] with a rating of E-9.

---

[5] **SUBRON1**—**Sub**marine Squad**ron 1**.
[6] **MCPO**—**M**aster **C**hief **P**etty **O**fficer.

And that alone was three stripes down and a "rocker" above with an anchor and two stars. So yeah, a pretty big deal, at least in military circles, and almost all of it skimming the troughs and bottoms of the clear blue seas of the Caribbean and the far Pacific in a submarine for seemingly months on end. Year after absent year.

After his service retirement, an older and much wiser Mr. Strunk had happily returned to his beloved New York City roots, perhaps just for the very verve and excitement of it all—to perhaps enjoy a "spirited" kind of retirement that he felt he so richly deserved in his latter years. And so now it was indeed some fifty years later, and yet he walked the late-night streets of Greenwich Village, even now as he turned the corner onto Minetta Lane from busy MacDougal on his way home from a late-night meal at a place simply called the Cookery on Fifth and University Place. Then there'd been the near-obligatory stop for a quick nightcap at the Surf Maid, his favorite jazz piano bar on Bleecker, the one with the al fresco tables and the attractive blonde playing old favorites on the keyboard. And thus only now might he teeter along, slow-stepping his way home through light rain, much in his cups, and truly feeling no pain.

Still feeding a warmed feeling and a foggy upbeat mood, the good master chief could be seen lumbering down Minetta Lane with a discernible limp that, over the years, had been exacerbated by his recurring bouts of metabolic arthritis and the such. He guessed it was just called "old age," but who could be sure? Turning left now onto the secondary Minetta Street where he lived, the eighty-year-old navy vet continued halting along the narrowed lane, almost impervious to all and thinking only of spending some quality time with the grandkids that very weekend in upstate Westchester County. And oh, what a time it promised to be too: a full backyard, two boys, a pack of yapping dogs, and even a model railroading diorama set up to run in the basement. Small, small wonder then that the old codger might have been entirely unaware of his very surroundings—and of the pale hooded figure that stood tucked just in the dark recess of a doorway midblock waiting for his next prey. And that prey was now set to be none other if not the aged Elon Strunk himself.

But nothing at all had escaped the evil purview of the Village Slasher himself, as even now the unsuspecting old man came abreast of the deepened doorway where the killer sought to spring his very trap, the Ripper now making ready to spring his own planned and calculated trap. And thus would come soon the rude embrace, the brute force attack, and the choking grasp about the unsuspecting victim's neck. Only thus would come the sharp stretch of knife and the double slash of blade as the ripper's shiv struck home and cut deeply across the throat—once, twice—then done.

Now the old navy chief's slouching form began to weigh heavy in the arms of his attacker as the flailing man's struggle began to fall away ever noticeably, the eyes wide with fear and disbelief, feet kicking and body thrashing only momentarily as he began to bleed out and slump to the ground. But even then there came a disrupting noise, a sudden and troubling sound on the near horizon, an unmistakable sound perhaps, of footsteps clattering on the sidewalk, slowly ambling along—a strolling late-night couple just then turning the corner and entering Minetta Street itself. The Ripper's work had thus been rudely interrupted, without the killer's full laying-out and staging of the kill scene itself, now much without its more "formalized" presentation and trademark placement of objects.

So quickly now did the killer take to heel and fled afoot, heading south to Houston Street to escape detection and the very carnage of his kill scene, leaving behind the besieged Elon Strunk in an ever-growing pool of blood. And only the heavy *clack, clack, clack* of the man's very footfalls in flight might be all that was heard along the deserted corridors of old Minetta Street.

It was only once he'd fully turned the corner at Houston that he even began to hear the blood-curdling screams of the woman from the strolling couple that must by now have stumbled rudely upon the very body of the fallen elder.

And so he stepped up the clip of his pace, now in a far more hurried flight from the scene of the muddied killing, then quickly turned the corner onto a well-trafficked Houston Street and simply disappeared into the press of the crowd. And in an instant, the ruffian killer was already gone.

Captain Fuller's Major Crimes investigative unit had always had its sharpest focus on aggravated assaults, violent high-end armed robberies, and every type of homicide imaginable, as even now both Pomeroy and Robles were dispatched to the scene of the third Elon Strunk killing, not at all knowing quite what to expect. Now but a tick of the clock past one in the morning, it was only hours after the murder scene had itself been discovered after a resident walking his dog had simply happened upon the lifeless form just in the lane beyond the emptiness of Minetta Street itself.

By the time the two detectives finally did pull up to the location, ME Pimleur was already there squatting down on fat haunches examining the man's body and doing his best to hold the crime scene techs at bay, not at all wanting even them to disturb his scene just yet. An uncharacteristic end-of-summer nip and chill had somehow come early in the season and now hung in the air like a damp mop, disturbed only by the minor gusts of wind blowing in from the Hudson River that seemed to envelop the entire area in full. Pomeroy turned up the collar of his light jacket, and with Robles shadowing close behind, the two began their survey of the Minetta Street kill scene in total.

Toward its southern edge, leading down Minetta Street toward Houston itself, the lane was still desolate and unpeopled. To its northern end, it married up with its sistered venue Minetta Lane. Now both streets were almost completely cluttered with all manner of first responders that had already crowded the scene with spinning lights and yellow tape. Sifting through all the hubbub and activity, Robles finally spotted the medical examiner and bristled almost on the instant as he steeled himself for the taunts and jibes he knew were coming but decided to lead the charge with his dig anyway.

"Well, well, Joe," he said to his partner Pomeroy, "I see our old friend Mr. Back-from-the-Dead is already here. Shouldn't you be at some hoagie joint somewhere maybe stuffing your face with some 12-inch sub?" Robles jabbed, taking his best shot, now with a smothered snicker that just as quickly seemed to explode into a full throaty guffaw.

"Eat shit and die, Robles, and don't mess with me tonight. I've got my hands full right now and I ain't in the mood!" ME Pimleur squawked as he squared off against the man with a sharp squint of the eye and a manifest dislike of the junior investigator. "How about we all just get back to the job at hand and keep our focus on the work instead?"

Well, looks like our friend is all business tonight, thought the two, with apparently no time for games or the usual tête-à-tête bickering that both men had come to expect from each other.

"Okay, okay, I'm just pulling his leg, Sarge. You know how this guy gets under my skin," protested Robles, now perhaps shrinking away from the remark after having been reprimanded.

"Well, I'd imagine we have enough on our plates already with this murder scene—and the two previous. How about we dispense with all the sniping and low-blows here," Pomeroy warned, now doing his level best to get beyond the ever-ongoing feud and hoping the matter was resolved. "So how about someone maybe telling me just what the hell we have here? Doc, is this another one of your homicides?"

"Yeah, nice seeing you guys too," responded an indignant Dr. Richard with a wrinkled brow, then moved on. "So I got the call about a half hour ago myself and got here as fast as I could—only to find this poor soul laid out here in the dark."

"*Dios lo bendiga*—God bless the poor soul," said Robles and whistled as he swept a disgusted gaze all across the scene of the killer's latest ghastly attack. "Not another one of these grisly scenes."

Overhead, a late September sky almost crackled in the night with its minor flashes of sharp cloud-to-cloud lightning that emanated from a high thermal just above. Now the sound of rolling thunder could also be heard reverberating in the near distance from an electric storm that might already be rolling in from the Hudson River just to the west.

Much of the narrowed Minetta Street venue was still empty, the hour being what it was, and only the hastily erected police lines had been set up to cordon off the entire area, this to keep back those few late-nighters who might still be out and about from getting too close to the crime scene itself. Even the carbon arc lamps themselves that had been set up by the investigating police stood alone, looking for all the world like the large klieg lights of World War II, set to illuminate the narrow lane just west of old MacDougal. Then Pimleur stood up with a heave and a groan and inched his way toward the two detectives to begin his analytical narrative.

"What we have here, people, appears to be an almost identical crime, and an almost identical crime *scene*, as the one we had at the earlier Grove Street location, and again in Washington Square Park just a couple of weeks ago. And the one thing I can tell you right now is that *none* of this is a coincidence in itself," said the studied medical examiner with what might only have been a hint of melancholy in his voice.

"Of course, I've only had time for the most cursory of looks at things like blood spatter analysis and patterning throughout all of the kill scenes. With an eye toward specifically things like impact angles and directional flow, such as we see right now," Pimleur said with a tap of his finger on several older photo images of spatter found at each of the previous locations.

"The attack could only have come from behind based on this checker patterning and spray markings. See? Here, here, and here," the ME said, pausing only long enough to wave his hand in a wide and sweeping arc that skimmed across the floor and down along the narrow siding of the portal entry leading out from the very doorstep itself.

"Your victim was probably attacked right here and bled out exactly on the spot, most of it finding its way out to the curb. A hell of a mess, that much I can tell you."

"Yeah, and it's not especially easy on a queasy stomach either, Sarge, to be sure," agreed a still-rocky Robles, amazed that he could even find anything he could agree on with the stodgy coroner but was equally assured that there must be a first time for everything.

Then he found himself looking away if even for the moment only, chiding himself for the umpteenth time about why he hadn't channeled all of his energy into something else—some other field perhaps, whether banker, baker, or just candlestick maker. Then he rudely came back to the moment and the very horror of the scene and made his way to the edge of the curb and threw up his guts, for now, a second time.

"It's the crazy ones that scare the shit out of me, Pomeroy—they always do. Too unpredictable. So how about we just concentrate on getting this bad actor off the streets as quickly as we can? I want his ass in cuffs or a coffin—you catch my meaning? And for that matter, if it comes down to either you or him, you put a toe tag on the bitch and I'll be glad to meet you at the morgue," said Fuller, a full-figured gal with a short bob of a haircut that was rich with dark hair and only a shock of white that ran across each temple.

The head of the MCU was still discernibly upset with the prospect of their offender having gotten away yet again. And she was not content to simply sit on her laurels and wait for developments to pan out, or worse, for another body to drop. She was also making no bones about it, and for that reason alone a jet of hot steam could almost be seen coming out of each ear. Or at least figuratively, if not literally.

As the recognized captain of the Major Crimes Unit for much of Manhattan south, Fuller was already known for many things: her strength of character, her dedication to service and to her community, having an uncanny head for numbers and stats, and most notably for her knack for flashing a certain fire-coal look that could laser-burn anything in its path. Just like the one she cast in the direction of her two top cops even now.

"And just so we're clear, gentlemen, I want you both out there pounding the pavement from dawn to dusk if you have to. And I want your best people working the streets right alongside you to hunt this guy down—whatever you need, you let me know. You run him to the ground and bring this killer in.

"Close out this case, people, and get some of this heat off my ass. Maybe even solve a murder or two in the process. Now go work the case and drum up some leads. You're detectives—go DETECT. Find me a suspect—find me a solid suspect and wrap this thing up!"

Pomeroy could only grimace quietly to himself after he and Robles had just had their asses chewed out and handed back to them, then the two had left the stationhouse and made their way out to the street. After fuming for a few precarious moments, he was finally the one to speak first to his partner Robles.

"I think what pisses me off the most about this case is this guy treating our city like some kind of target-rich hunting environment and a virtual dumping ground for his kills. And all of it almost at leisure. *Dammit.* In the best of all worlds, I'd be able to put an end to the whole affair, nab this guy, and punch his ticket myself—if it came down to it. But this guy is slippery and always one step ahead of the best of us at every turn."

"Well, I'm with you on that, boss, thick and thin, you know that—but where do we even start at this point?" asked Robles, absent-mindedly scratching his head. He too hadn't been too keen on having his ass reamed out any more than the next man, especially when it's the crabby captain of one of the largest Major Crimes Units in the city. But it was what it was, he thought, perhaps to only console himself, even as they found themselves once again back at jump street with little tangible evidence, no forensics, no biometric tracing, and no weapons ever found at any of the crime scenes—so far. And upon his better reflection, he knew that probably did not leave much else for them. So what then might be left?

"Well, we have what we have, Robles. How about we just go back and start at the beginning, maybe starting with our first murder scene with that Paul Novaks's case. This whole thing is just another rinse-and-repeat of the same horrific crimes that all come later ... and all of it pretty much right in our face.

"So what do you say, how about we just work on moving the investigation forward, even if it means going back to square one. That said, how about we just go see a man about a murder?"

☙☙☙

Ellen Macklin's stodgy newsroom boss, Jim Prysock, was a worldly man and an old-school journalist of the first order. He was also a nervous and fidgety type, a condition undoubtedly aggravated by his recently having stopped smoking for yet a third time. Yet it was clearly days like today that he might almost have missed his beloved *Aranga* and *Panatela* stogies.

The senior editor's office was a complex beehive shuffle of newspapers, files, tapes, documents, and dusty old bookshelves that were crammed into every square inch of his office. But in all regards, it was more a kind of ordered chaos and more a badge of honor than a fault of any real sloppiness—a mark perhaps of the old-guard newshounds who sniffed out their stories the old-fashioned way by the sharpness of the nose, due diligence, and arduous legwork. Plus it was probably a safe bet and a foregone conclusion that he knew exactly where everything was and could put a finger on whatever he might need in seconds.

"Ellen, you realize of course that you've now got me stuck here in the middle between two polar opposites," the senior editor said to his best cub newsie. "On the one hand, we have a very clear obligation to our viewers to report the facts, to tell the truth, and to maybe get the word out about all of this to the citizens of this town."

"And on the other hand?" inquired Macklin as she sought to conclude the man's sentence while also carefully prodding her otherwise by-the-book boss.

"I'm getting to that, Cubby, I'm getting to that. As I was saying, on the one hand, we've got that and on the other, it is also clear that we might be compelled to simply keep a lid on the whole affair, in the interest of *not* kicking off a full public panic. So yes, I can maybe almost see Pomeroy and Robles's point."

"BUT—and I know there's a big but in there somewhere," said the unflagging Ellen Macklin as she continued to push forward, patiently waiting for the other shoe to drop, however softly. "I mean, this is a case of such imperative and circumstance that it's almost intimidating," continued the junior newscaster after a moment of good reflection. "Who's to say the people of our city aren't at the very least entitled to a heads-up about some Ripper type out there in their midst and freely roaming the streets? Jim, my journalistic gut is screaming at me right now, and it's telling me that we need to step up here and get the word out—quickly but responsibly."

"Okay, Ellen, I don't entirely disagree with you on this but—" said Prysock before interrupting himself. "But no matter how you slice it, this whole thing's got crisis and catastrophe written all over it, a real powder keg just waiting to go off. And I would have thought that you of *all* people could see that. We have a clear and irrefutable obligation here to our readership and viewership—so what would you have me do?"

"Simple, go live with it, Jim. Just run the story in full—as is," proposed a stoic Macklin, a woman who, if nothing else, was known for her fearlessness and a knack for sticking to her guns if she thought she was right in a thing. Much like she was feeling right at this very moment.

"I understand your eagerness to do more here, Cubby—I really do—but you also have to look at my dilemma as well. Unmasking the existence of a possible serial killer running wild in the city, *before* its time, might actually be the even more irresponsible thing to do," countered an unshrinking Prysock to his mentee reporter as he watched her squirm about uneasily in her seat.

"Especially if all the facts aren't even in yet. Imagine the panic and widespread fear such an irresponsible act could bring about for this city. All of this can only blow back on us in a way we would not like—and, might I add, open us up to any number of adverse legal actions. We don't want to go down that road."

"So you'd have us wait it out and only *hope* there are no more killings?" asked an incredulous Macklin with an almost measurable pause. "But aren't we compelled to look at the even bigger picture here? Aren't we almost mandated to offer a public advisory, a warning—*something*? I mean, in the interest of our viewers—and for the very citizens of our greater metropolitan city itself?"

"No, but it could be a mistake that can only come back to bite us is all, on the bad end. The whole thing's a ticking time bomb that could just as easily go off in our editorial faces as it might serve any valid purpose. My fear is that if we don't, we'd only be feeding into an even greater hysteria than anything else. We can throw out a prescripted teaser up front, a lead line or something—even if we don't release any full headlines on the story—but c'mon, this thing's got the potential to be a hot potato. It's settled, Ellen."

"Understood, Jim, but let the record show where I stood on the matter. This story's already too big for us to keep under wraps. It'll take on a life of its own soon enough—and someone else will snap up the byline. So do we even have a choice here? The station is probably already chomping at the bit and demanding that we go live with it before we get scooped by some other network."

"Well, pretty much as expected, I can see you're not going to go easy on me, and present a convincing enough argument as usual," Prysock said as he seemed to perhaps cave in, finally, however reluctantly. "In fact, if it is indeed your contention that we absolutely go live with this Ripper story, I'll even let you have a go at it and run with the full coverage. After all, you've earned it. Plus you know Pomeroy best and most of the case facts already—probably better than any of the rest of us. You've stepped up nicely on this story, and you've been with the story virtually since day one. You run with it."

"Wait, you're *serious* then?" asked a disbelieving Ellen Macklin with raised eyebrows as she cast a puzzled look at her senior editor and almost let out a shriek, then chided herself for having done so. *You're probably going to need to work on that*, she thought to herself, then spoke again. "In that case, you won't be sorry, boss. I promise you," she said, then quickly hustled out of the man's office and made immediately for the phone on her desk.

❧❧❧

"In an exclusive interview with Captain Fuller, the head of the Major Crimes Unit itself noted that her investigative team has continued to work closely with both crime scene technicians and the city's senior medical examiner, Dr. Richard Pimleur, to solve the swell of Ripper slashings that have been terrifying the city for days on end now.

"Captain, would you care to say a few words?" Macklin said, deftly handing off the interview like a fast quarterback snapping the ball and finding a good tuck-and-run play right in front of her. The reporter was directing herself to the often-gruff head of the very teams that took on the heavy-duty cases themselves, the homicides and crimes of a more capital nature that no one else wanted, now finally concluding her own somewhat lengthy opening remarks.

"Thank you, and good evening, Ellen. I'm Captain Angie Fuller of the central Major Crimes Unit for much of the Manhattan South area, and all I can tell you at this time is that last evening police found the body of an unidentified senior citizen in the Greenwich Village area, a man who appears to have become yet another victim of an attack of what is still of an unspecified nature.

"I can only confirm that the body of an elderly man was found on Minetta Street just west of MacDougal, with wounds that might appear to be consistent with those found on at least two previous victims."

The shoulder-held camera seemed to jockey about for better vantage, looking for that perfect-angle, perfect-light shot, its operator cued in full by off-camera content managers, studio producers, and a cranky film director. But at all times it continued to roll on and roll on, now capturing all.

"Of course, Major Crimes must continue to hold back some, shall we say, more explicit details of the investigation since the case is essentially still ongoing at this time. But that said, Ellen, I can tell you that the department is looking at, at least one person of interest—one we believe may have figured in all three killings.

"I might expect to have more information for you as the case evolves and the investigation moves forward, but for the moment that's pretty much all I can release at this time."

"Well, Captain Fuller, I thank you for the opportunity to have spoken with you, and for your updating us on the scope and progress of that investigation."

"And I thank you, Ms. Macklin, for the opportunity to address the issue. The people of New York can rest assured that our Major Crimes Unit—and the NYPD at large—will continue to carry this investigation forward until we have the offender fully in custody," concluded the captain as she wrapped up her recitation with a somewhat predictable but otherwise optimistic narrative that had essentially said very little.

Fuller had at once simply halted her statement with little embellishment or fanfare—and little else to say—then nodded at the camera and turned on her heel as she made ready to leave, but was pulled up short by the persistent young reporter.

Seemingly not to be deterred in her indefatigable pursuit of the facts—and to not be so quickly fobbed off by the head of the city's most important Major Crimes arm—reporter Macklin decided to even further push her luck with her hook of a question to yet a second source right there on set. Quickly turning her attention to the dashing Pomeroy, who was also standing on the precinct steps just next to his boss, the homicide detective looked up and caught the reporter's gaze. already knowing that he might be called upon.

"And what about you, Sergeant Pomeroy, do you wish to add anything further to the captain's official statement? Something perhaps that can shed some additional light on the case at this time?" asked an expectant Macklin, hoping to elicit some response—any small response, really—from the man who had so quickly piqued both her professional and personal interest. And even that almost all at once, even if the man himself hadn't realized it. Yet.

"Well," the detective sergeant began as he plied a slow and thoughtful answer, looking long and hard into the handheld TV camera directly before him with a square-jawed resolve, "I can only repeat what the captain herself has said—the NYPD Major Crimes Unit remains fully committed to identifying the perpetrator, or perpetrators, of these horrific series of crimes. And rest assured we will not slow our pursuit, or flag in our resolve to track this offender until he is found, arrested, and taken into lockdown custody."

The handsome homicide detective shifted his stance ever so slightly as he squared off against the gaping eye of the TV camera.

"Well, can you maybe at least tell us if you have any working leads in the case at this time, Sergeant? I mean, anything viable or specific—" she queried, doing her level best to pose the question as open-endedly as she could, the better to elicit a more expansive response from the otherwise laconic detective. "I mean, what do you see as your current strategy at this time?"

"As you know, Ellen, I'm not really at liberty to speak to any specific leads we might have in the case at present since much of the case is still ongoing. I can only reaffirm our unwavering commitment—and frankly, the department's best efforts—that will all come into play in locating the suspect we believe is at the core of these terrible crimes being committed against our city's most venerable senior citizens. Therefore, in my mind at least, our strategy is still pretty clear."

"Oh, and what's that, Sergeant?" prodded the relentless Macklin as politely but as firmly as she might. "Exactly what kind of strategy are you planning at this time?"

"Simple: hunt him, find him, track him, then take him down—with extreme prejudice—to bring him as quickly to justice as we can. This guy just made our Top 10 list in spite of himself. He can run but he sure can't hide—not forever. Sooner or later, his ass is mine."

Macklin seemed to almost wince at the man's mild profanity, then spun up a finger in the air and the cameraman quickly cut the feed and all simply faded out to black.

🙞🙞🙞

"Looks like we're back to the numbers again, Captain. We're convinced the numbers might mean something special," Pomeroy began cautiously, knowing that the whole concept might itself be a bit elusive for his boss to grasp in full, so better to parse it out in snatches rather than to blunderbuss her with a full shotgun load of information.

Pomeroy composed himself, not wishing to appear foolish in front of his stickler of a boss, but much of it might be of her own doing. After all, she was the one who had authorized the assignment of the news team to his investigative unit in the first place, and now she was entitled to hear the full truth, however speculative and however much was out there.

Captain Fuller herself seemed unfazed but still mildly intrigued by the detective's opening remarks and soon found herself asking her leading question anyway. "Yes, I've been kicking the idea around myself, but perhaps you and your team have found something new?"

Robles and Pomeroy exchanged quick glances, then the senior cop slid a small sheaf of papers across the conference table to his captain.

"Then you'll probably want to take a look at this for yourself. We're beginning to see a clear pattern of facts and coincidences weaving in and out of the case, Cap—much of it perhaps a little too coincidental to even be so.

"So far, Captain, we've got dates, names, locations, and similar individual initials on all of the victims—and even the method of the killings themselves. And don't even get me started on the meaning of the playing cards themselves."

Fuller's eyebrows arched ever so slightly at the comment, with a piqued interest that was hard to disguise as her gaze skimmed over the analysis reports that Pomeroy had just put in front of her. "And you say you got all of this from Macklin? Hell, if that's the case, then what am I paying you guys for?" said Fuller with a jostle of uneasy humor that gave them both pause for a moment.

"Put in a call, somebody. Let's see if she can stop by for a quick powwow. Don't know about you two, but I'd be keenly interested in having her shed some light on all of this in her own words," Fuller ordered, then added her codicil. "And get Pimleur in here as well. Something tells me we'll be needing his perspective as well."

"I'm all over it, Cap," said an obliging Robles as he snapped to and made off in the direction of the bank of phones to begin putting out the several notification calls as requested.

"It was Macklin and her people who raised the issue in the first place, you know. Nice having a second set of eyes on the case. Ellen stumbled onto the numbers thing pretty much by accident—but I'm thinking we're kind of glad she did. Last week it was the thing with the names and initials. And it was only then that we were even able to more effectively stitch together a timeline and a profile."

Then, even at the moment, it was Detective Robles who bolted back into the captain's squad room office nearly out of breath and waving a clutch of papers in one hand, much to the surprise of Pomeroy and Captain Fuller.

"Good news. Pimleur and his pit crew of lab techs hit pay dirt on some forensics obtained from that last Strunk murder scene itself."

"Oh?" answered Captain Fuller, perking up and now curious to distraction as she yanked off her glasses and jerked her head up from the buried huddle she'd been in with Detective Sergeant Pomeroy, who was still perched just on the edge of her desk. "So what do we have exactly? Did our guy Pimleur find something important?"

Even Pomeroy looked unusually pleased with the unexpected update and found himself tuned into the news even as Robles opened up about the findings.

"What we got was lucky, Captain—apparently. The ME found evidence of a hair transfer on the last vic, plus he got fibers and blood. Pims said he was able to lift a couple of friction prints, with a possible five-point match on at least one—all from the same crime scene on Minetta.

"Forensics is looking at all of it even as we speak, but so far nothing's popped yet. It's possible we could have some more definitive results back from the lab later this afternoon. Guess we'll all just have to marinate on it until we hear back from the ME."

Fuller and Pomeroy thought about what was being said, reluctant to bask in the moment for too long lest it slip only too rudely away. Then Pomeroy found his words and finally spoke out.

"Well, that might jive with what we originally thought," he explained. "Remember our first working theory was that Strunk's was the one event where the killer might actually have been interrupted by the late-night couple returning home and just turning the corner."

Fuller seemed to catch on right away and quickly ran with the thought herself. "I see. Then maybe our killer did get sloppy after all—I mean in his moment of distraction with the homecoming couple just around the corner. We've seen this kind of thing before, you know. It takes only one slip-up. But maybe putting that aside, let's get back to Macklin's numbers thing. How are we supposed to see that?"

"That's the interesting part, Captain—and Macklin seems to have her theory on it. She's convinced they're latitude and longitude markings—yes, latitude and longitude. In fact, they're grid number plottings on a map, and all of them tracing back to a very specific series of dark locations and events in London, England. And I have to say that all of it's every bit as macabre."

Having finished a more studied view of the pages, Fuller quietly set the papers down and sat back in her chair, placing her fingers in teepee fashion in front of her face, now with a light-bulb look in her eyes. Then, after what must have seemed like a clear eternity, she looked up and finally met the gaze of the two detectives sitting in front of her saying simply, "Well, I'll be damned." Then all went silent.

Bogdan Volstad was seething and dispirited. His killing lust had not been assuaged, his anger remained unchecked, and the thirst for the rip-and-slash and the letting of blood had only continued, even through his series of heinous attacks made thus far. He was a swarthy wight of small mercy and a man possessed, a night wraith and a patron of the dark lanes and back alleys. And still, it was clear that the killer's work might not yet be done.

Dressed all in black, Volstad sat in a darkened, dusty room all by himself, a hooded menace with an edged blade and a dark mission, a man still unshakably in search of yet another victim, yet another kill. He'd been hard put and put off not to do so. And in the face of past events, and still rankled by having been so rudely interrupted in his prized third takedown on Minetta Street, he thus had so desperately needed his fourth on Bedford. And had not old Saucy Jack done much the same himself on the thirtieth day of September, the night of the double murder itself on dark London streets of old?

Now an overwhelming feeling of incompleteness hung over the killer's head. This was as he continued to devolve and spiral only further down into a black abyss with an even blacker cloud anchored just above that could not so clearly be dissipated or too easily purged. And all signs indicated that he would be almost *compelled* to kill again, and all that remained was the who, the where, and the when. And then he'd have his own Catherine Eddowes and Elizabeth Stride—just like Old Jack, the old Butcher of Whitechapel himself.

BERSERKER: THE DOUBLE EVENT: ENDERS

30 SEPTEMBER—PRESENT DAY

Old Carlton Enders had always known that he wanted to be a "Coastie." As far back as he could remember, he'd often stand on the shore as a young lad in New England, where he'd watch from the beach just beside his family's home. The large, smooth-bearing coast guard cutters would silently sail by on the far horizon, and he longed to be aboard each and every ship that passed.

Salt air, rolling seas, and good seamanship are what he longed for even then, but could not yet have. Then the years passed quickly by as the scruffy, knee-high kid with the beachfront view would soon himself become the same young man who would now finally get his shot—indeed, his chance of a lifetime—enrollment in the famed U.S. Coast Guard Training Center at historic Cape May, New Jersey, in late 1950.

The young lad had done well and excelled, graduating within the top-five percentile of his "A" program training class with a full rank of petty officer. How rare indeed. And soon enough, he was already fast-tracking his way up through good nautical skills and his own applied learning in his area of occupational specialty—"Target Acquisition Systems"—he had advanced through the ranks at near-lightning speed, getting "4-Oh" marks on almost every evaluation he'd ever been given, and still keeping up his meteoric military rise.

After that, of course, it was on to a long and outstanding stint at the USCG's own Boston-based "1st District" HQs for most of his term of service. Only then did it finally occur to him, even now all these years later, that he'd finally lived up to his dream: serving on that fast white cutter that had always been his first love, even all those years before as he stood on a stretch of beach as a child simply watching ships pass over the sea.

And it was only now, after many years spent in the service of his country, that he found himself finally rounding yet another corner on an uplifting and well-deserved retirement, now with nearly twenty-eight years of superior performance in his chosen branch under his belt.

He was exuberant and clearly comprehending—perhaps even upbeat to a fault. *Semper paratus*, his very service motto, becoming more a code to live by than just a simple organizational slogan. "Always prepared!" it admonished, and Enders had always been so—proud to have served his time and to have achieved a final discharge rank of E-9, master chief petty officer of the "Littoral Guard."

And now much of it was happening precisely in its own time, even at the moment, with a bucket-list itinerary right in front of him and every road wide open and beckoning him on. How sweet would be this next of life's phases: "retirement." Perhaps now indeed could be a whole new chapter and plateau for him: a time for skiffs and fishing poles on cold mountain lakes, a time for ice cones and cotton candy with the grandkids at the county fair whenever it came to town. Or maybe simply just a time for an even more "life-affirming" adventure with an all-out assault on a whitewater rafting run down the wild rapids of frigid Colorado itself.

And all these things indeed did the good Enders mull over, allowing his mind to freely wander on his return trip back home across the lane. He was already quietly assured that he'd planned it all out—well down to the last tent peg and canteen—and it was his avowed wish to do it all, all within the very time he might have left.

Just maybe not today ...

※ ※ ※

The black-hooded Volstad was beside himself with spleen and fury—apoplectic almost beyond all rhyme or reason. His work had been so rudely disturbed, his signature placement of the calling card message and cryptic numerics almost totally confounded, and his delight in the very blood of the moment had truly been frustrated in full. The Butcher was beside himself, still with a bloodlust that had essentially gone unslaked, and a ritualistic killing that had itself only been stunted and left wholly unfulfilled. And much of it simply maddened the killer all the more.

And thus the Ripper's urge had very much carried over, still dark and unslaked, a pitch-black void that still lurked deep within the man's umbrous soul, and he knew on the instant that his tasks were not yet done. He'd been rudely interrupted, his beautiful work dispatched by a brace of careless interlopers who'd only stumbled upon the scene on a lover's lane stroll that had only randomly opted to turn onto his street just on the moment. And now they had barred perhaps his even greater work and greatest pleasure, even at the height of its most savored moments.

All this he pondered while still much in flight, even as he fumed and fretted his way quickly from the venue of his last attack on dark Minetta. And the frightful killer knew that his work was not yet done. The urge was far too strong, and in him still lies a dark and unsounded bottom of hunger that he knew he dare not resist. He must be on with his handiwork and would so enjoy his deadly hunt were he able. And thus he set out now for even newer prey, much as Red Jack himself had done with Stride and Eddowes in old Whitechapel all those many years ago.

"DEAR BOSS," the killer muttered solemnly to himself as he lumbered along with menace and stealth, now with a right leg that he seemed to disfavor and slightly drag behind as he moved through the darkened back streets of late-night Greenwich Village.

"DEAR BOSS," he echoed for yet a second time with a gnashing of the teeth, shuffling off slowly afoot on a sinister circuit to seek out more victims, more prey. Now as he fast approached his next poorly lit venue of the night did he find exactly what he'd been searching for, even as old Carlton Enders himself ambled slowly onto the scene on his late-night stroll across a deserted Bedford Street just near its quiet intersection with Christopher.

The time was now well past 10:30 p.m. on the thirtieth day of September, and if at all the fast-moving Christopher Street was itself populated with a flurry of passersby and light traffic on an already-congested one-way street, Bedford itself was not.

The very width of the street might itself not have been more than some thirty to thirty-five feet in full at its widest point, and might only accommodate the parking of cars on one side. It was an eerie and ghostly passage of a street, a walkable alley that seemed to be fraught with any number of dangerous dark spots and recessed doorways that ran along both sides of the entire lane.

For a hooded predator on a targeting stalk might it be nothing if not precisely the perfect hunting ground for his next victim, the unsuspecting old veteran Enders himself. And only Volstad knew that the selection of his next target was entirely a matter of circumstance and design.

But the killer knew his mind and what evil deeds it sought to digest— the hunt and bloodlust sport for which it now so avidly hungered. Such that would always move through the hunt and end in the kill itself. And thus he settled back into the dark of a recessed archway and tilted back the head with nostrils flared as he savored the deadly lead-up to his noxious deed. He shunted back, almost disappearing into the comforting pull of darkness, soon lost to the view of all.

Quiet now the stalker stood, poised on a precipice of intent and execution, a thug with quivering orbs that almost rolled about in his head, much as if to almost expose the very whites of his eyes as he assumed a kind of ghoulish pre-attack posturing. He was everyone's bad guy and the idyllic fiend of every Saturday afternoon hooror film of old. Only worse.

The killer steeled himself and made ready the fang and sting of his sharp cutting edge, set taut the nerves, and flexed the muscles as he dangerously fingered the lethal blade. With ears pricked up and carefully attuned, he listened only for the cadence of the coming footfalls, as soon indeed the sound did meet his ears and graduated in sound.

The stage was now set for Citizen Enders' and the Ripper's paths to cross, however short and brutal that meeting might be. And only then would come the leather glove and muscled arm, the lunge and tackle that would so cruelly catch old Enders by surprise ... then once-twice across the flaccid neck as the edge of blade swept silently across the victim's throat.

The hush of Bedford Street was only mildly disturbed by the gurgling death throes of the old man himself, even as he began to succumb to the violent attack of the Ripper, this on the very night of old London Jack's own "double event" itself. And in an instant the old soul had expired, his last sad and conscious thoughts now centering on the bucket-list retirement he would now never realize in full.

And so indeed had yet another eighty-year-old life been snuffed out by the insane Volstad, even as the ruffian slasher quickly made his way through the dimly lit backstreets of the Bedford killing zone and faded off into the late-night shuffle of Christopher Street just at the end of the block and was gone.

☙☙☙

The three men were meeting for yet a second time on the same night—the night of September 30 itself, only this time over a *second* body that would be found only blocks away from one of his earlier victims, old Anton Chapel himself on Grove.

By now a light rain had already been agitated into something far more unrelenting—an interminable pelt of a drizzle that grew even on the moment to a steady downpour that splattered everywhere and everything —and now horribly mucking up their very crime scene.

Gathering in small uniformed clutches throughout the whole area, a troop of officers moved dutifully about attending to the many tasks that might most be needed to process and secure the crime scene itself, ramping up their crowd-control efforts, canvassing the immediate area for any first-person leads, and streaming the long banners of yellow crime-scene tape to mark and cordon off the area in full.

Busied by the mandated protocols already in play in the near distance, another contingency of uniformed officers quickly set up a makeshift tarp and canopy to secure the very area *in situ*, and to effectively preserve any viable evidence from being contaminated—or worse, being lost in full. Then Pomeroy took the first opportunity to speak.

"I know, I know, Pimleur—I suppose now you're going to say I told you so," the detective began with a customary jab that might more have been expected from a snippy Robles. "So what the hell? What is it this time—same night, only a different victim? I go around the corner for a coffee and a bite to eat and come back and it's World War III out here again? What gives?"

"Trust me, I don't like being right about this any more than you enjoy hearing me say it," said a visibly upset Pimleur. "And I sure as hell don't like standing around out here either. You know I hate the rain."

"Copy that, Pimleur. So we got anything new on this one or what? Any ID on the guy, I mean—any idea who he was?" asked Robles, curious to a fault and perhaps a little too anxious to hear the coroner's response. And then he got his answer ...

"Well, we were lucky enough to at least find a wallet on the body here—it's probably our best place to start," Pimleur offered in reply as he carefully handled the evidence of the moment.

"Name says he's an ENDERS—a Carlton Enders, or so it says—and his ID seems to indicate that he's eighty to eighty-one, much like most of our other victims. I'd estimate about 5'10" in height, and a buck-40 in weight, maybe—soaking wet. Apparently lived right here in the Village as well since this address of record here says that he lived somewhere right over on Thompson Street."

Pomeroy thought about that for a moment, then asked the obvious connecting questions, "So let me guess, you found the same MO with the signature tattooing on the forehead, the note, playing card, and cryptic numbers, all just like those we saw with our previous victims?"

Pimleur looked up, slowly removing the half-shell glasses from the bridge of his nose as he stood to wipe them off in the gentle cascade of rain. "It's scary how you can almost read my mind, Pomeroy," noted the chief forensics specialist. "But you're right, that's exactly what we've got here, Joe. It's the damnedest thing. Pretty much a mirror image of each of the previous attacks," said the medical examiner with a certain deadpan look. "Oh, it's the same guy all right."

૭૭૭

"Detective Pomeroy," began an eager reporter Ellen Macklin with a hidden smile that might have said she knew more than she let on, this as she riffled through a small sheaf of papers and looked up. "I've been reviewing some of the data you've pulled together with your team, and I think I might have something of some good use to the investigation. Some new insights, perhaps, into the case—such that might be of keen interest to you."

"Oh," said Pomeroy with a quizzical look and an involuntary scratch of the head as he spun around. "Okay, I'll bite. What exactly do you mean?"

"Well, Sergeant, just as I was led to believe earlier on in the case, those numbers might mean something after all—and after a little background digging, I'm convinced they do.

"So following that same train of thought, I decided to take a closer look at all of the individual *names* of the men attacked, only this time paying better attention to the initials of each victim. There's something going on here, Pomeroy, almost to the point of being just a little eerie and Halloween uncanny. And I think I know what it is too."

Pomeroy chewed on the information being offered by the reporter for a moment, carefully digesting the reporter's observations, then finally met a matching gaze from her direction as he asked the obvious, "Initials? What exactly do you mean *initials*?"

Later, after she had explained her running hypothesis, he stood transfixed and amazed, unaware of the fact that they might have crossed a whole new threshold in the case. And even as the dust settled thick after the storm, and the reporter had finished with her detailed explanation, Pomeroy's eyes had already gone wide, and the only thing he could manage as he reached for the phone was "Holy shit!" then he punched in Captain Fuller's number and sat down in absolute disbelief as he waited for his boss to pick up the other end of the line.

࿇࿇࿇

Now it was some three days after the third Elon Strunk killing on Minetta Street itself, and neither Pomeroy nor Robles were any further along in their investigation than they had been previously, even after the second attack. Clues in the case were scant and leads were almost nonexistent. The two had gone through every file and every profile they could find, scanning every criminal record in their databases for a similar MO,[7] and turning over every rock in a methodical pursuit of a viable suspect. But all of their efforts had thus far met with only negligible results and yielded little.

---

[7] MO—*Modus Operandi*, a literal Latin phrase and legal term for "the way in which something (or someone) operates," contemporaneously used to describe (i.e., a criminal enterprise).

The senior investigator looked around his dusty work area and surveyed the pile of folders and papers that crowded every corner of his desk like so much erudite litter, then scratched his head in seeming disbelief. He couldn't get a handle on any of it and could not quite figure out a way to get ahead of this offender, and it seemed to aggravate him to no end.

Both he and Robles knew they would need something soon, some kind of break in the case, whether a hot tip, a new lead, or in the best of all worlds, an actual suspect, when just then the phone jangled off the hook, startling the senior cop almost out of his seat. It was Robles himself, calling with an update directly from the lab.

"Sarge," a thick and resonant electronic voice injected, as it trailed over the phone into the ear of Detective Sergeant Joe Pomeroy, the man's very news a kind of soothing music that might for all the world have sounded like a bright chorus of *Hallelujah* itself.

"Looks like we got at least one possible, Sarge—finally. A single hit on a clean partial print lifted from our last crime scene. And that's not the end of it either," the deep-baritone voice of Robles reported over the phone. "We might even have gotten our hands on a little storefront video as well. I'd have to say it's almost a win-win, boss."

❧❧❧

"You mean we might have film on this guy?" a hopeful homicide detective asked of his junior partner.

"Sure—granted, it was taken from a block away on a dark avenue on Eighth Street, but we managed to get our hands on some film. Maybe it'll give us something useful," said the sycophantic Paxton as he now delivered the full thrust of his brief. He'd stood the while bobbing his head up and down throughout his entire report, but it also served as a cue for the sergeant, who'd also been closely following along.

"You see, it's like I always say, there's nothing like good forensics, digital enhancement, and the luck of the draw to make our day. Could we have just caught our first big break?"

"Good—and not a moment too soon either. I could use some good news right about now. I've got four homicides just looking for a home, and my gut tells me they all go straight back to this one guy," replied a bridled but impatient Pomeroy, still chomping at the bit in advance of the patrol officer's continued words.

"Sarge, the good news is our tech guys were able to pull a little video feed from somewhere near the last crime scene at the Mews. The bad news is that even after some enhancement and filtering, much of the footage is still a little too grainy and unusable for our immediate purposes. But that said, with just a little luck, we might be able to finally match up a plate to a name."

"And if we can get a name, we can maybe get ourselves a face," said Pomeroy, almost completing the man's sentence and dove-tailing smoothly into his thought. "Okay, so now you've officially got my attention," advised the sergeant with just a tincture of anticipation and a hopeful perk of eyebrow that said the voice on the other end of the line might have just made his day. "So who's our guy then?" he asked finally.

"The prints came back to a name of Volstad," began the junior partner with a measured deliberation. "A 'Bogdan Volstad' to be sure—hell, there's a name. And Joe, there's more too—it appears as if our guy's already in the system. Looks like he's already known to both local and state authorities. Our records indicate that the man's thirty-eight years old, with an LKA[8] going back somewhere to the ass-end of Red Hook, Brooklyn, down by the river somewhere. And Sarge, there's more ..." continued a cautiously elated Robles.

"What?" Pomeroy prodded, now momentarily looking up from a mound of unread papers and staring off into short space as he listened carefully to Robles on the phone that was still glued to his ear.

"Well, you're probably not going to like this, but we just dig up another old address on this Volstad character—our person of interest," began Robles with a measure of apprehension as he ruffled through a small sheaf of papers in consultation. "An old address that came back as a 1743 West 43rd Street."

---

[8] LKA, in law enforcement circles at least, means Last Known Address.

"Wait, did you say—**1743**?" queried a disbelieving Pomeroy.

"Yep, you guessed it, boss—middle of the Hudson River," added Robles with a half chuckle.

"The sneaky bastard. I'm starting not to like this guy already."

"Something just doesn't feel right about this one, boss. This guy's an evil seed for sure, but on paper at least, he doesn't really look like a killer. The man's rap sheet just doesn't hold up, and nothing points to this kind of aberrant behavior, Joe—certainly on this level. He doesn't come across as your average garden-variety strong-arm thug type. The guy's a brawler for sure, with a slew of A&B[9] charges and a whole sheet of nasty priors that'll probably have us up most of the night just checking into. But one thing's for sure, Sarge, I might still like him for it, but we're going to need to dig a lot deeper on him."

"You did good, Junior. You keep going like this and you'll make detective sergeant yet."

"Yeah, right, boss, I'm still holding my breath on that. But anyway, listen, I'm sending all of it your way now—just thought you'd want to hear it from me first," concluded Robles with a commendable thoroughness and polished professionalism. Maybe one day he'd actually get those stripes yet.

"I appreciate the heads-up, Damien. You stay there and wrap up with ME Pimleur, just in case he comes up with something else that might be actionable for the case. But you made my day here—hell, maybe even my week!" the senior cop said for the first time since he'd taken on the case itself, even as he hung up and swept a cautious eye over the ordered array of notes, factsheets, and photos mounted on the room's "murder board" with a contented half chuckle and a now discernible gleam in his eye. And for at least that one moment only, things were definitely looking up, perhaps even for the very first time.

---

[9] A&B in police jargon implies a charge of assault and battery.

❧❧❧

"Absolutely not, Macklin, no way. You know as well as I that our network has an obligation to carry the story virtually as is. In fact, the network is planning to lead with its first installment this evening," Jim Prysock had said almost matter-of-factly with a priggish sniff of his nose as he spun about in his chair and rummaged through a dusty old credenza directly behind his crowded desk.

The curmudgeon of an editor resurfaced with two glasses and an old bottle of *Dewar's* Scotch that he'd always kept on hand for just such occasions—whether to lament his occasional failures, to celebrate his many small victories, or to simply take the edge off a high-pressure day when his world seemed to be closing in on him. He poured out a couple of modest drinks with a measured one-fingered stinginess and slid one glass across the desk in Ellen's direction. Not much of a drinker herself, she hesitated for a moment before even accepting the alcoholic beverage, until her boss gave her a small go-ahead nod, then she raised the glass to a point beneath her nose and sniffed the full-bodied aroma before sipping.

"Jim, you know we've both given our word to Captain Fuller and the folks down at the 6th Precinct," she began, slowly nursing her drink, shivering one eye shut as she digested, then shuddered at the delivery of the drink's secondary punch and very potency. She paused after only one sip and found herself curiously enjoying the trademark malted toffee nut taste of the Scotch, savoring its robust flavor almost to distraction, then continued with her more pressing thought.

"Take it as you will, boss, but if you do decide to go ahead with an exposé *before* the police can follow up on any of their key leads in the case, our credibility with Pomeroy and the captain will be shot all to hell."

"So just what are you trying to say here, Ellen? I know there's a point in there somewhere."

"That going live could only be seen as a breach of trust, Jim—on a scale that could place our even greater relationship with the NYPD in even more peril than it might already be. I should think we'd be well-advised to consider the value of that relationship and to honor our standing commitment to the unit. This whole thing *could* be an easy win-win for everyone, boss. We keep our exclusive on the story and still come out on the right side of the whole affair—WITH our relationship intact."

"Are you really telling me that—the right side? Truth is, I'm not even sure any of us really know what the right side is in this event, but it still doesn't release us from our even greater responsibility. And from where I sit at least, it's pretty much a no-brainer: We report on the story, release a very few salient details to our viewership, and above all else, we warn them of a possible stalker in their midst.

"In its final analysis, I'd expect it all comes down to a more common-sense approach, Cubby—an informed public is far more alert and on the lookout to help the police. Surely you can see that, can't you, Ellen?"

"I know, I know, but if we tip our hand—at the expense of our relationship with the Major Crimes Unit—what'll we wind up with? Jim, you don't pay me to just sit around here and be a pretty face and never speak my mind. We could very easily be looking at a serious compromise of our good standing with the law enforcement community—and especially with the very liaison people we have to work so hand in hand with on an ongoing daily basis. Not to mention a serious breach of ethics with a pretty bad trickledown for all of the rest of us involved. They'd never trust us again.

"Boss, this is as much about principle as it is about credibility—you drummed that much into my head from day one yourself—and it's about integrity and trust, and relationships," Ellen said, driving her point home with acuity and aplomb.

"Ellen, I don't entirely disagree with what you're saying here, but I'm still catching a lot of heat upstairs from the managing editors themselves and they're dead set on running with the story later tonight."

"I have to say, Jim, this can only end badly. It can only be a reckless move to go live with anything just yet, and we're not sure," Macklin ventured, taking another small sip of the top-shelf Scotch the senior editor had offered her earlier, then wrapped up her soliloquy with a warm smile as she concluded with, "Of course, you're the boss and the one calling the shots here. Let's just hope we don't live to regret it."

❦❦❦

"And none of it seems to provide us with any better results than we had already. So far that is—nothing actionable, I mean. Not a hair, not a fiber, no prints—which could mean our killer simply wore gloves. But we still have nothing that even begins to point us to a suspect. Sadly, that seems to be the long and the short of it for right now, Captain.

"But be assured," continued the almost contrite coroner, "that my office is working around the clock to uncover anything that might at all be actionable for your investigative team. And while I might be covering some old ground here, I did find some pretty striking similarities between all the cases—much as we did with the earlier Novaks, Chapel, and Strunk slayings. And now again with this fourth victim, our Mr. Enders—all occurring over the course of little more than three to four weeks, if that."

"Seems more like an eternity, all cards on the table," observed Pomeroy a bit dryly, scratching absentmindedly at an annoying itch just behind an ear.

"Well, whoever he is, our killer's certainly been a busy boy, almost enjoying his work, I'd say, and daring us to the teeth to do anything to stop him."

A nod or two of assent from the others told the medical examiner that he must be on the right track in his analysis.

"In fact, it is my sober opinion that these brutal attacks will only continue, perhaps even accelerate and intensify, over the course of the coming days and weeks," concluded the portly forensics specialist, pausing only momentarily as he struggled to catch his wind, then opted to continue.

"All four victims appear to have been the focus of a series of classic grab-and-slash attacks, such that must have been both sudden and extremely violent—obviously. The attacks were swift and explosive, probably carried out in less than a minute and always occurring within low-traffic, poorly lit backstreets that all seem to be located in the same Greenwich Village areas over and over.

"In fact, we have no real evidence of any previous attacks—on such a scale, and with such a degree of ferocity—occurring anywhere else in the entire metropolitan area. Certainly nothing like this and concentrated in only this one area. We have to ask ourselves why?"

"I think, Dr. Pimleur, that that's a question we would ALL like to have answered," said the captain with a nod of agreement from Pomeroy.

"Oh, and one other thing you should probably know: it's also my firm belief that this offender is already quickly devolving, apparently moving down a one-way street of no return—and fast. This doesn't end well for anyone, I'm afraid."

"So what else can you tell us about him," queried an interested Detective Pomeroy.

"Well, our killer's calculating and smart—able to stay a step ahead of us in spite of our best efforts. And don't be fooled, he's not done either. In fact he may only be getting started and still perfecting his craft. My guess? We're in for a helluva ride and a devil of a time just trying to keep up with the guy, let alone nab him."

Eyes went blank in the room with the chilling words and there was a discernible hush that fell over the room, then it was the detective who finally spoke his small piece, hoping now to infuse his observations of the case into the roundtable discussion itself. Without fidget or undue delay, the senior investigator then laid out his soliloquy of the facts as best he knew them to be.

"Some pretty alarming words to hear, Pimleur. God help us if we don't get this guy before he strikes again. In order to move forward more effectively, maybe we back up a couple of clicks and review just what we have so far. Maybe we can nail down more of a foundation and amplify our timeline.

"First off, we know as early as 31 August that the body of our Paul Novaks vic was found on Grove Street near Seventh Avenue—and again on 8 September when we were called to the scene of the Anton Chapel assault itself in Washington Square Park. Now we have two more here with Strunk and Enders, both on a date of 30 September. So why these specific dates, and what's the significance of each?"

"Yeah, I've been asking myself pretty much the same question, but I keep hitting the same brick walls over and over," noted a frustrated Captain Fuller.

"Tell me about it. We also know that the interval between all of the killings has always been more at *weeks* and not months—we *think*. And yet all of the cases continue to show the same MO and murder profile: a double slash across the throat—thought to have been from left to right—done with such ferocity as to nearly sever each of the victims' heads. In addition, we found a number of unexplained contusion marks about the torso of the bodies, consistent with some measure of grappling and resistance, but no real evidence of blunt force trauma to any of the victims."

Now it was Captain Fuller who would inject herself into the discussion, interrupting Pomeroy's focused remarks to share a pointed observation of her own with the group. "But even on the face of it—and setting that much aside—it still brings us back to the bizarre series of clues that were found to be common to all four cases, namely the curious forehead markings, meaning the 'Dear Boss' scribblings, the notes, and odd number sequences. Oh, and don't forget the playing card thing itself, that red Jack—all trinkets, really—all of which appear to have repeatedly been found at each murder scene we uncovered. Do we have anything new on any of those? I'm thinking this is probably as good a place as any to start."

"Unfortunately, the very best of what we have so far," responded a still-eager Robles, maybe reading more into the moment than he needed to. "Is still only circumstantial at its core, I'm afraid, and none of it could really be considered evidentiary. In fact, all we've really got here are some loose odds and ends that none of us can account for. As to the rest, ma'am—the killing format and these weird rituals and post-mortem displays—none of us can be 100 percent sure of what *any* of it means."

Having waited her turn patiently, and not wishing to speak out of sorts, Macklin now found herself finally thrust to the forefront as she now tagged in to address the group, the reporter's very comments being directed mainly at Pomeroy and the captain herself.

"Captain Fuller," the petite and comely newscaster began, "and Sergeant Pomeroy—gentlemen," she acknowledged. "First off I'd like to take this opportunity to thank you all for allowing me to even be a part of the investigative team—and to bring to it what little I could to help resolve the case itself.

"I've been embedded with the team for some time now—from its inception really, all the way back to the first Grove Street attack—much with your sanctioning, of course. And all along, I've been asked by the team to yield on the finer point of never disclosing any of the salient details of the case and not leak the story to any of our media sources. Indeed time and again I've been asked to simply sit on the story in full, at least until the conclusion of the initial phases of the investigation. And I have done so, however reluctantly, without protest or resentment.

"But I'm sure you understand that I also have my own chain of command and bosses as well, and I'm beginning to feel a little conflicted here. In fact, I'm taking some pretty heavy flak from my own as any editor since I also have to answer to him at the network as well—unfortunately.

"And I can tell you, I've got a pretty hot-under-the-collar Jim Prysock breathing down my neck almost daily to go live with something before our station gets scooped by some other news outlet who might easily stumble bass-ackward onto the same story we're trying so hard to keep under wraps. With that in mind, I hope you can understand that I do have a kind of divided loyalty here, and I'm stuck in the middle here with a pressing dilemma of my own. How would you have me go forward on this, Captain?"

Fuller thought a hot second about what she was being asked, then offered her assurances to Macklin.

"Well, I guess all I'm asking is that you buy us a little time, Ellen—if that's even possible. It's probably the best way to handle the situation. Buy us some time. Maybe stay dark on the story for another few days is what I'm requesting," implored Captain Fuller as the rest of the team hung in the balance and listened attentively about the meeting table.

"Plus I'm sure we could probably use the extra time to maybe buy ourselves a little wiggle room to pursue some of the finer points of the case while we wait to get a lead on this guy. I do appreciate your helping out with the investigation here. I just need to know if our request is at all workable. Somehow just buy us a week, okay?"

"Captain, you must know there's no such thing as a WEEK—or even two *days*—in the news business, and I'm hoping you can understand my position here as well," replied Macklin, perhaps a deal more forcefully than she might otherwise have liked as she struggled not to offend any in the meeting. After all, she was still just finding her way with the team and learning the ropes. Plus she was still the outsider and a little unsure of her footing, particularly in this current group setting.

"But that much said, ma'am, I'll do as much as I can. I'll hold the story as long as I can get the exclusive rights to it later," said the fetching reporter, hoping that the concession was not being lost on Fuller and Pomeroy. "If you think it'll help move the case along and close the books on this *Slasher* fiend. But just a heads-up for all, and I'm certain you know as well as I that these things always have a way of getting out one way or another—often whether we will or not."

"Of course, Ellen—I understand completely, but I also know Jim Prysock to be a reasonable man," countered Fuller, not at all put off by the reporter's remarks since even she could see the cold logic of what Macklin was saying. Then a cloud rolled past her face when she finally realized what might have been said. "Wait, are you trying to tell us that we've got a leak somewhere? You mean right here in-house?"

"No, ma'am. I'm just putting it out there as a WHAT-IF only—but often it's someone who's close enough to the investigation themselves."

In all truth, it may have even been a foregone conclusion already, Pomeroy opined privately to himself as he coughed lightly into a cupped hand. *In fact, it was not too far-fetched to assume that it might only be a matter of time before it would become necessary to even do so—to release the story and run with some select details of the case perhaps. But all of it was simply the time they might not otherwise have if the killer were to strike again.*

But even more alarming, in the unlikely event that someone did decide to blow the lid off the story, what then might the NYPD—and the even greater City of New York itself—expect exactly in terms of fallout and a near-certain mass panic that might almost be certain to take over in the face of any reporting on the serial killings themselves? And none of it was terribly comforting to think about, but Pomeroy and his team still had a job to do, and they were all bound to duty to see it through to its logical conclusion. And now instead there was some odd talk of a conduit that might already be leaking info to the press? *Shit.*

"So where exactly is the leak in all of this, and how do we even begin to pinpoint a source in the first place? If it's even true, that is?" asked a now-steamed Sergeant Pomeroy.

"Hell, it could actually be someone right here at the 6th Precinct—someone right under our very noses all the time," growled a visibly shaken Captain Fuller, now with nostrils flared as she glowered angrily at everyone seated at the table "And God help the soul if I find later that there's been any targeted news releases leaked by *any* of my people to *any* live TV venues! That much you can clearly take to the bank!"

"Captain, I've got people already on the lookout and digging around on exactly this right now," offered Macklin in a weak attempt to defuse the captain's ticking time bomb. "Even if half of what you're saying is true, we might still be hard-pressed to root out an actual source for those leaks—*or* to find a way to shut them down—quickly enough. But I'm still looking into it anyway."

"Yet here we are, once again having to worry about some deep-throat in our midst," responded Pomeroy. "Whose unmasking is never as easy as you might think since they're usually deeply entrenched and always insulated from any pointing fingers. But this I can tell you, I'm sure it wasn't any of us."

"Yes, I understand that, and of course I'm inclined to agree with you, but to take it a step further," the captain said with a wave of chafing anger that seemed to still be building, "but to have those damn broadcast reports go on to even quote a series of 'confirmed confidential sources within the NYPD' itself—well, you can pretty much imagine my surprise. I was spitting mad and seeing double!"

"Well, none of us much like being blindsided by this any more than you do, Captain, but I have to say..." Robles began almost sheepishly before being entirely cut off by his boss. Now as the most junior member of the investigative team himself, he generally hated having his ass chewed out and handed to him, and over time he'd quickly learned to simply bite his tongue and keep his mouth shut whenever the captain was on the warpath. Pretty much like right now since it was shaping up to be precisely one of those moments. Perhaps better then 'twould be to simply zip the lip and listen in instead. But Fuller was still on a bit of a rampage even now and was making it well known, her anger seeming to mount by the moment.

"Oh, and don't think I'm finished with you two yet either—I mean, what the hell!" growled a still-miffed Fuller to the team. "You realize all of this adds only more fuel to the fire, don't you? And all of it will bring on only more of a media spotlight on all of us—and our collective activities. A spotlight our investigation simply doesn't need at this time, dammit!"

Pomeroy chewed on that idea of the lid blowing off the whole affair for a moment, then found himself speaking up, almost blurting out his suspicions before he realized that he'd even said it.

"Has anybody at all talked to either Paxton or Reid lately? Both officers were on patrol and first on-scene at least a couple of the homicide locations long before any of the rest of us even arrived. How about we pull their asses off the line right now and get them in here. Maybe, Captain, maybe it's time for us to have ourselves a little chat with both."

જાજાજા

"On a night that has already witnessed a double-event murder—namely that of two more elderly victims in the west Greenwich Village area—New Yorkers across the entire metropolitan area are understandably quite on edge tonight.

"Insider sources within the NYPD Major Crimes Unit now indicate that the killing spree appears to have been highly targeted, beginning late last evening with the graphic killing of one Elon Strunk, and ending with the early morning slaying of another—one Carlton Enders—both of whose mutilated bodies were discovered by passersby who then immediately notified police.

"Now, in an *Action9News* exclusive, we have further learned that the twin attacks now mark the third and fourth victims of a slasher that terrified New Yorkers have already dubbed 'The Village Ripper.' That the name itself might summon up only grisly images of the past—with the original Jack the Ripper of London fame from more than a century ago—is no surprise. So it might be expected that there'd be many cautious New Yorkers who are understandably quite spooked by the killer's very existence and elusive nature.

"Recent events seem to have only amplified the grip of fear across the city, and have somehow taken an already chilling situation and made it that much more harrowing and surreal. And much more so indeed for seniors within that Manhattan district.

"'We simply don't feel safe anymore—any*where*'," observed one Arthur Rankel, an official spokesman from one of the smaller community centers in the west Greenwich Village area. 'And now we're all afraid to venture outside at all,' Mr. Rankel told this reporter just earlier this evening.

"The police investigation seems to have gained some traction, however, and a number of new leads have been generated as police close in on a possible suspect—a person of interest as it were—but sources close to the investigation say that no further information can be released to the public at this time.

"Of course, your *ActionNews9* team will stay with you every step of the way with our ongoing coverage of this killer in our midst—and the trail of horrific crimes being left in the wake of his senseless spree.

"We urge our viewers to stay tuned for further updates as we receive them. With more to follow at 11, this is your coanchor Ellen Macklin signing off. Now for a quick look at the roads out there..."

There followed now a pregnant pause, such that might even have been longer than anticipated, almost as if the network itself had wished to allow the menacing words themselves to fully sink in before moving on. Then the distant voice of a second anonymous newscaster lulled on with a monotonic soliloquy about building renovations on the lower East Side as he delivered the network's mundane nightly wrap-up. Such was the nature of a "slow news" night and the very reason that the drab monologue continued, marching along in lockstep with its otherwise gloomy parade of news.

"In a moment we'll take a look at area traffic with a birds-eye report from our roving eye-in-the-sky helicopter and Chopper Dave, right after these important words from our sponsor."

Then the suspenseful TV newscast lessened its grip on its audience and faded quickly to a perky cosmetics commercial that promised clear skin and reduced wrinkles in five days or less.

IN THE HOUSE OF BUTCHERY AND CONTEMPT: KIRWIN

9 NOVEMBER—PRESENT DAY

"Foxtrot 7, this is Foxtrot Leader," USAF Lieutenant Colonel Maxwell J. Kirwin squawked as the flight leader of the famed 336th Fighter Squadron, out of the K-14 air facility just south of Seoul, South Korea, in late 1950. The "Rocketeers" had been the unit's adopted nickname, an air wing that was already made up of several fighter aircraft that were "state-of-the-art" in their own time: the F-80 *Shooting Stars*, the F-84 *Thunderjets*, the fast but already aging P-51 *Mustang* fighters, and even a small contingent of the larger work-horse heavy bomber B-29s that had been pressed into service even now, well after World War II.

"Foxtrot 7, this is Foxtrot Leader—do you copy? Come back," the call had been punched in from Kirwin to his wingman just over the skies of Changju, North Korea. The two F-86 Sabre jets had slipped quietly out of American-controlled airspace on a dead-of-night bombing run that saw him and three other fighter jets get in and out with their mission completed before the echoes had even faded. Then they'd moved up into "MiG Alley," just south of the Chinese border itself. It was already December of that same year, and Kirwin and his wingman, Capt. Dunston "Skip" Aldrin were all that were left of a "finger-four" combat formation of Sabrejets that had been jumped by a hunting pack of North Korean MiG-15s just at the Yalu River after the American fighters had baited them to maybe come out and play.

And so indeed they had, Kirwin recalled with mixed emotions, even all these years later—with nine MiG kills for his squadron, and sadly two of his own, both lost in aerial combat and shot down as well. And thus there were only two of them left now, Kirwin and Skip Aldrin himself in the Number 7 jet that had itself sustained some considerable damage, now with his Number Two man half slumped over his stick and barely responding to any of his commander's very hails.

"Foxtrot 7, this is Foxtrot 1. Skip, come back. Do you copy? Skip, can you read me?" he flashed back in a moment's slow walkthrough times past, walking slowly on his way across a West Greenwich Village venue in New York City's borough of Manhattan. And even now he could still hear the words rattling around in his head, over and over, even now as he was just returning from a reunion of surviving members from that same 336th Group. Those few at least were still among the living, even now some sixty-eight years later.

And so it was that the good Mr. Kirwin had continued, ambling along and reliving a horrid, torrid past that he might seemingly never escape. "Foxtrot 7, this is Foxtrot 1—come back." And so soon indeed did the old codger come upon the quiet old-world lane called the MacDougal Mews itself—an area just north of the now-gone Shakespeare's tavern of old. Very much a landmark tavern and eatery back in the seventies and eighties, the new digs had since been transmogrified and made hideous, now morphing into little more than an eyesore of a neighborhood laundry shop. And so sadly now no more Shakespeares, no more nightly readings and gatherings, and indeed very little even remaining from that very period of time.

Now a world away and working his evil agenda, the Ripper grinned meanly to himself with a measure of heavy appetite and good anticipation, almost immediately spotting the old man who was even now sauntering down the dark Mews venue just now approaching him. And he knew on the instant that he'd found his killing meat and forage—and his night's best target: an unsuspecting soul, the aged Maxwell J. Kirwin.

And thus the rabid Volstad pulled fast the hood and prepared to slake his grizzled lust to maim and kill in full, and so drew back the head to shroud the face from greater view. Slowly he turned a small corner in the Mews alley and melted back into a darkened doorway to contemplate the final moments of his stalking pursuit. Certainly, it would not be long now, he thought muddily to himself ... no, not very long at all.

And only now would come the final horrid event itself, much like that recalled from the very time of old Saucy Jack himself, under late autumn moons all those many years ago. Back during the dark fog hours of autumn 1888 within the confines of the squalid back alleys in a seedy underworld called Whitechapel. And therein lie perhaps another puzzle piece that might yet be uncovered by the police, he thought, and which might itself eventually solve the series of grisly murders themselves.

So now thrust the villain Volstad out of shadow, lurching forward with purpose and fell intent. Now would come the sinewed arm and harsh embrace that would thus rudely snatch the passing Kirwin in, dragging the old, enfeebled form back into the dark recess of the sheltered doorway—the villain's final killing zone. And thus would come the hook and grapple, the rip and deep score of the ripper's blade, the massive arm collaring roughly about the throat and stretching back the neck. Then would flash the edged bite of steel, the long blade hovering only momentarily in the night air, showing only as a sharp glint in the dim and yellowed light of a far streetlamp.

Now with a clean ripping of the fleshy region of both nape and throat, the evil Volstad could almost feel the snagging edge of the long knife cutting deep, deep, deep into the victim's body. Almost surgically did the studied slashing quickly penetrate the neck with near precision, slitting left to right in seconds. Overtaken by the hack and gurgle of his own death throe, such that was even now well upon him, the man knew the very moment would be his last. *But what is happening here—and WHY? Who is this man?* the vic must have asked in wretched pain. But the Volstad was a villainous and murdering Ripper—a thief of life who was fazed by naught—not by the muffled screams, and not even by the man's desperate struggle to break free from the chokehold that led to the laying open of his very throat.

The silence of the Mews had only briefly been disturbed by the murmuring death throes of the old man even as he found himself blacking out and slowly succumbing to the violent attack of the Butcher. And thus had yet another eighty-year-old life been cut short by the West Village Ripper. Now alerted to a sudden sound, however, Volstad shut everything down and made to leave, quietly repacking the satcheled "tools and instruments" of his murderous trade, then quickly set about staging the body and scene just so. With a furtive shift of eyes did he now sweep the entire area in full, then returned to his work in a haphazard fashion before shuttling off unseen from the dimly lit MacDougal Mews lane.

Surreptitiously skulking his way back into the shuffle and flow of footfalls that set the pace of the crowd on an otherwise busy Eighth Street, the killer knew he was still only a block away from where he'd last struck, and thus with a hurried pace, he quietly stepped off into the crowd.

And even to the abysmal shock of the many late-night viewers who later sat transfixed in dark dens in front of large TV screens, and even to those others who might later scan the pages of their local news rags—all would learn equally of the heinous killing that had just taken place only steps away from such a peopled venue.

And thus it appeared that a NEW and far more evil incarnation of New York's own Jack the Ripper had arrived on the scene and struck yet again. Indeed, it had not escaped the note of many that this same villain had not just slain the old vet but had also apparently "done things" to the unsuspecting Kirwin as well. Evil, dark, and *unspeakable* things, and none of it had been lost on Volstad the Butcher, even as he stood lost in the fog of murder and a long-ago dream that was itself a full century ahead of its own time and oddly reminiscent of a faraway London.

The slasher had now again become Old Jack himself—that nameless, faceless fiend that had so terrorized an entire city all those many years past—and all of it seemed much like "old wine in new flasks," but always precisely the same kind of carnage.

And thus had this old man too been dispatched in signature fashion—a quick and silent double slashing of the throat, followed by a horrid devolvement into even other more leisured, "play-time" deeds, the terrifying acts and feats of a maniac, such that almost always involved trinkets, blood-letting, and damnable disembowelment.

Cruising directly now into the quickened pace of the foot traffic on Eighth Street—much like blood coursing into a larger vein—the killer had for all intents and purposes simply disappeared. And in that same instant, both he and his lethal blade had slithered quietly off into the soppy murk of night.

ཤྲཱི་ཤྲཱི་ཤྲཱི་

Now the time is early on the morning of 9 November, and MacDougal Street on its north side was already crammed in with bustling activity, virtually overrun by first responders and emergency personnel that had continued to pour onto the scene of the Kirwin slaughterhouse, seemingly in minutes.

MacDougal itself had already been cordoned off and shut down in full—from Eighth Street just north of the Mews, all the way down to West Fourth itself—which meant that the crosstown streets of Waverly Place, Washington Square West, and West Third, respectively, had all been shuttered and locked down as well, while uniformed officers canvassed the whole area in a hectic, door-to-door search for a viable suspect or a guilty runaway.

Now entering what could only have been a scene of seeming ordered chaos and high activity, Detectives Pomeroy and Robles arrived at the location as quickly as they could, the team's black unmarked Crown Imperial screeching to a halt just a half block out on Eighth.

"Dispatch, 20-David Sergeant. 20-David checking in," radioed the dutiful senior cop Pomeroy as he punched the comm button and spoke to an anonymous voice somewhere back at the Sixth.

"Go for Dispatch," replied the tinny electronic voice coming back over the airwaves from the nearby Tenth Street precinct.

"Dispatch, show supervisory sergeant in service at Eighth and MacDougal investigating a 10-54 major crimes alert with possible fatality. Looks like a bad one too," Pomeroy observed, then clicked off the line as he and his partner quickly exited the unmarked vehicle and made their way to the Mews area, only to find the ME Richard Pimleur once again already on the scene. Even before the two of them—again.

It was kind of a thing between the three, and each cop felt that the beefy coroner was somehow bound and determined to show them both up in responding to each particular crime scene whenever they had the occasion to meet, as indeed he had already once again done here.

A more subdued Manhattan medical examiner this time only nodded to both men and made with an olive-branch overture to maybe pass on the usual darts and barbs that might normally be traded back and forth between him and the junior Robles. Instead, the three investigators got right to work with the matter at hand and huddled together with a concentrated focus.

"Hell of a scene here, boys, as you can probably see for yourself already. And this is no ordinary killing either, gents," the rotund doctor of forensic sciences said with almost a hint of melancholy. "This is something else entirely. This is well outside the bounds of what we might normally see." Pimleur seemed to be somewhat distracted and not quite himself as he stood and began to uncomfortably shift his weight from foot to foot.

"I mean, in and of itself, it has all the hallmarks of the act of a pure ritualist—a kind of ceremonial killer—or so it would seem. But this one's far worse than any of the previous murder scenes, I'd have to say. Maybe even worse than all the others combined."

The grotesque, almost mutilated form of the one-time Maxwell J. Kirwin was only partially laid out in one of the darkened thresholds within the cul-de-sac that was the MacDougal Mews itself, now almost entirely obscured from view by the spinning-light cars and stepped-up police activity. The body had oddly been propped up—somehow with the head bobbed down and tilted askew, slightly favoring the right side. Yet visible almost immediately were the twin ridges of the double slash marks that had been left behind by the violent swipes of the Ripper's sharp blade. Only this time there were even other wounds as well.

A disturbed and mystified Robles surveyed the area in full with a look of certain disgust, aghast at what he was seeing, then only slowly found his words when he finally uttered a phrase in his native language, "¡Madre de Dios!—this is the devil's work for certain, Joe! This scene is WAY different from any of the others we've worked before, chico. Hell, the carnage alone speaks volumes here, in terms of the man's present state of mind and how he stacks up mentally I mean," grumbled the junior detective, perhaps still trying to suppress the unhealthy gag reflex that now lurked somewhere in the back of his throat, trying to choke him up, and taking his best shot not to lose his cookies right there on the spot.

"You know the thing that really bugs me the most about this case—the psychology of the whole thing is what. None of this makes any sense, gentlemen—none that I can see. None of it makes sense," the Pims repeated, almost as if to himself only. "Don't you see it?" implored the ME with a scrunch of a face that said even he might be slightly put off and repulsed by what he was seeing himself.

"I mean, just look at this guy's handiwork here. This time our suspect appears to have plainly taken his time with this particular kill, almost to a fault, and even *ceremoniously* so one could even say."

Pimleur himself could not believe he was even being compelled to admit to what he found himself saying. "Only this time, our guy appears to have also *done things*," he said, as he pulled himself up short for good emphasis. "Done things to the body, probably post-mortem."

The three men had gathered in the Mews and had continued to labor their way through the medical man's studied presentation and analysis, but it was only the two cops that were at once both repulsed and drawn in by the words of the learned doctor.

"You want my opinion—for what it's worth? None of these killings appear to be random at all—in any way—and all of them involved a good deal of planning, premeditation, and flawless execution—as much as that's even possible under the circumstances of such an open-air attack," the ME said almost matter-of-factly to the two probing detectives nearby. "And incredibly violent—unquestionably. I mean, just look at this here," the pudgy coroner offered as he swept an arm in an arc all around the lurid crime scene. "I've got high-velocity blood patterning and arterial spray all over the walls here like some kind of blood-red mosaic. Jesus, this almost gets to me, and I've pretty much seen it all."

"Yeah, we guessed as much, Doc. The guy's probably just running only on fumes and blind luck—or he's just getting started. And he certainly seems to have luck on his side too, with some remarkably good timing to his crimes, I'd say," noted the youngest of the three men currently on the scene. "Somehow always managing to be precisely in the right place at precisely the right time—and apparently the same for every killing," concluded Robles. "How the hell is he doing this?"

"Yeah, something's peaking with this guy, for sure. Almost as if all of his wildest rages are somehow being triggered from some dark, dark place inside him. But who can even know what this killer's full endgame might even be?" asked the senior Pomeroy with a certain deadpan look, then turned his attention back to the other area sweep-and-recovery tasks that he knew could also be just as important to the case.

"Well, you're dead right about one thing," the ME remarked, perhaps indeed more to himself than to anyone else, then blew hard out of billowed cheeks as he forged on with his briefing. "There is a certain undeniable malice of forethought here—there can be no mistaking it—a kind of pure, unsounded evil that appears to know no bottom. This is the work of a madman, and I'm damn glad all of this policing is left to you guys, but where do you and your people even go from here?"

The three men surveyed the ruddy spillage all about them—the whole blood-soaked scene itself—a scene that was already causing many of the greener cops who knew to hang back on the periphery to have to suppress even their keen urges to "lose their lunches" and almost chuck it all up right there on the spot. Now itself but a dark effusion of cascading life's blood, a thick crimson fluid ran from the victim's throat, neck, and gaping chest cavity, which had itself been laid open in full, and made into a kind of irregular U-shaped cut that extended from the upper left area of the torso, and down in a jagged line sharply across and back up the opposing side.

The entire visual presentation itself was a kind of ruddy long-ago look at some old *seppuku* ritual perhaps, in some old *Samurai* movie from years gone by. Only then such an act of *hara-kiri*, or "stomach-cut," had only been the sad and illogical end of a dishonored swordsman who had been rudely cast out of service to only become one of the *Rōnin* "wave-people" of medieval Japan, compelled to wander about with two sharp-edged swords, no purpose, and a bad attitude as a new kind of highwayman besieging all. Committed by those who disfavored some angry *Daimyō* warlord, such an act could only result in the very *hara-kiri* ceremony itself, such that the disgraced warrior would then be compelled to carry out to assuage the lost honor of a former lord.

But this was not even that ... this was far, far worse.

"What in the name of Jesus Christ nailed to the cross?" cried a doleful Damien Robles, as much in disbelief as having to once again look away from all the mayhem. "I'm beginning to think these killings are only made to LOOK random, even staged—but all have a seeming premeditation to them. I mean, what *didn't* this guy do here?" asked a still-disbelieving detective.

Now the three men shifted their consultative huddle and edged only farther out of the rain as each man struggled to shake off the sudden damp chill of an unusually cool August evening.

"Looks like the attack came quickly, I should think—with a level of extreme violence, unlike anything we've seen before," Robles resumed as he tipped his head away from the body and scanned both curb and sidewalk in search of a careless or forgotten clue ... a sloppy discard perhaps, or maybe just a single scrap of evidence left behind by an unwary killer who might have lacked a keen oversight in policing up his crime scene after the fact. Or perhaps he simply didn't care.

Pomeroy let out a slight chuckle as he stood with hands on hips and looked at his two counterparts. "Somebody should probably write a book about all of this, I'd imagine. Maybe call it *Descent into Madness* or something like that. A descent into madness that must have been fueled by a deep hatred and obsession with this particular demographic, this specific target group," the ME said, ending his soliloquy with a dismissive wave of hand. "Hell, if I wasn't looking right at this guy's handiwork, I wouldn't believe what you're telling me!"

"Well, either way," injected the Manhattan coroner, "It pretty much sums up our situation here, gents. But perhaps the even better question might be how'd this guy even have enough time to carry out all of his activities?" he asked. "I mean the slayings themselves, the disembowelments, the staging, and very *presentation* of each scene—with ample time to do all of it without discovery or interruption? Very curious to say the least, wouldn't you agree? Oh, and let me guess, no one saw or heard a thing right? Right. So how's that possible—and who even does this, Damien—and even more importantly WHY?"

Now there followed a disconcerting silence that seemed to ensue for some several seconds, then Pimleur spoke up to break the palpable barrier of quiet as he continued with his detailed report. "And what else is new is the fact that the killer might have used *two* different cutting blades to carry out this specific attack.

"Wait, what—TWO blades? Well, there's a twist that none of us saw coming. What exactly do you mean?"

"Two different cutting edges, one smooth and one serrated. The man's trademark calling card and the note itself, the double cuts across the throat with this series of deep penetration cuts, and especially the ritual disembowelment all seem to be unique to this killer and to this vic only—*why*? Hey, you two guys still with me so far?" Pimleur said almost jokingly, hoping that both were still at least on the same page as him.

"Yeah, we're still with you, Pimleur—please go so we can maybe finally get out of this sop," urged the senior detective. "So far I find myself agreeing with the gist of your findings—for the most part anyway."

"Well, you can see it for yourself: the opening of the chest cavity, the removal of organs, and the placement of those organs on top of the body, in what we call a kind of 'extracorporeal display.' My God, man, some of these cuts were so deep they severed the hyoid bone—right at the base of the neck, "the ME said with a crude gesture that seemed to draw Robles's attention to the victim's throat.

"The grappling alone between the two men appears to have almost cracked the third and fourth rib cage with such a force of violence that both seem to have punctured the man's lungs."

"All of this is a clear escalation from anything we'd seen before," noted a clear-sighted Robles to the two men standing nearby. "From all of the killer's previous attacks, both in its strategy and in the manner in which it was carried out—the killing format itself, as it were. But this—this is unusual, even for our guy. There's just something ghoulish about all of it not that we did not see with any of the other slayings."

"Frankly, I can't help but think we might be running out of time here" was all Pomeroy could manage with a doleful look when he was finally able to speak. "Both for us and for any number of the other poor souls that might still become victims going forward. This guy's not done yet."

Robles thought about what the sergeant had said then piped in with his keen insight. "It also takes it up a notch too—to a whole new level and a whole new category all by itself, boss. Just who is this guy anyway, some kind of modern-day reincarnation of Jack the Ripper or what?"

"Maybe—or that's exactly what he wants us to think, Junior. At this point anyway who can tell? We don't know anything for sure yet," answered Pomeroy with a bit of a stiff lip and a twinge of pretension. "But all of it keeps coming back to this guy being a stone-cold killer who's somehow now become completely unhinged, a thing most monstrous, a kind of modern-day madman who thinks he's been reincarnated for some higher purpose, almost as if transported from another place and another time and brought here."

"Hell, is any of this even real?" said Robles, posing the remark more as a question and less as a simple what-if, but found himself still looking away with a noticeable distaste for the bloody outcome of this fifth kill scene itself.

"Hey, I never said I was a criminal profiler—and none of this is really in my wheelhouse. And none of it's exactly cut-and-dry here," Pimleur began in slow response, perhaps again poking fun and hurling a veiled jab at Robles as the jerkwater junior detective he'd had to put up with time and time again.

"In fact, for all we know, we could be looking at some Jekyll-and-Hyde thing going on with this offender. This guy's shifty, much to his own best advantage, and just cagey enough to avoid detection, slipping our net again and again," Robles added, oddly commanding the stage but also wanting to simply get the information out to the entire investigation team.

"And angry to a fault—apparently," added Pims, not wanting to be left out of the conversation and hoping to contribute.

"And it could well be that same anger," parried the senior detective to the surprise of the other two. "That might well be the man's undoing in the end. Just saying. Plus, he's got to be some kind of chameleon, I'd expect. A modest man of means passing himself off as either Joe Happy or John Q. Public one minute, your best neighbor from next door, but a thing of horror in the next.

"But we must also understand that only too quickly can this man also become a kind of monstrous Butcher of Whitechapel, a fiend risen from the dead from a time long past, slipping in and out of identities like a soiled shirt."

Pomeroy's chilling narrative had been spot-on and had nearly sent a cold shiver up the junior detective's spine. But both he and Pomeroy remained transfixed and locked in on much of what the pudgy coroner had to say—knowing only that there might indeed be more. And of course, they were right.

"Judging from the man's predisposition for killing—I mean, the ritual format of ripping and disembowelment, and even the staging of the bodies themselves—it makes this guy all the more dangerous and unpredictable. This is truly the stuff of nightmares." Pimleur shifted his stance now as he knelt beside the body and studied the form of the fallen victim. "And right now I think our even greater worry is that we may have allowed the offender to slip right through our fingers, again—now for the third time in a row."

Pimleur and Robles tried to digest what they could of the good doctor's studied discourse, then Pomeroy swung an inquisitive look over at his partner. "And what about you, Robles, you're still kind of wet behind the ears and learning the ropes here. What's your take on all of this?"

"Who—you mean me?" the junior cop said, almost surprised by the comment imprimis and not fully aware that he was even being listened to. But he'd venture out onto the high wire anyway with no fear.

"My guess is we're probably looking for an older man, slightly graying at the temples—or at least *passing* as someone who is—and a man who's always cautious to a fault. Our guy's methodical too—did I mention methodical? Sly as a fox and damned patient as he plans and waits for his next kill. In fact, I think he even thrives on this shit: the hide-and-seek and the hunt-and-kill of it all. The sick bastard!" Robles had addressed the remarks to both men with a kind of guttural grumble, but it might indeed have been more to himself for his very own edification.

"A commendable observation, Robles. Can't say I'd agree 100 percent with everything on that, but much of what you said had already crossed my mind as well," conceded the portly ME, actually paying the man a rare compliment that might otherwise have seemed out of place. "So—you guys releasing the body to me yet or what?" Pimleur asked, still keen on getting it back to his forensics lab for a more detailed examination. "That and the fact that it might be good to just get the hell out of the rain itself. What do you say?"

"Sure, it's all yours, Pimleur," stated the detective sergeant, "We're done with it for all intents and purposes now. The crime scene boys have mostly wrapped up their work as well, and knowing them, they've probably been at it for most of the night sifting through all of this just trying to make sense of it all," Pomeroy observed dryly.

"Sure, I understand. And a great job they're doing too, Sergeant," said the ever-accommodating medical examiner. "Looks like the sweep teams have already come and gone and have pretty much gone over every square inch of the area anyway. I'd imagine if there was anything to be found here, they probably already found it.

"As for your other consideration, I'd have to estimate TOD as being somewhere between 11:00 p.m. and 1:00 a.m., with only a two- to three-hour window as our most workable time of death. Your body here is no more than a few hours old, chaps. In fact I'd have to say it's still even warm."

"Looks like we also have the same trophies as we had before as well," said Robles, only too quick to point the matter out as he gestured with a sweep of the arm at the possibility of finding even a tidbit of evidentiary material that might have been left behind by the killer.

"I mean the whole scene, complete with the trademark Jack of Diamonds and the 'DEAR BOSS' crap scrawled across the victim's forehead in blood. But why the card—the *same* card—a red card, and why a Jack of Diamonds in the first place. What the hell does any of it even mean?"

It was still a sober Manhattan medical examiner that now leaned away from the conversation just long enough to wave a commanding hand to catch the eye of the attending EMT responders that had been standing by on the scene. The gesture gave a go-ahead nod that told the men to come ahead to cover up the body a final time and prep it for moving. Now the two stretcher-bearers emerged to drape a vinyl cadaver sheet over the body that was still laid out on its morbid litter, then quietly carted the deceased man away.

Sergeant Pomeroy remained behind to more carefully survey all of the minor puzzle pieces that had conveniently been left behind by the slasher and think about his response to Robles and the ME. "The card thing still beats me too, and much of it's got us all pretty much at a dead end. Personally, I see all of them as just a series of calling-card clues that were set to only taunt us, maybe trip us up and leave us hanging with only a trail of illogical but tantalizing clues.

"The significance of the Jack of Diamonds thing is obviously something we'll need to look at more closely of course, and frankly no one's got a clue on what it means yet either. I think we *might* actually have figured out that REDRUM word thing being stenciled on each of the victim's forehead, however. It's some kind of cutesy trick with the word MURDER being spelled backward. So no real mystery there—except maybe our being right back to the why and the who—with us left pondering the imponderable: who *next*."

"And therein lies another truth for sure, I'd expect," mumbled Robles, not certain anyone had even heard him since he'd mainly made the point only for his hearing. "Even as we try our best to solve yet another angle of the mystery."

The cool night rain seemed to noticeably dissipate, the thick night clouds just overhead now pulling back slowly like a drowsy bear lumbering into a darkened cave to hibernate. And just up the block, a still-busied Eighth Street continued to only echo its hectic sounds of light traffic and an occasional din of honking horns.

"In its final analysis, gentlemen," Pimleur concluded with a quiet flourish that was all his own, perhaps wanting to simply wrap up the whole sordid affair and slip back to his lab. "This is pretty much all we've got on the victims so far—and not much of a lead on any viable suspects either. But that's more *your* department than mine, so I'll just leave you to it.

"Sorry, Pomeroy, but much of what I have so far is at best a best guess, and all I can give you for now is only guarded speculation, for the time being at least."

The portly forensics expert seemed to be standing his ground only tentatively, now with a searching hand scratching at the back of his head. He felt almost contrite for the sparsity of information he could make available to the investigators and almost seemed apologetic. But perhaps he wasn't done yet.

"Of course, I might expect to have a full soup-to-nuts report on all of it for you guys later, after my team's had a chance to run a few analytical tests back at the lab."

The well-manicured medical examiner was now seemingly spent and had finally stopped his incessant pacing, as he now leaned heavily on a parking meter, exhaling loudly with an almost audible huff.

"I'm afraid much of the rest of this is for you guys to sift through on your own," said a still-winded ME, now turning his attention back to the deceased man still lying covered on the ground. "Maybe just a word of advice: Figure this guy out quick and get ahead of him before it's too late. If you don't, I fear a return to violence. He *will* be back, and he will strike again—so maybe be prepared and be on your guard. As for me—hey, I've got my crosses to bear as I try to put the pieces together myself."

"Roger that, Pimleur—don't know what I'd do without you," Pomeroy jibed, feigning a wry half smile, such that even allowed Robles a shot with his final dig, as one who was ever reluctant to simply let anything go. Besides, thought a very wise Pomeroy, even the great and noble Pimleur himself might need to be taken down a notch or two every once in a while.

"Yeah, and thanks a bunch too, Doc," ribbed Robles. "You get to go home and duck out of this rain. We get to stay here and tromp all around this god-awful crime scene. Say no more, Pimleur, there's a fair trade."

"Yeah, love you too," came the reply from the rounded Pimleur, who smiled broadly as he spun on the balls of his feet and made ready to exit the crime scene. Pulling deep the floppy rain hat over his brow to shield the face from a new and reenergized drizzle, the good medical examiner looked back one final time and tipped his head in a silent goodbye.

"I know one thing, gentlemen, I wouldn't want to be you guys," he said. "And I'm glad I'm not in your shoes. Heck, I wouldn't walk a mile in them even if I could—certainly not for this case.

"The storyline of your killer, I'm afraid, is still evolving, you heed my words. These attacks can only build with greater momentum." Then the ME click-clicked his automobile key fob on the instant, causing the vehicle to chirp twice and the doors to open and then continued with his own brand of a farewell soliloquy.

"And you guys better get a quick handle on this situation too—and soon! Otherwise, I fear that all of this'll blow up in our faces and somehow find its way out to the press. One way or another, we all know there's always the possibility that something might eventually get out. You can almost bank on it. "Some full doc dump perhaps—or maybe just something leaked out in dribs and drabs to some hungry media source anxious for a good story. Point is, we won't even know it until we read about it in the newspapers or turn on a TV."

"Yeah, I hear what you're saying, Pimleur," agreed the senior detective. "They're already sniffing the air and poking around almost all of our murder scenes. They've been hot on the scent of this story from the very beginning, I'd imagine, hungry for any news at all. In fact, it might only be a matter of time before they either break the story in full themselves or something leaks out from some unsanctioned source. But by then it'll be too late, and we won't be able to put that genie back in the bottle."

"So I see we're on the same page then," said the stocky coroner. Now back in his official vehicle, Pimleur wrestled with the ignition of his car before it turned over then clapped on the windshield wipers as he softly gunned the engine and began to pull away from the curb. He paused only momentarily to peek back from the driver's side window and added, "Be warned, Pomeroy, this story will easily take on a life of its own, you mark my words—the likes of which none of us will even want to be in the middle of."

Then the laid-back ME smacked his lips and ended his winded liturgy, "That said, gentlemen, God be with you," he added, then hit the gas and sped off down the rain-soaked street on his way back to the forensics lab still much in the dead of night.

Dr. Richard Pimleur, the consulting senior medical examiner for the NYPD—and truly most of south Manhattan itself—carefully pulled off his plastic examination gloves and shed his protective lab coat, then waddled over to the basin to wash and scrub out after his preliminary view of the Kirwin body itself. Slowly then did he even begin his studied discourse, speaking to Robles and Pomeroy only over a busied shoulder before he'd even finished at the sink.

"Gotta say it's a crying shame what I'm seeing here, gentlemen," the ME began, a shaded look now sweeping across the man's lightly bearded face. "And what a ghastly piece of work it was too."

Robles glanced at his partner with a quizzical and disgusted look, almost visibly shrinking from the sight of whatever was left of the Kirwin cadaver. To the view of both policemen, however, it was clear that something unspeakably dark and gruesome had taken place here, now with a mutilated form and a bloodletting ritual that had left another old man dead—and much of it quite taken to its farthest extreme. And neither seasoned man could ever recall having seen anything so macabre, certainly not since that horrid spate of machete hackings up in the Bronx just the year before.

For weeks, in fact, that bloodbath fiasco had almost exclusively been bannered across the news headlines and networks, perhaps even crudely so, only then it had been "gang-related," supposedly carried out by members of a known drug cartel in a local turf war that had been touched off to perhaps make its deadly point to a rival crew trying to muscle in on its "perceived" territory. And *this* was even worse than that. So both investigators simply switched back to their more studied view of the crime scene particulars, however unpleasant a task that might itself have been.

"The poor guy was gutted and laid out like a stuffed pig," observed Robles in a decidedly vulgar vernacular, soon with a sickened look that wobbled his gaze away almost dizzyingly, more in the direction of Pomeroy and the ME.

"Indeed, my friend. But I'm afraid it only gets worse," countered Pimleur, the celebrated Manhattan ME, with a straight face as he pointed to the prostrate form on his examination table.

"MUCH worse—at least as we see here with the very placement of organs outside the vic's body, in fact exposing the heart and much of the intestinal coil itself, clearly now with both removed.

"This was of course then followed by—dare I even say it—an *extracorporeal* placement of both on top of the man's body, obviously post-mortem. This is a savage business, gentlemen—a most savage business, classic mayhem done with expertise and an almost unfathomable pleasure."

Pomeroy and Robles thought about the off-the-cuff remarks being made by the forensics expert and exchanged a knowing glance before the junior investigator finally spoke up. "I think our guy's seeking his truth and wants to become some kind of enigma for the ages. He's a madman with a frightening agenda and a bankrupt mind that is somehow revisiting the deeds of one of the most notorious historic figures.

"In fact, I suspect he's even further devolving, almost striving to become some kind of modern-day Jack the Ripper caught up in his fantasies and getting away with yet another killing—and yet another victim. Even worse, right under our very noses. Why is it we always seem to have an abundance of clues and round evidence, but we're somehow always short on any solid leads at every turn? Are we just going in circles here?"

"No, not really, we're still certain of one thing at least," said Pomeroy with a small fade of hope that must have been lost to the shadows of his face as he looked up at the other two men. "He's our darkest of nightmares and the worst offender we could expect to run into—too crazy to care, too smart to get caught, and too hard-boiled to even give a damn. This one's a loose cannon and a slasher. I fear that this might be a long summer and we're going to have our hands full until we can nab this maniac and close this case out."

ତତତ

Senior homicide investigator Joe Pomeroy approached Captain Fuller's office in the 6th Precinct with Robles and Pimleur well in tow—and even Ellen Macklin, the *Action9News* reporter, following close behind. He rapped twice on the door frame, now with two coffees carefully hoisted in both hands and clutched with a ham-fisted grip—apparently a courtesy cup for his boss and a second for himself, each of the others having already fended for themselves and bringing their morning joe.

"Pomeroy, I see you're still quite the incurable brown-nose, aren't you? Well, it'll get you nowhere," the captain said, doing her best to suppress a half chuckle that clearly said she was only joking and really did appreciate the kick-starting java. "But thanks for the unexpected treat anyway. I can probably use the caffeine infusion."

"I know what you mean, Cap, even when I was a nipper, my mom's favorite morning phrase was that she always needed TWO cups every day just to wake up—ONE FOR EACH EYE, she said!"

"Ha!" Fuller said with an outburst that was probably genuine and pretty hard to stifle. "That's actually kind of funny, Joe—I'll probably have to borrow that for future use with my morning repertoire of wit. I'm pretty sure I fall in the same category myself, but I think it probably just goes with the job."

"Sure, feel free, Cap," Pomeroy acquiesced as the police captain ushered everyone through the door and into several semicomfortable chairs around a small conference table. As they looked around the lavishly furnished office, they could see that it was a comfortable den with a lived-in look that might have even been called lavish—*lavish* that is, by police command standards at any rate—and they all nudged themselves around a small boardroom table on the second floor of the 6th Precinct, with Joe Pomeroy himself plopping down into the seat nearest Fuller.

"So how about we just get down to the brass tacks of it then," Fuller began, cutting right to the chase and getting immediately to the real reason her senior homicide team's lead detective and a gaggle of others were even here crashing her door and sitting in front of her, especially this early in the morning. Something must be up or else all of them wouldn't even be here.

"So just where are we on this case, and what's so all-fired important that it's got you up at the crack of dawn and foaming at the mouth here?" she asked, as she ran long and slender fingers through a lock of unkempt hair and struggled to shake off the fatigue. Now a muddling look of bewilderment seemed to oddly twist her face and plant there instead a certain question mark look.

But the captain was also wise enough to bide her time and simply wait for the man's more detailed explanation. Pomeroy had long been her most senior investigator, an integral part of her Major Crimes Unit and her team's top performer for some several years now. He could even boast of having the highest case closure rate in the borough, were he of a mind to, but he wouldn't. And if the man said he had something on his mind that was so important that he was even here in her office at this hour with his full team, she knew she might damn well take him seriously and make the time to hear more about it—and even that with no undue delay.

"Okay, so lay it out for me, somebody. What's this all about? You guys all look like you maybe have some new info for me, is it something related to this—this *Village Ripper* case?"

"Well, it's the damnedest thing, Captain, I can tell you that much. Robles and I have been all up and down this thing, and only now are some of the case facts actually beginning to come together and even make sense," said the brawny, square-jawed Sergeant Pomeroy. "Our own ME Pimleur—and even our reporter friend Ellen Macklin here—have all stayed the course and each in their own way have been extremely helpful every step of the way in our pursuit of answers here. And it was only within the last couple of hours that Macklin has advanced a pretty radical theory to explain some of the more salient points of our investigation."

"*Salient points*, Joe? I'm not quite following you. Sounds like you're trying to tell me something—so what is it? C'mon, spill it."

"Well, we've stumbled upon some interesting new developments for one thing—maybe, such that appear to be quite compelling, maybe even *actionable*. A quick understanding of which might help us to resolve at least some of the crime scene clues found at each of the kill sites in the past. Best of all though, we could have our first good look at a viable suspect."

At this news, even the normally reserved captain pricked up and arched a single eyebrow, her innate curiosity and native cop instincts already kicking in. Then, Pomeroy and Macklin exchanged a casual glance, but it was the police sergeant who spoke up first.

"As you know, Captain, Ms. Macklin here was kind enough to assist us with this *numbers* thing—those sets of numbers we kept finding scrawled on each of the playing cards left behind at each of the locations we've investigated. We were all pretty baffled by them at first, and none of it seemed to make any sense—clearly. But I think you might be quite surprised to hear what she might have uncovered. What each numerical sequence might mean, that is."

"Okay," responded Fuller with unfeigned interest. "So somebody maybe enlighten me then."

Now it was the reporter Ellen Macklin who seemed to step up her game and moved to the forefront, instinctively flashing her trademark warm smile and tossing her head back ever so slightly to flip off a stubborn wisp of hair that would simply not stay out of her eyes.

"Captain Fuller—Dr. Pimleur—Detectives, good morning," she began almost too formally for the current forum, looking in the direction of each as she acknowledged the meeting attendees. "First off, please understand that I only chanced upon the information pretty much by accident, even though I had my suspicions from day one. And thanks to Detective Pomeroy, I was prompted to take a very quick crash course in the whole JTR affair."

"Wait—suspicions? Suspicions about what?" prodded a deeply curious Fuller.

Macklin looked around at the small assembly of people, carefully surveying the room in full then squared off on Captain Fuller, almost feeling the hesitation and fence-sitting fears drain away completely in the face of her good conviction. She knew she might just be right, and she had to stand by her very findings.

"Go on, finish telling her," urged Pomeroy, dividing his gaze between Macklin and Fuller. "Tell her what you found with all of the numbers you worked—EXACTLY. Captain, you're probably not going to believe this."

"Try me, Pomeroy. I'm open to all and any suggestions at this point in time—*if* it means we can move the investigation forward" was all Fuller said, quickly focusing back on the cub reporter.

"Well, for me at least, it all began with the first Anton Chapel killing itself," Macklin resumed, being sure to choose her words carefully and to maintain good eye contact with the team lead. "And the numbers series we found on the playing card recovered from the body at that time.

"I was never quite sure what they might be, but something seemed just a little hinky to me—both with the numbers series themselves and with the very format on each of those Jack of Diamonds playing cards. Something about it just seemed all too familiar. Then it hit me square in the face when I was tinkering with a random map series on a geo app on my iPhone. I think they're all about latitude and longitude!"

"WOW, here's a whole new spin—and a pretty big leap for sure!" snickered Robles with seeming disbelief to a sea of shaded faces, then wisely piped back down in the face of the group's collective looks of disapproval.

"Let her finish, Detective Robles," ordered Fuller as she spun on the junior cop to quash his wry humor, seemingly miffed at the man's very outburst *imprimis*. It was a look that was even further backed up by the disapproving glare of the senior Pomeroy himself.

"A new spin?" echoed Macklin as she looked in Robles's direction, seemingly unaffected by the remark. "Perhaps you're right, Detective Robles, but just bear with me and maybe hear me out a little further. First, let's look at the numbers themselves, remembering again that the first series we got from the Novaks murder scene were recorded as **515200 00605**," said Macklin as she glanced in Pomeroy's general direction. "Am I correct in that, Sergeant?"

"Yeah, sounds spot-on to me—*and* it seems to jive with our numbers as well," said Pomeroy, dovetailing closely with Ellen's findings. "So tell them what you were able to find."

"Well, if we work with the assumption that these are all in fact map coordinates, I asked myself WHERE is this location at, and what did any of it mean? So I decided to zero in further and look at each in terms of an actual *lat* and *long* plotting. Care to hazard a guess as to what I found? Anyone? It may surprise you."

"I'd imagine it's a location somewhere—probably," ventured Fuller, perhaps wearying of the guessing game and growing more and more impatient with the cub reporter's building delay, ever mindful of the fact that time itself was still an imperative in their ongoing investigation.

"But not just *any* location, Captain—here, take a look at these," she urged, producing the first of two handheld maps.

"Here," she repeated, quickly unfolding what appeared to be a plotted map extract of the North Atlantic countries of Great Britain, Scotland, Ireland, and Wales. Now a slender and well-manicured finger tapped softly at one chart area in particular.

"Okay, so I see a map, but what exactly am I looking at, Macklin—and what am I supposed to be seeing here?" chimed in the pudgy Pimleur, perhaps sounding a bit more disenchanted than he should and reservedly speaking up for only the second time.

"Dr. Pimleur, what we're looking at is London, England," she began, now studiously poring over a second, even larger blow-up of the earlier chart that seemed to provide even greater detail of the target area in full. On that second map were a series of superimposed markings—bold red circles to be sure—all highlighting different areas and different events.

"Specifically a location, sir. In this case, our **515200 00605'**, which very quickly rendered itself to a map coordinate that was set at **51° 52' 00" N—0° 06' 05" W.**"

"Okay, but granted that much, what's the significance of it? What does any of it even mean?" asked Fuller in a choppy fashion, as if in pursuit of some logical conclusion just slightly out of reach.

"What I found was that it was specific to an area near a Durward Street in London, Captain. At a place that had once been called Buck's Row."

"I'm still not following you, Ellen. Should that mean something to us—in terms of this case, I mean?" queried Fuller.

"It's the site of an old rundown area that was once known as the Whitechapel district, ma'am—in old London," replied the young reporter with no seeming hesitation, much like a gatekeeper about to loosen a leash of greyhounds from a racing slip. "It was the scene of *his* first murder—involving the rather ill-fortuned Polly Nichols to be sure—on the last day of August in 1888."

"1888? Ms. Macklin, all of this makes for a pretty intriguing history lesson, in the long run," observed Fuller. "But can we maybe just move on? Who are we talking about here?" the head of the Major Crimes Unit persisted, feeling for all the world like she had one foot in and one foot out. Was she more tired of Macklin's monologue, or was she simply afraid to even hear the truth? And what it might all mean to her, her elite team, and her city. "And just who is this JTR person you mentioned earlier?"

"Why, Jack the Ripper, of course. It was Jack the Ripper, Captain, in an 1888 time frame. Only the victim Polly Nichols THEN is, in this case now, our own Paul Novaks."

"But how is that even relevant now?" asked a casually frustrated Captain Fuller.

"Because I began to find that there was more—much, *much* more, ma'am, in close parallel with each of the cases we're looking at right now. And what I keep finding here is puzzling—very puzzling. In more ways than one, Captain. So maybe just bear with me a moment more."

"Okay, I'll bite," said Fuller. "Please continue—and maybe slow it down a bit, you don't need to be so nervous."

"Yes, ma'am. Well, first off, it was only after Major Crimes had been called to the scene of the *second* Chapman killing, here in New York, that I really began zeroing in on a possible meaning for ALL of the numbers we kept encountering, and from there things somehow just fell into place."

A general hush fell over the crowd, over each of the meeting attendees squirmed in around the small conference table, each looking askance at each other and probably running 50-50 on all of what was being said.

"In fact, the second series of numbers that we got off the body of our second victim were—let me be sure here," the reporter said, pausing just long enough to consult her working notes. "Yes, **51311335 042120**. Everyone confirm that as correct?"

Pomeroy and Robles tipped their heads down slightly as they referred to their scratch pads, with the senior detective eventually nodding his agreement. "Affirmative, that corresponds to our figures as well. So go on, tell her what you found," prompted a still-confident Sergeant Pomeroy.

"I found that the numbers all translated to **51°31'13.35"N** by **0°4'21.20"W**—this time a Hanbury Street location. An area known to also be in that same Whitechapel district, where on the night of September 8 would be the very killing of Jack the Ripper's *second* canonical victim, Annie Chapman. I know—I know how strange it must sound.

"But note how that London killer's second victim now only too perfectly juxtaposes itself to our victim Anton Chapel—oddly also an **AC**? It was at this point that I found myself already drawn to the coincidence and beginning to see a completely different picture."

"But how much of it is just weird coincidence, Macklin, and how much of it can we take as being anywhere near accurate?" queried Captain Fuller, still intrigued even if her brow might otherwise have said that she might only be annoyed. "I could see myself maybe embracing the idea, but I don't exactly see it as a slam-dunk, Ellen, by any means. What else you got?"

"Well, that's pretty much when I found this, our next series of numbers presented this time as **515137 00655**."

"And was there any importance to the numbers of that set? Did you find anything unusual?" asked Robles, trailing off on his question but still chomping at the bit for some simple recognition and a little well-earned inclusion.

"As you might already suspect, what I found was that this same **515137 00655** sequence we're seeing on our side was a **51° 51' 37" N-0° 06' 55" W** longitude and latitude location—a distinct one, to be sure. In fact, a Berner Street location in old London that had once been called Dutfield's Yard, only then the killing was on 30 September, now with a *third* Whitechapel victim on their hands, one Elizabeth Stride. On our side, of course, we had our guy on Minetta Street that we now know was Elon Strunk. And here we have yet again another uncanny set of initials—in this event, **ES**."

The perky newscaster tossed her head back with confidence and a studied nonchalance to seemingly whip another stubborn clasp of hair out of her face to better see.

"Okay, so now you've officially got my attention—*maybe*, but please proceed," declared a now far more impressed Fuller with a curious peak of eyebrow that said she might be listening to all that was being said. In other words, just maybe this Macklin person could be on to something that the rest of them had not at all seen in their investigation.

"So is anyone else beginning to see a clear pattern emerging here, some diabolical and ritualized practice that seems to be recurring again and again?" was all the captain could ask under her breath, even if accompanied by a crass slide of eyes that slid in the direction of Pomeroy and Robles. "So why didn't any of my people catch this? I mean, if we're not making any measurable progress on this case, guess whose fault it's going to be? And much sooner than any of us might expect."

"Our guys did try, Captain," replied the somewhat offended homicide detective with a level of defensiveness that might have said he could be protecting his own. "But none of us ever saw that angle, and we never came close to wrapping our minds around any of these numbers things—let alone crunch them out enough to find any real significance with their format or intended presentation."

"But wait, Captain, it seems to only get better," offered an overly enthusiastic Sergeant Pomeroy as Macklin got back on her roll and resumed her discourse with an irrepressible excitement that seemed to only keep building.

"Well, we marked our crime scene as number four—the one with the Carlton Enders slaying, right there on Bedford Street on the same date. And it was at that same location that we found yet another set of cryptic numbers that at that time seemed to present us with a '**515138 0078**' series. Everybody recall that?" asked Macklin, hoping that everyone might indeed still be on the same page.

"Sure, I seem to remember the numbers series, but again who knew what any of it meant," Pimleur blurted out, still drawn into the analysis that was being so competently outlined by the news reporter. "But so far I seem to be following your every word closely—admittedly with a great deal of fascination. Please, go on."

"Well, upon even closer scrutiny, I quickly found that this same **515138 0078** sequence was actually a **51° 51' 38" N** by **0° 0' 78" W** locale—in its final analysis a location once called Mitre Square—and might still be so today. But again on the night of 30 September—the night of the 'double event' itself—we witnessed Jack's TWIN killings, beginning with Elizabeth Stride and ending with Catherine Eddowes. And in at least the latter event, all of it seems to entirely coincide with our own Carlton Enders, Captain Fuller, our victim number four."

The head of Major Crimes might still have been a bit put off by the young reporter's ongoing analysis but remained steadfast in her pursuit to explore all alternate options on the table. "I'm beginning to think this is a bit more complex and convoluted than we might initially have thought," she ventured. "It also means we'll probably need to update our working profile as well."

Pomeroy beamed at his superior, perhaps seeing that she too had been duly impressed as he continued to enjoy his own "Aha" moment, then added, "I somehow thought you might be interested, Cap."

Could Macklin be unstoppable at this point? Indeed it might seem so, at least in her studied discourse, such that had been so evenly presented and brought to a quite natural conclusion.

"Of course, all of this would now bring us to our final series of numbers, which, of course, came to us as '**5131716 043047**', with the Kirwin killing itself. So here we are again, and history tells us that this was the location of the Ripper's *fifth* and final victim.

"It would also be the fiend's most horrific killing frenzy of all, with all of it occurring in a seedy inner courtyard called Miller's Court on a date of 9 November—again all within that same 1888. And here the map coordinates were also conclusive and quite impeccable: **51° 31' 7.16" N—0° 4' 30.47" W**. And that victim's name we now know was one Mary Jane Kelly … our own identified victim was Maxwell J. Kirwin. Anybody else seeing the curious 'MJK' initials in there as much I do? I think it's fairly obvious, and clearly more than mere coincidence."

The cub reporter paused only long enough to give Fuller and Pomeroy just enough time to put their tongues back in their mouths, then brought a quiet end to her soliloquy.

"This then would conclude, and pretty much account for, each of the five killings that we've seen so far. So perhaps what we really need to do is ask ourselves if everyone else is seeing the same striking parallels I am here," she said, ending on an upswept interrogatory, entirely pleased with her near-flawless recitation of the facts as known. And then she dropped the mike.

☙☙☙

Blanketed in the dark cocoon of his dank and filthy basement flat in a secluded area of Red Hook, Brooklyn, just off the famed "Buttermilk Channel" waterway itself, the killer was not at all a happy Volstad. In fact, he stank of decaying anger that seemed to almost immobilize him in full, even as he roughly tamped out yet another unfiltered cigarette from the crumpled pack that sat on the littered table in front of him.

He was inflamed with steeping anger that might observe no bounds, now with a restlessness that simply would not leave him alone. He lit the end of yet another coffin nail with a heavy Zippo lighter and heaved the pack back onto the coffee table, even as he clutched at a beer can and tossed back another deep swig. Then he grabbed the television remote and bumped up the volume for yet another time, already not liking what he was hearing and thinking of how best to seek an outlet to vent that welling anger. Then the broadcast returned from its "20-ad" commercial break and he spun his attention back to the talking head on the TV screen.

"And still with no appreciable leads in the hunt for New York's own Village Ripper," the news co-anchor began incisively. "The frightened citizens of the borough of Manhattan have been rocked by this latest slashing incident, and all of them continue to walk around on edge, almost fearing for their very lives..."

But there was something else wrong here, the black-hearted villain thought to himself in a heated snit, something far more than just the words alone to despise. Something in the tone of the woman—a certain trick of the eye perhaps, a detectable lilt in the voice—or maybe just its very intonation.

But indeed there was something else he didn't like, but he couldn't quite put his finger on the pulse of his anxiety. All this even now as he continued to grimace at the telecaster pontificating on air, for all the world like some great provider of truth whose best opinion must of needs be their own, with himself now growling like a rabid dog protecting turf.

Abruptly changing the channel for now a third time, he looked on at the coverage that each news network had presented over and over, with each running similar stories that touched upon only some of the details and key points of the murders themselves, and could only be heard in choppy half sentences.

"And so New York City has once again been caught in the vice grip of yet another ripping victim found in lower Manhattan's own Greenwich Village. Police describe the murder as being particularly heinous and noted that the incident now marks the fifth such slashing victim to be found in one of the most heavily frequented and most historic of New York City's districts.

"Of late, there has now been a discernible citizen outcry, both to the mayor's office directly, and to the police commissioner herself, with many wondering why someone would even perpetrate such heinous and barbaric acts. So the citizens of New York only continue to ask who is committing these crimes—and when will it all end?"

Volstad hissed loudly through blown cheeks and angrily stubbed out the burnt end of another filterless cigarette, tossing the remnants into a half-filled coffee cup, each discarded butt floating about in a crush of others to almost create a kind of disgusting baby logjam that all seemed to float at its very surface. Then he chain-lit another coffin-nail, gnashing down unevenly with a rack of stained and yellowed teeth as he angrily flipped the channel for yet another time. And again he didn't like what he was hearing.

This it was that same fool cop being interviewed on the steps of the police precinct by some sprightly, rose-cheeked reporter that he'd already decided to despise on the spot, almost without basis or foundation.

"And you say you are still working to identify a person of interest in this case?" asked a straight-faced Ellen Macklin with a slight arch of an eyebrow, as part of her second publicized interview with the senior detective, Sergeant Joe Pomeroy, this time on the steps fronting the tired stateliness of his own home-base 6th Precinct.

The fact that she looked positively electrifying in blue might itself have been entirely lost on the evil Volstad, and for the moment probably only mattered to Pomeroy, who sought to only keep his tongue in his mouth and his eyes in his head. But as for the haughty deviant himself, the Volstad could not even fathom the depth of his anger—an anger that rendered itself only in a certain shade of deep red—in fact, *blood*-red to be certain. And in his disturbed mind, a spine-chilling plan was already fast taking shape.

"That's correct, Ms. Macklin, but as I'm sure you can already guess, I'm not at liberty to go into any great detail on the matter, other than what we talked about earlier," concluded Pomeroy, dodging an interview bullet and looking sternly official at the camera.

"And Detective, can you maybe tell our viewers if you and your people have been able to develop a working profile on this fugitive yet? Any viable leads as to just who this suspect might be—in your mind, I mean? What kind of person even does this kind of thing to our city's seniors? Any special insights?"

Pomeroy chewed on the reporter's clutch of disjoined questions that had been fired at him in rapid succession for the better part of a minute before even committing to a response. He paused only long enough to lean in closely and square up directly on the TV camera's very screening monitor.

"Well, first off—and I'm pretty sure we can all agree on this—this man's a coward. And nothing if not a monster of the first order, and of the worst kind—other than a child molester himself. I mean who, in a truly civilized society, do we most hold in close regard if not our vulnerable young and our revered elders? And this attacker—this vile, marauding beast—has just crossed another threshold and taken his infamy to a whole new level. I am confident that the Major Crimes Division will not stop until it has turned over every rock and looked in every rat hole to find this man. Then he will be hit with the full force of the law and bear the brunt of his due punishment without question or an audience of protest. There's already a pretty hot hole in hell just waiting for this offender, and that is all I wish to say about that."

Then the tony, well-dressed police detective stepped away from the mike and took a breather in his soliloquy, as much to let the powerful optics of the interview itself sink in as to also continue glaring deeply into the still-rolling camera, the one with the steady red light. Then he exhaled lightly and found his footing in time to move back to the forefront when prompted, only to continue with what was quickly turning out to be but a sharp and stinging invective ... like the business end of a double-barreled shotgun aimed right at only him, a now-enraged Bogdan Volstad.

"So in conclusion, Sergeant Pomeroy, is there anything else you'd like to add? Assuming of course you could speak directly to this suspect?"

"Certainly—and let me be clear about this and take it even a step further. To the fugitive perhaps watching this PSA, maybe hoping to hide and lay low—I see you—I see you. In fact, if you're within the sound of my voice and listening to this broadcast, you're about to feel the full force of the NYPD coming down on you, and I'm pretty sure you're not going to like it. In fact, there'll be no hole in hell big enough where you can hide.

"It's your move, but I gotta say that I might only urge you to proceed at once to your nearest police precinct and simply turn yourself in—and do it on the moment. Otherwise, we will hunt you down and bring you to justice ourselves. It will not be pleasant, and you will *not* like me when we meet!"

Now still a bridge and tunnel afar and a river crossing away, just by the western edge of the Red Hook jetties of Brooklyn itself, the Volstad had finally fathomed the ugly underside of his anger and had grabbed it by the horns in full. "Screw you! And know that I *will* have my revenge soon enough," spat the oily villain underbreath with a heated venom as he continued to watch the police spectacle unfolding on the TV screen in front of him. And when he'd finally had enough, he stood abruptly in a stew of violent anger, lunged forward, and put his entire foot squarely through the television screen itself. Then he grabbed his sheathed ripper knife, a light jacket, and a Makarov .380 pistol that he tucked neatly in his waistband and headed for the door. It was time again to hunt, only this time his intended target had just changed. Now that target wore a badge and was the same smug cop he'd just seen on TV. And yes, he too would soon taste the sharp bite of his steel blade, after which he might simply shoot the son-of-a-bitch in a femoral artery just to watch him bleed out slowly and die.

"And then I will kill your girlfriend too," he warned. "And I will make you watch as she dies in the fading light of your own eyes." Then he slammed the door to his basement flat on his way out to only further scream at the rain itself.

※ ※ ※

"Maybe now you can understand more clearly just what we're up against, Captain. So I've asked Ms. Macklin here to give us a little historical background on the whole thing if you'll just bear with us and indulge a whim," said Pomeroy as he turned in the direction of the perky journalist.

"Okay, I'm game if it'll help the case," said Fuller, eager to hear an alternate perspective. And so she found herself gladly turning the floor over to the cub reporter who'd come such a long way since she had first met her.

"Ellen, how about you give us a quick rundown on the historical perspective of the London killer's profile, perhaps in parallel with a look at our guy as well, if you would."

"Sure, I'd be glad to," Macklin conceded, content to even be included in the conversation as the team's newbie.

"Captain Fuller, I began to notice a pattern emerging even as the detectives moved through the initial phases of their investigation. My team and I were obliged to do a little background research on our own—you know, just to make sure we got our facts straight," offered the *Action9News* network reporter, now exhaling almost audibly.

"And so we did a bit of a deep dive ourselves, poking around some old archives that looked at precisely this: the historical persona of Jack the Ripper himself, a man thought to be perhaps one of the most prolific and well-known mass murderers of all time. Indeed, also a killer who was thought to have gotten away with all of his crimes.

"Of course, it was never about the number of women killed, but more about the MANNER in which the killings themselves were carried out and the degree of mutilation with each victim. This from a man we know stalked the seedy lanes and backstreets of East London's Whitechapel district during the fall of 1888.

"In fact, each of those historic killings would happen in an August to November time frame of that same year, during the course of which time, an unidentified, unnamed assailant attacked a number of women within that very district, always with the same *modus operandi*. And always with the same end for each: a deliberate series of cuts to the throat of each victim, often with a trademark series of ritual disembowelments that seemed to always accompany each of the murders themselves."

Now, the casual dialogue flipped back to Pomeroy, who broke an uneasy silence to speak up, wagging a finger at his laptop keyboard. "Captain, she's right. I've been to a couple of those online forums and blog sites that study precisely this one specific casebook and killer. I've done the research and I must say, I've become a kind of an amateur sleuth myself—in this particular area of study, that is. I'm sure it's probably just a cop thing, with those native instincts kicking in. You know, never quite being satisfied and always compelled to try to solve a cold case—in this event, one that's probably the coldest of them all. I'm pretty sure you of all people might understand, Cap."

"So who else might know about this?" injected the captain, as she too, stepped out onto the high wire of bold speculation.

"For now, just the five of us, ma'am, even if some minor details of the killings themselves may have already been leaked to some local news outlets," Macklin said as she paused in midthought. "But none of them seem to have made any real connection to the older historic killings themselves."

"So far, that is," Pomeroy chimed in as he read Fuller's body language and gauged her close reaction.

"Certainly not with the same level of clarity that we might have now, Captain. And with Macklin's continued assurance of a measured news blackout on the findings of the case, there really has not been any release of news that might compromise any of our investigation details. My hope is that it'll pretty much stay that way too," the detective said with a glance at the newscaster. "At least for the time being anyway."

"Well, we'll need to continue to keep all of these details as close to the vest as possible, for sure, and keep all of it in-house as best we can. Word of this leaks out and we're sure to have a citywide panic on our hands, and I'm pretty sure we can all agree with that assessment. So it's worth repeating: our investigation needs to remain as much under wraps as we can keep it."

Macklin was first to respond, saying, "My people and I have been doing our best to slow-walk any release of the case facts as best we can. But even with full network support, things have pretty much been touch-and-go on my end. We're already beginning to feel some public pressure for a release of something even now."

"Understood," Captain Fuller noted, maybe stating the obvious even as each of the meeting attendees leaned in just a little closer, careful not to miss a beat. "But since you seem to be on a roll here, Ms. Macklin, maybe you can fill us in on the significance of the red Jack playing cards themselves—in your own studied opinion, that is. It's something that kind of plagued us all along from day one."

"Best guess, Captain? The image of the red Jack is presented at each of our crime scenes only as a *nom de plume* for Jack the Ripper himself. You must also remember that during the time of the actual 1880s London killings, the slasher was already known in Whitechapel by many fearful names: *Jack the Ripper, Saucy Jack, Dear Boss, Leather Apron,* the *Butcher of Whitechapel,* and often simply *Red Jack* itself—you name it.

"And all of these names appear to have stuck over the years—some more than others. But history itself would go on to most remember only Jack the Ripper as the killer's name—and the time period itself."

"So those 'DEAR BOSS' note scrawlings we've been finding on each of the bodies might only allude to a vernacular name of the man himself during the time of his London rampage?" queried Pimleur yet again, quietly thrusting himself into the mix. "Then, clearly, our offender is somehow identifying himself with the historical killer—by itself a pretty scary prospect, if I do say so myself."

"And by extension, I suppose, that the 'Redrum' word we found tattooed on each victim's forehead must figure into all of this as well," noted Robles, subtly wheedling his way back into the discussion, never one to be left out, hopefully, this time without stepping on any toes, or his tongue, again.

Macklin was quick to respond, almost as if anticipating the remark in full. "Well, as the captain mentioned earlier, this was probably the easiest of all the clues that we delved into. Now, of course, we know that the REDRUM scrawl found on each of the victims' foreheads was but a simple anagram for the word MURDER—only spelled backward as it were.

"But here again, you should know that this same Redrum word was only another pseudonym given to the London Ripper by many in the Whitechapel district at the time of the actual killings. So an argument might be made either way that we may have come full circle on that one as well. But again, we can't be 100 percent sure about any of it, really. Much of it still remains highly speculative at this time. That said, Captain, I feel we're only getting closer and closer to the bare truth."

Fuller sat quietly for a moment, perhaps stewing in a prickled heat and drumming her fingers with an irregular cadence on the tabletop before returning to Macklin. "I see" was all she could manage for the moment, then swung her gaze over in the direction of the chief medical examiner.

"Okay, but how about we take a step back and look at yet another aspect of the case, namely the knife our killer seems to have used. Dr. Pimleur, you've had a chance to examine the bodies and you've seen the cuts, I'm sure. You care to make some kind of educated guess as to just what type of weapon may have been used in each event?"

"Certainly, Captain. For sure it was some kind of bladed weapon, obviously. But absent our being able to get our hands on the real knife used, the best I can do is venture an educated guess. I discussed this earlier with Pomeroy and Robles, and I'm of a mind that it would have to have been some kind of angler's filleting tool, a surgeon's instrument perhaps, or an upholsterer's knife, although a butcher's blade might have done quite handily as well. At this point, Captain Fuller, nothing at all can be ruled out as a possibility."

The senior Manhattan medical examiner paused only long enough to purse his lips, swig deeply from a fresh bottle of water, and lock his gaze in deep thought on a far corner of the room. Then, just as quickly, he came directly back to his train of thought and the moment.

"In my opinion, the blade was long and narrowed with a straight taper, most likely six to eight inches in length with a single- or double-edge presentation that may or may not have been serrated. It was also equipped with a cutting surface that must have been honed to a point of some considerable sharpness, such that would easily allow for the kind of deep angular cuts we've been seeing in all of our victims."

"I gotta say, you make it sound like some kind of modern-day Mack the Knife going around ripping people," added a still-irrelevant Robles as he seemingly continued to only lose his footing in the conversation.

"Only much, much worse, Detective Robles," came the ME's terse reply, clearly infused with a measure of sarcasm and dull innuendo. "But back to the knife: in my studies of many of the older London cases mentioned earlier, history seems to suggest that even the original Jack might himself have had *multiple* bladed weapons at his disposal. A motley assortment of knives and even surgical tools, as it were, that might have been used interchangeably during the commission of his several crimes.

"In fact, many of the old London police files tell us that at least one well-known doctor of the time," Pomeroy offered, adding to the curious flow of the conversation, "was himself invited to review some of the autopsy files from the many victims of the original Ripper and laid out his findings on the case." The ME paused only long enough to consult his notes, then seemed to read its verbatim content.

> " The instrument must have been a strong knife, at least six inches long, very sharp, pointed at the top, and about an inch in width. It may have been a clasp knife, a butcher's knife, or a surgeon's knife. But it was no doubt a straight knife.[10] "

"Yes, I came across the good doctor's notes and findings myself—in my research, that is," added Pomeroy, speaking now more as an amateur Ripperologist than an actual modern-day professional investigator. But having already read much of it, a lot of it might indeed have been in his wheelhouse, even if this was his first Ripper-styled serial killing.

"Dr. Thomas Bond's insights were quite illuminating, to be sure, even if a little skewed to his interpretations. In fact, my research found that in at least the case of Mary Jane Kelly—the London Ripper's alleged fifth and final victim—the extent of the butchery and disfigurement to the body could only have come from something more resembling an

---

[10] Extracted from the 10 November 1888 report from a Dr. Thomas Bond—as presented to Dr. Robert Anderson at the latter's request—in which Bond discusses the type of knife used in the slayings of Nichols, Chapman, Stride, and Eddowes. The doctor's findings were then actually presented in a formal brief and was listed as item #9 in an itemized list of eleven. The source, in this event, is cited as being the "Jack the Ripper Tour" site at https://www.thejacktheripperwalk.com/tools-used-jack-ripper/.

axe, or even a crude hatchet or cleaver of sorts, more than an actual knife. But again, this was only the doctor's best guess, not mine."

Macklin found herself digesting all of the information in full for a moment, then signaled her desire to push on with her line of thought, saying, "Then there was also the case of the contemporary senior detective Donald Rumbelow, a former Scotland Yard police official—a man already acknowledged as one of the most accomplished and key experts on all of the Ripper's inactive case files.

"Here, after all, was a modern-day investigator who had described the slasher's weapon as being a 'twelve-inch-long, double-edged amputation knife with thumb grip'[11] and further spoke of actually having the weapon in his possession for some years thereafter. But here again, perhaps none of it may ever have been confirmed to anyone's real satisfaction. So our guess, and the ME's best projections, might not be too far off the mark."

---

[11] In the year 1937, a knife that was then described as a "twelve-inch-long, double-edged amputation knife with a thumb grip" was given to one Dorothy Stroud by editor Hugh Pollard, an associate of one Robert Churchill, a Scotland Yard ballistics expert, which was then later alleged to have been in the possession of that same Donald Rumbelow and purported to be the actual knife used in the Ripper killings, much of which claim was notably provided with a measure of some plausible provenance.

BOGDAN VOLSTAD: REVENGE TACTIC

10 NOVEMBER—PRESENT DAY

The rain had finally tapered off, after an almost full week of precipitation and murk. The lingering storm front had now cut short its flooding of the northeastern corridor and was instead beginning to move off from the greater New York area to points north of the city. Almost reluctantly did it now seem to only slowly drag its wet feet like a child facing bedtime at night or chores on a weekend, as it stamped its way out over the North Atlantic just off Martha's Vineyard. It had last been tracked as far out as the Kelvin Seamount, and its departure had been a welcome change of pace for the people of the New York metropolitan area who, much like wet-mopped, long-haired Spaniels, now stood and vigorously shook off the drench of the previous weeks. *It was enough already!* most citizens must have thought, and only the setting of the day's sun, however pale and unwarming, was still much better than the previous wet alternative. And even this as yet another front threatened from the near horizon and was already poised to move in with its drench of rain in the coming days.

And thus the Bogdan Volstad sat quietly, squirreled away in a sidebar window seat in front of a Bohemian bistro in a quaint old Greenwich Village, just near the corner of Bleecker and Tenth Street. For him, at least it was a nice open-square area for sure, with an impeccable view of everything he needed to see.

He had continued watching with a wary eye and bated patience to catch even a glimpse, however briefly, of the haughty, insulting detective who had fast become his avowed enemy—the son of a bitch. And so he had resolved to find out as much as he could about the man who might now be hunting him, and it was only in due course that he finally understood that it might simply be time to turn the tide and become the hunter instead.

The Ripper had killed five times already and had taken an odd and grotesque pride with each bloody undertaking—even now already planning a sixth, his last slaying perhaps. This, he knew, might now be proposed for two reasons: one to closely mimic the black-hearted killing of Carrie Brown in 1891 at the old East Side Hotel right there on Catherine Slip in a turn-of-the-century Manhattan. And second, to simply plague and confound this cop, this Detective Pomeroy chap who'd already risen to the pinnacle of his native dislike as quickly as he did. And he would tell him as much to his face if he saw him too—just before letting his blood run free in crimson red on the very spot where he stood—which he hoped to do only too soon. The man, and the news reporter who always seemed to shadow his every move, had now become a nemesis and archenemy, a sharp prickle of thorn that he could not quite pull from his craw. *And as I breathe, I will be revenged on him,* the Volstad thought dangerously to himself, then consoled that very anger by knowing even that might be far sooner than later.

The Volstad had thus been stewing in his juices for much of the day and the better part of the evening, this right after seeing the earlier television broadcast with the saucy afternoon interview between Ms. Pretty, as he now referred to the bubbly news reporter herself, and the cop that had seemingly gone out of his way to taunt and mock him. And much in public view too. And now he only relished the idea of preparing to see to both of them, if nothing but to slake his vaulting anger. And only then was he rudely jostled from his dark rumination by the clatter of approaching footsteps on the parquet floor of the café.

"A refill perhaps, on your drink, sir? A small *biscotti* maybe, with your café—yes? They're fresh-baked each morning—right here," came the cheerful, soliciting question from the bistro waiter himself. In performance and presentation, the waiter was well-coiffed and endearingly effeminate, being at once quite prim and proper. He was dressed to only mild ostent in a frill of a white shirt and a faux bowtie, ever carefully balancing a small serving tray just over his head. The angered Volstad would just love to stick out a foot and trip him up, just for jollies, but truth told the whole Parisian affectation of it all only seemed to rub him the wrong way. That and the annoying nasal twang the man had cultured in his voice even as he posed his question through a toothsome smile. "More, sir?" he asked again.

"Ya—I am fine! I am fine, I say. You will please leave me alone here, yes?" growled the unpleasant Volstad as meanly as he might dare, rudely waving off the waiter with a swipe of the hand in midair. He would much rather obey the crave and call of his tobacco habit with one of his imported cigarettes than endure the unwanted attention of this sugary fop.

"You may leave now," he said dismissively as the waiter cast a final disgruntled look at the hulking man who'd now been seated in that same window seat for most of the afternoon, then left in a huff with a final "how rude" glance over his left shoulder.

Then the Volstad swung back in his window perch and continued his sly surveillance of the activities that seemed to all be centered on the 6th Precinct building, itself but a short half block down from the vantage point of his current sitting, just where he'd been all day—waiting, waiting, waiting.

And then he saw his man.

❧❧❧

It had already been a grueling day for both. Pomeroy was entirely spent, while Macklin could only see herself in luxury enjoying a long bath, served up with a tall glass of wine and a good book, curled up in bed. But for the moment, both she and Detective Pomeroy were mostly just hungry: a full sit-down, blue-plate-special kind of hungry perhaps, a condition that might itself only be remedied by food and slaked by a fine wine—such that had both their stomachs grumbling.

Now exiting the old precinct building, Macklin used the somewhat transparent excuse of navigating the small flight of steps to gently grab Pomeroy's arm on their way down. It was a cute and spontaneous ruse that, for the moment at least, was not at all lost on the sergeant. It had been a long day, one capped with meetings with both Captain Fuller and the full investigative team itself, and now it was simply time to clock out, unwind, and knock off, perhaps to simply call it a night already.

"I'd imagine after the kind of day we just had, you must simply be beat," said a gracious Pomeroy as he turned to look at a captivating Ellen Macklin, this time clad all in pale blue, spruced with an accenting gold scarf that seemed to carry it all off for her and suited her to a tee.

"Plus, I'm sure it didn't help to have the captain grill you as much as she did during the meeting. Just know that she can be a little bullish sometimes—and for that, I'm sorry. Lord knows she's got this certain knack for coming across like a bull in a china shop—and that's only when she's in a *good* mood. At other times, she's simply charging straight ahead in a hard-hitting manner that's almost always in your face. Either way, it's just her style. It's not you personally or anything like that, it's her way."

"Oh?" remarked Ellen with just a hint of the same natural curiosity for which she was so famously known.

"Well, I wouldn't want you to take offense at anything said. I hope you understand."

"I do now," responded Ellen with an easy smile, a quiet titter, and a decidedly adorable crinkle of the nose. "But hey, I'm a big girl and I don't ruffle too easily." She also seemed to be taking her sweet time in releasing the man's arm. The evil Volstad had continued observing from afar, even once they'd already cleared the bottom stair of the precinct steps.

The two stood long on the sidewalk now, just in front of the building, loitering inconspicuously in place as they casually glanced up and down Tenth Street itself, both probably thinking about what to do next. To their immediate view, everywhere the "blue and whites"—the very lifeblood cruisers and patrol cars of the NYPD—crammed every square inch of the block up and down Tenth Street. But also crowding the streets were the many personal vehicles belonging to the on-duty officer, all of which made parking an insufferable bear for anyone else living on the crosstown thoroughfare. And always with the ever-present cadence of the normal hustle and bustle just a block up on Bleecker, which also fed into the ambient noise that permeated the small side street. All of it turned much of the narrow one-way avenue into a very corridor of lights, siren blasts, and a general hubbub of activity, this for virtually all of the shift-changing cops that were coming and going out of the precinct at all hours of the day and night.

"So you hungry or what?" Ellen asked finally with a sincere smile that she was maybe using as a way to break the ice or simply as a means to some other desirable end—the very least of which might be eating food itself. "I mean, you haven't had anything to eat all day, have you?"

"Well, I didn't know you were watching, but now that you mentioned it—sure," answered Pomeroy. "I mean, a guy can't be expected to survive only on vending machine candy and stale pretzels now, can he? And believe me, no assortment of Mars bars, chips, and cream sodas can be expected to carry a growing boy all day," he said, ending his odd soliloquy far more feebly than he might have wanted to. But hey, things can happen when you go a little weak in the knees perhaps, which was precisely where Pomeroy was right now—with her eyes, star cast and steady and now also a warm shade of hazel, were already weighing on him and wearing him down.

And it was also wearing down whatever semblance of order or resolve he might formerly have had, even now where he stood: a man almost drunk with infatuation and the haunting beauty of her very presence. And him being all smiles and giggles probably didn't help much either and might have been the very tip-off for sure. But Lord, if there were ever four fine women in the world, she'd sure be *three* of them. And all of it, Pomeroy thought, embodied right here in the soft art of her person.

"Well, if there's an invitation in there somewhere, I'd be happy to tag along. Mind if I join?" he asked with a hopeful lift of an eyebrow, then followed the question with a further point of clarification. "There are quite a few good places right here in Greenwich Village. Perhaps you have a particular preference for food. I mean, what cuisine are you? Are you more Chinese than Japanese, Italian, Korean—*Ethiopian* perhaps? What exactly are you in the mood for?"

"Oh, I don't know." A shy Macklin shrugged with a knowing glance at Sergeant Pomeroy. "Just about anything at this point."

"So let me guess, you're one of those mung bean fries kind of gals, am I right?" he said with a chuckle, seeming to very much enjoy his good-natured ribbing of the cub reporter. "Eating tree limbs and bark with a side of kimchi? I know your kind!" he said, immensely delighting in his ribbing and fun jostles.

"No, no, that's not me, silly. Can't say I like any of that stuff, Sergeant Pomeroy. Really? I think I'll just let that slide for now, but what do you feel like?"

"Anything but bouillabaisse, I'd imagine—and probably no raw fish either. I'd rather leave that kind of thing to the otters. Me, I'm more of a *tortellini* and *orecchiette* type myself. I'm predisposed to Italian. But do tell me what you're in the mood for."

A reserved and quietly bashful Ellen Macklin looked up at him just long enough before answering, perhaps making sure he'd indeed understood her full unspoken answer, which he must have, now betrayed by his own chagrined blush of sorts. Only in good time did she finally speak up, saying, "I think I'm feeling a little more *exotic* this evening, but probably not Japanese—at least not tonight, Joe.

"So let me ask, are you more the traditional type, or do you lean more toward food on a more *nouveau* side? Either way, I think I might have just what the doctor ordered for you, that is if you're up to trying something new?" she offered, extending the invitation almost good-naturedly as the two continued with a subtle kind of courting dance that was reflective of some even greater and wilder attraction ... with both, of course, still afraid to even admit to any of it.

"Nouveau *what*?" said Joe Pomeroy with a crackling laugh. "Okay, I'll bite. Let's say we go with the *new*. So what exactly did you have in mind? Go ahead, impress me!"

"Okay then, how about some Basque food, silly?" she said to Pomeroy with a teasing jostle of an arm that might have said more than he could have imagined. Hey, you're *listening* but not *hearing* what I'm saying, the body language said, but wound up only as, "You mean you've never had Basque food?"

Ellen beamed at him with a cute little owl face, now landing a one-two punch of her own in what seemed to be a flurry of comeback questions. "Let me guess—never, right? Well, I suspect you don't know what you're missing then," she concluded, with the comment itself accompanied by a light poke of a finger against his massive chest. "It's simply a feast both for the eyes and for the mouth. And fortunately—*fortunately* for you, Pomeroy—I know of such a place right here on West Fourth, and we can probably even walk there from here. Sadly, parking anywhere in the area is always a bear."

"Not when you're a cop, it's not," said Pomeroy, almost jokingly, but maybe also being dead serious. After all, he reasoned quietly to himself, rank must (or at least should) have *some* privileges indeed—or so at least he'd been led to understand—and parking should certainly be one of them.

"Oh, that must be nice! But you have to know it's probably also the very reason I don't drive a car in the city," Macklin said, now dovetailing her witty remark with a kind of perfect timing, as indeed the cute courtship ritual danced on.

"So okay, this Basque food place you have in mind here, just where is it—and how far away? I'm starving here!" he probed, maybe feeling fifty-fifty about the whole thing, but also bound and determined to entertain at least one last impromptu end-of-day recap meeting with a good colleague who was now also a very curious love interest for him.

And Detective Pomeroy thought quietly to himself, *if that meeting just happened to be over margaritas, then what indeed could be the harm?* he asked himself as he continued to wrestle with his temptations, however futile the effort. And with Macklin, he reasoned, perhaps he need not even rush things too quickly along, since what indeed might be said of two people who would prefer to take their time and enjoy the journey more than any actual destination they might later find together?

And so the gruff cop went on and on, almost rambling foolishly and feeling much like an amalgam of a smitten kitten and a giddy schoolboy ... or simply a man in awe of his budding feelings for this fine, fine woman sitting just before him. And one, he reasoned with a measure of hope, who might be just as interested in him. *Imagine that?* he thought. The hulking investigator could not help but feel as though he was oddly being drawn into some kind of amorous web—only a web of seeming infinite warmth and alluring invitation. A web, indeed, from which he actively sought no real escape.

"It's a nice little out-of-the-way place just near Cornelia Street on West Fourth—the *Alhambra*—specializing in an incurably romantic atmosphere and delicious cuisine from both the Basque region and continental Spain, sprinkled with some Mexican. Have you ever even tasted Basque food, Pomeroy? *Sopa, almondigas,* and those delicious little *chorizo* sausage thingies—the kind they serve up right at the table, you know, in those charming little mini cast-iron frying pans? How cool is that?" She paused in her exuberant chatter just long enough to catch her breath and rethink her unbridled exuberance. Fearful indeed that she might come across as being a tad too loopy, Macklin decided to maybe simply dial it back a notch.

"C'mon, you only go around once. How about we live a little? I'm sure you'll just love it!" said Ellen with a plea that sounded a lot like half flirt and half invitation and maybe just the right amount of twinkle. "It's simply the very best *paella* this side of town, other than Barcelona itself—or so I've been told," the charming off-duty reporter said with a casual titter and a slight tug at his arm. "We can probably even catch up on some loose ends and discuss the case in greater detail … only over a carafe of chilled *sangria*."

"Or maybe we don't," came Pomeroy's studied and well-thought-out reply.

"Don't?" queried Macklin with only a hint of momentary distress. "Don't what?"

"I mean, it's possible that we don't have to discuss the case at all—if that's okay with you, that is," he answered, perhaps sounding a bit harried and maybe a little too rushed, with the remark itself accompanied by a soft and almost imperceptible squeeze of her hand. And both knew on the instant that the stage was already being set for something far more significant, something perhaps well out of each one's wheelhouse that neither of them had even seen coming or even ready for its very consequences.

"If that's what you'd like" was all Macklin could manage for the moment, finding herself to be far more excited than she even dared to let on.

"Swell. Then maybe we should just go see a guy about a little frying pan at *Alhambra* then," Pomeroy said with a natural cleverness that could only have been wittily shot from the hip. "Hell, I could use a double of something anyway, but I expect that whatever it is, it'll probably have a very short lifespan for sure!"

Now arriving at the car, Pomeroy moved to the passenger side, carefully opened the door, and held it until Macklin was comfortably seated inside, then circled to the driver's side and slid in. Oddly, he found himself uncharacteristically fumbling with his key fob before finally turning over the engine, then idling for a moment before slowly pulling out into a light flow of traffic that was headed down West Tenth.

It would take him yet another full minute to realize that it was the first time in the past weeks that he found himself not thinking about police procedures, mounds of paperwork, or even murder most foul. Instead, his eyes could only cloud over, and for the moment, at least he could see only her—Ellen Macklin. Then he gunned the engine and slowly made his way toward his new horizon, his new plateau—a small out-of-the-way bistro called the *Alhambra*.

༄༄༄

The stalking Volstad strained his view with sunken eyes to more clearly see through the opaque façade of the bistro window, now bathed in light and ablaze in a wash of deep golds and soft siennas. The sun-drenched glow was made all the more vibrant by an early evening squint of the sun just as it began to settle low in the sky. The pale of the sun's light still glimmered its way in from its low station over a far horizon, even as a now-setting orb slipped down behind the western edge of the Hudson River, just a short few blocks away. But yet, the Volstad had continued to watch his man.

It was now but a tick of the clock past seven when the stalker first spied his police detective target just exiting the station house on West Tenth. What was his name again—*Pomeroy*? Now he could see the man coming down the precinct steps, all puffed up and self-assured—perhaps much even to a fault. And look, he was not alone.

The villain could see that the man was far too friendly-like and nearly arm in arm with some young biddy who could only have been that very vixen he so despised. That same newswoman type he'd watched pontificating on her soapbox platform on that TV news broadcast just earlier in the day. The haughty, insulting bitch.

Seemingly quite invested in what looked to be quite an animated consultation, the scrunching villain could easily observe the unmistakable cues of body language between the two that were far too cozy and too coy, especially in such a public venue. Easily could he spot the artful dealings and close interaction of the two: the subtle telling gestures and the inadvertent touch-ups and rubbings between the two.

As if no one knew.

It was the small things, really, that he could see—even from the close vantage point of his window perch—such that first gave him pause and gave rise to a piecing together of his most nefarious of ideas. Carefully watching both, the supervillain had already begun seeing with even greater clarity—discerning carefully that the exchange between the two was not just a random congress of minds or some minor confab between casual associates. Nor was it simply some polite tête-à-tête consultation between colleagues either, obviously. No, there was something else going on here, clearly—something perhaps just beyond the pale of something of even greater import, such that might play right into his hands.

Only now did all of it seem to present him instead with a clear and optimal advantage, such that might also provide him with his best chance to avenge himself in full. Deride and defame me, will you—and in a public forum too?

And it was only then that a secondary attack strategy began to indelibly take shape in the killer's mind, a strategy that might now clearly involve BOTH—and with both bring each to the same deadly end—the slender edge of his killing knife's point. And would that not be deliciously evil, culminating in a most excellent end for both his tormentors indeed? It was a maniac's revenge that could only appeal to the mind of the already insane—in short, a murderer much like himself, but ever more in spades.

On the instant, he'd already begun planning his next move carefully, perhaps first a devious act of isolating, abducting, and sequestering the girl, then luring the fool cop in on what was sure to be some classic end-run rescue attempt. Certainly, such an action, he already knew, would be wholly irresistible to the cop—that ever-predictable cowboy—and then the Volstad could lay hands on both.

The drugs he knew he had at his disposal, those he'd used in the past, might work well with a good application, coursing its warm intoxicants through their systems and probing deeply into the psyche to only further heighten their sense of pain and lower their very threshold to it. In other words, it could only be a win-win for a cold and bankrout sort much like himself. And only then when the darkness had fully come upon them would he embrace them both—well, after he'd had his *fun*. And only then would he be ready. And in the end, when just we three were thus strikingly alone—ah yes, with just we three—only then would he finally introduce them to the keen edge of his ripper's blade and bleed them both out in full, but only slowly, slowly.

Now he stood in haste and stepped over to the bistro counter, paid his table bill in full, and briskly made for the door. In his wake, he'd left a wad of crumpled napkins, pieces of soiled silverware, and no tip for the effete garçon with the charming bowtie. The killer left the coffee shop with the withering eyes of the miffed bistro waiter boring a hole in the back of his head, as the villain purposefully moved off to his car, left by design just at the curb where it had been all evening, then opened the driver's door.

Dropping silently down into the seat, he turned over the engine and slid carefully out into the eastbound flow of traffic as he began heading down Tenth Street, making sure to remain a good two-car length behind the unwary cop in his own oversized Crown Victoria.

"Yes, you, too, shall have a taste of the ripper blade as well. Soon, my friend, perhaps even sooner than you might imagine," the Volstad muttered to himself with a tweak of eyebrow and a face that was scrunched and contorted with dark anticipation. "Then will I kill the girl slowly—in stages as it were—right within your sickened viewing. And I will make you watch in wretched sorrow … and it is only then that I will help you die."

ஒஒஒ

Once Pomeroy and Macklin had finally arrived at their Village eatery, the quaint restaurant was already abuzz with a full house of primetime patrons and casual diners. Decidedly both of them happily found the lighting to be superb and quite suitable and the ambiance ideal enough for the small seating-room bistro that had turned out to be everything Ellen had said it would be and more. Pomeroy was secretly glad that she'd almost insisted on dragging him here in the first place. It was a delightful little out-of-the-way nightspot with tables set out in a glass-enclosed alcove that even extended out onto the sidewalk.

Luckily, even without a reservation, the two were still accommodated and happily ushered off to a table that was already "quite appropriately" tucked away in a cozy corner just by the window between a complimenting pair of decorative palms that seemed to afford them even more privacy, or at least the *illusion* of such. The table itself was neatly decked out with its almost "standard-issue" checkerboard tablecloth, a small condiment tray, and a single red candle flaming almost invitingly between the two, seeming to only further beckon each into the other's eyes.

The two settled in cozily and ordered cocktails and tasty appetizers, now quite content to only continue with the harmless back-and-forth banter that, for the moment at least, seemed to center entirely on the day's work and the many twists and turns of the case over the past weeks.

Now comfortably putting down roots for an evening of fine dining, however exotic (Basque INDEED), the two had decided to shelve any greater discussion of the dossiers and particulars of the crimes, even if for the moment only, even as two salt-rimmed margaritas arrived quite in the nick of time.

Pomeroy bobbed his head in thanks to the doting waiter as the man nodded, turned on his heel, and returned to the bar. Then both he and Ellen took a long and savoring sip of the ice-chilled beverage. *Whoa*, Pomeroy couldn't help but think, *here's a little something with the kick of a mule.* Indeed, both could only squint an eye at the drink's very tartness, causing each to almost comically gag on its very potency, affording them both a good laugh. Finally, they tore themselves away from the mirth and giggles only long enough to pore over their menus, carefully fingering through the bistro's several celebrated offerings.

"Whew," exclaimed Pomeroy to an equally startled Ellen Macklin. "These drinks pack a punch, don't they? I swear this could curl hairs on a mustache. But that said, it does go down smoothly enough. I suppose I can look forward to one heck of a headache in the morning for sure."

"I think I see what you mean, minus the mustache and headache, of course," Ellen said, accented by a hint of a titter, backed by yet another quenching sip of her Margarita, with yet another darling squint of the eye at the very potency of the drink itself. Then both began picking at the *chorizo* appetizers that the waiter had earlier brought to the table.

The chatter was still light, and the companionship was marked by good cheer and a quiet kind of flirtation, as they opted for one of the bistro's trademark *Paella*-for-two entrées, then placed their order with the doting maître d' who had magically just returned to their *al fresco* dining roost.

"So, Joe, what you said earlier in the captain's office, is that true?"

"True? What do you mean?" asked Joe with a queer and inquisitive look between bites of *paella*.

"The thing about the historical Jack the Ripper case files, I mean, and those websites you said you checked out," a quizzical Macklin noted with a fetching owl-face look. "You some kind of Ripper fan?" she asked, then chuckled. "And maybe, more importantly, do I need to be worried about tonight here or what?"

Pomeroy tried his best to contain his mirth, almost choking on his food after having heard the Cubby's comedic remark. "Hardly, plus that's a pretty big leap there, Macklin," he began affably. "But thanks for the vote of confidence nonetheless." Then laying down his utensils, he placed his hands in front of his face in a teepee fashion and looked closely at her.

"Sure, I've heard the JTR name, in passing, at least. Who hasn't? And yes, I've even been to several of the more credible Ripper blogging sites online. Did you know these people call themselves 'Ripperologists'—student detectives of the crimes and the cold case itself? The victims, timelines, and even the suspects themselves? But all of it is harmless enough, though. They're pretty much all just amateur sleuths trying to solve perhaps one of the most profound cases that history has ever known: the Whitechapel murders. And to be truthful, I've dabbled. I admit it freely, I've dabbled myself."

Pomeroy's inquisitive dining partner paused only long enough to "breathe in" her food and to attempt yet another sip and squint of her muscled margarita drink, then settled back farther in her seat. "Ha, small world then," she observed with a flash of her hazel eyes. "So you might be one of them?"

"What—a *Ripperologist?*" he asked as he thought about what she had said. "Yeah, you got me, that's me. I guess I am. A kind of macabre side hobby, if you will. If you can even call it that," Pomeroy concluded, still oddly feeling a compelling need to provide an even greater explanation for her.

"Hey, I'm a cop, remember? So for me, it was an almost native instinct—an irresistible urge as it were—to delve into the case files to maybe seek out new answers to some old, old questions. For me, it was an easy move and a natural inclination, I suppose, to try to solve one of the greatest cold cases of all time."

"I think I understand, Joe," she said as she quickly turned her attention back to the hefty portion of their delicious rice and seafood dish.

"But more importantly, it's my understanding that you, too, have paid a visit or two to some of those forum websites yourself. So what's a nice girl like you even doing in a place like that? I mean those blog sites. Or for that matter, even knowing anything about *any* of this stuff?" Pomeroy asked with what some might have called an uncharacteristic measure of humor.

"Oh, so you find that unusual, do you? Well, let's just say I found myself recently having to take a crash course in the historical Ripper casebook. I thought it important enough to more clearly understand just what we might be dealing with here. I mean, you can see that, can't you?" Macklin said, pausing only long enough to perhaps regain a level of composure.

"Yeah, I suppose. Better to know the monster you're dealing with now than to remain in the dark and be caught off guard later by the very lunacy of both the historical killer—*and* our own. I don't imagine anyone will ever be able to fathom the depths of depravity found within both murderers, then or now—the historical London killer or the very butcher we find ourselves hunting even now."

"And here I thought we were going to keep it light and not discuss any casework, Ellen. But hey, I guess it goes to your point."

"Well, I've been told I have an often-dangerous curiosity. I'm thinking it just kind of goes with the territory. But you're right, Joe, maybe we should forego the shop talk and simply concentrate on this splendid meal for two. What do you say?"

"I'd say it sounds like a very workable plan, but I must say, all of it's so incredibly interesting, sometimes it's hard to get away from it all."

"Okay, then let's talk about YOU then," she said with an impish twinkle of the eye, obviously surprising Pomeroy and catching him off guard. "So what's your favorite color?"

And Pomeroy could only smile.

❧❧❧

The black-hearted Volstad was bent on some measure of retribution and had been feeding the black dog of revenge all day, however irrational it might seem in his mind. His head was a bad neighborhood to be in at the moment, even as he carefully matched the speed of his pursuit car while also continuing to hang back a good two cars from Pomeroy and Macklin in their vehicle just ahead.

Dropping gears and slashing back on his forward roll, he could see that the vehicle in front of him was just now turning off Tenth Street and onto Seventh Avenue South, just as the line of cars began crossing Christopher Street to access the narrow one-way lane that was West Fourth. *Where the hell were they going anyway*, he thought urgently to himself, *and when might it be best to strike?* Ah, but no matter, he would hook on and follow them nonetheless to await his best opportunity to pounce and make good of his attack. Surely there would be some small window of opportunity for him to best exploit, he reasoned well, and time could only be on his side.

Now sitting un-busy at a delaying traffic light, Volstad the Butcher reached down into his waistband and withdrew the *Makarov* PPM pistol to examine the weapon in full. He snapped out the clip and checked the magazine—a full twelve rounds now at the ready. *Good*, he thought quietly. Then he mechanically slid back the action to chamber a round, but still ensured that the safety was on, even as the traffic's forward roll began to resume. Tucking the automatic pistol carefully back on the seat between his legs, he hit the accelerator gently and grappled the wheel to negotiate the unruly traffic on the well-traveled street, then watched as the target car up ahead began to slow on West Fourth. Then he pulled to the curb a half block up just near the corner of dark Jones Street.

Everywhere, the dazzling neon lights buzzed in the night, illuminating the many bistros, coffeehouses, boutiques, and knickknack shops that dotted the West Village street. The lights spilled out onto the early evening lane with a spectrum of colors that splashed across the tapestry of the night in a brilliant palette of blues, reds, greens, and every other carnival color one might ever imagine. But all of its beauty was already lost on the shadowy Volstad, even as he paused to observe the two arriving at some destination, just as the vehicle soon slowed to a halt.

Ach, where are they going? thought the ruffian stalker as he watched both doors open and the pair exit the car. Quietly, he watched them cross over West Fourth to its south side to enter a small restaurant just near the end of the block. For all the world, the two looked far too upbeat and happy, too fully absorbed with each other's company, and even that perhaps a bit too obvious. *Good, let them be off guard.*

And thus, the sinister Ripper now found himself anxiously waiting up the block and parked at the curb just west of Sixth Avenue, his rage unchecked, still fueling his resolve and stoking his fires. At best, he knew it might just be an insufferable waiting game, but he was prepared to bide his time in search of just the right moment. And thus, with the sly passage of time, he found exactly that—the two of them seated in a window alcove of the restaurant, now presenting him with perhaps his best moment to strike.

Strategically, he waited for much of the downstreet traffic to pass by his current location, then pulled out from the curb only when there were no cars in sight. Reaching down, he carefully fingered the small black handgun, flicked off the safety, and made sure to keep his speed steady as he checked his rearview mirror for yet a third time.

Rolling inconspicuously forward, he hit the door button and lowered the passenger-side window as he slowly raised the lip of his gun just as he drew abreast of the dimly lit restaurant window. Then he fired twice as flames of fire almost licked out of the open passenger window, the bullets crashing violently through the thin pane of glass fronting the bistro eatery only a few yards away. Then he hotly gunned the car's engine and sped quickly off to Sixth Avenue, spun left wildly in a careening fishtail that almost took the car up on two wheels, then headed north in loose traffic ... and in an instant, he was gone.

"Oh, how grim, Joe. How utterly grim. Aren't we supposed to be here to simply enjoy a nice meal and good company? How'd we even get started on all of this *Jack the Ripper* stuff anyway? I find much of it to be just a little too morbid for my tastes," said a somewhat uneasy Macklin to her law enforcement liaison as the two sat in their cozy alcove at the Basque restaurant on West Fourth. The comment seemed to have its desired effect and prompted Pomeroy to rein himself in and realize that he was *supposed* to be off duty like that was ever going to happen. Besides, he reasoned, he'd had more than enough of this ghastly stroll down the often-dark streets of his very job, and the even darker historical accounts of more than a century past with the grisly murders of Whitechapel itself. Perhaps he, too, had had just about enough of old Red Jack. Summoning the very best of his resolve, Pomeroy decided to switch up his tack and maybe simply brighten the direction of the conversation altogether.

"So I've been thinking about it and I'm pretty sure you can just call me Joe at this point—especially after all we've been through. So far, I mean. I will say, it's been a rough couple of days here. What do you think?" he asked, making his best case, perhaps just a little anxious to finally dispense the last vestiges of "formality" in their working relationship. A relationship that now appeared to be going in a completely different direction for the moment. A direction that found him wanting to only further "explore options" with her. Perhaps even as much as Macklin herself.

The remark had caught Ellen a little off guard, but was oddly not at all distasteful to her, even if being near him did otherwise seem to disrupt her general train of thought. She actually kind of liked it—and him—but found herself returning to her point of focus, almost in spite of herself. It was better to be safe than sorry, she must have reasoned to herself, and maybe play a little hard to get in the process. Yet she was still drawn to the man even if she couldn't quite put her finger on it or clearly understand any of the why.

"Then perhaps you should call me Ellen, if you'd like, that is" was all she said in response, now raising her margarita snifter in a mock toast in his direction. An elfin twinkle was oddly couched in her eye as she briefly locked her gaze with the man. Her face, however, seemed to entirely betray her rather subdued response, with the woman now beaming with a certain question-mark look and a subconscious wetting of her lips, coupled with an almost playful and involuntary reddening of her cheeks. And the alluring display was not at all lost on a still-smitten Joe Pomeroy, even as both now began playing coy "finger games" across the checkerboard tablecloth. Perhaps the great "secret" they'd both been harboring so privately for so long might now actually be out after all. The two had somehow managed to find each other, even in spite of all the darkness and mayhem of the case at hand. And as such, she, too, returned his warm touch and sat basking in his warm eyes. And then the shots rang out, as just beside them, the restaurant window itself shattered inwardly with a shower of a hundred deadly shards of glass, and in seconds, both were on the floor.

Captain Fuller was still hard at work back in her 6th Precinct office when the call first came in over the radio. She had just been logging off her computer network and packing up her attaché case to wrap it for the day when her police scanner came to life with a sharp crackle and spat out its own deadly words. She recognized the voice almost immediately.

"Dispatch, this is 20-David Sergeant. Shots fired; shots fired at the police. Location: West Fourth Street and Cornelia. Requesting backup and roll an ambo. See the man at the restaurant and be advised a plainclothes officer *is* on the scene. No serious injuries or casualties at this time. Roll on Code 3!"

Then the radio snapped off with a final click, even as Captain Fuller haplessly jammed her knee into the corner of an open drawer on her desk as she quickly jumped to her feet and made a dash for the office door to stick her head out into the hall.

"Heads up, people, heads up! We've got an officer-needs-assistance call coming in at the moment," she advised and was met almost immediately with multiple responses.

"On it, Captain. We've got multiple units dispatched and already rolling on it. Interceptor units are already en route," said one anonymous voice on the main precinct desk, rattling the words off like so much automatic gunfire in a heavy-exchange time of crisis.

"We got anybody hurt, any casualties?" asked a composed but wide-eyed Fuller of her desk sergeant. "Any line on who or what might have been targeted? I thought I heard the call had gone out from 20-David. We got any further word on that yet?"

"Negative on either injuries or casualties. Units are just now arriving at the scene. I'm afraid there are simply no other updates at this time," the wire-thin-framed desk sergeant replied.

"Ah hell," yelled Fuller. "20-David *is* Sergeant Pomeroy, dammit. He must be in trouble. Get me my car and driver—NOW! I'm rolling on this one myself," Fuller commanded as she ran quickly back to her office to retrieve a few items she knew she might need. Then turned in the doorway and shouted back over her shoulder, "NOW, dammit—now!"

એએએ

A terrified Ellen Macklin stirred only slightly while still hugging the floor of the crowded restaurant, now strewn with shards of window glass, upended chairs, and spilled plates everywhere. In retrospect, almost all of the other patrons in close proximity to the windows had been compelled to immediately abandon their tables and quit their standing on a hail-Mary merge with the ground, such that had been both quick and reflexive. And few, if any, had even thought about dropping to the floor. Now in full survival mode, they simply followed basic instincts.

Now, Ellen raised her head slowly to survey the extent of damage and maybe seek out her dinner companion, but she could only catch a quick glimpse of Pomeroy even as he had rushed out of the front door with gun drawn.

She had been both concerned for, and slightly impressed by, the man's responsive actions, but she had to also understand that all of it was purely a reflex action, much as the man's training kicked in and he moved to neutralize the threat. He was already heading out into the street in pursuit of the shooter and had raised his gun at the speeding car even as it drove out of sight and spun around the corner. Instinctively, he knew he had no clear shot and refused to endanger the lives of any other civilians with a wild shot that might otherwise go wide of its mark or even ricochet off who knew what.

Damn, Pomeroy said, almost upbraiding himself. The son of a bitch had managed to somehow slink away yet again. And gone with him was also any clue as to who he was or why he'd even been targeting them imprimis.

Macklin was stunned and still rattled, much in fear for her life, to say the least, and yet she had just watched Pomeroy react so well under fire like no one else she'd ever seen or known. For her, it had been the scariest thing she'd ever been through in her entire life. For him, it was just "Tuesday." And yet he had protected and virtually shielded her with his own body as they had both dropped to the floor.

"Joe..." she called out almost in a daze and still somewhat out of sorts, now looking up just in time to see the detective as he ran back into the restaurant still holstering his weapon. She could even sense him moving quickly to her side and kneeling beside her as he spoke to her in a calm and soothing tone.

"Are you okay, Ellen? Were you hit?" he asked with a look of deep concern. "You okay?" he said, repeating the severe question for yet a second time. Then, sensing that she was unscathed, he turned to the restaurant waitstaff and began barking out a series of orders that would quickly get them all mobilized into action to check on the others, then addressed the crowd at large.

"Okay, people, stay down. Everyone, stay where you are until you get the all-clear! Everyone'll be fine, but just keep your heads low. Anyone else hit or injured in any way?" asked Pomeroy, dutifully trying his best to restore some measure of calm that might itself offset the chaos and ease the fears of the people. He assured the crowd that he'd already put in a call to his station and that his team would be there in only minutes.

Remaining well on point, it was clear that Ellen's half of the love-interest equation was still a man very much in control of the situation, now ordering up a first-aid kit and bandages to dress some of the patrons' minor wounds as needed—including Macklin's own—then leered at the staff as he pushed them further along, slapping on his codicil of instruction, saying, "And light a fire under it—MOVE!"

Sweeping the reporter up into his arms from where she still lay crouched on the floor, he drew her close and held her tight for the moment, trying to calm the subtle tremors that in time did seem to subside. Pomeroy gently cradled her face in his hands and spun her head about slowly, checking her neck, arms, torso, and legs to make sure she had not been hit or injured in any way. Over the right eye, he could see a small cut and a minor abrasion on her left arm, both of which must have been sustained when the window had shattered and crashed inward. Taking a clean cloth napkin from a nearby table, he daubed at the superficial wounds, thankful to no end that nothing more serious had happened to her, or indeed to anyone else in the restaurant upon his even closer inspection.

Then they heard the distant sound of sirens wailing through the night air, as even now, an assortment of police units began rolling up on the scene. Having already traversed Seventh Avenue South, the responding police vehicles shot up West Fourth from its east end, entering the wrong way on an otherwise one-way street, right up to the eatery's location. Then the door went wide and the men in a blue burst in with their guns drawn, clearly uncertain of just what to expect until they saw Pomeroy himself standing by and helping others in the restaurant's small interior.

"You okay, Sarge?" said one of the several responding officers. Two of whom happened to include Paxton and Reid—the same two beat cops who had been with Pomeroy at the very first Grove Street crime scene.

"We got here as fast as we could, Sarge. 'Leastways as soon as we got the call," Paxton offered. Both men had recognized the plainclothes cop fairly immediately, with each now asking after his condition and finding out what exactly had happened.

Having helped Macklin to her feet, Pomeroy dusted himself off, then looked around at the mayhem and confusion of the small space that but a moment ago had been a restaurant, now all a rattling jar of chaos and disorientation brought on even as the first of the shots rang out. And then all eyes swung back to the entrance just as the doors swung wide and even more cops stepped inside, and alongside them entered Captain Fuller herself. She stood framed in the doorway as she quickly oriented herself and made her way into the interior of the bistro with an unfathomed look of distress that seemed to etch itself into the very lines of her face.

"Jesus, Mary, and Joseph, Pomeroy!" she said with a good-natured twist of humor, perhaps simply trying to alleviate the stress of the moment itself. "I can't leave you alone for a minute without you getting into some kind of trouble. So much for crisis management and a quiet dinner for two. Is Macklin okay?"

☙☙☙

Volstad the Butcher now found himself slowing his speed some five blocks north on Sixth Avenue building into the double-digit streets and stopped his ill-advised weaving in and out of traffic. The better to *not* attract the attention of any stationary police units that might otherwise be watching the road for speeders. It simply would not do to have come this far in his studied treachery and fell deeds, only to stumble upon some local yahoo traffic cop on the prowl and have to shoot his way out of a sticky dilemma, knowing just as well that he'd easily do so had he no better option at hand.

Inside the vehicle, there still lingered the rank smell of smoke and acrid cordite, both due to the fact that he had fired the gun from inside the car on his drive-by past the West Fourth Street bistro. He was not at all certain if he'd even met his mark with any level of accuracy. He'd been rushed, impulsive, and pressed quickly into action by a push of traffic that was already entering the lane behind him far back but building quickly as seen from the vantage point of his rearview mirror. It was better to take his shots when he could before the vehicles behind him closed in too closely.

So he was compelled to take the unpracticed shot as is. And even if it did not kill, the very audacity and impact of the shots would at least terrify, if nothing else, and thus might it indeed serve its very purpose in the end. He was neither nervous nor was he afraid. He had killed before, clearly, and had immensely enjoyed the task without true guilt or even a twinge of remorse. But still, he knew that he must be cautious and avoid any rash, impulsive actions. But even that might already be a foregone conclusion.

By now, he'd just come off Sixth Avenue and had turned unnoticed onto an east-west Fourteenth Street with noticeable haste. He had shuttled along quickly eastbound in the stolen car, still wary of being spotted, then throttled back and took a slow right onto an even darker Avenue C. The cops had not yet caught up with him, and there were no chase cars to be seen anywhere behind—no spinning lights and no sirens wailing after him in hot pursuit. Dare he think he'd even gotten away, again?

After he evasively turned back south, it now became clear that he might even be poised to do the unexpected, returning to the very scene of the crime, however circuitously or illogical that might even seem. Now sailing through an intersection with East Houston Street, the Volstad knew he'd gone as far as he could. He'd probably need to ditch the car on the belief that it may have been seen by someone back on West Fourth or even by snooping cameras up on Fourteenth, much as they already had.

Slowing to a stop just at busy Houston, he waited at the light and then cruised through the crosstown hub while continuing south on Avenue C in New York's own "Alphabet City." Just up ahead then, the Williamsburg Bridge.

The Volstad had thus driven almost roundabout north on Sixth, then crosstown on Fourteenth, and finally back south again down Avenue C, all in an attempt to fully throw the cops off his trail. He knew they must all have expected him to exit the city just as quickly as possible, either through a series of side street venues due north or by heading "tunnel or bridge" the hell out of town. But in fact, he'd in effect made but one big U-turn and simply traced his route right back down the concrete spine of New York's east side and directly into the mouth of the dragon with a heavy police presence for yet a second time.

And thus, he found himself leaving the car parked just on the western edge of small Downing Park just on the southern edge of the Williamsburg Bridge and ironically only one short block east of NYPD's Seventh Precinct, the latter perhaps to just stick it to them and flaunt his very escape right back in their "stupid gaping maws."

He laughed to himself as he inconspicuously exited the car and dusted off his prints as best he could or cared to, then decided to simply walk the rest of the way to his next address. It was an address that was just at the corner of Catherine Slip and Water Street, then he steadied himself for his next fell and violent predator attack.

He crossed over yet another narrow backstreet and entered the small *Tanahey* Playground, moving to its grassy southern end, which is an area of overhanging canopy and steeping darkness. His time was near. He could sense it in his soul. It must be right here, and so he stood now just near the site of the now long-gone East River Hotel of old, its chilling history quickly exciting him and bringing back memories of the ill-fated Carrie Brown. He fingered the sharp and hungry blade he held just at the waist, then obscured himself in darkness. He had another important date to keep and he would not wish at all to be late, and indeed might it soon be "Old Shakespeare" all over again. In fact, it would be "DEAR BOSS" for yet a second time.

⁂⁂⁂

Assured that both were all right, the captain sauntered over slowly and addressed her senior detective with a look of unease and genuine concern. "Pomeroy, Macklin," she began, her eyes widening and maybe just a little more than surprised to even see them both together here, even if off duty.

"Seems you two might have had a pretty rough go of it here. I mean, just from the look of things. You guys okay?" she asked, now further investing her thought with, "So what the hell happened here anyway?"

"Beats the hell out of me, Cap. One minute we're sitting here enjoying a fine meal and a bottle of wine, the next minute we're under fire with shots rocketing through the glass here," Pomeroy observed dryly, pointing to the remnants of the blown-out casement behind him.

"I got out to the street as fast as I could and gave pursuit, but this guy's vehicle spun around the corner onto Sixth almost up on two wheels and headed north at a clip. I didn't have a clear shot, at the moment at least, and there were far too many civilians in the line of fire, so I had to hold my position. Hell, the whole thing happened in the blink of an eye, Cap!"

Fuller studied the scene a moment longer, then looked over at several uniformed officers as she barked out new orders. "You men help with some of those people in there and move them to the back of the restaurant. Nobody leaves until we have a little chat with each and every one of them. See that they're comfortable but keep all of them corralled in one area. It's imperative, people." Then, turning around she said, "Just maybe someone else was being targeted here or maybe someone might have seen something of note."

Then she swung her attention back to Detective Pomeroy and asked, "So did you get a make and model on that vehicle? Maybe pull a plate number for us?" the captain asked with a hopeful glint of an eye. "Anything could be helpful, Joe." *Hell, any clue in a storm*, she might have been thinking to herself, then waited for the man's certain answer.

"Silver late-model SUV, Cap. A four-door to be sure. Tinted windows and some sort of roof rack. Possible partial plate coming back as a Nine-David-Whiskey-Seven something, but that's all I was able to get. The shooter was gone in a flash. Simply took his shots and fled. Last seen headed north on Sixth. He could be just about anywhere by now."

"Paxton, Reid, on me!" she yelled, shifting her gaze to the two junior officers nearest her across the room. "I need you two to pull the video from every store in close proximity to this location. Somebody somewhere had to have eyes on this street, gentlemen—*something*. I want some film!"

This she ordered as she pointed up at the several building-mounted surveillance cameras that could be seen just along the small street, one or two of which might have been angled down just enough to capture a speeding car and a gun being fired out of a window just below them.

"Also, get a couple more uniforms up here as well. Maybe carry out a few knocks and talks up and down the block. Canvass the entire street if you have to but find me something. I want door-to-door on this one, so get your people on it ASAP. And I want it YESTERDAY!"

"Yes, ma'am," Paxton said with arched eyebrows, expecting the very continuum he knew might be coming. He found he needn't wait too long.

"And when you're done with that, see if you can maybe scare up a few witness statements as well ... ASAP, gentlemen, ASAP. 'Matter of fact, kick it in the ass! Clear?"

"As a bell, ma'am" was all Paxton could manage. "We're rolling on it now," he replied. "The order's already gone out and we've got most of it in hand," assured a now-redeemed Officer Paxton, the senior patrol member of his group.

"All of it's out on the wire now, Captain," the man said over a shoulder as he turned on his heel and made to step off and carry out the boss's new orders, only to be pulled up short by her further comment.

"Pax, I want a hard perimeter set up around this whole area, copy? Have your people take that radius out to five blocks and set down a grid search that'll lock down this entire zone. I want it tighter than a drum!"

"Roger that, Captain" was all the officer said as he tagged a couple of other men in blue and corralled the bistro manager inside the doorway for a chat about his restaurant cameras. Two others began taking statements from the several restaurant patrons on hand themselves, all of whom sat like a huddled mass of humanity hovering just in the rear of the restaurant, each no doubt sitting about with some trepidation, each hoping for just a moment of recovery from the shock of the flying bullets.

"And while we can't be sure," resumed Detective Pomeroy, now again quite serious, "I suspect our guy's already long gone by now, Captain.

He took off like a cheetah, it the corner there, and spun up Sixth like a hound after a fox! Five blocks is probably not going to do it. We might need a citywide on this character. For my money, he's probably already somewhere up in the Bronx by now."

Now with the officers gone and each dispatched off to their several assigned tasks, the captain turned her attention back to the two in front of her. "Hell, you could just be right, Pomeroy. Who knows? But for right now, all I can do is take it all under advisement. What say we just go with a short-radius coverage for the time being? We can expand that search zone later if we need to."

Pomeroy couldn't help himself thinking that the captain might indeed be throwing out far too loose a net to catch this particular shooter. A short five-block radius might inherently have holes in it the size of the island itself. This guy had probably already slipped through every roadblock out there, well before they'd even had a chance to set them up. What the brawny detective didn't mention was that he couldn't help but wonder who'd have the balls to even attempt to pull this off in the first place.

"So how's our Ms. Macklin holding up here, Joe?" Fuller asked the detective, now changing the subject with a subtle nod toward the journalist who, by now at least, was comfortably seated in one of the restaurant chairs in the front-area dining room. "I take it you two must have had quite a bit of excitement for one evening, no?" asked Fuller with a decidedly impish look on her face as she stood with arms akimbo and swung her gaze toward the still-edgy newscast journalist. She'd even come to *like* the young woman and so seemed to be genuinely concerned for her safety and well-being.

"I'll be okay, Captain," Ellen said as she looked up, having heard her name mentioned and now a little more than anxious to explain things her way in full. "I'm still a little woozy and shaken up is all, but I suppose that's kind of understandable. What I can't understand, though, is why HERE and why NOW? I mean, it does make you think, doesn't it?"

"Think about what?" the captain asked pointedly, seeming to echo Macklin's very remark with a measure of her unmasked curiosity.

"Well, for one thing, about who was being targeted here EXACTLY, I mean. Ah, maybe it's nothing, Captain, but maybe it *is*, or I'm just thinking to myself out loud here. But I still think our two toughest questions must remain the who and the why of this whole thing, I'd imagine." Ellen paused only momentarily to wince at a minor discomfort she felt just then at the hands of one of the EMTs, this as she turned to the young medic who was treating her.

"Easy there, Doc. It still stings a little. Well, just a bit," she reported as the med tech knelt beside her and daubed at what seemed to be a minor cut just over the left eye. She was probably responding to having been poked and prodded a bit too roughly, her face contorting with a stab of pain from, in her view, being slightly manhandled just during his examination.

"Well, we're following up on all leads and taking everything into account, Ms. Macklin," observed a crisp Captain Fuller, seemingly now lost in deep thought.

"Whoever the shooter is, we must have been getting a little too close for comfort and spooked him out of his hole. Or maybe I just hit a nerve in my report and made him feel uncomfortable, causing him to want to strike out. Point is, we've probably got him squirming on a hook on a short line," noted a shaky Ellen Macklin, still a bit of a nervous wreck and perhaps just looking for a handle to safely hold on to.

"My thought?" she continued, "He can almost feel us hunting him— worse, getting closer and closer as we narrow the gap. This could just be his way of telling us to back the hell off. But oddly, something tells me we're not going to be doing that at all, are we, Captain Fuller?"

"What, *back off?*" the captain said, making a soft clucking sound with her lips to maybe show her disdain and to savor her "pshaw" moment. "No, I'm pretty sure that's not going to happen. I can only guarantee that things will only be getting worse for him in the coming days. So far, we've got this guy for discharging a weapon in a public space—at police, no less—which translates almost automatically to attempted murder, driving a vehicle at felony reckless speeds, and a whole laundry list of other charges to pile on top of those. All of it only moves this guy higher up on our food chain—right onto our first-level hit list."

Fuller stopped only long enough to catch her breath and cough into a cupped hand, then resumed and ran the table of the conversation. "Personally, I'd like to see the guy's head on a plate here in front of me, but I'll settle for his ass in jail—or better yet, under it. Now, all we have to do is find the son of a bitch!"

Now, on the very next morning after the shooting on West Fourth and the apparent attempts made on the lives of both Pomeroy and Macklin, Captain Fuller stood in brief conference with a squat and beefy little man who seemed to favor loose clothing and skinny ties. Now oddly hovering just near the station commander, the man seemed to pace restlessly back and forth behind the meeting room table, even as many of the others were content to just sit and size up the very brass of the newcomer.

This was going to be another of those "don't mess with me" kind of mornings for the precinct captain herself—and for those that might be forced to work around her—and everyone braced themselves for the storm they knew might just be around the corner.

Fuller hesitated for a brief second only, then stepped forward to introduce the man who'd already been the object of much collective curiosity, and who was himself chomping at the bit for his intro, and perhaps even that without much of a lead-in. And yeah, Pomeroy knew the guy for sure and had even worked him a few times in the past on a couple of other cases of some good import, such that they had indeed been able to see the case through to a successful conclusion.

Here was a man who was good at what he did he knew and probably had news of some kind that might itself be related to their case, such that it needed to get out as quickly as possible to the teams that might most need the information. Thus, with no real hesitation, the ample-waisted Fed started right in and kicked off a careful litany of analytical profiling.

"Good morning, people. Okay, okay, so let's settle in now. Maybe grab your coffee and settle down, please. We've got a lot of ground to cover, and we need to get started here. My name is Special Agent Don Marshall, and as some of you might already know, I'm an FBI profiler consulting on this New York Ripper case here. You guys can just call me Argyle—everyone else does," he said quietly. "Hey, what's in a name, right? But don't ask, that's a story for another day," the FBI man said with some good levity, but also brimming with a measure of tempered authority.

"Okay, so I've carefully looked at both your suspect here and his signature killings, all trademarked by the man's very actions and the systematic way in which each crime was carried out by the killer himself.

"You're looking for a male Caucasian, thirty-five to forty years old," said the strange, new-faced Agent Argyle Marshall, a beefy boisterous type who spoke too loudly like a stentorian on steroids. *Well, WTF?* might Pomeroy have even thought to himself, looking over at Robles and Macklin with a studied look of surprise. For sure, this guy must have worked in some god-awful megaphone factory somewhere, yelling like a banshee in the rain.

Maybe take it down a notch or two, for Chrissakes. At least this early in the morning! he and the others must all have been thinking, each person wincing in their way at the man's loud and booming voice. Pomeroy already knew him to be a man who saw everything through only one window at a time, and even that with but one perspective available to him—that of always being right. Truly, it was annoying as shit.

Pomeroy dropped his head in seeming resignation, knowing both the man and his call-in trade—all Fed, all the time. *Good old Marshall Mincewords*, he thought. That prick from some FBI profiling unit who was now here snooping around the 6th Precinct for a probable lead on something. Undoubtedly the hottest case they had, his—the Village Ripper. Here, after all, was a man who saw the world with only one perspective—"his way or the highway" —and even that with no real room for greater discussion.

Now sporting what appeared to be a tacky tweed jacket over jeans and a prison-blue button-down shirt with, of all things, an orange tie, the man might almost have pulled off the dapper, too-cool look and seemed oddly well-coordinated in spite of the otherwise eye-blinding colors. Then he resumed his studied discourse and addressed the group at large with a halting delivery, in spite of all the hype.

"Our profile is building your guy out to be about five feet ten to five feet eleven, dark-haired—again, male Caucasian—who might be anywhere from thirty-five to forty years old. We see him as a definite sociopathic loner type who is probably armed to the teeth and has already demonstrated a keen homicidal tendency.

"He's also showing us physical victimology that, for some reason, is almost always old octogenarian men. But to what end and for what reason we are yet to determine. A fetish or death wish for eighty-year-olds only? So why the rage and why that age bracket? we keep asking ourselves, but clearly, much of it remains anyone's guess." Profiler Marshall paused in his presentation to let that much sink in, then picked up the tab of his conversation.

"We think our guy is someone involved in some heavy trade, something requiring intense manual labor, whether working in a loading dock, construction, or even as a longshoreman of some kind, but clearly, something strong-arm and extremely physical. Our guy likely works with his hands, we believe, and is extremely strong and able to subdue on the moment, then grapple his victims from behind each time, and this with seeming ease with much of it occurring in seconds only."

Captain Fuller herself seemed pleased with the criminal profile assessment and said as much to Marshall when she said, "So this is good—a good working paradigm that I think we can use almost as is right out of the box, people. So please listen up and pay attention here."

Then Argyle Marshall concluded his brief update by saying, "Your guy is not going to stop. He will not quit. And while we don't know why he's doing what he's doing—or why he's even choosing this demographic—we just don't know. I mean, why elder abuse and why murder only old men? It could tie back to some childhood thing, perhaps, some physical or sexual abuse by a senior guardian after the individual's primary parents were somehow no longer in the picture. Such might account for the gerontophobia we're seeing here—a general fear or hatred of the aged somehow.

"Hey, all I'm saying, people," said the FBI profiler, "is that at this point, your guess could be just as good as mine, and the bare truth of it is that we just don't know anything for sure. But just a quick heads-up, you folks keep your eyes on and your heads on a swivel. Our

FBI Behavioral Unit believes he will turn and fight if cornered, and might even be harboring some weird death-by-cop wish, since, indeed, we do not believe he will allow himself to be taken down easily. Work your leads, tap into your CIs, pound the pavement and canvass. Find out as much as you can about this guy before you move headlong into a battle with this particular bad actor."

"Now, if we could only find an actual witness who might have had eyes on our shooter—exactly at the time of the attacks themselves—we might even be able to generate a composite sketch or two, which we know could go a long way in helping us step up our hunt for the guy. We need *leads*, people. We need viable new leads here," Captain Fuller said with a still-flustered tone and look at each of the attendees in the room. "And thanks to the FBI consult on this case. I hope that our combined efforts can make up for some lost time. Special Agent Marshall will be hanging around for a while, and we've set him up at the Sixth if anyone wants to pick his brains and take advantage of the man's keen insights into the case."

Joe Pomeroy looked over in Macklin's direction, now half-raising his hand, not knowing if he even needed to do so—much like a kid in a schoolroom hoping to be noticed and called on and maybe given center stage to field a relevant question for which only they might have the answer. "That's all well and good," he countered, "But even if this current profile holds up as workable, the question remains as to whether he might be the same guy we like for the Village killings. Is he our very own Ripper?"

"We'd be smart to move forward on that basis, I should think. What else do we have for the moment?" asked an edgy Captain Fuller, not entirely bending under the stress, but still beginning to feel its very presence. She had lately been feeling much like a middle-aged woman with a slight heart murmur in a high-stress job that seemed to give her nothing but heartaches and head throbs. And all of it—*all* of it was taking a hell of a toll on her own greater "quality of life" plan and leaving her nothing if not depleted and at wits' end. Now as she was nearing the end of both her career and perhaps even her tether, her eyes still nonetheless sparked out at the world, knowing always that the scrutiny of her superiors might already be locked on her at all times ... in fact, probably just her alone.

She could also clearly see that her people were already getting just a little antsy and put off by having to even endure this guy's wordy ramblings, perhaps even wasting time with this profiler hack when there might be some real police work out there that needed to get done. There was a manhunt underway, and this guy running on endlessly here might not be helping quite as much as initially thought. But yet, she was thankful for the quick consult anyway if even one small characteristic detail could be brought to the forefront to shake a tree or a thought or two from her people.

"We also find no evidence of bullet fragments, no trajectories, and no spent rounds ever found or left behind at any of our crime scenes," said Robles, presenting his bit of the report.

"In fact, no type of firearm appears to have been used in any of the cases at all, with no evidence of GSRs[12] either, just the killer's trademark edged weapon assault," the junior cop continued. "But the staging of the sites, the locations were chosen for each attack, and even the very body angles of the victims posed at each of the kill scenes still match up almost identically."

"Also, it's clear that each of our crime scenes seems to tell us a completely different story each time," added the studied forensics specialist Pimleur. "Each scene presents a completely different kind of struggle, but always with the same result—grapple, control, submission, then the brutal killing itself," the ME concluded, perhaps also adding to the build-out of their full criminal profile.

Then Pomeroy took up the baton and ran with the theme, coming in with his own. "Also, note that there's never been any real sexual component to any of these crimes—no evidence of any kind of a sexual violation in any way—until the very evisceration 'activity' that we encountered with the last victim, of course. Perhaps that in itself says something, no? I mean, maybe this is indicative of some kind of a patricide-parricide thing: the killing of a father figure or a parent. Yes, no, maybe? Frankly, we just don't know."

"Well, we at least have a what, a where, and a how," advanced Macklin, now a good deal more composed and tossing off the jacket that had

---

[12] **GSR**—Gunshot Residue.

earlier been draped over her shoulders by Pomeroy. "Unfortunately, we got our WHEN at the time of each killing, now with this guy having FIVE such events under his belt. All of which seemed to always fall on a series of critically historical dates. Distinctively, dates that in every event seemed to correspond directly with London Jack's ripper killings of 1888."

Then, Don Marshall, the FBI criminal profiler, added his addendum with the comment, "And we still don't have anything on facial rec for this guy either—not yet at least. We have nothing coming, nothing going, nothing from a block away even. He's always either looking down or away—probably both on purpose—almost as if he knows precisely where the cameras are."

"That and he's always being hidden under either a hat or that damn black hoodie thing, we just can't seem to get a good angle on this offender," said Pomeroy with a tone whose harshness might have summed up the collective frustration of all. "And nothing at all that we could call a full-frontal throughout all of the killings!"

The wise medical examiner thought about what had been said for a moment and then tossed in his professional insight, "In my own studied opinion, what we have here is a clear and classical psychopath who is 100 percent incapable of feeling any empathy or remorse for his very actions. He will continue to kill almost as a blood sport if left unchecked, and afterward will probably just sit down for a good meal."

"And now," added Pomeroy, "the rage of his fragile, hair-trigger condition has at length now externalized itself, such that has been allowed to now show its horrific face—now a monster most unmanageable and one we must find quickly and put down as fast as we can, much like the rabid beast that he is."

ক৵ক৵ক৵

"Sergeant Pomeroy, Sergeant Pomeroy!" came the spirited call from Officer Paxton as he quickly reentered the small restaurant like a man bearing only good news and glad of it.

"We got a hit on that partial plate they gave us earlier," the patrolman said as if relishing some small victory that might even now be close at hand. Then came a static crackle of the man's shoulder comm as the uniformed officer punched in to receive a momentary update, then turned abruptly back to his superiors with his further report.

"Wait, run that by me again!" blurted Pomeroy as he realized what the man had just said as he cast a sideward glance at his captain. "You mean something came back on the partial? Well, maybe things are beginning to look up after all. Here's a spot of good luck, and I'll take whatever I can get at this point," the sergeant noted, being sure to check his excitement and struggling to keep his own emotions bottled up as best as he could.

"Yessir. That partial—for at least that particular make and model—was initially traced back as a still-incomplete Nine-David-Whiskey," advised an eager Paxton to the group that now consisted of Pomeroy, Robles, Pimleur, and Fuller.

"And when you ran the plates, who'd they come back to?" queried a hopeful detective sergeant, knowing fully well that he might not wish to get his hopes up too high.

"Stolen, Sarge. The plates were stolen. And the vehicle itself comes back stolen from a—" the eager beaver of a beat cop paused only long enough to consult his notepad—"a Mrs. Joanna Vitale—grandmother, resident of Bay Ridge, Brooklyn, reportedly visiting a grandson on the Lower East Side when the vehicle was hijacked at an intersection near Catherine and Water Streets, but no indication of the victim having been roughed up by the assailant. Apparently, the vic only had some minor scrapes and bruises after being pulled from the car, but she's understandably still not a happy camper. She's being interviewed even as we speak, Sarge."

To most who knew him, it might already be obvious that Paxton might indeed have had good expectations for his upward mobility within the police force—no surprises there. But it was also clear that he seemed to know instinctively when things might be working in his favor—much as he could sense right now. For the junior officer, it was always about the WHO and the WHERE of every situation—when to speak and when to keep his mouth shut. And right now, even he could see that he'd captured their collective attention, if even for the moment only. And so he'd decided to carry the torch for just a bit longer.

"Sarge, I've got more coming in now," Paxton said to the curious entourage of listeners as he gently tapped on his communications earpiece. "Current update is now telling us that a couple of mom-and-pop stores up on Eighth Street might have snagged a westbound view of our guy as well, for what it's worth. Seems at least two store cams were trained out on that cross street and might have caught something for us. Several cams might have picked up your fugitive vehicle heading west, apparently at near-felony speeds when last seen.

"Sarge, this guy's hauling ass out of town—probably headed directly for that FDR, sir—which means he could be headed either north or south," the informative Paxton concluded. Then he paused his studied delivery just long enough to let all of it sink in and to perhaps gauge the combined reaction of his bosses when Pomeroy himself cut in.

"Nice catch, Paxton. Maybe things are finally beginning to fall into place here to help us catch a break. Maybe we can begin earning our paychecks for real now. Okay, you seem to be on a roll here, Paxton. So what else you got?" asked a gratified Pomeroy, perhaps just glad to finally have a tangible lead, however slim. Could the far-ranging dragnet they'd set down for their slippery fugitive be closing in at last?

"Sarge, the store cams were finally able to get eyes on a full plate this time. We've got a revised tag number that's now coming back actually as a Nine-David-Whiskey-Seven-One-Five-Lima on a New York tag. Patrol's already been notified, and I made sure to get the word out, sir."

"Then let's not lose his trail," blurted the lead detective, looking for all the world like a man who'd had an immense weight lifted from off his shoulders. Maybe even a man who'd finally been allowed the luxury of free air or at least a single breath of it.

"Copy that, Sarge, but we also got a second hit from a traffic unit on routine patrol up on Fourteenth Street only ten minutes ago. The call came in reporting a vehicle matching your description being spotted driving crosstown at a pretty good clip heading straight for the FDR. The last word we had from the units in pursuit, say it looks like our guy's trying to beat a hasty retreat out of town just as fast as he can. He's getting the hell out of Dodge, sir."

"Could be, but where's he headed from there, to the north or the south?" injected a pensive Robles, scanning the faces of both superiors. "A few minutes ago, this guy was on West Fourth firing shots at you and Macklin through a window. He was already a lot closer to the Hudson River west-side corridor than he was to the FDR over on the other side of town, wasn't he? The guy's only blocks away from his best escape route, so why would he head east instead? Where the hell's he going anyway?"

"Agreed, and probably a good question too," the senior detective responded. "What I can't wrap my head around is this guy's very endgame. What does he want and what's he after? I mean, what's his plan here? What I do know is we'd better find this killer before more people get hurt. We're gonna stay right on him 'til he's caught and we can take him down."

Then it was Fuller who spoke up and chimed in with her insight. "But on the flip side, this fugitive is now pulling us into another jurisdiction completely. I'll have to put out a call to the Seventh precinct. Sounds like our offender's moving right into their backyard. We'll need to coordinate our activities with them now, and they'll need a heads-up on our investigation efforts and the pursuit. And we'd better do it damn quick too."

"Roger that," noted Pomeroy. "I've got some of our people rolling on it already, Captain, even as we speak. But we might still have another problem—Ellen Macklin. What do you want to do with her?"

"I already thought of that. She's a big girl, Sergeant. Are you really worried about her?" queried a pensive Captain Fuller as she keyed in a quick communiqué into her phone to make ready for the very arrangement. "I'll dispatch a unit to make sure we get her home safely, just to be sure. She's a good kid after all. Does that work for you?" she asked, posing the question with a decidedly amenable look on her face.

Fuller must also have been loathing to leave the young reporter in the lurch, alone in the face of the night's very shootings that had impacted both of them. After all, who could know for sure if it was even Pomeroy who was being targeted—or her—or indeed BOTH of them at once? Or was it just some random act of violence that was simply being carried out for some other unknown reason entirely, such that seemed to touch only their lives?

"I'll also have a unit sit on the house, if necessary," the captain assured, then swung her gaze over at Macklin. "Miss Macklin, I can set up a rolling watch in shifts on your house and one that'll be parked on your doorstep for best coverage. You'll be safe and sound for the night, trust me."

"I appreciate that, ma'am" was all the reporter Macklin could manage, and even that with only a blush and a wan smile. "I don't think I'd object to the extra security."

Fuller looked around and took a final sweep of the chaos of the restaurant seating room, then glanced in the direction of her two detectives. "But right now, I need my two best cops over there at the Seventh, pronto. Touch base with the detective squad at the meet point. They're expecting you two already. Team up with their squad and see what you can dig up and coordinate the pursuit. We need to keep our eyes on this guy.

"And Joe, don't worry your head too much with Ellen. She'll be okay. We've got everything in hand," Fuller said as she nodded at Pomeroy as the man let out a subdued sigh of relief, presumably glad to know the journalist would at least be looked after and safely escorted home. In her mind, however, she was chiding her sergeant for even having invested himself as much as he had with the comely reporter. Then she was struck by the idea that she had no way of knowing if it might be the last time she'd see one of the two left alive ... she just didn't know which one.

BROWN AND BRUNER: CATHERINE AND WATER STREET
10 NOVEMBER—PRESENT DAY

It was an act that was wholly unexpected, a heinous and unanticipated event that might otherwise have been uncharacteristic of the current slew of killings to be sure. Holding that the real Jack the Ripper was known for only five *acknowledged* canonical murders back in old seedy Whitechapel, this "new world" killing should not even have been, perhaps, except by some cruel and curious twist of history and fate: that of the killing of a SIXTH Ripper victim. Only now it was all occurring right here in present-day New York City. And only too quickly had 1891 perhaps become the present day with a meeting of the two mutual killings and an accounting of the Carrie Brown murder.

But Volstad the Butcher was battling his demons and trying to channel his better angels if he had any, but all to no avail. The need to kill was simply too strong and far too compelling. Now his breath came in heated snatches, slowly, each with a measured push of air much like a readied sniper preparing for his thousand-yard shot. And thus, the dark villain in darkness waited, now at a place near Catherine and Water Street, both nestled on the Lower East Side of Manhattan, just near the Bowery and the murky waters of the East River.

The villain was still spurred on by his anger and an unslaked urge to kill and had shuttled quickly over from the Greenwich Village shooting scene where he had taken the potshots at the restaurant window where the cop and his girlfriend had been sitting, not at all sure if he'd even hit his intended targets. Now with hackles up and itchy palms, he was bathed in cold sweat and consumed by a standing impulse to once again attack. He had arrived almost blindly at this very spot, not knowing how he'd even gotten here, other than the fast flight from West Fourth itself. And thus, this would be the *second* double event of his full killing spree, only this time he'd be sure to make it count in all events. Maybe it was simply time to provide those that chose to hunt him with yet another irrefutable "history" lesson ... something perhaps from Old Jack's time itself.

The night was still in its infancy, having quietly shuttled over the cusp of early evening and finding its way to now meet its darker cousin night. The Ripper crouched warily in the shadows of the small green space that passed for a park just at the confluence of the two side streets and steeled himself for his next kill. Indeed, he need not wait too long.

Volstad could not help but believe that he'd somehow been here before, perhaps now more than a hundred years ago to be sure, he felt. Only then had it been a much different venue and a much different time as much under a different guise, but always with the same fell purpose. Had Jack the Ripper come to America and had he walked these very streets—perhaps just HERE, even near the place where Volstad was standing now—just at the confluence of Catherine and Water streets? Only then the time had been April of 1891, already some three years after all of the London butchery.

So what otherwise might be said of the ruthless killings that were even now being visited upon a terrified twentieth-century neighborhood on New York's Lower East Side? Volstad was a sheep of never and a brother of none. A villain and a victim almost all at once, driven by his rage and burdened with an unshakable urge and a blackened heart that spared nothing and cared for none. He was one who'd ever paced unevenly through life, lurking ever on the fringes of good society, a modern-day *nogoodski* who could only be found looming and loitering his way through his existence, embracing little and attaching himself to naught.

And thus, it was this same villain now shrewdly walked among us, surreptitiously blending in with stealth and good concealment within the heavy throng that always made up the seamy underside of backstreets and dark alleyways that were all an integral part of the Catherine Slip docks just off the East River, very near the dark underworld of New York's Lower East Side. Much as it might have been with "England Jack" as well, much as with the man's final rip and last goose. Even then in 1891, as the original Jack himself caroused with the drunken sorts that peopled the dark downtown brothels that dotted the turn-of-the-century south Manhattan landscape within this same area, his very victim that night was but a fallen waif of a night creature named Carrie Brown.

And thus, she too had become Red Jack's next and final victim in an all-too-surprising series of *six*. "Old Shakespeare," as she was oft known in her drunken states, ever quoting her learned lines from the many lost sonnets and deep Shakespeare plays while well in her cups and cavorting about the night haunts and steamy sawdust taverns that must have made up her world—and *oh*, the houses of ill repute. Perhaps then, indeed, must the poor wretch have been easy prey for easy pickings, at least for Red Jack and the blade of his dripping dagger. And by the early morning hours of April 24, she would coldly be found in old room 31 of the old East Side Hotel, now itself long gone but very near the area's jagged waterfront, where in minutes her wretched soul had been dispatched and horridly disfigured. And once again, even in death, the villain had further done things to her still-warm corpse, crudely posing the body and leaving it to profane and common view, then simply leaving her for dead.

Her killer, now himself a New York-based Jack the Ripper, even then back in 1891, just in from London and—still steeped in blood and savoring the comforting reminders of his several kills in old Whitechapel—knew at the moment that he must again set a new and different guise for his new-world incarnation, whether patron, pedant, or even doctor perhaps, but always more bawd and cutpurse than any other. The cold, cold grip of murder must have come almost instantaneously, and the fateful "Old Shakespeare" would indeed be no more.

And now would it be the Volstad's turn to carry off his ghastly murder, once again right here at Catherine and Water streets, just like his bloody predecessor in 1891. And once more, "just for jollies."

అంఅంఅం

Carlton Bruner had always been troubled by a clipped and halting gait, one that for all the world came across as a "*ssh-clomp, ssh-clomp*" as he shuffled along, dragging a disfavored left leg with only great hardship. It had always been a dark complication that had its deep roots in an old war injury that had been sustained during the embattled retreat at the port of Pusan just during the opening months of the Korean War in late 1950. In fact, it had historically been August of that same year when the bulk of the defending ROK forces and an Allied UN infantry unit had been ruthlessly driven back by the NKPR[13] and pinned down in some far southeastern corner of the Asian peninsula.

---

[13] **NKPR**—North Korean People's Republic, a fictional name for today's Democratic People's' Republic of Korea.

Now with their backs to the sea, things could only have looked quite bleak for his Twenty-Seventh Infantry Regiment even as they dug in deep and held the perimeter just near the Naktong River. Cautiously, had they awaited the fierce enemy push that to a man they knew was coming, the old man remembered almost as if still yesterday, now steeling themselves against the very real possibility of a position overrun by an ever-aggressive force of NoKos that had continued to push south ever nearer their very position of standing.

And now, much like the brave expeditionary British forces at Dunkirk in the early 1940s at the start of World War II, they had all desperately hung on and sought their timely relief. "A rescue—a rescue for the men," Bruner now recalled, thinking even back then, hoping against hope that one would be forthcoming. Returning to the moment, the old man might indeed have continued musing over these past events had he not heard a sharp crack of a twig somewhere behind him. And just that fast had he been snapped back to the present.

The strident and sudden sound had been disturbing to his remembrances, quickly bringing him back from his foggy distractions even as he trudged slowly along and navigated the dark lanes of the park just near his home. Had he also seen a shadow? Just there, perhaps? No, maybe? But who else indeed might even be out and about this late in the evening? Old Bruner was not at all sure even as he looked behind him but still saw nothing.

Crossing over now, slow and halting, the man continued, moving deeper toward the darker shrubs that dotted the small neighborhood park just at the press of night. It was a still-pensive Carlton Bruner who looked around and surveyed his late-night surroundings with eyes that were still unmindful and only half alert. His pathway was poorly lit and overgrown with a seeming canopy of camouflaging leafy oaks and low-hanging limbs, such that might have served to only further obstruct his late-night view.

Still glossed over from a minor spatter of rain that had already ended some hours ago, the narrowed lane glistened now with a dark and resplendent glow that shimmered up from its still-wet surface. There were no sounds, no movements, and no distractions to abrade the ear or beckon the eye to view, all owing to the late hour and the quiet unpeopled park, save for his shuffling gait and the telltale cadence of its ever-continuing "*ssh-clomp, ssh-clomp, ssh-clomp.*" But even now, he'd heard a crunch of leaves and a faint rustle of activity in the bushes, much as his aged eye did finally catch a shiver of movement just there at the periphery of his vision. *Was there actually someone there?* the old man must have thought to himself with a taut hesitancy that was laced with only a mild tremor of fear.

And only then would come the deadly snatch and vicious grappling hook from just behind the elder man. Only then would come the hot embrace and choking grip with a large mugger's mitt of a hand that cupped the mouth and instantly stifled the sound. *My God, he is much too strong. Too, too strong*, thought Bruner. His eyes now going wide with fright and mute surprise, with both legs soon completely off the ground as the man was pulled back and almost hoisted up into the air, the harried extremities thrashing wildly about in the air almost from the moment of his very abduction. And even with the darkening of the old man's eyes, he could still catch the dull glint of steel and its thrust forward with a long and sharpened blade that seemed to shiver only momentarily in the night air and menace him in the same moment.

Something deep inside the old man told him darkly that his demise might now be near an end, perhaps even sooner than expected. But he also found his very strength at that moment. And almost as quickly, he was back to his former self—a fighting man and a ground pounder, an old army grunt much in spirit and in his heart. He'd not given up any ground at Pusan Harbor all those many years ago, and he damn well wasn't giving up any ground now. He would not go down without a fight. And much of it was not at all expected by the attacking slasher even as he made ready his sharpened knife as he was a man-killer simply accustomed to stark terror, blind conformity, and enforced compliance. He was not equipped for unquiet rage or hot defiance.

Now, somehow slipping his tormented hold for but a moment only, Bruner jammed a hand deep into his pocket and fingered the Buck knife he knew he always carried with him. It was now clearly a race against time, the man knew, even as he could already see the brandished knife coming for his throat, even if he could not fully see his attacker's face.

He'd have only half a chance at a viable defense were he to even survive the moment and only half again at even getting away unscathed, but he knew he had to try. So he swung back viciously with his Buck knife blade, just as his attacker made his first move to strike. Bruner jammed the short blade blindly into the only area he could reach—the attacker's upper thigh.

And then came the man's very deep-throated howl, much like a cornered, wounded animal, a sound that pierced the cowl of night itself. And even on that instant, the Volstad could feel the almost-spontaneous pain in the fleshy upper region of the right leg, perhaps now becoming even more focused on his injury than his blunt attack on the old man. In fact, he'd not even seen it coming. The quick flash of the blade had been surprising—even unexpected—at least coming from the old man, the codger who was supposed to be objectified only by the killer's attack.

The very act of resistance and very boldness, at least on the part of the old Bruner, now only further fueled the killer's taut anger, causing him to strike with even greater resolve. His butcher's knife was much as long as it was sharp, and so quickly now found its fleshy mark, probing deep into the throat of the thrashing old vet. And thus, would come the gorging cut and double slice, once-twice, with all of it now a horrid roll of gurgling sounds escaping softly from the old man's mouth.

The deed now done, the killer paused only long enough to scan the immediate area with a broad sweep, and content to find no one in sight, he could now only hastily step through his ritualistic acts of postmortem disfigurement and placement of objects about the scene. There would simply be no time for such now. There could only be the red Jack playing card, the bloodstained "Redrum" marking on the furrowed brow, and the "Dear Boss" note itself—always scribbled, folded, and placed carefully in the dead man's mouth. But not today.

All this now must the Volstad seemingly forego, almost disallowing himself the very leisured moments he so keenly desired, now placing in angry abeyance the very macabre and methodical calling-card rituals that he so richly enjoyed. So he did only as much as he might dare, lest he, too, soon be discovered before his time or worse captured outright. And in a snit and angry shake of a tail, the Butcher was simply gone, dropping the knife as he made good his escape, painfully halting off with a pronounced limp, nursing a gashed leg wound, and vehemently cursing his bad luck.

ॐॐॐ

"Okay, people, I just got off the phone with the captain over at the Seventh and I've looped them in on our pursuit. Pomeroy, I want you and Robles to hustle over to the precinct there and talk with their dispatch. You'll be checking in with Detectives Crouse and Kincaid. Find out what you can about this fugitive's most recent movements. Maybe get a last-known on the guy if there even is any. Maybe something'll pop," said the captain with a measure of optimism that was still tempered by the passage of time and betrayed by Fuller's dour look. The whole thing was a long shot and she damn well knew it.

"And how about this time you keep those phones turned on and maybe keep me in the loop for once? Just in case they've stumbled onto some new sightings. We clear on all of that?" asked Fuller, expecting full compliance and surveying her two subordinates with an almost chilling glare.

She had hoped to spur her people on with greater incentive but was now concerned that much of what she'd said had come across as being only more of a kind of "whip and lash" invective than anything else. But yet, she forged on with a message that was brimming with hope and good prospect.

"Maybe we can actually leapfrog ahead of this clown and finally put an end to all the madness, maybe even tonight."

"Copy that, Captain," answered Pomeroy with a look of certain irritation and the pull of deep exhaustion, both feelings deeply etched in the man's dark eyes and rich, burnished face. He looked around at the chaos of the Greenwich Village bistro where both he and Macklin had been dining just earlier and that had then been shot up all to hell, then turned back to his boss. "Sounds like something might have popped in the case, Captain. What do you know that we don't?"

"Just go hook up with Crouse and Kincaid on that side. Word is they might already have some news for you by the time you arrive. They'll fill you in on the details once you get there," the head of Major Crimes said as she began walking with them to the door and ushering them out.

"And you two listen up too: you keep your heads on a swivel and get your asses back here safe and sound, in one piece, savvy?"

She stood authoritatively in the frame of the office doorway, seemingly anxious to get back to work, then bristled up in her next remarks. "Remember, this guy's unpredictable. You guys listening to me? Keep your comms on and your lines open.

"And check in with me if you come across anything at all actionable. Let's make it our mission to get this guy already, maybe even tonight. I can almost feel him nearly in our—!"

"Sergeant, Sergeant Pomeroy!" said Officer Paxton at a dead run as he flagged the senior man down and cut in for now a second time, sidling up to a point just near the captain and reporter Macklin. "We just got another hit, Sarge!" the patrolman said evenly as he worked to quiet himself down, speaking now as if in confidence to just the small group of investigators.

"Looks like they just found your suspect's vehicle, Sarge. A roving patrol out of the Seventh reports finding a late-model SUV, the same make and model, abandoned just south of the Williamsburg Bridge, a block or so east of the Seventh Precinct. Seems this guy's just thumbing his nose at us, Sarge, and somehow managing to get away with it every time!"

"Not much longer, Paxton," an affronted Pomeroy responded with an absentminded scowl that ran as deep as his soul and scored his face with a furrow and a certain dread resolve. "Not for much longer he won't, if I can help it. He who laughs last and all that," the detective said with a snarl and a sniff that clearly bespoke his defiance.

"And now we have maybe our best lead on exactly where that suspect might be. It could even be our best chance to nab the son of a bitch and simply have an end to all the madness," suggested Pomeroy with venomous anger, perhaps no longer willing to even hold his composure. "This guy's been pissing me off since day one. I'll be just as happy when we've got his ass in chains and shackles!"

"Well, this guy's luck can't hold out forever," countered Captain Fuller, injecting her remark into the already combustible mood of the discussion with a measure of exasperation that was clearly all her own. "This fugitive streak of his simply has to come to an end. I want his ass in cuffs or coffin, one way or another, and let's see if we can actually make that happen sooner rather than later."

Captain Fuller tiredly removed the glasses from her face and gently massaged the bridge of her nose, then sat back slowly and closed her eyes in a moment of deeper reflection.

"And when it does go down, I want to be right there alongside you. I'll be the one slapping on the cuffs and looking him in the eye when he finally is in custody and we march his ass into holding."

"Copy that loud and clear, boss," said a surprisingly insightful Robles with yet another spot-on remark that was delivered only matter-of-factly. "I think this is a man trying to outrun his demons, but how far can he go? Probably all we need to do is wait him out and let him stumble on his own and fall, as we know he will inevitably. Give him just enough rope to hang himself and let him come to us."

"But how many more people might have to die before that actually happens?" queried a still-grizzled Pomeroy as he coughed lightly into a cupped hand, an unpleasant gesture left over from his former smoking days. He was clearly still hot under the collar and loathe to give in to a calmer and more rational side. "How many more victims might perish at the point of his knife and never even see it coming? I for one don't wish to find out. So how about we just round this guy up tonight and be done with the whole affair?"

Now, it seems to the loathsome villain that he might indeed have only three blind-alley options available to him at quick disposal. One, to attempt to flee and make off on a dead run back to his Red Hook flat, where in all likelihood they would already be lying in wait for him and even that much in force. Two, he could try to hobble himself off to some local hospital somewhere, *maybe*, under whatever guise or mantle of false pretense he might need to seek out treatment for the increasingly painful leg wound. Or three, he could simply continue in spite of injury and exhaustion, merely binding the wound and wrapping a small tourniquet about the thigh to at least stem the flow of blood.

Much as he had already done on the instant, he vowed only to push on much without rest or repair. He would need to find a safe haven from the storm.

Braga! the shifty assassin had cursed in regard of his black mood and dull suffering. *Shit.* The old man had managed to get him good somehow, almost *besting* him, the son of a bitch. And the most damnable part of it all owed much to his stupidity and blunt surprise. The old man's reflexes had been swift and sure, far quicker than anticipated. The very counterattack had not at all been expected and, certainly for the moment at least, it hurt like the very Dickens itself.

But the Volstad had already decided to simply refute the pain and internalize the throbbing pulse ... better 'twould be, perhaps, to simply grit the teeth and flash the eye and go with option three. Compelled to forge ahead, therefore, he did so with a kind of reckless abandon in pursuit of a single fell purpose—that of hunting and felling the two remaining targets of his keenly focused anger in his seemingly ongoing blood-drunk spree.

He was flustered and unsettled, wholly uncertain whether he'd gotten either or both of the two targets he'd engaged with the hasty wildfire shots he'd loosed at the *Alhambra* restaurant on West Fourth. And so, he was driven on by his death march of demons, darkly moved to try his hand at termination for yet a second time.

He had just killed his sixth and final victim in New York City, and even that much without chore. He'd completed yet another full cycle of slaughter and mayhem, such that history itself would uphold and always remember well, much as they would tremble much in fear of his very name and persona as "The Village Butcher," "The Slasher," and "The New York Ripper." And would not old London Jack himself have been proud of his handiwork thus far? Perhaps all the more for careful execution of his vile deeds without getting caught, much like Whitechapel's own "Leather Apron"—even then back in late 1888, leaving in his wake a trail of bodies, a quiet suspicion, and only a dark cold-trail pursuit that never went anywhere.

There would be time enough, the evil Volstad mused to himself, to finish the bloody task he'd so hotly hung out for himself: eliminating the two remaining thorns left alive—the cop and the newsie, that nosy lady reporter, both of whom could only too easily be dispatched, he believed, perhaps even before this very night was done. And thus, he stepped off as quickly as he could in the direction of dark Downing Park where he had last left the car, unaware of the series of surprises that might already await him just ahead.

Detective Sergeant Joe Pomeroy and the still-shaken reporter Ellen Macklin were both still dusting themselves off at the West Fourth Street Alhambra bistro, even as she found herself still shaking off the terrors of an evening full of violent twists and turns.

In the wake of the shooting, the crime scene techs had already completed most of their routine tasks, and once cleared to do so, the waitstaff of the small bistro had busied themselves as they worked to clear tables and upright chairs, cleaning up much of the debris that had resulted from the earlier drive-by shooting attack.

Captain Angie Fuller was just now preparing to leave, as were many of the other patrons who had already been fully vetted and debriefed by this time and released by the several law officers attending the scene. And thus, a small queue of diners, most of whom had long ago lost their appetites in the face of the de facto sniping attempts, now slowly found themselves being ushered out the door in a careful and ordered manner. But even this only after having their statements taken by Paxton, Reid, and a bevy of uniformed officers right there on the spot.

What did you see and when did you see it? Were you injured? Did you take note of the car at the time of the shooting? Did you get a fix on the driver? Which way was the vehicle going when you last saw it and where were you when the shots rang out?

These, indeed, were the poignant questions each patron had to field in the investigators' collective pursuit of exactly what may, or may not, have been seen by each of the witnesses on hand. In due course, then, it would finally be Pomeroy who would break the weighty ice of the moment.

unrelenting and incorruptible—much a force to be reckoned with in its time and feared by almost every bad actor in the neighborhood.

Dogged in its pursuit of the diehard criminals and hardcore felons that must have prowled the darker streets just between Canal and Chambers, his team had been there right in the thick when the bills came due in a dragnet of crooks that seemed to go on and on. And because of those very years of training, Pomeroy had learned all by himself to best navigate the arterial backstreets of the area as he rode the dragon alleys all those years ago. And even all these years later, he had forgotten nothing, as well the captain knew.

Those, he remembered, were the formative years, the early probationary years that had been lain at the feet of a much younger Pomeroy. Years spent as a rookie beat cop with a big heart, a no-nonsense attitude, and a good set of knuckles should he ever need them in a scrape. And even then, the word had already gone out on the street both about him and his team. Don't mess with them and run if you even see them coming.

Decidedly, the vote had come in on the effectiveness of that anti-crimes unit back then and the verdict was in: they had not been very popular with the local kingpins and drug runners in the neighborhood, but they were loved by the honest shopkeepers who only sought to make an honest living without graft or payout to unscrupulous sorts. So what else was new? Many thought it simply went with the territory, but most also knew that they were just good at what they did—from a law enforcement angle—whether a small pinch of local ringleaders or the takedown of both gangs and major drug factions.

As a result, his very anti-crime unit had risen quickly with local fame, soon developing a well-founded reputation for being both hyperaggressive and fearless to a fault with a well-oiled tactical assault team that relentlessly got in the face of the bad guys while battling both on the front lines and from behind the scenes.

Quickly then had they culled a name of some repute, with a propensity for coming in hot with a series of trademark "knock knocks" and breaching entries that somehow just seemed to be a normal part of the job. But much of it could have gone either way in the blink of an eye whenever there was any unforeseen gunplay.

In its time, Pomeroy knew that the crooks already called them "heavies," "devil dogs" and "door kickers," and the team had quickly become a force majeure and feared by the area's criminal element, and they could not be bought off. Over time, Pomeroy and his anti-crime team had more than made their numbers in violent felony arrests, fast making them a force to be reckoned with in a neighborhood that stretched from Canal Street north and south.

Even in its second year after its very commissioning, his squad had already become a fully functional unit, a no-nonsense task force of cops whose approach to law and order was short and sweet: Don't do the crime if you can't do the time. And Lord help you if they had to come find you, you were probably already well behind the eight ball. Pray God they didn't get a green light to land on you with two feet in force. It might just ruin your entire day.

All this and more came rushing back like a surge of memories that flooded his mind as he spoke to the captain, much of it allowing him to remember both the good and the bad, and then he capitulated to her suggestion. The decision wasn't too hard.

"Okay, Captain, I'll see she gets home safely" was all Sergeant Pomeroy could muster for the moment as he snapped back after his brief walk down memory lane with Fuller. But he was also secretly pleased with the notion that he'd even been presented with the pleasant escort assignment imprimis. He couldn't have asked for better.

"Looks like we're pretty well wrapped up here for the night anyway," the burly sergeant added. "Robles can handle things here while the rest of the team ties up a few loose ends. Which I guess frees me up, Cap. I'll touch base and report back once everything's settled," he said. Then he began heading for the door when Captain Fuller pulled him up short.

"And Joe," said Fuller as she flashed a look of genuine concern in his general direction.

"Ma'am?" queried Sergeant Pomeroy as he stopped in his tracks with an inquisitive tilt of the head.

"You make sure you watch your back out there, you hear me? I mean it," Fuller said.

"Copy that, Captain. Will do," responded Pomeroy, almost dutifully, a remark that seemed to dovetail neatly with her final instruction.

"Barring everything else, you make sure you keep your eyes on and one round in the chamber."

⁂

Bogdan Volstad, the sinister Ripper who had long terrorized much of the Greenwich Village area of lower Manhattan, now seemingly reveled in the night's fiendish deeds. He had carefully avoided much of the city's daytime hustle and bustle and had moved only by night, confining all of his monstrous midnight deeds to only the southern edge of the island, much in an area that had already been long wedded to the envelope-pushing idea of "weird" and truly "out there." Yet even now, in his greatest moment of thumping pain, did he still feel unfulfilled *somehow*, even with his recent spate of deadly dealings. He had much to settle yet, and two were still very much alive, he criticized himself harshly, and would still need to be dealt with, with good prejudice, however harsh its ultimate outcome.

The dreadful butcher had moved unsteadily and was still slow-stepping his way clear of the crime scene where he'd just slain his sixth and final victim, the battling Carlton Bruner. He was already beginning to make his way back to the car that he had deliberately parked some blocks away, knowing that it was now a clear and dire imperative that he leave the area as swiftly as possible, and that even in spite of his throbbing injury.

Now, a crowd of blue seemed to press in precisely on the moment, the running killer Volstad could see even from afar, with a team sweeping in just on the moment to nearly encircle the abandoned car where he'd left it. Soon, they were fanning out in a clear search pattern that took in much of the small Downing Park area as well, he saw. How long before they'd look beyond and how long before they might find him? Instinctively, the Ripper knew he'd need to avoid the probing cops at all costs lest he was indeed seen and apprehended *in situ* by what he knew could only be the long arm of the law. Might they indeed not already have a viable, working description of him, in addition to having the vehicle itself now in hand?

Overwhelmed now by their very numbers, Volstad the hunter had now become the hunted but knew he'd still dare them to the teeth should he need to and battle them to the end to shoot his way out if he were even cornered and compelled to fight. The murderer had already made a pact with the devil that he would not be taken alive, and if the issue was forced, he would take as many with him as he could. *Send anybody you want*, he thought blackly to himself. *Just don't send anybody you want back.* But all such foolish bravado aside, he reckoned quietly to himself, he might still prefer to circumvent the thorny problem in full and simply find another way around the police barricade that seemed to go up on the instant and stretch itself for a full city block, only he better do it now if he were to even survive the night. And so, he quickly turned on his heel and stepped off, heading back toward the same Tanahey Park and the very kill scene he'd just left only moments earlier.

Now, the bloodied villain had but one mandate and motive in mind: FLIGHT and a quick escape from the heavy police presence that was already building and virtually flooding the street where he'd last parked the stolen car on the eastern edge of the small Downing Park near the Williamsburg Bridge. And so, the villain hobbled along cautiously with a halting gait while still nursing the dull and nagging leg wound he'd suffered in the botched scuffle with the contentious Carlton Bruner.

Everywhere, the red and blue swirl of police lights shimmered and spun, piercing the deep veil of night and bathing the entire area in a sweeping arc of light that could only mean one thing: the law was here in force and already snooping around his vehicle stash point just by the bridge. *Damn.* Sooner or later might they not soon expand their search radius out even farther, ever closer to his very point of standing?

He would need to get his hands on another vehicle in the instant if he were to, at all, be able to safely exit the area with quick-time dispatch. Perhaps now might simply be time to get the hell out of Dodge. The small cadre of cops was like a sea of blue uniforms, a constabulary of guns and searchlights in the night that he knew must all be looking only for him. And all of them soon enough converging in this one area in full, perhaps even closing in on him now were he to do nothing at all.

The butcher was driven now only by a clear survival instinct and his urgent need to avoid the considerable police presence that he could see building up only blocks away, and to simply flee the scene in full and let the devil take all as well as he might. Now concerned that he might indeed have overstayed his welcome in the suddenly too-hot police search zone, the killer now only wanted out as quickly as he could. Indeed, had things gone precisely according to plan, he would already have been long gone from the scene and well on his way to his secondary site.

A man downcast and now cast down, he was a fugitive much on edge with a level of discomfort that was only building by the minute. A quick look about and luck would once again grace his wretched lot when at long last he spotted a lone, late-night vehicle stopped just at the corner of the same Catherine Slip he'd fled just earlier in haste. His arrival at that intersection also meant that he'd managed to come almost full circle in the erratic swiftness of his very flight. And now an escape that had itself been blunted by the stepped-up police presence near his only way out—the car.

Slowly then did he approach the car from the rear with an element of stealth and good surprise as he hugged whatever shadows the street might afford. Carefully avoiding the small-capture wing mirrors, the villain crept almost heel-and-toe from behind and made ready as he desperately brandished the gun, leveling up the lethal lip of the *Makarov* pistol, its presentation at the car window came almost at the last minute, just before the unsuspecting driver could even gun the engine in quick flight or run the very light at which she now sat.

Without compunction then did he use the weapon to ruthlessly commandeer the old Buick from the unsuspecting motorist sitting just there at the traffic light. It had been a middle-aged woman just returning from a late-night market shop, even as a look of fear and stark terror contorted her face into a trembling grimace. Quickly did he fully subdue the luckless driver right at the red, then displaced the terrified woman much at gunpoint, leaving her dazed and shaken— virtually standing in the middle of the road—then sped off into a dark labyrinth of backstreets and dusky byroads. And in minutes was the deadly villain already heading back to the scene of the earlier shooting at the café on West Fourth, seemingly right back into the very mouth of the dragon itself. In Volstad's mind, it was perhaps the best and only course of action at his disposal for the moment—perhaps even the very least of what a killer on the run might be expected to do.

And thus did the committed felon soon find himself slowing to a roll just as he reached broad Canal Street, where he hung a sharp right and began his trek due west back into the maw of the Greenwich Village nocturne. And even in that very instant his trail might have already gone cold, and the Volstad was quickly lost to the sheltering mantle of night.

൞൞൞

By now, Macklin, Robles, Pomeroy, and Captain Fuller had all rejoined each other back on the sidewalk in front of the debris and splintered glass of the *Alhambra* restaurant. All around them, a small crowd of nonplussed onlookers pressed in from all sides, trying to nosy their way in for a better, more grim view of the crime hotspot. *What happened? Who got shot? Had the cops arrested someone?* they must have been asking each other as the busied crowd buzzed among themselves. And even as the area of the earlier shooting was still being scrutinized and fully processed by a team of sharp-eyed crime scene techs, Pomeroy found himself consoling a still-shaken Ellen Macklin, just as the two approached the sergeant's Crown Victoria parked at the curb.

"I can't really say, Captain," said a cautious Pomeroy, anxious to ensure that his facts were entirely accurate. "I only heard the two shots, both of which appear to have been fired at pretty close range. My guess is from the passing car we saw pulling out of here at an extremely high rate of speed."

A ring-eyed Sergeant Pomeroy must only have looked bone-tired and seemed to be in a state of near-exhaustion, with neither him nor Captain Fuller really knowing when last either of them might have slept. *Now there's a concept—a good night's sleep,* Fuller mused to herself in the back of her mind, then was immediately wrenched back to the moment.

"Both shots pretty much shattered the whole front of the bistro here. Then the guy peeled out like a thief on the lamb," growled the rough-edged detective. "The son of a bitch! Anyway, the rest you already know."

"Okay, just make sure your follow-up report reflects all of that, Joe. I want to capture as much as we can on this one. Eventually, we'll catch up to this guy, and when we do, I want to be 100 percent that everything we have on him sticks. But how about for now we just concentrate on getting Ms. Macklin home safely, then maybe call it a night. Sound good?"

"Captain, if it's all the same to you, I'd rather just stay here and work the case. I'd imagine I might be of a lot better use right here on scene."

"Pomeroy—*Joe*," urged the captain with a look that lingered only long enough for him to slowly catch on. "We've got it handled here. Just take your cue and get her out of here. Go home already—no discussions. That's an order!" said Fuller, half wanting to wrap up the scene and half wanting to simply protect two of her best investigative assets for the moment: Macklin and Pomeroy.

"Copy that, boss. Then I'll see you tomorrow" was all the senior detective could manage as he squeezed gently on Macklin's arm and guided her off in the direction of the unmarked police car.

The street outside the bistro was still heavily dotted with first-responder vehicles, and the small side-street venue had essentially remained closed to all through traffic, a move that must itself have peeved those few drivers being held up by the delay just trying to get home. Now ushering Macklin into the vehicle, Pomeroy could only glance up and down the street and simply thank his lucky stars, now almost glad now to finally be able to just call it a day.

He entered the car, exhaled loudly, then turned over the ignition and pulled slowly from the curb as he moved into West Fourth Street, proceeding east toward the slow-moving traffic of Sixth Avenue. And neither one of them ever took note of the nondescript car sitting in the darker recesses just at the end of the block facing out onto West Fourth, unaware of the shadowy, hollow-eyed driver who sat just at the edge of Cornelia Street already watching them like a calculating deadly bird of prey.

❧❧❧

"Ah, so there you are," snarled the evil Volstad as he surveilled the group of police elite standing just in front of the same restaurant he'd left just earlier. And with them was that same hussy reporter he had so intensely come to dislike. Small surprise then that, in his mind at least, he had already vowed to be revenged on all of them.

A light rain had once again picked up, pelting an already wet pavement, making for a slick base of fuel and motor oils that had seeped out and mixed into the street asphalt. Now making road surfaces even more dicey with the onset of yet another wetting downfall, it had also caused them to become oily and slick, offering only the poorest traction.

This was made even more obvious just as the unmarked police car peeled off from the curb with a sharp fishtail to the left. Pomeroy apparently accelerated too quickly as he sought to merge out into the light traffic of West 4th Street, even at the very moment he passed the villain's parked car just up the street.

Volstad hunkered down in his seat only long enough to not be seen just as the Crown Victoria slid by on uncertain footing. And it was only then that the sinister assassin eased his car into drive and pulled out after the detective's vehicle. And much of it was itself a bit too surreal and oddly reminiscent of the earlier tail he'd already placed on them but a few hours earlier.

The Ripper's hijacked Buick from Catherine Street had now become the chase car, and the hotly hunted had become the hot-footed pursuer, and the killer's second slow-speed pursuit was already underway. And where it might lead was anyone's guess, at least in his mind. And like the rabid, driven man he had already become, Volstad was sworn to have his revenge on both or to boldly die trying.

❧❧❧

Pomeroy tapped on the keypad of his handheld phone to end the incoming call just as he hung up with his boss, Captain Angie Fuller. His junior partner, Damien Robles, eyed his boss with caution and good expectation, but when he did speak up, his voice was just a little halting and betrayed his greater concern.

"Sarge, you don't look so good. What was that all about?" he asked with a mounting curiosity that would not be assuaged without disclosure as he absently scratched at the nape of his neck, perhaps in search of his best answers.

The evening air was damp and alive with an unseasonal nip for this time of year. And a drizzling rain had already poised itself just overhead with a scurry of clouds that wrung out like a wet towel dripping water in a shower stall—now again almost on cue and soaking all. *Dammit.*

"It's pretty much as we suspected all along, Damien. Looks like our worst fears weren't too far off the mark," offered Pomeroy, not entirely sure of his footing going forward since most of what he'd just heard might indeed have the potential to break new ground for their lagging case.

"Forensics came back on the knife we got from our last crime scene—the Carlton Bruner attack we had in that crosstown park over in Alphabet City," said Pomeroy. He was, of course, referring to an area of east New York City where Avenues A, B, and C all ran roughly north to south and ended somewhere around the towering Williamsburg Bridge. Pomeroy paused only long enough to sharpen his focus and recenter his thoughts, then continued on.

"Looks like the captain is convinced by the evidence she got back from the ME that the same guy who took the potshots at me and Macklin might be the same guy we liked for all of the Ripper slashings we've been looking into all these past weeks."

"Wait, are you saying what I think you're saying?" asked a keen-eyed Robles, still maybe a little stumped by the new spin and the sudden turn of events. "So we think he's one and the same guy? Hell, what do I know? Maybe she's right. It's no real stretch since both MOs seem to match up. All of this can't be just sheer coincidence, boss. Plus, I think all of these killings were made to only *look* like random crimes of opportunity," Robles ventured, surprising the other man with his apparent sharp grasp of the situation in full. "In fact, I'm convinced they're all somehow connected ... and have been all along."

"I'm convinced all of our previous killings had to have been rage homicides, Damien, undoubtedly. We know this from the viciousness and very malevolence of the crimes themselves—the staged scenes, even the consistency of evidence found at each site. And all of it is driven by animus and a bottomless and all-consuming anger. But I suspect we all knew that going in."

"This guy's smart, boss, and he's devolving quickly. But he's becoming more and more careless as he moves ahead, I think. It's possible he's beginning to slip up," the junior cop chimed in, deftly picking up the tab of the conversation. He liked the direction they seemed to be headed in for the moment and instinctively believed that some great truth might be just around the corner and about to break. And he fully expected to be there when it did.

"There's a certain focused hatred here that our killer harbors deeply in his heart, Sarge," added an insightful Robles as he closely followed the senior detective's lead. "But always involving only old men, and I can only help but wonder why, but there's no viable explanation why."

Pomeroy thought about what his partner had said for a minute before responding, then offered his best explanation. "Our killer's committing his string of violent attacks in pursuit of some hidden goal, some insatiable need he'll never really be able to fathom or even satisfy. And that's what makes him even more dangerous.

"On the surface, all of his crimes might only APPEAR to be random—almost *desperately* so—like Eppes's axiom of coherent states on *Numbers*. But none of it has ever fooled me for a moment. I've always thought the killings were somehow all related."

"So is this our guy or not?" asked Robles with a flurry of thoughts flickering through his head, but still quite anxious to simply get to his boss's bottom line.

"He's the serial killer that no one saw coming, Robles. He's the boogeyman and a cryptid, the creature in your closet, the monster under your bed. Our guy's probably all those things combined. Who can know for sure? We have to find this guy."

Detective Robles mulled over the series of metaphors and macabre images around in his head, perhaps even recalling his series of frightful memories from his childhood, then offered his version of light at the end of the tunnel.

"But even if all of what you say is true, our offender had to have made a mistake somewhere. We just need to figure out the what and the where, Sarge. Then we have to find that one chink in the man's armor."

"Then we'd better get busy on it then, Damien. We haven't a moment to lose!"

TENDER MOMENTS DISPIRITED

10 NOVEMBER–PRESENT DAY

"You okay, Macklin?" asked a still-unsettled Pomeroy as he drove steadily along and navigated his unmarked Crown Victoria through the back-channel streets just north of Canal and east of Hudson, as he headed for Broome Street. The route itself, now very near the famed Holland Tunnel, was probably best known to most native New Yorkers as NoHo, an upscale locale that was just north of Houston Street. A dull roar could be heard in the far distance with a sudden surge in early evening traffic, as cars entered and exited the broad under-river tunnel on its way to and from the far shores of New Jersey. A hot sirocco breeze now kicked up as well, making the night sticky and uncomfortable, reminding all that July was July no matter where in the city you were.

"Yes, yes, Joe, of course, I am now. Thanks in great part to you. It's just that I felt so mortified back there for having fallen apart at the restaurant, especially in front of the captain the way I did. You think she'll ever forgive me?" asked a genuinely concerned Macklin.

"Forgive? Hey, we were shot at, remember? That'd pretty much rattle anyone's cage, I'd imagine. Plus, I was right there with you on the floor, Ellen, or did you forget that small detail? Hey, there's no shame in it. I just had to make sure we both hit the deck when the bullets started flying and the glass started shattering the way it did. So maybe stop beating yourself up over it already."

And then he said the seemingly magic words that he knew might put a Band-Aid on the whole affair and maybe calm her down when he said, "Actually, I'm the one who feels kind of responsible for the whole thing, Ellen. It was my job to watch out for you in the first place. It was my job to make sure nothing happened to you—at least not on my watch—and I failed. I came up short."

Macklin mulled over the detective's soothing words for a brief second, then offered her own secondary observations.

"No, Joe, it was not something either of us could have controlled. Don't beat yourself up already," Macklin advised. "But why would anyone even shoot at us anyway? I mean, what'd we ever do?" the reporter asked plaintively, dropping her head to her chest and shuddering with a soft sob that seemed to disappear almost as quickly as it had come on when he gently touched her hand.

"None of this is your fault, you have to know that. You're still just a little shaken up is all," a consoling Pomeroy said sedately, trying to assuage her fears and pleased to see her coming back from the edge.

Now a splash of light streaked through the window of the car as they drove slowly under one of the halogen street lamps that lined both sides of the small side street, just as they turned onto a now-revived Broome Street, itself still a tepid mixture of the old and the new come together.

"That's it there, Joe, right there, just up on the left—the brightly lit building midblock."

"THAT?" Joe said with a muffled guffaw that he was probably already too late in stifling. "Wow!" he almost whistled, still amazed at what he was even seeing. "Geez. You rich or something? This thing's a real palace of a high-rise!"

The building was tall and reaching, a slender, glass-and-chrome-looking structure that was comprised of beams, balconies, and cantilevers that seemed to hold the whole thing in place and make it a near thing of beauty. It was a virtual steel finger that stretched up toward the very heavens, a sheer urban marvel and a truly upscale marriage of grandeur and functional architecture that immediately caught the eye without distraction.

It stood out visibly on a street that still contained its several prewar buildings from a time long past, many of which had already been converted to spacious lofts in the early 1990s. And even on that instant, Pomeroy found himself completely bowled over and more than pleasantly surprised by the unexpected turn of events, and his eyes indeed must have said as much to a tittering Ellen Macklin.

"Hey, don't hate me for living well, Joe. I hope you don't think any less of me," said Ellen with an uneasy squirm as her eyes looked up and met his. "Daddy comes from old money but also went on to make a killing in the bond market with some pretty wise investments made along the way in futures and precious metals. I can't apologize for who I am or where I come from, Joe. You have to know that."

"And I'd never want you to, Ellen. And no, I don't hate you. Let's just say you can color me impressed," Pomeroy said with a half chuckle that was smothered in his smile.

"And here I thought you were just another pretty face working her way up through the ranks of a popular network news station," he said as they smiled softly at each other.

"But I'd also have to say that I'm glad to see you're so capably making a go of it on your own as well. That's impressive," he offered, followed by an affectionate squeeze of her hand just as the car pulled up to an empty parking spot that was, a miracle of miracles, right in front of the building itself—a true stroke of luck that the detective attributed entirely to simply being with this warm and intriguing woman.

"You know, I just realized something," Pomeroy said as he threw the car into park after easily backing into the spot.

"Oh," responded Macklin, her interest now piqued in an odd kind of way. "And what's that?" she found herself asking with an arch of the eyebrow and a discernible twinkle in her eyes.

"I just realized that if there were four beautiful women in the world, you'd be three of them," the off-duty detective said with a warm smile that seemed to indicate that he might have meant it. Then he got out of the car and made his way over to the passenger side to hold the door for Ellen and found himself graciously extending a guiding hand to help her up and out of the police sedan. *Might as well be polite*, he mused to himself.

Now exiting the car, still shaken, Ellen found her footing unsteady, tripping lightly on the curb as she softly careened into the policeman's waiting arms, cleverly excusing her "oafish clumsiness" for having done so, even if the action itself might have had its desired effect, now finding herself pressed closely to Pomeroy as he held her to prevent the "imagined" fall.

"Oops," Ellen said out loud like in some quaint old *Betty Boop* movie with an almost impish grin that might have been considered out of place, much perhaps to let him know that it might even have been on purpose. "Oh, clumsy me," the cub reporter said as the two enjoyed another mutual laugh, knowing that both might already have seen right through the posturing ruse.

"Yeah, right," chuckled Joe Pomeroy as he pulled her nearer to him, then leaned in ever closer as he drew to the moment and kissed her softly right there in front of the Broome Street "palace." She did not resist. Indeed, she seemed to almost welcome the detective's soft approach and returned the man's kiss in full.

And so he tasted her lips as the two seemed to hold the kiss for a time that felt more like an eternity, but neither one made a move to pull away or to break the embrace. Then, when they finally did part from their tenderest of moments, Joe found that he could only manage a wan and sheepish smile like a lad caught with fingers in a cookie jar.

Perhaps, indeed, they might already have reached some new and far plateau even if neither one was entirely aware of it happening nor willing to admit it. Or, indeed, perhaps they had.

"Joe, don't leave me alone right now. Not now, Joe. Please. I don't want to be by myself tonight. It's just too much and I've already had the craziest of days," said a shaken and still apprehensive Macklin to an oddly unsurprised Sergeant Pomeroy.

"I feel like I've been stalked most of the evening and shot at for no reason—if it was even me they were shooting at," the newswoman said plaintively with far more concern than her face might otherwise have shown.

The two had ended their studied kiss and broken their embrace long enough to stare into each other's eyes and almost sigh. *Oh, how cliché*, the two might even have thought to themselves, both having been lost in the moment and feeling for all the world like giddy schoolkids who'd been seen smooching under the bleachers just behind the football field. In an instant, their brief moment had truly been nothing but magical for both. The kiss was transcendent and far more than just rewarding. It had been a wondrous moment. A moment that seemed to only seek more like its own upon which to happily feed—lover to lover and self upon self.

"You'll be fine, Ellen. No one will get to you now," assured a cautious Pomeroy to best calm the woman's nerves as much as to lighten his burden of surety and self-assurance.

Perhaps Joe Pomeroy might even have been able to savor the moment even longer had he not had his "Spidey-sense" police training kick in and his tingling curiosity drawn to a dark vehicle that he'd just seen turning onto the street up the block with lights off. Was it just his imagination or was it, once again, danger close? Was there, in fact, something that might not bode well or be quite right, or was it all owing entirely to an active imagination? And yet the dark unlighted vehicle still sat and made no attempt to move at all. The strange car seemed to only linger just at the corner, idling roughly as it sat and seemed to rev its engine, almost rocking in place, much like a horse in a starting gate, straining at its very tether.

And now, the hairs went up in full and the alarm bells went off as the police detective switched now to a different mode entirely, remaining cautiously on guard.

Then the shadowy vehicle accelerated forward with an astonishing burst of speed even as the driver's window suspiciously slid down just as it drew abreast of the building itself. And then the shots rang out again for yet a second time.

ஃஃஃ

Bogdan Volstad, the infamous man-killer, now with a measure of new-found celebrity, had almost flippantly been portrayed in the media as "The Village Ripper" and had already perpetrated multiple horrific murders. The man had taunted the police and fled in the face of his crimes in at least two high-speed pursuits, the last of which had involved at least one carjacking. And all of it, he thought angrily, all of it to only wind up here but a few blocks north from the *Alhambra* restaurant yet again.

The villain had only loosely tailed the police detective and the plucky female reporter at a short distance, the better to arouse no real suspicion and to entirely avoid any telling glimpse in the cop's rearview mirror as he followed. Pomeroy and Macklin had tooled along in their off-duty unmarked car almost aimlessly, it seemed to him, shuttling quietly through the several darkened streets just north of Canal decidedly on the area the assailant himself was not terribly familiar with.

Volstad had been careful not to seed the suspicion of the two he'd fired at earlier, deciding instead to wisely hang back a full two-car length behind with another car between, even as he nervously drove along in the same stolen vehicle he'd commandeered crosstown on the far eastern edge of Manhattan just south of Alphabet City. And now, his very rage and obsessive urge for vengeance had driven him right here to some obscure backstreet area just near Broome Street. He was but a half block's distance from the two targets he'd been scoping as the pair now stood in front of some fancy new high-rise in the middle of the block—kissing. *Really? Shit.*

The car's engine idled roughly and seemed to only sputter and cough in the old stolen Buick SUV, but it also had ample power, enough he'd found to at least push the pistons up and down and move off with good speed should he even need it. The old car decidedly had just enough under the hood to maybe power its way out of any untenable situation he might find himself in. But he also knew that the authorities might indeed be looking for the car by now—by plate or description—its displaced driver perhaps having already called it in to report its very loss but moments after the high-jacking. As a result—and as a matter of good caution—he knew he might need to swap vehicles and soon dump the car, this for yet a *second* time were he to indeed stay a step ahead of his dogged trackers.

Inside the car, he pulled the visor down to shade any full view of his face and hunkered down only further in his seat as he watched and waited, watched and waited, watched and waited. Then the villain saw his best opportunity and slowly placed the car in drive and began inching forward off the curb and out into the street, gun up and safety off.

Pomeroy was having none of it this time around. Someone had fired on the two of them yet again, and the whizzing bullets had this time been far too close for comfort. Someone was trying to get his attention, and now once again they had it. But who *was* this guy and just what the hell kind of axe did the demented assassin have to grind anyway? The detective sergeant could only help but wonder and could only forge on in search of truth, however bizarre.

Now even more motivated by the very thought, he found himself quickly hustling Ellen Macklin into the police sedan, entering the vehicle, and driving off as he hit the lights and siren. He swung about on the instant with a U-turn that peeled off sharply from the curb and left a rubber swirl on the street, almost coming up short in its wrenching turn.

The old Crown Imperial pursuit car overcorrected erratically now with a hard fishtail spin that rattled its passengers violently first to the right and then to the left. The tires finally catching a good grip on the damp pavement, the aging sedan now took off with astonishing speed, flying like a screeching angry bat from hell after the unknown assailant in quick-time pursuit.

In the back of his mind, the detective already knew he was probably breaking protocol by even having a civilian in the vehicle with him in the first place, this while also conducting a high-speed chase, much as he was right now. But Pomeroy's options, at least for the moment, seemed limited and he was not about to leave the reporter standing alone on the sidewalk in front of her building while he gave chase. What if the maniac came back for yet a *third* time for even another kill shot attempt? Perhaps he might not miss it the next time around. No, leaving the woman behind there in the face of an active threat was itself an untenable option that he simply could not entertain.

"Buckle up and stay the hell down, Ellen," Pomeroy ordered, perhaps more harshly than he might otherwise have intended, then reached for his police radio, fingered the lateral button, and shot his ident over the unit's squawk box back to his precinct headquarters.

"Dispatch, this is 20-David Sergeant. 20 David Sergeant going out to any units in the vicinity of Broome Street and Canal. Shots fired at the police. Repeat, shots fired at the police! Need assistance. Any units in the vicinity. 20-David is unmarked and in pursuit at this time." Then the airwaves went dead and Pomeroy nearly put his foot through the radiator as he stomped the accelerator in search of a last desperate burst of speed. Hell-bent for leather, he'd nail this son of a bitch this time or die trying.

❧❧❧

The night had been a clear and constant friend to the Village Slasher, the Butcher Volstad. Still a man driven by his demons and his dark designs, the Butcher had carried off yet a second drive-by attempt on the two, but had again foolishly taken his shots wide—and wildly—much without rehearsal or good aim. He could not even be sure if he'd hit either of his marks at all, much of it owing mostly to bad timing, bad luck, and perhaps just his bad aim. He'd rushed his sighting and taken his shots high and wide of the intended targets, perhaps more to terrorize and strike fear in the heart than to truly maim or kill—much indeed like an alerted dog's bark being far worse than its actual bite. Only these were live bullets fired at live people, not just the disarming howls of a foamy-mouthed beast under a dark moonscape sky in late October.

The Volstad checked his rearview mirror twice with but a fleeting glance each time, surreptitiously checking his six just behind him to be sure. Was he being followed? Had he been seen at all in those fleeting seconds just as he sped past the targeted couple and opened fire? Had a fleeting image indeed been captured perhaps in the brilliant splash of light from Macklin's Broome Street condominium, a building that stood like a lighted beacon in a sea of the night? Had either of them been able to even latch onto a plate number or see but a fleeting blur of his face just as he roared by in the stolen car? Certainly, he must have triggered one or more of the several unseen cameras flanking the very building walls along the block he'd just left as he careened roughly down the road, no?

Ah, but no matter, he cared not. And whether a hit or a miss, the flight of the very bullets must have made his point roundly enough. And so the madman simply gunned the engine with a leaden foot and sped up, nearly choking out his carburetor as the runaway Buick throttled up with a laboring sputter before the wheels dug in and found their hottest traction.

Soon reaching the end of the block, the fugitive hurtled around the corner on angry tires almost as fast as he could, negotiating the turn almost up on two wheels as the heavy-centered SUV shuttled on with near-reckless abandon.

Assured that he'd been able to successfully duck the tail and flee the scene again in full, perhaps, the crazed felon was almost at the end of the next block before he even looked up and caught the first telltale sign of pursuit—a splash of headlights in his mirror far behind. At first, it had been but a distant blur, a dull flickering of light that was coming up far too fast to be something other than what he knew it to be already. Yes, it was unmistakable now—he was being tailed and someone was right on his ass and closing fast.

ಶಿಶಿಶಿ

"So what's eating at you, Detective? Looks like you've got something on your mind," asked a curious Captain Fuller of her junior homicide detective Damien Robles. The two had remained behind at the West Fourth Street bistro for several additional moments, as they supervised the details and processing of the full crime scene.

"Well, for one thing, this whole affair is taking far too long here, Captain. Hell, these crime scene boys should have wrapped all of this up by now, don't you think? What are they doing?" inquired a decidedly impatient Robles, almost chomping at the bit to do something—ANYthing—more than the nothing he was doing right now.

Fuller paused momentarily, looking down only long enough to kick at a shard of glass left over from the imploded window, then picked up the tab of her conversation with Robles. "I suspect it'll take as long as it needs to take, Robles, you know that. We have to let them do their thing and finish gathering as much evidence as they can while the scene is still fresh.

"And maybe, just maybe, our boys can sniff out a clue or two that can help our investigative team. In the long run, it'll only help firm up our case when they move to prosecute, but first, we have to catch him."

"Say what you want, Captain, but I still can't shake the feeling. Like I'm sitting here on my thumbs when I could be doing something more relevant to help the investigation further along," suggested the junior man, his growing anxiety showing perhaps a bit more than it should for the moment.

"I should be out on the street with my partner, Captain, at the least. And I sure as hell don't like leaving him out there with no backup, other than Macklin ... and she's not a cop, boss. You know I'm right."

"Well, you can stop your worrying Robles. Pomeroy's a big boy and I'm pretty sure he can take care of himself. Plus, he's been at this much longer than you have," Fuller upbraided the man, perhaps her awkward way of assuaging the younger man's worst fears. Whether or not it was working for him was pretty much up for grabs and probably anyone's best guess.

Outside, a full troop of forensic specialists and uniformed police officers still busied themselves as they moved about feverishly working to ferret out all and any clues they might be lucky enough to find. And both Fuller and Robles knew that could be anything, anything at all: from the random and unsought to spent shell casings. And everything from canvassing for potential witnesses to pulling camera feeds from videos taken from adjoining buildings. And even checking tread marks on the road that might have been left behind by the suspect vehicle after it had peeled off and sped away so quickly after the villain had fired his shots into the crowd at the West Fourth Street bistro.

"Hell of a thing, Robles, when a person can't even sit down for a nice meal at the ass end of a hectic day without being shot at. Question is, who was being targeted here—Pomeroy or Macklin—or perhaps just someone else inside the establishment at the time? Maybe someone we might not even be aware of? It's something that just keeps bugging me here," submitted an obviously tired captain to her junior sleuth.

"Beats me, Captain," said an unsettled Robles to his boss. "If you ask me, the entire shooting thing could have been unrelated. A personal feud, perhaps, a vendetta, a grudge shooting. Hell, maybe even some kind of Gambino-style hit for all we know. At this point, your guess is as good as mine, but the forensics team is staying right on top of it, ma'am."

Fuller made ready to answer, posturing subtly with a finger still wagging in the air, when the incoming call burst in over the airwaves like a sleek greyhound coming out of its slip with a burning desire to win.

"Dispatch, this is 20-David Sergeant going out to all units. Shots fired at the police. Say again, shots fired at the police..." Then a dreaded silence fell over the two of them like a wet curtain as their entire world stood still for yet a second time.

"Faster, Joe, faster! Stay on him, stay on this guy. Don't lose him now!" shouted an agitated but still courageous Ellen Macklin, much like a backseat driver, only planted right up front on the passenger side just opposite the detective and buckled in tight.

"Don't let him slip us again. If we could only close on him, we're so close. Here, turn here, Joe. Turn HERE," she said, accompanying the animated instruction with arms that seemed to flail in the air in the direction they could both see the getaway car heading.

Gone now were the irrational fear, the bouncing jitters, and the soft trepidation she might have shown before. Gone now was the anxiety and wary disquiet that, for Macklin at least, might normally inhibit her world and her every move. And all of it—all of it—now replaced instead with a steely gaze, a clench of teeth, and a certain dead resolve to see the daunting task through to a successful conclusion.

Now both she and the plainclothes cop could see that they were right on the getaway car's track, even as the faint taillights up ahead told them they were bearing down quickly in their unmarked chase car. And both might easily agree that catching the bastard was probably the only clear imperative at hand, all other options weighed on the moment. After all, a bird in the hand and possession being 9/10 of the law might be a good thing. *Therefore, better not to lose the tail at all*, she opined, the most viable option being of simply staying right on his ass much as they were doing right now.

"This is 20-David Sergeant in vehicle pursuit of possible West Fourth Street shooter from an earlier report," the street-smart sergeant said. "Unit is currently westbound on Broome Street just north of Canal. Suspect heading for the West Side Highway corridor at felony reckless speeds. Any units in the vicinity are ordered to respond at best speed and intercept. 20-David out."

Still egged on by a hard-charging Ellen Macklin who seemed to only daringly go about the business of earning her stripes, he could almost not help himself focus, even in his hot pursuit, as she continued to push and prod him on with a kind of newfound intensity.

Brave girl, Pomeroy mused to himself, allowing himself a small moment of levity, but still surged ahead with his tailing track, knowing fully well he would not so easily give up the chase, or the hunt, until he'd nabbed his man—the son of a bitch who'd seen fit to shoot at him twice so far in one night.

The car chase was now fast evolving into something else entirely, a true bear of pursuit and only one with another name—stark flight. In fact, it was already becoming a white-knuckle ride at top speed on a hot run through backstreets and side roads, and much of it with a near-reckless abandon like a page ripped out of some old gothic novel or some old cops-and-robbers sprint with two cars on a hot block-by-block chase that had quickly morphed into its fast-paced action scene. It was now indeed a fleet-moving image that moved at a speed of its own, a strange and unusual sight that could have been lifted right out of some scripted TV police drama set in an old black-and-white format from many years ago.

Dead ahead, the tough homicide detective could almost see the driver of the other vehicle, dodging and weaving dangerously through light traffic and trying to shake the tail that he clearly must have seen by now in his rearview mirror. But he sure as hell wasn't stopping, the two could see, certainly not now with a clear shot at a wide-open West Side Highway just a few short blocks ahead of them with nothing else in his way. Indeed, he might just get away once again. Or would he?

Still in the final phases of wrapping up the investigation into the earlier shooting at the *Alhambra* crime scene, Captain Angie Fuller and Pomeroy's partner Damien Robles, were just preparing to leave when the second call came in. They had both listened intently as the senior detective's "shots fired" call echoed over the police band radios, and both had been startled and almost totally unprepared for its urgency.

Tender Moments Dispirited

The two seemed transfixed at the moment and stared knowingly at each other in sharp disbelief. *This cannot be good*, they both must have been thinking, and in quick seconds, Fuller had already dispatched a number of responding units, all of which seemed to already be en-route. Then she headed for the door, virtually dragging Robles in tow. The captain had insisted on responding to the call herself, and in person, truly in spite of Robles' best objections, and would not be dissuaded from doing so in the least.

"I'm going out on the call with you for this one, Robles. I want in and I'm riding shotgun. I want a firsthand look for myself. Then hopefully we can find out just who the hell keeps taking potshots at our people.

"This is twice in one night. Hell, something's not right here," she observed dryly, now approaching the car and opening the door. Then she slid into the passenger seat with Robles as her driver. It had been a hot minute since she'd been an operative out in the field, and it was probably time she pounded the pavement and got back in the game.

"Things could, at any moment, get hairy if we finally do run this guy to the ground," advised Robles, almost instantly regretting the remark even as he said it. "You know that. I mean, a cornered rat is most dangerous when trapped and all that."

"Robles, don't you worry about me. I can handle myself well enough," said Fuller as she shot a darting glance at the man, which in its way said everything it needed to Robles, who wisely picked up the cue and quickly slammed the unmarked car into gear. The junior cop peeled off from the curb and drove off at a clip to join up with the hot pursuit that was already in progress and fast moving up the West Side Highway.

"It's not my first rodeo, you know. I was riding shotgun in a squad car as a rookie while you were still chasing your high school diploma," she said with a chuckle and a look of righteous indignation. "Just find out what his '20' is so we can maybe pick up the guy's trail," she ordered, still fairly miffed at Robles as she inquired about the sergeant's last-known location. Then the car sped off at high speed with a flash of light and a wail of the siren, such that fractured the very stillness of the night.

A PERSECUTION MOST REAL

11 NOVEMBER

"This is 20-David Sergeant requesting backup—any units vicinity of Spring and Greenwich. 20-David currently in high-speed pursuit of the suspect vehicle with shots fired at the police."

Now looking over at Ellen Macklin, Pomeroy could see that all remnants of fear had drained from the woman's face as she continued to hunker down in the front passenger seat next to him, even in the face of the white-knuckle ride they now found themselves in.

"I just can't figure out who this guy is, Joe, or why he's even coming after us. I mean, what did we do to him? This is twice in one night we've been targeted and shot at, Joe. Not exactly something I want to get used to," the reporter said, now almost bristling up with subdued anger, but still finding a way to gently touch his arm for reassurance.

"One thing I learned a long time ago, Ellen, was that there's no sense in trying to explain CRAZY. But that said, my greater instinct still tells me this just might be our guy—maybe. For all we know, he could even be the very killer our people have been looking for over the last few weeks. All evidence we have so far seems to point to him being the Village Slasher."

"But Village Slasher or not, why target us, Joe?" asked a still incredulous Macklin, even as she was flung hard against the car door with the very momentum of the car's next sudden turn, this time widely to the right and leveling up due north. Up ahead, the wavering, fishtailing lights of the fleeing vehicle driven by the mad Ripper could still be seen from the vantage point of their unmarked car. But that lead vehicle was still, in fact, several blocks ahead of them and only slightly now in view.

"Looks like this guy's all over the road up ahead. We don't seem to be closing. For sure he's going to either wrap himself around a pole or worse, just run somebody down, the reckless son of a bitch," grumbled Pomeroy to no one in particular, then followed the dry comment with an angry punch on the radio comm button.

"Dispatch, 20-David Sergeant; Whiskey–Tango–Foxtrot, Base; where the hell's my backup?" Comms are spotty, comms are spotty. I cannot read you! 20-David still in pursuit of the suspect vehicle. Now westbound on Spring and approaching the West Side Highway. Roll units, roll units in this location. And tell 'em to kick it in the ass too!" he spat as he squawked into the handset mike.

It was clear that Pomeroy might be tired of the game and the reckless pursuit. He was about to punch in on a call for a second time when he was stopped dead in his tracks by what he saw just ahead of him: two blue and whites spinning about on a sharp axis as they shot out of a side street and came into view, almost materializing out of nowhere, now with lights spinning in a bright array and sirens wailing far into the night.

"Dispatch, 10-David-7 and -9 now joining pursuit," came the heated obligatory call from the secondary team, the two police vehicles charging ahead but falling in quickly behind Pomeroy as the lead chase car bore down on the runaway vehicle still much in flight and still two blocks up.

"'Bout damn time" was all Sergeant Pomeroy could manage as he spun the wheel hard to the right and almost put his foot through the radiator as he punched the gas and shot forward with astonishing speed. Ahead now, a display of distant taillights that seemed to further disappear only deeper into the night.

❧❧❧

Approaching Manhattan's lower West Side Highway, the Volstad had barreled off Spring Street like a bat out of hell and merged wildly into the northbound traffic lanes at near felony-reckless speeds with evil intent. Fearful that he might yet be caught, the evil Ripper could sense both the net and the noose tightening about his neck, and could well intuit that the end might indeed be near at hand.

But an even deeper part of him knew he would not be so easily apprehended and perhaps not even taken alive. He was prepared to inflict as much harm as he could before his own assured and bloody end, as indeed it had been his plan all along.

For now, however, the man could only wince in pain, reeling from the still-fresh and throbbing stab wound he'd received from the battling Carlton Bruner during his final scuffle in the park at Catherine Street, now seemingly so many hours ago. He was a madman on the run, staying only one step ahead of the law even as he gunned the engine of the hijacked car and stole a fleeting glance in his rearview mirror to see if he was still being tailed. For the moment, there was nothing, but he found himself still waiting for the other shoe to drop and for the pursuit to resume at any moment. He found he need not wait too long, as almost in the instant, his worst nightmare was again being realized, now with distant lights strobing wildly in the night and closing in fast behind him.

Midevening traffic on the northbound highway was surprisingly light and fast-moving for the hour of the night. There was a loose but steady push of cars heading uptown, each filled with an early-night contingent of tourists, diners, and party people, all seemingly going somewhere in a harried rush—somewhere in the night, whether bistro, bar, boutique, or jazz club. And then there was him, more like a desperado in an El Dorado from Colorado trying to leave a cold trail while trying to shake a hot tail.

Odd then that the man's bloodlust urges would kick in even now—again. His mind reeled with heinous thoughts of heinous deeds. Time perhaps to slake his bloodthirst yet one more time. Time for him to feed on the carcass of another kill.

But why now would I even think of such a thing, the Volstad must have been asking himself—or perhaps not—this even as he veered sharply to the right. He'd done so without having been seen, he was pleased to believe, as he fled the busied highway, fully doing the unexpected, spinning wheels, and shooting off onto a darkened side street under the shielding cover of night. Still sharply into the turn, the overhead street sign now said Bank Street. He'd just traveled nearly ten blocks due north up New York City's westernmost spine in under two minutes and had not once slashed speed or slowed his roll. Now his only concern was whether or not he'd ducked the hot chase that seemed to so unrelentingly follow close behind him.

The turn onto a now eastbound Bank Street was not immediately seen by the pursuing police, still some blocks behind. If left undetected, his unpredictable move might have bought him a modicum of time, but it had also brought him back almost full circle yet again, right back to the western corridors of Greenwich Village.

The Butcher was back in his element and now quickly about the business of getting "lost" in a minute's time. Still in the stolen car he'd snatched just earlier, he bolted in three blocks and found himself right back on Bleecker, almost to the very prowl and killing zone he'd so enjoyed all these nights before. Next stop, perhaps even Grove or Bedford for yet a second run ...

Oh, the delicious insanity of it all, the fugitive found himself thinking, almost enjoying the run, duck, and hide of the chase and the slaking element of staying just one step ahead of the police. Soon, indeed, he knew it might come down to a full and violent battle between him and his dogged pursuers. But he'd already steeled himself for just such an event and for the inevitable encounter he knew was coming. Knowing also that he would not shy away from the final confrontation he knew could come at any time, were it even in the cards for him.

He would not go down without a fight and he would always defiantly beard the face of foul surrender, knowing all along that he would not go easy.

※ ※ ※

Coming off small Bank Street in west Greenwich Village from the steady press of traffic he'd just left on the West Side Highway, the Volstad cruised with stealth and good speed past the Greenwich and Hudson Street crossover points, then made his way farther east. Turning now and again on numerous side streets, he finally found himself arriving at a quieted, clandestine spot where he pulled to the curb on one of the street's darker corners and discreetly nestled himself some four cars in from the corner.

Rightly did he suspect that it might simply be time to ditch the stolen car he had now and simply bail on foot? He was certain that a broadband police call must have already identified his vehicle by now and clearly, something must have gone out over the airwaves about the shooting at the *Alhambra* by this time. He'd have to sever all ties with the SUV, however reluctantly, and simply improvise on the fly, at the end perhaps to take another route or *car* entirely. But for now, his best option might be to simply step off and disappear into the night. He must do his best to blend in with the window shoppers that ambled in all directions on the shop-lined streets right there on Bleecker, now navigating his way across the many darker feeder streets that led out onto the main.

It was then that he began to discern the strobing lights from afar and hear the chirping, wailing sirens of sharp pursuit that even now menacingly pierced the shroud of night and closed in seemingly on all sides around him. Perhaps the chase teams might even now be bearing down on him and making their way up the narrow lanes, straight to his point of hobbled walking even here. Had the cops picked up his scent and sniffed him out, perhaps while also following a trickling, telltale trail of blood that may have been left behind? Was this them arriving even now, just up the block nearby, seemingly almost everywhere at once? And always closing, closing, closing.

Somewhere, tires screeched to a halt and doors swung wide, but even at that moment, the evil Volstad was already two blocks up and moving quickly away as ably as he could manage on a gimp of a leg. Now, he realized quite ironically that he need not even feign a halting limp since, indeed, he was already nursing a throbbing wound that pounded away ever and again at his very sanity and hurt like hell. And thus, the fugitive felon faltered along without attracting great suspicion, but had the ruthless killer, indeed, managed to slip the noose for yet a third time?

༺༻

"Well, here's a piece of good luck," offered a still-guarded Sergeant Pomeroy as he spotted the suspect vehicle parked just up ahead, bearing to the left side of the street. "There, right there. That must be it! That's the same SUV I saw on West Fourth, Ellen, and again on Broome Street in front of your condo. And the plates match too. Look—9-David-Whiskey-7," he observed with a pointed finger even as he and Macklin arrived on the scene and drew abreast of the fugitive vehicle.

Just now rolling up to a screeching halt at precisely the same moment was both responding units 10-David-7 and -9, the two patrol units that had earlier joined the pursuit just when the first call for assistance had gone out, even as still other units began rolling up as well.

"He can't have gotten too far away, Joe, can he?" Macklin asked as Pomeroy slammed the car into park and waved to the other officers in their cars. "I mean, how far could he get on foot anyway? We might still have a chance to find him, no?" asked a subdued but still hopeful reporter of the lead detective, who now looked over at her with a look of surprise on his face.

"Sorry to be the one to break the bad news, Ellen, but I'm afraid there is no more WE in any of this, at least not going forward. This'll, unfortunately, have to be the end of the road for you, however unfavorable it might be for the pursuit of your byline story," Pomeroy said with a look of urgency while gently placing both hands on her shoulders. "Look, you've been in the line of fire *twice* tonight, either directly or indirectly, and we've both been shot at four times.

"Right now, home is probably not a good option for you, and I'd blame myself forever if..." the detective sergeant said, almost stammering his way through the slipped remark. He was a man struggling in unfamiliar territory and unsure of his feelings. Much of what he was experiencing was still new to him: the strong and heady attraction to Macklin, the unsteady emotional footing, and his budding feelings for the appealing news anchor.

"And?" asked the curious newsie, wondering just where the entire conversation might be headed. "Blame yourself for what?"

"Let's just say I'm concerned for your well-being is all, Macklin, and I think it would make things a lot easier for all of us if you would simply get in the back of that police unit and stay put. And no arguments either, understand?" the brawny homicide cop seemed to order, maybe going a bit too far with his actual tone, but not far enough to mask his true feelings.

"Joe, we've come a long way together already, and—and don't forget he shot at me as well, remember? Now you're going to bench me?" she asked with a certain look that weighed in somewhere between melancholy and betrayal.

"Well, maybe it's because I *do* care, Ellen. Did you ever stop to think of that? So now you'll just do as I say, please, and let the police take it from here. Let us do what we do best—it's our job."

"But Joe," Macklin protested before being interrupted once again by Pomeroy.

"Listen, we've seen this guy up close, Ellen. We know he's got some kind of sinister agenda and he's unpredictable. All of which could make him twice as dangerous, plus we know this guy's trigger-happy and highly unpredictable. He's a bad actor acting without a moral compass and daring us to the teeth, Ellen, and apparently, damn the consequences. I won't put you in the middle of any of it," noted the beefy police sergeant. "Not on my watch."

"Then at least let me," pleaded a surprised Macklin, concerned that she might be getting chucked from her story.

"No, Ellen, you're already up to your neck in this. Plus—*plus*," the detective continued, determined to make his point, "I'm already in more trouble than I can dig myself out of for a year or so, just allowing you to tag along for as long as you have already."

Still frustrated, the detective could only end his soliloquy by holding up the palm of a hand to quash the very protest he knew would be coming from the striking newsie, then gently caressed her shoulder in a gesture that could only show just how much he cared. But even then, as if to almost entirely disrupt their leading discussion, a cavalry of blue began to arrive, now more and more in force.

Screeching to a sudden halt almost in hot unison came 10-David-7, now with 10-David-9 closely following behind, the same two units that had just earlier joined the pursuit. And now even other units began rolling up as well, and soon the entire area was swarming with cars that were now emptying with uniformed officers spilling out, some even with weapons drawn. The uniforms knew instinctively to rally just at the point where Sergeant Pomeroy would now brief them, and each officer circled up around him to get the word.

Pomeroy was already finding his way out of his unmarked car and walked back to one of the follow-on police cruisers, then spoke to one of the uniformed officers just as they exited their vehicle. Moments later, Pomeroy was already depositing a still-protesting Macklin into the back seat of the police car with stern instructions to stay down, stay put, and stay out of sight.

If indeed this was the same guy who was behind the wild shots fired at them already twice before in the same evening, there might be no telling what the slippery felon might do next. Clearly an ounce of prevention, he had thought to himself, might be far better than a pound of grief after the fact were something to at all happen to the civilian in his charge, Ellen Macklin.

Now locked in her little world of safety and security, Ellen was still noticeably rattled as she sat nervously in the back of the squad car watching on as the watch sergeant stood locked in an animated huddle with a bevy of police officers providing background on a plan he'd only had minutes to devise on the fly. Better to err on the side of caution than to come up short in a clutch.

"The good news is that we already had a pretty good fix on a make and model for the car that took the shots at us on West Fourth. A couple of crosstown store cams gave us that much, but the question remains as to whether this is the same guy that paid us a visit on Broome Street as well. But this car here," he said with a broad sweep of hand in the direction of the suspect vehicle that had been simply left at the curb. "This is it—*look*," he said, "9-David-Whiskey-7-1-5-Lima right on the plate."

"Assuming this is even our guy, Sarge," offered an eager Paxton to his boss, "how much of a lead do you think he's got on us by now?"

"Can't be more than ten minutes, I suspect. This guy's still in the neighborhood. So we're going to divvy up into teams of two and fan out. I need you people to get out there and beat some bushes, comb this entire neighborhood. What we're looking for here is a full grid search and a quick takedown to nab this thug once and for all!"

Then the team of man hunters split into smaller search groups and began moving off, each with a different assigned search zone and pattern, and each pausing only long enough to hear the sergeant's final words as he began moving up toward the end of the block. "And I want this guy tonight!"

A wary but still unshaken Volstad could still hear the sirens screaming and almost see the lights that he knew could only signal the arrival of the cops precisely at the location where he'd last left the stolen car back on Bank Street. He could nearly envision much of the stepped-up activity and the scrambling of a multitude of uniforms in a sea of blue even from his vantage point blocks away. How could he not? But he hustled on nonetheless, knowing instinctively that his best and perhaps *only* recourse at this point might be that of a classic fight-or-flight action. And for the moment, at least, knew he'd have to go with the only viable option at hand—*flight*.

Perhaps then, a move to disappear for the moment and simply drop off the grid until things could cool off might best suit his immediate needs, and so he moved to do precisely that—to covertly get off the streets and find the quickest route to a safe house that he knew was near.

For the time being, however, the villainous sprinter simply edged his way down Bleecker, still doddering along with a pronounced limp, furtively shifting from light to shadow, shadow to light. And this only blocks from where he'd had his first kill on *Grove Street* with the elder Paul Novaks victim, the unfortunate wretch who even then had been but a murderous avatar for Jack's first-acknowledged kill, Polly Nichols.

Approaching the intersection of the very next side street, the Volstad turned abruptly east and headed down the oddly unpeopled residential end of West Fourth Street and walked past the big bank on the corner of Seventh Avenue South. Now, his eyes were curiously drawn to the emblazoned neon lights just overhead as he saw the sign spelling out the name of a small out-of-the-way pub called Jekyll and Hyde. *Oh, how apropos indeed*, he thought to himself, still much in pain, for one such as he. Then he pulled fast his coat and deepened the brim of his hat as he sauntered by the empty tavern. Stopping now *anywhere* might be too risky indeed. He'd simply take a pass and move on.

❧❧❧

Pomeroy was just in the process of firming up the deployments and movements of the search teams, setting up a tight screening perimeter that would effectively scour the entire area in pursuit of the violent criminal who was still very much on the run. At the moment, he was surprised to see the captain arriving on the scene in tow with his partner, Damien Robles. The search teams had already formed up and were about to fan out, even as Pomeroy hooked up with Fuller and Robles to brief them both on developments as they all gathered just at the corner of Bank Street and Bleecker.

"You okay, Pomeroy?" asked the captain. "You look like shit," she ventured as part of her opening remarks. "I gotta say I'm kind of at a loss here trying to figure out how you managed to get shot at TWICE in one night and still walk away in one piece. I'd imagine you must have pissed someone off. So what gives, anyway?

"And I'm not real crazy about her being here either," the captain added, not in the mood for mincing words as she nudged her head angrily in the direction of the police patrol car that held Macklin in protective custody and planted in the back seat.

"This is an active crime scene, Detective, and we're trying to hunt down a known violent felon who's still very much on the run. You know as well as I do that we can't have civilians anywhere near any of our task force activities. It's not in the plans."

"Long story, Captain. I'll explain later. But after those shots rang out for the second time, it just didn't feel right leaving Macklin there to fend for herself in front of a building on Broome Street. There was a very real possibility the offender might return a second time.

"Everyone's got a line they don't want to cross, Captain, and I guess that one was mine. You can have my head in the morning, ma'am, if you're still so inclined, but this guy's about to learn not to pull the chain unless he wants the whole junkyard dog. I'm here to introduce him to the dog if you catch my meaning."

"So you saw fit to take an unauthorized civilian on a high-speed chase up the west side of Manhattan at breakneck speed? Never mind. I probably don't want to know. Let's just get on with the business at hand. What do we have here?" Pomeroy's boss asked as she flung the back half of her protective vest over her head and pressed the Velcro tabs firmly in place, strongly resenting even having to wear the damn thing in the first place, but did so anyway. After all, she reasoned rightly, there was no sense in taking any unnecessary chances.

PARLOR GAMES

11 NOVEMBER

"Our shooter is holed up somewhere right around here, Captain—I'd almost bet the farm on it," hissed Pomeroy to Fuller and Robles as the three manned the makeshift command post they'd set up just near the corner of Bleecker and Bank streets. "He's probably hunkered down somewhere in less than a four-block radius of where we're standing. Where else could he go?"

"Problem is we don't even know who we're looking for, really," noted a glum Robles with a shake of the head. "Boss, we don't have a single solid lead or even a working description on the guy, if it's even him. I mean, who exactly are we tracking here?" he queried.

"I expect we'll know him when we see him" was all Pomeroy said in response. "Our guys just have to look for someone who seems a little out of place."

"Where—here in Greenwich Village, Sarge? That's going to be a pretty tall order, I'd imagine," chuckled Robles almost halfheartedly. "Everyone kind of looks out of place when it's anything goes out there."

"Point taken, Robles, but we gotta run down every lead. The guy's stolen car was highjacked from a driver over by Alphabet City and just found here parked on Bank Street. So yeah, he's still around here somewhere. All I know is we can't just let this guy slip the net—" Pomeroy stated as he was about to elaborate further before being interrupted by the harsh jangling of his phone.

"Pomeroy," the homicide detective sergeant answered in a hushed tone. He spoke only briefly to an anonymous voice on the other end and then clicked off the line after only a few seconds.

"I'll be damned. That was our liaison team that we had go over to the Seventh to talk to those case detectives at the precinct. Captain, they've got another Ripper homicide over there—apparently, a bad one—with a body found in some local neighborhood park just near Catherine and Water streets."

"Jesus, Mary, and Joseph!" exclaimed the junior Robles, almost stung by the very import of the new report, then had his lightbulb moment. "Then—then if this is the same guy who's tied to both the killing and the carjacking, he could just be the same offender we've been looking for all along, namely the Village Ripper, Sarge!"

"Whoa, whoa, let's maybe hold back on that and not jump the gun just yet," advised a sober and far more cautious Captain Fuller. "I mean, there's still a lot here we don't know about. But if true, it can only be good news," she was about to conclude. Then the second call came in, which was a static crackle that punched in over the police band radio.

☙☙☙

Volstad the Butcher had managed to somehow slither down into his ground-floor hovel just on Grove Street with no detection and virtually no time to spare. His ability to even walk steadily afoot was compromised not just by the injury he'd received from Bruner but by something even greater, a condition aggravated by an innate sense of disequilibrium, one that had plagued him for much of his life: benign paroxysmal positional vertigo or BPPV. A trick of an imbalance of the inner ear, the doctors had told him, and he had believed it wholeheartedly, now moving through life always rocky and slightly off-kilter.

The villain's small stash-house flat was a shamble of old lockers and storage bins, ratty newspapers, soiled ashtrays, half-eaten sandwiches, dusty shelves, and tumbledown furniture that spoke of both filth and sharp neglect. More a crash house than a home, it was only a place he might use in the manner of a storeroom only, never as a place to truly hang one's hat, turn on a TV set, or enjoy a glass of wine with a late-evening meal. It was in fact but a pit stop and a dive whose only intended use was that of being a waypoint between his several heinous murders. The seedy hovel had only ever been used as a refuge and stopover point, more of a simple holding area for his murderous accoutrements—the tools and weapons and instruments of death—as much a place to slip in and out of identities and clothes.

For now, however, the oily villain was most concerned with only checking the taut dressings that had been only hastily applied by the trembling Dollarhyde at the "stiff house" just a short time ago. But no time to dawdle, he reasoned, and no time to rest. Surely, the cops must be still hot on his trail. A quick change of clothing then, perhaps, and back out the door. Better than to face his adversaries outside and have a chance to engage, were that even a choice, than to wait submissively within and be caught unprepared, he thought. Then he slid back the bolt of a small Makarov pistol and headed back outside.

Now, just up the block on either side of the police cordon lines, a horde of nosy, rain-soaked onlookers and sidewalk detectives stood in quiet fascination with the police activity unfolding on both ends of the search zone. They were civilians trying to crack the case from fifty yards away behind a police line, but it was almost amusing to watch.

Having already gathered most densely at the northern end of the marked police cordon just at Tenth Street, one particularly aggressive crowd had almost elbowed its way to the fore and had to be urged back and restrained. All this as the curious horde of pushy onlookers continued to gather in small groups of twos and threes throughout the area.

Gee, who might the cops be looking for? the busybody onlookers must have been thinking to themselves. *What could have happened and what'd they do, whoever they were?* an uneasy push of the crowd now seemed to ask, soon with the even more important, *Maybe somebody got shot.*

All this seemed to be most in the mind of every man gawking on, probably something most had already speculated about, however much to themselves. *Maybe there was a body somewhere, but where's all the blood?* yet others in the unruly crowd kept asking in harsh whispers, and all of it with a kind of reckless and macabre curiosity.

By now, both plainclothes cops were already in the wind, both now on the corner, both now swerving sharply to the right and almost nearing Bleecker. Pomeroy was now like a man with a scent or a fox with an olfactory fix on its very prey, as the two men doggedly pressed on.

"20-David Sergeant, Paxton-Unit 12 calling. Blood trail here, I've got a blood trail. Two hundred block of West Fourth near Tenth. Looks kind of bad, Sarge."

For the detective sergeant and his captain, it was precisely the wake-up call they had both been hoping for. A blood trail could only mean one thing—their fugitive was somewhere close and probably injured. "Deploy the search teams and saturate the area, Pomeroy," Fuller said, giving the order with what might only be described as a burst of adrenaline. "I need you to concentrate your search efforts here, here, and here," the boss said with a furrowed brow as she tapped demonstrably on an unfolded street map.

"Make your perimeter FOUR blocks square, from Seventh Avenue South out to Hudson and north and south from Fourteenth Street to Grove. You copy?"

"20-David Sergeant," the call went out almost as soon as he got the word from the captain, holding the comm unit up to his mouth. "20-David Sergeant to all search units. We have a new deployment order: Team 3, continue to secure all corridors east to west. Team 4 will lock down areas of egress north and south of the command post, and all others converge on Bleecker near Christopher, extending over to West Fourth. Do it forthwith. Let's kick it in the ass, people. Acknowledge your copy."

Quickly in turn now, all of the units came back quick and dutifully, each responding one after the other, each answering with the obligatory "10-4," "strong copy," or simply "roger that." Then the senior investigator turned back to his captain.

"Grid search is up and running, Cap. All units being redeployed as we speak," Pomeroy noted with good compliance and a level of competence that was astonishing. "Assault teams are two out and will be on scene shortly. We'll pigeonhole this madcap and reel him in, hopefully within the hour."

"Now I see why I keep you around, Sergeant, but let's not get ahead of ourselves just yet," warned Fuller, almost prepared to say more, had she even the greater option of elaboration when suddenly, everything hit like a ton of bricks.

"20 David," Paxton came back feverishly for yet a second time, sounding far more urgent than he had before. "Sarge, I got a clear blood trail here, probably looks worse than the last, now coming off West Fourth and moving over to Grove. Your guy must be hurt, Sarge. NEGATIVE, negative, I've got movement. I've got movement in this location!"

༺༺༺

"GO, GO, GO!" shouted Captain Fuller to her close team with an impatient wave of a hand, just as the double doors of the inconspicuous undercover black van swung wide and opened onto the dark side street, even as a clutch of cops emerged out of the back almost at a dead run.

"On him, on him! You two—Pomeroy, Robles—I need you to get ahead of this. You meet up with Unit 12. Paxton and his team are already on the move," Fuller said as she slapped down hard with the palm of her hand on the console table just inside the open-doored police van.

Both detectives turned on their heels and made to leave, stepping down heavily out of the rear of the makeshift command post van when both were pulled up short by the trailing voice of their captain.

"I need eyeballs on the ground on this one and I want you and Robles to check the situation up close, maybe size up our options as it stands. Find out what you can and report in, then get your asses back here on the double, hopefully, all in one piece," Fuller said, nearing her best conclusion. Both Pomeroy and Robles were rearing to go but had both paused in their tracks, held back much like hounds locked in a slip preparing to run. "And make sure you lock that bitch down tight, Joe. You savvy? No one in and no one out without a check. Hell, do a cavity search if you have to, I don't care, but nobody gets through!"

"We're rolling, Captain. Let's hope we don't have to go that far" was all Fuller could hear as her two top cops moved off at a clip into the night, hopefully dodging only raindrops and not actual bullets fired in anger. Fuller was doing her level best not to worry about their very well-being, but she couldn't quite shake the telling trick of a bad feeling about the whole call. It was a nagging intuition that somehow kept her quite on the edge like a fanged and rabid beast that would simply not allow her to relax.

Back outside, the teams emerging from the van now quickly met up with others from other squads, each unit redeploying themselves in new lines as the orders came down. Then they began to move up the street, soon approaching the corner of a fast-moving Seventh Avenue South and the sleepy back end of a side street just as it merged with West Fourth.

ఞఞఞ

The injured Volstad was hanging on but a tether of relief from the pain he felt and pretty much running on fumes as he made his way back to Bleecker. Instead, he might now be compelled to simply move on to the second safe house he'd already set up well in advance, one that he knew might be closer and far more accessible right now in his moment of desperation. But first, he'd need to tend to the throbbing wound that was still essentially his leg. He'd already bypassed two all-night pharmacies where he might have sought some measure of medical aid but found himself checking the urge, much with the press of cops so close behind. A box of Band-Aids, a bottle of hydrogen peroxide, and an over-the-counter assortment of painkillers would by no means be the best possible solution for his most immediate problem, namely a gashed and lacerated thigh. He'd simply be compelled to seek other venues, other options that might be more outside the box. And he had just such an alternative already in mind.

Still very much exposing himself to untold danger, the fugitive continued tripping down Bleecker, finally arriving at the doorstep of a quiet, nondescript location, such that he might have been seeking all along. The subdued backlit sign just above his head confirmed that he'd indeed found his best medical mother lode, for the time being, at least. *Eternal Light Funeral Services*, the sign blared out to all in the night who passed beneath its message. And for a wounded man quite on the run, the very publicness of a local hospital might only add to an even greater risk of discovery, as much he feared and simply would not do.

Such a treatment center must of needs remain off-limits to such as he in his circumstance. He had much to hide and much to lose and knew he might not bear up well under close scrutiny. He'd have to go another route. *Perhaps then a veterinarian, some local downtown clinic somewhere with open doors, or maybe just some trade-competent mortician then,* he thought to himself. A man perhaps who might be just adept enough with his hands from years of doing previewing prep work on the deceased. And now, much in the interest of expediency and his anonymity in full, he knew he'd be well advised to simply go with option three ... a mortician. Indeed, he posited, *any* port in a storm.

Cautiously approaching the quieted location, therefore, and stepping only tentatively up to the dimly lit doorway, the injured man slowly twisted an ornate knuckle of a doorknob and quickly slid inside. Now finding himself standing in a darkened foyer of a receiving room, he surveyed the area at short range and waited for his eyes to adjust to the dark. It was not long before a shadowy figure emerged from a chamber of rooms that seemed to be secreted somewhere in the back. Bowing deferentially to the unexpected late-evening guest, the curious old mortician ventured forward with a slight shuffle to amicably greet his off-hours visitor.

"Good evening, good sir," the pleasant man proffered with a studied look of concern and mild surprise. Volstad quickly sized up his man and viewed the reedy funeral director before him as a dandy and a fop, a well-groomed and nattily dressed popinjay with a receding hairline and badly mottled skin. Even at first glance could the injured Volstad tell he was the retiring type—easygoing enough, perhaps, to cajole and menace with a heightened brow and a deep-throated growl. And that would be precisely how he would proceed to control the man and keep him in line—to browbeat him with a hard line and torment him with a sharpened knife like a bully tactic on steroids.

"You are welcome, good sir. I am Dr. Dollarhyde—Dr. Malcolm Dollarhyde. Here to serve you in your hour of greatest need, as you wish, sir. If it pleases you to know, you should understand that we are committed fully to soothing your grief and safeguarding your very privacy during your hour of darkest sorrow.

"How may we be of service this evening? You have lost a loved one, perhaps, yes? Only recently?" the small piping voice questioned as the man stood with arched eyebrows and hands clasped dutifully in front of him. And all of it but a ruse and a sly, commercial affectation to show some mock compassion, to show, perhaps, that he was only too ready, willing, and able to serve ... especially for the smallest of large fees.

"I can assure you, good sir, that we here at Eternal Light stand ready to serve your every funeral need as you go through your time of loss and deep grieving. Come, come in. You must sit. You are welcome," offered the tony and well-groomed funeral home spokesman to his prospective client. Now with an almost effeminate gesture of a hand, Dollarhyde ushered the man even deeper into the maze of the parlor. Or so precisely he thought. And might, indeed, have continued with his practiced soliloquy had it not been for the cold lip of the black-muzzled *Makarov* pistol rising and being pressed into the fleshy patch just at the nape of his neck.

TERROR STALKS THE NIGHT

11 NOVEMBER

Now Pomeroy and Robles—and virtually every other officer in close proximity—were already converging on an area where the blood trail seemed to end—a simple red brick façade of a building with a recessed doorway. The address was somewhere on the west end of Bleecker and the sign just overhead said Eternal Light something or other in a neon sizzle that flickered with a slow repetitive flash, as even now a specialized breaching team prepared to make entry into the building. The trail led here, and here is where their best suspect must be.

"7-David-50, SWAT team leader to all teams: move in, move in!" ordered the beefy, well-sinewed crash team honcho, Sergeant Taylor "Bulldozer" Runyon. The command was given by the SWAT insertion team leader in a coarse whisper to a huddled mass of operatives clad all in black, just as they began their penetration into the target location. Months and even *years* of training now kicked in on the instant with each of the men—those who always went in first with the sharpest surge of adrenalin—as all of them now strong-armed their way into the U-shaped reception foyer up front.

The greeting area was oddly rounded in a tight arc as if to draw its mourning visitors from its center and force them back into two wing areas that seemed to embrace both sides of the reception area. It was a kind of big open-ended "U," therefore, with only poorly lit hallways and a spate of shadowy rooms that sat off to either side entering to both left and right. To a SWAT team leader, Runyon knew that simply meant they'd have to be fully cleared one by one, however dangerous and painstakingly slow. After all, in its final analysis, lost time was far better than lost lives. And to a man they forged on, impervious to the danger and fearing nothing.

❧❧❧

"You will shut up, old man! You are understanding me now, yes?" growled the fleshed and bloodied Volstad as he continued in his violent devolving trek to nowhere. Now with a flash of an eye and a hiss of breath that must have seemed almost serpentine, he brusquely collared the terrified undertaker by the neck and forced him back against the counter.

"You will listen and you will listen very carefully, if, indeed, it is your wish to live to greet another sunrise. You must do as I ask and you will do so without question and delay," the villain instructed with a stern and deadpan face that struggled to mask its actual evil intent.

Terror-stricken even in the moment, the bespectacled mortician had been frightened almost from the first, now all atremble with a paralytic fear that must have shaken him to the core. After all, this kind of thing simply never happened to one in his trade and certainly never to him. And thus, he knew not what to do, what to say, or even how to act under the present frightening circumstances.

The two dilated pinpricks that had earlier been the man's very eyes could now only stare back at his assailant with anxiety and a shivering trepidation that must have bordered on stark fear and disbelief. A feeble attempt to now somehow edge back and away from the posed threat only found him being pulled up short by a sinewy grapple around the collar and even more pressure from the business end of an automatic pistol being applied just at the crown of his head, causing him to freeze almost where he stood.

"I have been injured," said an unsteady Volstad as he waved off the man's anticipated next question. "And no, you may not ask me how or why.

"You need only know that I have sustained a rather nasty leg wound—most regrettably, indeed—which, for reasons I cannot go into, does not allow me to go to a hospital. I cannot simply walk into a doctor's office either, certainly not without question or great suspicion. So you are, perhaps, understanding then what I am saying to you, yes?" the menacing villain asked heatedly of his captive audience of one. Then he gave the mealymouth even further instructions and growled out his detailed orders as to what precisely must be done in the next minutes.

"But you are asking me to perform a dangerous, near-surgical procedure in a backroom setting, which can only be dangerous. Surely, you can see that. My tasks here are to only dress and prepare the dead, sir.

My specialty seldom has much to do with the living. I am not equipped to do what it is you ask of me," the old man advised, perhaps thinking it at least worth a shot to try to defuse the situation in some small way. A subtle poke of a repositioned gun barrel that now threatened to splatter his brains across the floor decidedly gave him the answer and sharp motivation he most needed to find in very quick order. And it kept his assailant still moving and talking without shooting.

"You will treat the wound quickly and properly within reason. You will clean and dress the leg and stitch it up as best you can," the killer said, pausing only long enough to let that much sink in.

"And you must begin the work immediately," he ordered with a crass slide of the eyes that told the shaken undertaker that his hollow-hearted assailant might just mean business after all. "And then I will decide if you will live or you will die!"

"I am no medical doctor, sir. I seldom use any of these procedures on ... on *live* clients. But since I am obliged to do as you ask, I will try, sir. I will try," the mewling man said, the dapper director of the funeral parlor probably still hanging on to a thin thread of hope that he might yet be able to escape with his life intact.

"Come, come, good sir. I know. Yes, we both know. You have a good-enough grasp of surgical procedures, a working knowledge of anatomy, and the skill to see it through, yes? Your business demands this of you. And you will do more than simply try, sir. You must succeed!" urged the strong-arm villain with yet another prod of the gun barrel as he gnashed a row of brown, uneven teeth, then continued with his menacing soliloquy.

"You will find, sir, that I have no time for pleasantries, and you would be well advised to not test the issue—or my resolve. I will, therefore, either pay you well or I will kill you well, and that is all the choices I will give you. And you will make your decision now. Scrub up, there is much work yet to do. I have done, sir. Now scrub up!"

☙ ❧ ☙

The door to an even dimmer inner sanctum of the funeral parlor was now found to be slightly ajar—already not a good sign in any regard for a SWAT team on the move. But on and on they pushed, Lieutenant Runyon and his breaching team moving deeper and deeper into the recessed darkness of the mortician's innermost world.

Now, the long candlelit shadows seemed to dance and ripple eerily like a silhouette of dancing slender-nailed fingers, and all about them hung the mulberry and eggplant purple drapes of mourning and sorrow, each hanging with deep furls and folded pleats, such that seemed to fully block out any light from entering. ALL must be dark in a place like this in such a somber line of business.

Strewn across the room, a scattering of floral sprays and wreaths of purple and white flowers soberly adorned the room, each petal cluster exuding a sickly sweet aroma that hung in the air like jasmine or hyacinth. And much of it worked in a kind of macabre harmony to make the place only that much darker than it already was.

Runyon, the salt-and-pepper-haired SWAT team leader, gestured silently ahead now with two fingers, chopping at the air to communicate his orders to the rest of his team as he whispered, "Move ahead. Breach, breach, then split right and left. We go in three, two, one!" The very cadence of the utterance seemed to signal a kind of countdown and a movement forward, as much to indicate that the two teams should split after insertion and push off in a coordinated two-prong assault that would then sweep the rooms that sat off both to the left and the right.

Now with the two detectives Pomeroy and Robles still in tow and bringing up the rear of the crash team, Runyon's elite door kickers now entered at a crouch behind ballistic shields, each pair of operatives moving off into the darker recesses in a single-line column-ahead format as they made their way up to a reception area that led off from both sides of the rotary to the back rooms.

Tap, tap, said the hand on the man's left shoulder in front of them as the SWAT team began snaking forward in a serpentine column.

Tap, tap, proceed to the first door, this in a long hall of doors that led down to a red-bulb end as they approached the viewing rooms and rear offices of the deceptively larger-than-expected funeral home.

There followed now a quick search of each room—left and right, north and south throughout the funeral home. A keyed-up Runyon was working at his very best, now ushering his SWAT team carefully through each area, clearing each room with both a flashlight and a quick sweep of a long gun. And each entry would simply end the same; repetitively backing out of each room, only to rejoin the team and move on to the next door and the next room with each action playing out like a moment suspended in time.

"CLEAR!" said a voice just up ahead on the right and to the front of Runyon. The SWAT team lieutenant steeled his nerves and repositioned the lightweight Heckler & Koch he held, then placed his hand on the man's shoulder in front of him. *Tap, tap,* the gesture said, proceed to the next door.

The cadaver prepping room was operated exclusively by Dr. Malcolm Dollarhyde, the shy and balding mortician who now stood stark still and trembling in his small foyer. Now, the director's captor ushered him at gunpoint through a suite of large rooms toward the back where they finally arrived at a small and brightly lit examination facility. The small lab was not at all the same sleazy back-room hovel like those that had been carefully shielded from public view in funeral homes in the past but only half a century ago. It was instead now a high-tech facility that could easily boast of a good degree of practical modernization and a full tabletop suite of state-of-the-art embalmment equipment.

The prepping room now came equipped with only the most sophisticated prepping paraphernalia in the industry and hosted all of the tools of the trade that might otherwise be needed to conduct the work that the mortician might need to perform during the normal course of his business. As such, all about the heckled funeral director now stood the embalming tables, mortuary stretchers, transport trolleys, and even the large "scissor lift" devices that would be used to hoist and elevate a body to situate it in a desired position during the cadaver-readying procedure.

All else aside, however, Volstad continued only to live in the moment and realized that he was pretty much running on fumes and hard against the clock. Indeed, perhaps his only focus for the moment was getting his wound treated quickly as best he could for the moment. Circumstances had disallowed him access to an actual hospital or even a local doctor, so he knew instinctively that his most workable alternative and next best option might be standing right here in front of him in a gown with a surgical mask hanging loosely below the chin line. Perhaps the good doctor was either just scrubbing in or simply scrubbing out after a procedure, but Volstad knew he had his agenda, even if Dollarhyde the undertaker didn't yet know it.

With his lethal *Makarov* pistol held steadily at the man's head, the wounded killer ordered the still-gowned mortician into one of the back lab areas and urged him to begin the wound cleaning and dressing work that he knew would now be needed to mend the bloody consequence of the attack on his right thigh, ensuring with his automatic weapon that he gets it just right with his every move. Unmistakably, he'd even invited the little skink to only carefully understand just what was at stake and that his best (and perhaps ONLY) reward for his competent service would be his *not* cocking back the hammer of the gun and sparing his life. But even that might still be up for grabs if things went too far south. But he also knew it wise to incentivize the man, letting him know that there'd certainly be some considerable financial gain in it for him as well *if* all went well. Either option seemed to be more than enough to fully motivate the easily shaken undertaker, now as he carefully went about the business of patching up the interloper's leg.

Nine stitches and several excruciating moments later, a recovering Volstad pulled himself together and shook off the remnants of pain. He had talked his way through much of the treatment process—oddly—if, indeed, one could even call it that, with comments like "do it this way" and "do it that way," almost as if he knew what needed to be done and how. He had winced only once just as the wound was examined and cleaned, and had almost grunted outright when probed and sutured, but all had surprisingly gone well. And all from a man who had said that he allegedly only worked with the dead. So yes, the good Dr. Dollarhyde had done well—*quite*—successfully stemming the flow of blood and cleaning the wound, then stitching up the jagged edges of the deep cut as best as he could.

"I have done all you have asked of me, even if against my will and better instincts, sir, and all without question. Will you not now hold to your word and spare my life? I have a family and I only wish to live," petitioned the still-suspicious and terrified clerk of the deceased.

"So you are perhaps wondering about the money, yes?" taunted the Butcher as he exhaled with a priggish sniff. Hurriedly, he dressed as best he could, careful not to disturb any of the bandages on the upper thigh.

"Then, indeed, you shall have it for, shall we say, services rendered? Much as promised, sir, much as promised," the Butcher hissed deceptively with a slight chuckle as he continued to study the frumpy undertaker through the dark eyes of a crouching predator. "And so, indeed, you shall be handsomely rewarded."

His dark soliloquy now at an end, the predatory raptor of a villain paused only long enough to draw the man's attention away, if ever only briefly. And in that one fractional moment did he grapple the slight-statured man from behind. The very strength of the arm was at once both brutish and swift, choking with a sinewy pull that almost immediately cut off all air—the closing of the killer's fatal grip now embracing the smaller man in total as he throttled him just at the neck. THEN came the cutting edge of the blade on the man's exposed fleshy parts. *Then* came the Butcher's best strike, slicing deep—*once, twice*—until done, and the debt itself was paid in full, just as promised.

And the luckless Dr. Malcolm Dollarhyde had never even seen it coming, even up to the moment of the fearful strike—the attack, indeed, now coming from the *second* blade he didn't even know his killer had. And neither did the cops.

ॐॐॐ

Pomeroy and Robles could only watch on in quiet amazement, both men struck by the precisely orchestrated movements of the SWAT insertion team just in front of them. The two detectives had hung back and stayed low as the strike team almost crept in on silent haunches, moving further in, in, in toward that final door that would then clear the entire floor in full.

"CLEAR!" said one SWAT team operative with a gravelly voice that was designed to be heard only by those in close proximity to his sheltered position. *Tap, tap.* Proceed to next.

"CLEAR!" barked another dark-helmeted SWAT team member to their next in line.

The crack team had continued to hug the wall, eyeing every shadow with a deepening suspicion, indeed soon spying a small sliver of light just breaking out from under a door directly ahead. It was an odd, oblique shaft of yellow shooting just through a crack at the base of a door only yards up on the left. But something still wasn't quite right and all the hairs went up. As did all the small sidearms and long guns to sharp aiming as well, as the team prepared to make its quiet entry.

The door to the dark interior of the funeral home—and the very last of the offices set in the back—was even now slightly ajar, already not a good sign in most regards. But the crash team inched forward nonetheless, undeterred and still at a slight crouch, each left hand clapped on the shoulder of the man to his front.

"Down, down. Stay low!" said the barrel-chested Runyon to his team of six, more as instruction than simple observation. "DOOR!" the voice intoned in a coarse whisper to the man to his immediate front.

That man was perhaps the most hulking member of the insertion team, John Boxer, a man the rest of the team simply called "Striker." Now the Goliath advanced from his third spot in line with his six-foot-five, 240-pound view of life. Easily grappling the large steel *Blackhawk* breaching tube, appropriately stenciled with the two words "KNOCK KNOCK," the man held the tool low in hand like a battering ram waiting to do its bidding. Then, with a quiet visual cue from Runyon, the heavily muscled door kicker hit the entry portal with enough force to almost knock it cleanly off its very hinges, then he stepped back and dropped the battering tool by design, allowing the next operator in line to slide past him and catch their own low-profile peek into the lighted room.

And then they saw the body.

Bogdan Volstad, the ruthless butcher of New York's west-side Greenwich Village and a Ripper to all, had often traveled with many knives, such that he must have carried to slake his unreasoned urge for edges. And thus, the cutters, the dissectors, and the gutting blades alike might all be brought along should he ever need them or be presented with an opportunity that might beg their use. Or, indeed, should one simply be lost or foolishly left behind by mishap or misstep, much as he had done just earlier, back at the crosstown park just after the harsh and defensive attack by Bruner?

Thus, might he ever carry several such blades on him, all being the man's very working tools, but always secreted about his very person would also be the compact and lethal Makarov .380 automatic pistol as well. He favored its touch and feel, he comforted himself with its heft and balance, and secured himself with its rapid blowback slide and quick-loading action, just in case he might ever need its dark, dark services.

Having done with his work and dastardly deed in the dispatching of the unfortunate Mr. Dollarhyde in such a horrific manner, the villain Volstad now wiped clean the greasy, blood-soaked knife on the victim's own soiled lab coat. The Volstad did so almost methodically, as if hoping to stem the drenching flow of blood, perhaps to clean away the crime by wiping it on the victim's white linen shirt in full. *Aye, and here's the rub*, the killer thought, indeed perhaps the even greater contradiction of it all, all in all, and there an end. And like a harsh soliloquy or page right out of *Hamlet*. It was indeed all out, out, damn spot! Or so at least it might have seemed to the evil Volstad. Then he carefully returned the murderous weapon to its sheath, secreting the blade back on his person, where he could always keep it close.

Then the villain quickly set about the studied task of staging the scene, the odd but insatiable ritual he always embraced with the placement of objects on and around the body. It was an odd and almost celebratory custom he simply would not deny himself, and even if he knew it not, it had already become his most telling signature move, his very trademark and calling card ... the objects.

Still only blocks away, a now-stitched and hastily patched-up Volstad found himself slithering stealthily out of the funeral parlor, sluicing quietly out onto a hushed Bleecker Street with only a cursory look to left and right as he fled the building. In his wake, he had left behind only mayhem and the ripped corpse of the too-accommodating Malcolm Dollarhyde in a stiffening state. Still unseen and undetected by the very pursuit team he knew must be close on his heels, the violent felon simply lowered his head and pulled his hood up against a drizzling rain, then turned on his heels and began hobbling off in the direction of the safe house on Grove Street.

જાજાજા

The small pursuit squad of detectives, patrol officers, and SWAT rapid-response team members had only casually happened upon the minor blood trail by chance some blocks back, and tracking it to its source found that much of it seemed to end just at the doorstep of a local neighborhood funeral home, but how and *why*? Now with only the greatest caution and the best of the procedural standard had they even entered the building, already alerting to the crimson trickle that seemed to lead directly to its very doorstep. Was this even their guy? Was he still armed? Might they meet any resistance? And what was this guy's full endgame ... and did he even have one?

Now led by an insertion team that ably spearheaded the advancing search group, they soon found a body in the funeral home's innermost sanctum, stumbling upon the mangled remains steeped in blood. The heavily armed SWAT team was still all about its own hot business and loaded for bear as they thrust themselves into the room with shocking speed and a good element of surprise, and to a man they knew that Trouble itself might have a new name and might indeed lurk just around the very next corner. And so they moved in with ears on and guns up, prepared for whatever might go down in the coming hot minutes.

જાજાજા

Now a throng of six men all clad in black fatigues, steel helmets, and weapons at the ready slowly edged around the corner, inching forward on padded paws like a stalking feline, with Pomeroy and Robles trailing right behind. The human shield of cops continued in its forward push, warily tracking what was now only a diminishing blood trail that seemed to lead to only one location—a recessed walk-in that was bathed in soft light just in the midriff of Grove Street. Surely, now they might soon have their man.

"Fan out on two sides," ordered a deadpan Pomeroy as he gestured with a sweeping hand that took in both sides of the street. "Check every doorway, every alley, every dumpster, every crevice."

Then Robles piped in with his critical update, which he threw out as an aside to Pomeroy. "Looks like we've got some new information coming in pointing to this guy as the same offender we liked for all of the killings in the past few weeks, boss."

"Good. We should probably get a full surveillance package on him—house, car, financials—whatever when we get back to the office. I want eyes on him until we can reel him in, savvy?" Then he turned his attention back to the men on the ground. "And people, listen up, all of you stay alert and keep your head on a swivel going in."

"Copy that, Sarge," came the reply from the mass of helmeted first responders in near unison with a collective nodding of heads as they each pushed cautiously ahead in their pursuit of an anonymous killer, a faceless man and phantom target that they all knew must be brought down.

"We will consider this offender armed and extremely dangerous. He's killed before and has had his taste. He won't hesitate to kill again, so you watch your six and the man next to you as well, understand? Six men go in, six men come out, we good? Now move out and gimme two, gimme two—north and south on both sides. Let's get this SOB before he strikes again!"

ತನತನತನ

The fugitive was quickly running out of steam and out of options, and he knew he'd have to make a move sooner rather than later. And much like the hunted spy of fictional fame, he simply had to "come in out of the cold" and seek some badly needed medical attention for the injury he'd sustained to his leg, hence the visit to the mortuary to greet his sacrificial lamb, the ill-fortuned Dr. Dollarhyde, all of it now already a faded memory in his mind. The Volstad's circuitous journey had had him already on a dead run for the better part of several hours now.

And all of it had only led him right back here, just two blocks from dark Grove Street and the surety of the safe house he now so desperately sought. Fast afoot on his flight from the funeral parlor and the police, he was now almost there.

The sham dead drop of an apartment that he had maintained back in Red Hook, Brooklyn, was simply a ruse, a dummy stash house and a crash pad that he'd used only occasionally as a drop-off and pick-up point. Indeed, much of it had been on an as-needed basis, much at his leisure. But now might be a time to stay away, since he knew by now that he might already run the risk of the location having been discovered and fully compromised by authorities. And as such, he knew instinctively that he must not return there under any circumstances. He would now instead be compelled to move on to a second safe house that he'd already set up well in advance in anticipation of exactly this event. Plus, he knew the location was closer and far more accessible to him in his time of need, and in fact, leaving the seedy Red Hook dive behind, he already knew it would be far better to have "blocks per minute" rather than "miles per hour." Better to be here rather than having to navigate his way through bridge and tunnel somewhere just to get to Brooklyn.

Now the cops seemed to be only blocks away, he reckoned, fanning out and expanding their grid search activities and probably going door to door as they slowly closed in on the very place where he stood at the moment. By now, perhaps, they'd even stumbled upon the fiasco of the bloody murder scene he'd left behind at the Eternal Light stiff house and funeral parlor. Indeed, he could even see the distant reflection of lights, hear the sirens, and even sense the very *closeness* of the mad scramble of law officers as they went on a wild search for apparently only him.

Better to get the hell out of Dodge while he still could, he reasoned correctly, even as he quickly put as much distance between him and the funeral home as he could, again approaching the corner of Grove Street at Bleecker, soon enough turning the corner as he began to head west.

Making his way now down a street curtained in deep shadow and poor street lighting, he could make out a late-night couple casually strolling along hand in hand, a man walking a brace of small terriers, and even a shade being pulled down over a second-floor window somewhere, but still no police. *Good.* The pain was now abating somehow and downgrading itself back a notch or two to a pang from a throb, having already been roughly treated by the terrified Dr. Dollarhyde just earlier. But the fugitive, nonetheless, found that his ability to walk steadily afoot was still somewhat compromised, not just by the injury he'd received from the retaliating Bruner earlier, but by something even greater.

He knew it was a condition that was already aggravated by an innate sense of disequilibrium for the man—almost unavoidably—one that had plagued him for much of his adult life. "A trick of an imbalance of the inner ear," the doctors had repeatedly told him, and, indeed, it had been his affliction ever since, now moving through life with a rocky gait that had always kept him slightly off-kilter and disfavoring his left leg.

Now, he hobbled his way down the narrow lane and made his way in midblock, stopping only long enough to furtively glance in both directions before slinking two steps down into a street-level brownstone flat just on the north side of Grove Street. He had managed to do so with no real time to spare, as even at the moment, a bevy of men in blue were already turning the corner and scanning the block from end to end. But by then, the Butcher had ducked into the shadows and was already off the street, managing to somehow slither down into his ground-floor hovel with no detection and virtually no time to spare.

The small lackluster flat in which he now stood was dusty and unkempt to a fault, steeped with a lingering musty odor that permeated all and sat almost entirely bare of furniture. The small tuckaway lodging had served only as a safe house of sorts, a warehousing stash point, and a place to quietly hunker down. A place perhaps to wash and purge the very drench of blood he must have carried about his very person, as much a place to change clothes, resupply, and sleep whenever he might, which was decidedly never often and never came easy.

But even more important was the fact that it had also been central to almost all of his kill sites thus far—seemingly only blocks away from each—save that of Bruner on the far eastern edge of town in Manhattan's own Alphabet City. That attack had been his one deviation, his one departure from an otherwise specialized killing regimen, perhaps even his one moment of greatest vulnerability when he'd dropped his guard and had been shanked for his troubles by the gutsy, counterattacking Carlton Bruner.

But far and away, the seedy dive might most have served as a kind of arsenal storehouse, a meeting place of guns and knives that he might ever use interchangeably as his Ripper needs might give rise. But for the moment, at least he could only make his way carefully to the small bathroom, where he checked the patchwork dressing that had hastily been applied to his wound by the funeral director he'd strong-armed only minutes earlier. Emerging just as soon, the Volstad began prepping himself for a second departure, and in moments, he was already slipping into a whole new disguise—indeed, a whole new persona—which in fact, was not so new at all.

So on he placed the old tattered rag of a coat, the shoddy pants, and torn shirt. Now came a smirching of the face and a tousling of hair, a scuffing of old shoes, and a careful tipping of the deep-brimmed hat far down over the face and eyes. Then he picked up the old wooden cane and a handful of plastic bags and headed for the door of his vulgar hovel. Edging his way out into the night's dark rain, the murky villain now headed back into the very fray, as it were, and few might have known him had they seen him on the street beside them. And most would have simply passed him by as nothing more than the muddy vagrant he professed to be, which was precisely his plan and best option.

☙☙☙

"Guns down and safeties off, people," said the senior homicide detective leading the hunt. He spoke in a low whisper as he guided the assault team methodically down a shaded Grove Street, just a block in from Bleecker and two from the busy passages of Seventh Avenue South. A persistent light rain was still falling and pelted the team of SWAT and elite ESU officers, quickly turning what was dry into a drench of wetness that seemed to eventually soak through everything and everyone, causing their clothing to cling uncomfortably to their bodies.

"Remember, people, this guy'll shoot you dead just to see if the gun works," warned the senior sergeant of the sweep team to his several operatives who were still on the hunt for the best suspect they'd had for weeks. Now two probing lines of police were fleet-footing their way silently down both sides of the narrow lane, looking for a man they didn't know and might not be able to identify even if seen.

"Damn, Sarge," piped in Robles, just at Pomeroy's elbow watching his six. "Sure wish we could have had this guy back on Broome Street, just when all of this began. It might've saved us all a lot of trouble, no?"

"Yeah, yeah, I hear what you're saying, but there's probably no sense in dredging up what's already past. Hey, welcome to my museum of failures, Junior, but things were happening pretty fast back there and he got too good a head start on us. Plus, I also had my hands full just trying to get Macklin the hell out of there as fast as I could."

He paused to survey the current situation even as it continued to unfold all around him. "Paxton, Reid, you two head up that column and close up those gaps. I don't want this guy slipping the net again." Then he turned back to his partner and hissed the next words under his breath.

"All of this is starting to really piss me off! Hell, enough is enough with this guy already. He's managed to vanish into thin air at every turn. The guy is taunting us."

Robles saw his chance and keyed in on his boss's remark by dovetailing into it with one of his saying, "Remember what they say, Sarge: 'He who holds the devil by the tail best hold tight. He will not be caught a second time.'"

"I hear that, friend," acknowledged Sergeant Pomeroy, marveling at Robles's keen insights. "Now, if we can just box this guy in, we should have him this time. Guess it's just on us to see that that happens. Besides, there can't be a whole lot of places he can go right now, so we should pretty much have him bottled up at this point."

The throng of lawmen was now approaching their midblock location, led on, and almost guided there by the very blood trail that was by now still visible if even seeming to trickle off. Pomeroy chopped at the air with a vertical hand, almost like a tomahawk held in midair as he ushered his men forward with silent gestures to the searchers on both the left and right sides of the street.

"By the numbers, people, by the numbers. Give me two. Get this guy and we all go home safe. Remember, we're executing a no-knock warrant here, so let's operate on that basis and keep your hackles up. Be ready, be ready!"

The slow march of man hunters had finally found their intended end-of-trail locale and was coming in on final approach to the suspect hideout. The brawny Striker hit the door fronting the ground-floor flat with the unforgiving *Blackhawk* breaching tool, almost cleanly dislodging it from its very jamb with the brute force of the blow. Then they entered sharply in groups of two, each breaking left and right as the team inserted itself without check or challenge. And in an instant, they were in.

ಶಲಾಶಲಾಶಲಾ

Everything was for show and all might have been a sham—all calculated props designed to only *look* like that, which it actually was not. The seedy tattered bags, the shopping cart, and ratty clothes—indeed, the very cosmetic smear of grease and grime placed just so here and there—much of it indeed but a calculated cover set to facilitate an unchallenged escape. But would it be so easy and might it even work? Was the strategy sound and workable enough to even carry it through? He would thread the eye of the needle and straightaway slip the police cordons and pass through the barricades, shaking off their canvassing patrols almost as if they were not even there. He would dare them all to the teeth and spit in every eye even as he passed over, always getting the last laugh. And in the end, if indeed it came right down to it, he was well content to simply shoot it out and swap lead if pressed. He cared not and almost welcomed death after years of dreadful living.

The Village Ripper—then become Red Jack and the Bowery Butcher—was now but a Grove Street vagabond named Bogdan Volstad, slyly again masquerading as one Howard Kettle. He was a man of many guises, of many sins and sobriquets. But all of it had finally come full circle and been revealed to all as truly being one and the same.

His very last victim had just been the ill-fortuned Carlton Bruner—the killer's reinvention of sad Carrie Brown in 1891. First, the two attempts on the lives of Macklin and Pomeroy—both at the restaurant and on

Broome Street proper—and now the senseless dispatching of the funeral director just earlier.

And all of it swam through his head like still-fresh photographic images he might choose to never forget. In fact, in his mind, Volstad the Butcher had reveled in each of his kills, much delighting in the hunt and spring of each attack. And he would continue to do so had he still the urge and a greater luxury of time. It was, for him at least, his unchecked lust and lone desire, but for the pressing moment, only evasion and flight could remain first and foremost in his mind. And so, the villain only continued with his slow-speed getaway, right into the mouth of the dragon.

Summoning all of his nerves and almost mocking them with his very disguise, the villain made good use of the shuffling limp he had all along, such that already seemed to always disfavor the right leg. Now, he crossed to the far side of the street and made straight for a row of trash cans directly opposite his own safe house, cane in hand and shopping cart in front as he scouted. He was now a city nomad, a soiled itinerant dressed in probably New York City's best disguise, that of a homeless miscreant and a foraging vagrant. And in an instant had he become the invisible poor, a nameless wretch, and a waif of the street.

But indeed, the real test might be yet to come … perhaps just up the block or around a corner somewhere. And soon he found he need not wait much longer. His worst fear might soon enough be realized, just as he busied himself conspicuously, groping hungrily through the bins just near the corner of Grove and Bleecker just as a search team of uniformed cops swooped around the corner in a mad rush and fanned out across both sides of the dark street searching, searching for a suspect they couldn't even find, and a man they couldn't even see. They were, in fact, all like blind men in a dark room searching for a black cat that wasn't even there. And the Butcher simply moved on …

THE KNIGHT-ERRANT

11 NOVEMBER

Now the good Howard Kettle, the alter ego of the vile Ripper himself as described in his one brief encounter with Officer Paxton, even back then on the night of the very first killing—the night of the brutalized Paul Novaks, left just there on the triangle end of Grove Street more than a month ago—was even by his own words a "liberator extraordinaire of trash and knight-errant of both alley and street."

And thus, the savage Volstad had once again assumed that very persona to smooth out the path of his escape from the very men who would now be so keenly hunting him down. Might he once again escape the clutches of his hot pursuers or would he simply be compelled to instead draw down and swap bullets with the small enforcement posse?

The villain's irrational need to continually reinsert himself into the police activities all around him, such that even now might lead to his very downfall and capture might have been astounding to some—indeed, even foolish to a fault—but criminal profilers might already have known that the man's even greater plan was to simply taunt the very lawmen who wanted to take him down and dare them to the teeth, then force their hand into some kind of final showdown.

He could easily have slipped their nets—several times over by now, in fact—but had chosen instead to remain and simply beard them to the face and beat them at their own game. But as he was, he might not seek a confrontation with any, nor as he was would he avoid one, fully expecting that his very disguise might be just enough to see him through his very flight ordeal. But deep down inside, he also knew that he would not shy away from a battle were one thrust upon him by his dogged followers, whoever they might be and wherever that fight might be joined.

And thus stood the mysterious, make-believe vagabond, a ruffian ragpicker who was hiding now in plain sight and continuing to stoop deeply over a row of trash bins just across from the seedy flat he'd been in only moments before. Now with but a crass slide of eyes did he even watch the police activity sidelong, casually eyeing both the scene and the circumstances as both continued to unfold around him, but he mostly trained his eye on the garbage cans for the moment, much perhaps as he should in disguise, the better to perfect his clever assumed role. And even as he did so, a train of cops had already begun their approach in staggered lines of two down Grove Street, now with a single man in blue already fast advancing to his very position.

Under the dark tree-canopied light of the small street, the killer could see in a flash that it was that bugger Paxton, the bloke he'd had occasion to speak to only once before, now itself so much a long time ago. The patrolling officers all steadied up with their continued sweeps, stepping forward in a slow survey of the entire area, and now even him, as the seedy vagrant Volstad pushed on with his rummager's ruse with seeming fervor.

"You, you there!" the lead patrolman said, now sizing up the shady unexpected character that both he and Reid were just then encountering there on the darker south side of crosstown Grove.

"Go steady there. Hold up a minute," Paxton ordered of the man, charging him to stand where he was and be further scrutinized. The officer was also compelled by close departmental protocols to keep at least one hand just on the sidearm grip itself at all times for his own best protection, should there ever be a need to use it. But to a man, they all hoped that no one situation would ever demand they have to do so. But this guy ... this guy, the cop seemed to almost recognize.

"Old Shakespeare, is that you? Kettle, Howard Kettle?" the cop asked almost curiously, now far less on the alert, seeming to already know the muddy vagrant from the area, then glanced over at his patrol partner, Reid.

Outwardly, neither officer seemed to express any real alarm since both appeared to already know the man as one of their denizens of the dark. To the two men, he was simply one of the harmless neighborhood regulars that they'd seen often enough in the area, such that had already tainted him as a purveyor of both basket and bin throughout much of their daily walking beats, causing them to even use a name of some seeming familiarity—"Old Shakespeare."

It had been a name that both officers had long ago knighted the harmless coot with as a kind of amusing title, a kind of local joke, and a term almost of some endearment. The old ragamuffin trash picker had never made any real trouble during any of his patrols and had even been polite to a fault, Paxton opined as the many thoughts of past encounters flashed through his mind. He was apparently well known in the neighborhood and was only seen as being a bit quirky and pretentious, but never tagged as being either a danger to himself or others.

Indeed, the odd nickname had been given the old cuss entirely based on the man's smooth British accent, his seeming eloquence of speech, and his endless quoting of the many scattered Shakespeare lines and iambic quatrains that the seedy hobo must have mastered long ago during a now long-buried past. Just like Carrie Brown in New York City's East Side Hotel in 1891: "Old Shakespeare" herself.

"C'mon, old-timer, you'll need to move it along now. We have to clear the street here. This whole area is now a crime scene," said the deep-voiced cop with no real suspicion of the man or his seeming trash-motivated pursuits. The cop simply wanted the man to move on as quickly as possible, and seeing his seeming compliance with the request, he simply let him pass and waved the fusty transient on into the night.

Paxton's eyes trailed after the vagrant as he watched him head east, now approaching the corner as he crossed Bleecker Street heading toward the loud push of traffic on Seventh Avenue South and turned left to head north. And neither cop would ever have seen the small automatic pistol held just out of sight and tucked into a snug waistband even as the tumbledown drifter forged on.

Then Paxton decided to give the man a second look. He had a gut instinct and just maybe something didn't seem right.

༺❦❦❦༻

"Captain Fuller," a small voice said from within the tight confines of the police cruiser in which she had been sequestered only moments earlier, just before any of the action had even begun.

"Captain Fuller, can I maybe get out of this car now? I'm a big girl and I can take care of myself, ma'am. Plus, I'm a reporter—it's what I do. I should be wherever the action is. I mean, not getting scooped on a

The Knight-Errant

story and all that. Plus, I could probably use a little fresh air as well," Macklin said, tapping lightly on the glass of the vehicle's rear window.

"Ma'am, can you hear me?" she prodded as she pushed her luck and stepped up her plea. "I'm feeling a little claustrophobic in here. I'd really like to get over to wherever this pursuit is headed. Captain? Captain Fuller?" she pushed, still tapping softly on the window. The cub reporter's pleas were also beginning to walk a razor's edge between a dangerous dedication to her work and just plain being a pest.

"Ma'am? I'd love to have a firsthand view of the story here, as it unfolds. Maybe see it up close for myself. A good story always keeps my bosses happy and helps me keep my job as well. What do you say, Captain?"

"I understand everything you're saying, Ms. Macklin, but all things considered, it's a clear security issue," the captain said as she sauntered over to the car door. "I can't very well have you running around all loose cannon on us now, can we? I'm afraid you'll just have to stay put for the time being or for at least as long as the threat is still active. So for the time being, this is your best—and frankly your *only* option—in the interest of your well-being, that is. Which is just another way of saying it's for your own good, I suppose," Captain Fuller observed almost sternly. After all, she reminded Ellen Macklin, it had only been a few hours since she and her lead detective Pomeroy had been shot at, and again, a second time, that same night back on Broome Street.

"Captain, there must be something you can do here. And aren't you the one who always told us all to follow up on a lead no matter how infeasible it might seem? Plus, I'd imagine we'd all want to know just what's going on with Pomeroy and Robles. Any word from the team, ma'am? Is everyone okay?" a still-pushy Macklin persisted, careful not to tip her hand about her true motive and concern, Joe Pomeroy himself.

"This area's not been secured sufficiently enough, Ms. Macklin. Plus, we've still got an active shooter on the prowl who's already popped several shots at you and the sergeant, in fact, TWICE. It's just not safe, Ellen, can't you see? And I won't run the risk of this guy's aim improving should he decide to come around here and make another attempt.

"We believe this guy's the same character who might also be responsible for the string of deadly slashings we've been having across the city over the past weeks. Now, he's been made into some larger-than-life character that some people are now calling the 'Village Ripper' and the 'Slasher.' And we just don't know where he might be holed up, even if we already know what he's capable of. So suffice it to say, you'll know when I know," Fuller concluded, abruptly slamming the door on both the subject and the beleaguered Macklin's request almost at once.

"Ma'am," Macklin proffered one final time as she continued to petition Fuller and make her best case.

"Okay, okay! Against my better judgment, you can exit the car and maybe move your muscles a bit. But I want you joined at the hip right here with this officer—and I mean right here. You don't leave her side for anything, *capeesh*?" ordered the slightly capitulating commander of the Major Crimes Unit. Then the news reporter finally exited the police cruiser and began stretching the kinks out of her legs, focusing entirely on her discomfort and oblivious to much else. And then the radio crackled and the call came in ...

ॐॐॐ

"Son of bitch!" hissed a still-harried Bogdan Volstad as he continued with his persona of Howard Kettle, fooling all, yet fooling none. He was aggravated to no end, having trudged more than a couple of blocks away from a hot search zone that he knew must still be under close scrutiny just near the old Grove Street safe house.

He'd managed to skirt his way around the fool cop who'd insisted on running into him seemingly again and again throughout the neighborhood. *If only the gull knew*, he thought to himself with a kind of knavish delight, but for the moment, at least he had other plans for the evening, other business at hand—a hastily protracted flight and a small favor to return to two old acquaintances—then a certain quick escape from the entire area, if at all possible. By car, by foot, or by subway, if need be. If not, he'd simply fight it out and tangle with his chances against the lawmen. By now, he posited bleakly, the cops must surely have stumbled upon his dead-drop hideaway and crash pad already, which meant they must have found all indeed.

The Knight-Errant

Now, might there be an even sharper imperative to simply slip the net and set up shop somewhere else, he reasoned smartly to himself while still much on the run, even now as he fast approached the eastern edge of West Tenth, only to find even more activity swarming in a blue beehive of police cars and command vehicles. GOOD, the man-killer mused to himself, unable to resist the taunting urge that seemed to drive him continually in and out of the mouth of the dragon in perfect disguise. And now, he was almost willing himself back again into the lion's den, only to come out the other side, wherever that other side might lead. It was almost too easy, he mused sarcastically to himself, the fool cops, wasting time and seeking out a bevy of pointless clues he never left behind. How curious, the fools.

All about him, the sharp blue and red lights deeply swirled across the building façades that lined both sides of the street, casting eerie shadows and wild afterglows with the spin of each strobing light. *But no matter*, he thought to himself with a kind of false bravado, his ratty handcart well in tow and floppy bags of plastic bottles clacking in the early night. *If I must, I will make a deal with the devil, but I will respond in kind if confronted. They'll not take me alive.*

Then he turned and began squeak-wheeling his way back down the street directly toward the several squad cars that were already parked at the curb and in the street, and even the much larger command vehicle that could be seen from his short block away. *Indeed*, he thought blackly to himself, *this should at the very least be interesting*.

Now only stopping on occasion to almost *dutifully* rifle through the odd garbage can along the way. He'd already decided to bank on his ability to live in the shallow confines of his alter ego persona, Mr. Howard Kettle—"Old Shakespeare," knight-errant, master of trash, and a king of the streets.

And even then, as he drew near the large police vehicle, he could already make out the silhouettes, two of them standing off on the sidelines just on the north side of West Tenth. And then he spotted the woman again, for yet now a third time. Yes, it was unmistakably her, he could not be wrong. She was the one—that same detestable soul he so disfavored. And yet there she was, standing just beside a police car talking to someone else.

Almost immediately, the posturing and very body language of the taller woman that the reporter was talking to was evident, and he could see even at a distance that she must be the one in charge. The very police captain he'd seen earlier that he immediately recognized now from the several television broadcasts of days past. Yes, the one always in the background gloating and glowering her grimaced face while the other two fops rambled on about the progress on the case and told their lies. That was regrettably all about him. But the other one—that *other* one—he could distinctly make out as that same nemesis of a news reporter that had just earlier vilely taunted him on public media—and in a public forum too—which truly might have been his chief complaint.

Perhaps, therefore, his work was indeed still not done, not quite as it were. Thus, the emboldened serial killer simply bristled up, knit the brow, and prepared to face head on his final moments of reckoning—either ALL of them or just himself.

ஓஓஓ

"20-David Sergeant," the call squawked in over the police band, crackling over the airwaves like so much static electricity at the height of a passing storm, as the senior detective touched base with a call to the mobile command center.

"Mobile command, 20-David. Put me through to Fuller ASAP," Pomeroy said, barking the order to the mobile unit's dispatcher. "Get the captain on the horn—now." Then, a single uniformed officer exited the mobile police van at a trot, bounding down the three steps and hustling off to flag down Fuller where she stood in a brief consultation with several other cops and flanked by a now-enfranchised Ellen Macklin.

"Captain ... Captain Fuller!" the winded runner said with a measure of urgency that must have been apparent to all as he approached the boss. "There's a call from Sergeant Pomeroy on a secure line for you. I think he's got some kind of update for you on the situation."

Fuller pried herself away from the small gathering of patrol officers and Macklin, then made her way up the steps and into the van. Grabbing the communications handset from the tech seated at the mobile console, she punched in and waited for the voice on the other end. "Sergeant, what's your 20 and what've you got for me?" was all she could manage as she waited with anticipation for the update she knew must soon be coming.

"Captain, the team's at the suspect stash house here on Grove, and all we've got right now are only more question marks and even fewer answers—so far anyway. We followed a slight blood trail from West Fourth to some funeral home on Bleecker where our insertion teams have just entered and found another body, Cap. Looks like more of the same kind of killings we've had all along, and this one's a pretty bad one too. Could be more of our guy's work—throat cut and body eviscerated, just like the others. Grisly but pretty much as you might expect."

Now, the ruptured silence was deafening as the captain seemed to wait for the other shoe to drop, now having to speak much louder as if to almost drown out the stepped-up patter of rain that, all of a sudden, had begun pelting down loudly on the very van in which she sat.

"Copy that, but tell me again how a funeral parlor figures into all of this? I'm afraid I don't understand."

"I'm getting to that, boss," the sarge responded, perhaps even annoyed at the ill-timed interruption.

"We found evidence of some unusual activity in one of the back prep rooms that seemed a little out of place or maybe just out of the ordinary—bloody bandages and medical instruments that appear to have been used for treating something, or someone, ma'am. We're thinking our guy might have been injured somehow and came here for a quick stitch-up. If it's our fugitive, he might have come here in lieu of some hospital or doctor's office."

"That might actually make sense, in a weird kind of way. What else you got?" Captain Fuller asked, her voice peaking as she followed along.

"I've got boots on the ground beating every bush and canine unit scouring the area scent tracking in a three-block radius. Aviation units are already up with the top cover, and search teams are going block-by-block on a tight sweep of the entire area. The dogs seem to have picked up a scent trail that took us almost door to door and ended at a midblock location here on Grove—the stash house I was telling you about. We're there now, Captain."

"What are you seeing?" asked an expectant Fuller, hoping against hope that this could pan out into something tangible, something actionable.

"Seems the whole place is a veritable treasure trove of stores and munitions of all kinds—old handguns to bayonets, binding ropes, tape. Hell, even body bags for quick disposal, I guess. And knives, Captain—lots of knives. Near as we can tell, it looks like some kind of waypoint stash house or crash pad. Looks like this guy's got one of everything in his flat, boss, plus it's pretty seedy in here. Not good."

"Then expand your search perimeter and fan out. Maybe get your people to conduct a secondary grid search. This guy couldn't have gotten too far, especially if he's injured. And keep that canine unit out on the street as well. Maybe see if they can pick up a hot trail again. You copy?"

"Roger that. Rain's picking up and washing up any tracks or evidence we might have had I'd imagine, but I'll see what we can get from a closer look. Oh, and Captain?" Pomeroy said almost as a codicil to his report in a moment of inquiry.

"How's our gal Macklin holding up so far? Is she still under lock and key with your people? Everything okay, I mean?" the detective asked, perhaps once again betraying his real interests and emotions in the matter.

"Like I don't see right through that. You just make sure you keep focused, Sergeant. Ellen's safe and sound and behaving herself. She's been begging to get out of that car you locked in since you left, so she's here with me getting a little fresh air. Now, how about you back to the tasks at hand? Mobile command is out," she was about to say.

And then they heard the two shots ring out as they echoed through the street like a clap of thunder shivering through a canyon, then shuddered its way over the airwaves back to Pomeroy before he could even punch off.

Things seemed to rapidly come into focus for the Village Ripper, Bogdan Volstad, even as the crazed felon had decided to keep up the pretense of the stodgy old thespian, Howard Kettle, only long enough to get closer to his most intended target, that haughty, insulting reporter, Ellen Macklin.

And what a piece of luck it was too that he should even find her here, even if clearly under police protection. He'd taken his first shot already, but it was a measure of the man's own deep-rooted insanity that he should even harbor such an unreasoned antipathy for a woman he had never met—but he did, and even that without conscience or sound logic. And he was sworn to take his second, even better shot, when he got his next best chance.

But he would have much preferred to have had access to both together as they were as one, and in his corrupted mind, he knew that harm to one might be harmful to both. And thus had the mad hatter continued with his wily shadowing of the still-unwary news reporter.

A shrewd and dogged killer by his very nature, he was now a man quite on the lurk and content to simply bide his time until the moment was just right. Keeping true to his guise and false pretense, the tattered man shuffled and staggered his way down the darker side of West Tenth Street, moving ever nearer the sidewalk perch of the hounding reporter who now stood sheltered in a recessed doorway, only steps away and dodging a light rain.

An unexpected clatter of trashcans now seemed to only quickly alert the one lone cop who stood just nearby, perhaps detailed to babysit the busybody newsie after the captain had entered the van.

A head swiveled sharply in the direction of the noise and Volstad could almost tangibly feel the policeman sizing him up, her eyes washing over him and his busied activities, even as she held the approaching bagman in a close survey. A quick assessment of the threat posed by the foraging picker by the alert police bodyguard seemed to tell her that this was not their man. So she had decided to simply stand down and resume her sentry post, casting only a dismissive gaze on the homeless man as he neared her very place of standing.

The cadent squeak of Kettle's battered shopping cart seemed to betray the man's very approach, the discordant noise of a broken front wheel spinning wildly only added to the orchestra of sounds that signaled this very movement as he edged his way farther down the street. And as he did so, he purposefully fingered the automatic pistol that was snug in his belt and tucked carefully from view. The reticent stalker was undoubtedly prepared to knock off the weapon's safety at a moment's notice, now still but a few yards from his intended target, the all-unknowing Ellen Macklin.

The sentry officer noted the man coming closer and closer, but was still not entirely thrown off by the man's presence or seeming movements as he continued down the small lane just on the other side of the street and now crossing. But the captain's orders had been firm and precise: "Let no one through and lock down the entire street. No through traffic, not on foot and not in a car."

"Sorry, sir," the policewoman finally said, looking over and moving to intercept the approaching vagrant and bring him up short. "Hold it right there, old-timer," the dutiful officer ordered as she stood sentry just near the reporter who was still sheltering in a doorway just out of the rain. "I'm afraid you'll have to turn around and go back up the block. This area's cordoned off right now. This is still an active crime scene."

"Why, I'm sorry, Constable. Of course, of course," the hidden villain said with a clear repetition of words and rhythm, the better to beguile them all. "I'm just a harmless picker of rags and riches. A harmless picker of rags and riches, ma'am," the garbage man chuckled once again with a repetition that was oddly reminiscent of Johnny Two-Times of cinematic *Goodfellas* fame. "Such as can be found, that is," finished the devious villain with a pretentious doff of his cap.

"Wrap it up quickly, then, and be on your way already" was all the accommodating policewoman said, allowing the indigent through and fighting the urge to perhaps even release a hidden smile and stepping even closer to Macklin's position.

And then the first of two shots rang out, each with a shocking report that cracked and echoed across the very canyon walls of the narrow street ... both reports now almost waking up the proverbial dead as one body collapsed to the ground.

꙳꙳꙳

"Captain, 20-David Sergeant, you okay over there? What was that, Captain? Captain? Are you still manning the command center? We could hear shots from here. Please confirm status. Captain Fuller?" bellowed Pomeroy over the airwaves with what could only be described as a heightening concern. And what made it even worse was the fact that he was not getting any answer.

He'd heard the two shots ring out, maybe more, each a split-second blast apart in its deadly report, perhaps with one round even ricocheting off some hardstand surface just nearby. And in an instant, all heads had simply stopped whatever they had been doing and swiveled north in the direction of the sounds, even now an area they knew was just up the block near West Tenth.

Right where he'd last stashed reporter Ellen Macklin, where he'd left her under the dubious care of a semiguarded patrol car just near the mobile command center by Captain Fuller. But he knew they were gunshots—*unmistakably* gunshots—and they were unmistakably close, maybe far less than the few short blocks toward which all heads had spun about to listen in.

"Robles, listen up," a winded Pomeroy said with dire instruction to the junior detective at his side. "You'll need to hold down the fort and head up the search team effort here. Narrow down our search radius and take it back to two blocks only. Then have your people push north to Eleventh Street and out to Seventh. I know this guy's around here somewhere."

"Copy that, Sarge," came the obedient reply from Detective Robles, his close friend and partner for the past five years. "I'm on it," he said, perhaps waiting for some further elaboration on his last instruction.

"Something tells me we're gonna need a tighter search pattern here. Hell, this guy's holed up somewhere, maybe just trying to wait us out. I can feel it as sure as I'm standing here. Deploy the searchers, Damien. Pull your people back a block, then move them north.

"And do it on the double! You copy?" Pomeroy instructed as he checked the younger detective, anxious to make sure his second-in-command had understood his instructions to the letter. "I'm pulling some of the team and heading north to Tenth. Somebody has to check on Macklin and the captain. Then I'll get right back to—"

He was interrupted now by a clear shattering of the hushed quiet of the moment, just as his team had huddled up around the radio, now came the dreaded punch of static that spewed out its deadly staccato of words over the airwaves, soon becoming the very call no one ever wants to get.

"OFFICER DOWN! Civilian down. West Tenth and Bleecker. Any available units, respond. Repeat, officer down—need help, any units!" squawked the radio call that few would ever wish to hear, least of all Sergeant Pomeroy. Quickly springing into action then, he and several other uniformed cops started at a clip hustling back up the block toward Bleecker. Then, it was a quick jog north to Macklin and Fuller.

Now less than a block out from where the shots had rung out, the seasoned detective stepped up his pace, soon reaching for his sidearm and holding it low, trailing tightly behind the right leg and knocking off the gun's safety as he softly padded on and ran headlong toward the danger. Pomeroy was almost halfway there before he realized that he could only wonder which one he might be more concerned about at the moment: the captain or his budding love interest Ellen Macklin. But in his heart, he knew.

❧❧❧

Much of it had happened in the blink of an eye ... in fact, all of it had. The Volstad had once again spent his best shots unwisely, and in a skidding fit of rage and frustration had done so right on the fringe of a large police presence that he already knew to be in the area. Even more so since that same search team might be only blocks south of the mobile command center that was parked on West Tenth under the watchful eye of Captain Fuller. Startled by the very approach and seeming challenge of the lone bodyguard officer that stood just near the shielded newsie, the Volstad had fired first at the cop and watched her go down in a crumple. What he could not have known was that his wild shot had only grazed her vest and only temporarily knocked the wind out of her and only hurled her to the ground.

Then, he slowly swung the *Makarov* automatic pistol back toward the startled Macklin, who was still trapped in a small doorway just out of the rain, then added an ounce of pressure to the trigger toward its slow release. The small automatic bucked for a second time with the bolt sliding back and ejecting its spent shell, just as the villain watched the second woman go down as well. And even as the silent wisps of smoke curled up from the barrel of the Russian-made handgun, he knew in his twisted mind that he might finally have been vindicated. He'd taken care of that bitch news reporter once and for all, and she had been dispatched to his satisfaction as he stood and watched her die.

&&&

The Volstad had fired two shots—perhaps *more* by his estimate—all fired from an awkward semi-crouched position just by the shallow ruse of some garbage cans close to the police officer. The two bullets had only carelessly been loosed, coursing wildly but with both still finding their marks cleanly and without deflection. Macklin, and the officer tasked with guarding her, had both gone down and were now not moving. And from at least the vantage point of the killer, it was still the civilian in the doorway that had all along been his prime target, who appeared to somehow still linger on, even if writhing in distress in her secret pain.

And so, the killer palmed the heft of the *Makarov* automatic in his hand and raised the pistol to deadly sighting for yet a second time. Slowly did he swing its lethal lip back in the direction of Ellen Macklin, who was still curled on the ground just inside the doorway, then carefully fingered its hair trigger, squeezing, squeezing, ever so slowly squeezing. Then he was himself jolted with impact and thrown heavily through the air to the right, virtually recoiling in midflight from the double-tap hits to his torso that he'd never seen coming.

THE CAPTAIN THROWS DOWN

11 NOVEMBER

Captain Fuller had hastily thrown off the console headset she'd been wearing and tossed them aside when she heard the first shots ring out, being only feet away outside the mobile command center. She moved at a clip toward the van's side doors, flinging them wide as she stepped out just in time to find both of her charges: Macklin and her loosely set bodyguard down and sprawled on the ground with neither one seeming to move.

Quickly all the years of training kicked in almost in the instant, and the undaunted head of Major Crimes had already unholstered her weapon in the time it took to even look around. And her very first target was the shadowy figure who stood just between her and the two fallen figures. Those were her people, she reasoned to herself, furious to a fault that this could even happen on her watch just outside the command vehicle.

Her service weapon was already coming up even at the moment she saw the suspect doing precisely the same with his small Russian handgun, and now might it only come down to who could steady up and fire first before the other. And the unflinching captain had already decided it would not be her who fired last.

Sergeant Pomeroy was now at the vanguard of a small contingency of cops and SWAT team operators that he'd managed to commandeer from the main search party to respond to the urgent call of "Officer down." Driven entirely by a gnawing dread and a deepening concern for both the captain and his reporter friend, Ellen Macklin, Pomeroy covered the two blocks in quick time loping, sprinting at a dead run from Grove Street to West Tenth in record time. His chest was heaving and his heart was pounding, now clearly with visions of a downed cop and an injured civilian, a civilian he could only hope was not Ellen. Was she even the one noted in the distress call that had just gone out over the airwaves only minutes earlier?

Fast approaching the dark intersection of Bleecker and Tenth, just where the mobile command center had earlier been set up, with Captain Fuller overseeing every aspect of the robust field operation that was even now in play, he was a man quite on the edge. It was also where he'd last left Macklin tucked safely away in a well-guarded police squad car—or so at least he thought. But he also couldn't be certain if anything had changed in the short interval of time he'd been entrenched with the second deployment team that had been only blocks away.

Turning the corner, Pomeroy quickly found himself assessing the situation and could already see two people down and his captain just exiting the command vehicle with a gun drawn. That alone was enough to push him to a higher state of readiness as he brought his weapon to bear should the moment even demand it, as it clearly might already have. Odd then that two shots should already ring out in the night, and even those almost simultaneously, each shattering the calm of the quaint Greenwich Village street as even the night birds fluttered timidly off into the air.

The captain burst out of the command vehicle loaded for bear and not knowing quite what to expect. Her eyes had quickly adjusted to the darkness and she could already see several things unfolding almost all at once: Macklin down and lying in the doorway of the small boutique shop where she'd last been seen, the patrol officer tasked with watching her sprawled on the sidewalk and just now reviving herself after being laid out by the killer's first centering shot to the chest, Pomeroy, Robles, Paxton, and a bevy of SWAT team officers just then rounding the corner to arrive on the scene and a third wild-eyed assailant who was even then leveling up his handgun for what could only be a follow-on kill shot for either or both of her people. Instinctively knowing it was time to act, she stepped through a single hampering moment of hesitation, then found her target and squeezed the trigger as the gun bucked back once, its very lip still smoking hot in the cool rain of the night.

Pomeroy surged onto the scene in a running crouch with stealth and his gun held outstretched in a double-handed grip that he held firm and leveled at a suspect he thought he might already recognize. Moving even closer to the suspect, he hand-gestured the SWAT advance team and had them slingshot off to the far side of the dimly lit street and dig in with the best advantage. *Hell*, he thought as his eyes quickly adjusted to the dimness all around him, was this that same smarmy bum they'd screened just earlier at the very first crime scene all those months ago on Grove Street? Or was he simply wrong and this was indeed someone else?

There'd been something oily about the guy from day one, he remembered thinking. Something just this side of shifty that he didn't like, even if he never could quite wrap his head around the very why of it. Unfortunately, no one at the time could ever definitively put a finger on him as a viable suspect at the time. And so, he had skated—this Kettle, this same Howard Kettle. The sinewy and hulking skink had gotten away cleanly with his nasty little bucket of nuisance crimes and petty thievery and had never been compelled to pay a price.

Instead, he'd simply disappeared and fallen off the grid each time, slipping away and conveniently falling between the cracks of an overwhelmed and otherwise distracted justice system. And thus, here he stood yet again, almost defiantly in full view, the snarky remnant of his former rabid self, with all of it leading now to the very here and now of these final moments of tumult. All of it was fast becoming a drawdown confrontation that probably didn't even need to happen.

The sergeant drove his team along, motioning with crisp animated movements, pushing each of them into more optimized line-of-sight positions, this as their long guns sprang up to steady, aiming directly across from the distraught as-yet-unidentified man still brandishing a handgun. Pomeroy could almost see that the very worst of his fears might already have been realized, now with one officer down and the slumped form of Ellen Macklin only now struggling up to one elbow in a doorway just at the feet of a man who was poised to take his second shot.

Now shaking off the torpor of a single clouded moment of uncertainty, Pomeroy slowly squeezed the trigger and loosed his do-or-die shot as well. He'd been compelled to do so, but he could only hope that he was not already too late.

The Captain Throws Down

❧ ❧ ❧

Bogdan Volstad could only grimace and howl like a wounded animal trapped in the pangs of a death throe, as he was flung to the ground by the force of just the first shot alone fired by Fuller. To his view, she was simply the heavyset woman steeped in the shadow who stood with a gun aimed right at him from the steps of the police van. Then he felt the blow and impact of the bullet. To his distress, Fuller's shot had caught him sharp in the left arm, causing the ruffian fugitive to fully lose his grip on his weapon, the Makarov pistol spinning away and clattering heavily across the sidewalk pavement.

"Go low, go low. Aim low," Sergeant Pomeroy yelled to all in good proximity, having just arrived on the scene. "We want this one alive!" the senior cop ordered, hoping against hope that they might still be able to take him breathing, the better to perhaps then find the man more amenable and compliant, willing to bargain and willing to speak.

Then Pomeroy's second round quickly found its mark as well, having been fired almost precisely at the same time as Captain Fuller's rapid discharge. The round had, this time, penetrated midrange, crashing painfully through the fleshy portion of the man's lower abdomen, deflecting off a single rib, and shattering bone and tissue as it meandered frightfully throughout his body, felling the would-be killer virtually on the spot. It was much like a bad habit being dropped and wiped away.

"Check fire, check fire! Suspect is down. Repeat, suspect is down!" the sergeant advised after confirming a firsthand view of the situation. The man would live, but he would surely be in a hell of a lot of pain. Then he inched forward in cautious approach toward the downed shooter with eyes trained out in laser focus, gun still up and safety off.

❧ ❧ ❧

Ellen Macklin had only had the wind knocked out of her per se, recoiling sharply as she reacted to the heavy punch of force that had hit her center mass in the chest in an instant. The molten slug had ultimately buried itself only lightly in the police protective vest that Fuller had insisted she wear, and thankfully even that without at all penetrating.

"Yeah, I know. I know it's not exactly the kind of fashion statement you might otherwise like to make, Macklin," the captain had said earlier almost curtly, cutting short the younger woman's easy protests. "But either you put on the vest or you stay in the car, savvy? Your call!"

And so, Ellen had complied, however begrudgingly, and it was only now that it had become the very thing that would save her life. And so, this was, indeed, how the reporter found herself coming to, reviving right here—wherever here was—now slowly pulling herself up, first from a fully reclined position to her knees, then up to her feet, however unsteadily. Macklin's head was spinning, her chest throbbing in heaves like she had been kicked in the torso by an ill-tempered mule, but she was still alive, even if a heavy canopy of confusion still hung over her like a shrouding fog. She was alive, but still looking up at the grimace of a disheveled man who was moving in for his ugly conclusion, now with a still-defiant Ellen Macklin clenching her teeth at the very prospect of maybe not seeing the morrow. And then the shots rang out.

The Volstad could sense the walls rapidly closing in on him, now with a searing pain that coursed through his left arm and pierced abdomen, both much like wild stallions of fire stampeding through his mind and body. He'd been shot twice and stood clutching his midsection with blood-striped fingers, a throbbing sting already causing him to slowly drop to his knees. Still not done and unwilling to surrender, the Volstad was still scrambling for the lost Makarov pistol just as the powerfully built detective raced to his side and pounced on him, forcefully so, thinking the man down for good. What Pomeroy had not seen was the villainous knife still secreted on the killer's very person, the ever-infamous two-or-more-blades ripper knife. And then the villain made his desperate move.

"Freeze! I said freeze and drop the gun. Do it NOW," Captain Fuller had yelled as she glared off in the direction of the man behind the two shots that had just rocked her world right there on Tenth Street. Finding no compliance from the shooter, she was only met with the cold defiance of black steel swinging slowly about in her direction instead.

"GUN, GUN, GUN!" she warned in a booming voice that seemed to carry across the narrow side street with a haunting echo.

Compelled to preempt the threat and clear intent of the man's planned attack, she had fired a single shot that was calculated to only disable and not kill, to subdue but not entirely put down. Indeed, only too clearly did she understand that the offender must be made to answer for the string of violent crimes he had committed, for all of the suspected killings past and present for which he alone was responsible. Why, indeed, should he be granted calm assuaging death at the end when so many had perished in the past weeks by the cold bite of his bloody knife? He must be taken alive and tried, then granted his appointment with a big sleep-inducing suite of drugs on an executioner's table as he sleepily awaited a death he so richly deserved. Or in the end, he simply hung from the rafters, and having his neck stretched was the option even still on the table.

Indeed, she might have speculated even further but was soon drawn from her observations when she saw Pomeroy and his advance team already rounding the corner and arriving on the scene. She caught a quick glint of steel in the detective's hand, then heard a near-simultaneous shot ring out almost at the same instant as her own. For now, however, she could only stand in awe of Pomeroy's seemingly rapid advance to the doorway in front of which the perpetrator now stood in a hunch of welling pain. Fuller could not quite make up her mind whether the move itself had been more reckless than calculated, since all of it was unfolding far too quickly to even check, the headstrong detective already making his move. And there just behind the battling men and still struggling to her feet was a stunned Ellen Macklin, now with the captain left to only speculate as to which might be the man's greater imperative: the killer or the cub reporter.

"Watch him, Sergeant. Careful with this guy. Watch him!" Fuller ordered as she edged her way down the steps of the mobile command vehicle and approached the arena of action. Then her eyes were drawn to a dull glimmer of metal that only too soon morphed into the ripper knife that she could see was poised to strike and find its home in Pomeroy's chest.

❦❦❦

A still-wobbly Ellen Macklin had watched the furious battle between the two men unfold before her very eyes, even as she got to her feet unsteadily and attempted to step out of the doorway in which she had so precariously been trapped.

Her eyes were glazed, still seeking good focus, and her body ached as she sought to recover from the severe blow to the chest from the single-point contact gunshot fired at her by the violent assailant Volstad. Vest or no vest, the sharp impact of the blow could only be measured by its own contrast of sharp pain and dulling disorientation. Were this a roller-coaster ride in a kiddie amusement park, she would not choose to board a second time, and she was only too glad to see a charging Sergeant Pomeroy coming to her aid, even through a haze of dizzying distraction, and knew her rescue could not have come a moment too soon.

Reporter Macklin now found that her eyes were quickly being drawn to the downed police officer who was still on the ground and heavily traumatized by the single round from the surprising handgun that had seemingly targeted her as well.

What in God's grace had just happened? Was all she would later recall, asking herself in disbelief in the shattering moments right after the shooting, even as she methodically went about the heavy task of patting herself down in a quick body check just to be sure she had not been injured. In an instant, she'd watched on with unbridled terror as Pomeroy seemingly came out of nowhere and roughly tackled the injured suspect, kicking the gun away and deftly warding off the man's secondary thrust of the knife.

"Joe, knife, knife. Be careful!" warned Macklin as the burly cop easily parried the slash of the blade and deflected the attack with his left arm while telegraphing a crushing blow with a right overhand of a hook that hit almost audibly, crushing flesh and bone almost as soon as it was delivered. "Watch him, Joe!"

"Let's see what happens when you pick on someone your own size, you son of a bitch," Pomeroy spat with hot venom and a clear sense of satisfaction as he dealt the man a solid knuckle sandwich for yet a second time, the blow immediately dropping him like a weighty sack of rocks in the water.

Down fell the wicked Volstad in a crumpled heap at the sergeant's feet, perhaps having well met his match and bested in battle, soon with a noticeable outflow of blood that slavered wildly from the corners of his mouth.

But yet the villain fought on, in spite of injury and setback, loathe to surrender and still angered by his current disadvantage. He was soon back to his feet, cupping his hand as he hit the policeman with the heel of his palm in an upward motion that glanced off the detective's chin with impact. The sharp and sudden blow had sent a shockwave of pain through the detective as he recoiled from the upward thrust that had momentarily stunned him and shaken him to the core, the attack being wholly unexpected.

Fighting to recover from the sudden hit, Pomeroy continued to wrestle with the felon on the sidewalk just near the shop doorway, clearly thinking that he'd had all well in hand, only to find himself still tussling with the villain in his attempt to subdue and cuff the man and end the takedown in full.

The dodgy villain had, in fact, already been winged twice by both his and Fuller's two rounds but seemed to persist in his life-or-death struggle not to be taken down. The Volstad had told himself that he would not be taken alive and seemed to only boldly seek that end. Other police operatives arriving on the scene could see for themselves the man's resistant brawling with one of their own. This was as Paxton, Reid, and even the captain all converged on the fray to assist.

Now, indeed, might they finally have their suspect down in full, most might have thought, with Paxton now also reaching in to perhaps grab an arm, a hand, or a leg.

The plucky homicide cop was now being quickly joined by the other three and now a posse of heavily armed SWAT officers dressed all in black who had all heard the shots and responded in kind. And all of them converging on the center of activity that was still unfolding just on the corner of Bleecker and West Tenth, their numbers seeming to grow by the moment—almost exponentially—even as Pomeroy prepared to move in for a final takedown and capture, reaching for his handcuffs with a plan to at last slap an iron grip on the grim offender's wrists.

Thinking he might finally manage a hold on the criminal, Pomeroy wrenched the man's arm behind him, perhaps thinking the task was done. But none, none had ever seen the second knife being unsheathed and brought to bear by the battling assassin until it was almost too late. It was only then that Paxton drew back in pain as the sharp blade quickly found its way home and plunged deeply into Paxton's arm as the officer grimaced and drew away, staggering back out of the skirmishing huddle. The vile Ripper had, once again, managed to lunge out and slash one final victim even as he was taken down, but the point was moot when a second backup officer stepped forward and hit him with a max Taser charge that came off like a *Star Trek* phaser set on heavy stun.

And even now was it only too soon "Goodnight, Irene" as the man's body flailed and convulsed with a fifty-thousand-volt hit that lasted only three seconds, and then the man went still. The fight was over and the cops finally had their man, the heinous villain who'd said he'd never be taken alive. And yet here he was, laid out, subdued, and sucking concrete in wild submission.

ఌఌఌ

Just now handing off a cuffed but still-combative Volstad to a couple of burly SWAT team officers, Pomeroy had struggled mightily as his charge had battled on, the violent man swearing and writhing about, ever resisting capture. Now, however, with a final safe transfer of custody to the two strong-armed door kickers, the sergeant ran in a beeline to the downed officer's side while keeping a wary eye on the still-kneeling Ellen Macklin. A quick slide of eyes between the two told him just how thankful she appeared to be and that she was simply glad to be alive.

"20-David Sergeant," a surprisingly calm Pomeroy reported as he spoke into his comm. "Confirming single downed officer, this location. Check that. Add one civilian, both with recoverable injuries. I'll need a bus here. Corner of Bleecker and West Tenth," the senior cop ordered as he put in his call for an ambulance, then quickly moved over to Ellen's side to check the extent of her injuries as well.

The Captain Throws Down

Seizing hold of the reporter's shoulders, Pomeroy gently helped her steady up to her feet, then did a visual scan of almost every inch of her body just to be sure there were no collateral injuries apparent, soon zeroing in on an obvious area of interest.

The protective vest he now inspected had just been tested to its limits and had held up well, and like the other cop being helped up from the sidewalk, Macklin, too, had survived. Helping her out of the vest must have been like a weight being lifted from her body, and he could see immediately that it had not been damaged much at all, even at close range, save for a single mid-mass concavity that had been punched in with the force of the killer's shot. But it had thankfully not penetrated.

Pomeroy knew it would probably hurt like the dickens in the morning, this as he draped a supporting arm about her waist and slow-walked her over to the police van past Fuller.

"Joe, talk about the cavalry riding to the rescue, I've never been so glad to see someone. How's the officer holding up?" Macklin asked with genuine concern, gesturing in the direction of the female police officer who seemed to be shaking it all off but was being tended to by a team of paramedics nonetheless.

"A word, Sergeant?" said a troubled and somewhat ominous Fuller if she stepped forward with a black and disapproving look. She was glad to see that both individuals were okay, but she was still pissed at Pomeroy for just about everything else. Mostly for holding the impromptu press conference, for taunting the volatile killer imprimis, up close and personal in a public forum over the open airwaves. Plus, she was still plenty miffed over her best detective, either directly or indirectly, involving the newscaster in three separate shooting incidents, culminating in this final injurious shooting.

"You two really take the cake," said a still-twisted Captain Fuller with a wag of a finger as the three stood just outside the command vehicle and moved over to the med team to check on the injured cop, then the boss paused in midstep. "And then some!" she said with flared nostrils. "And don't think this is over by a long shot either, because it's not," Fuller said with a glower in the direction of Pomeroy and Macklin as they all sauntered over to a second ambulance.

"That said, I'm damn glad to see you both alive and in one piece," Fuller said with a shake of the head and a hint of a chuckle as she watched the med teams fussing over her injured charges. "You two, I don't know what I'm gonna do with either of you. Jeez!"

Then, fully sizing up the situation and satisfied that all was well with her people, the captain turned around to her teams and spun up a finger in the air. It was a tacit gesture that seemed to signal a natural end to the operation in full and a cue to simply pack it up and take it back on the road. This hunt, at least for now, was over.

ENDGAME: A DEAD RECKONING

11 NOVEMBER

In the days and weeks following the shooting and apprehension of the unholy Bogdan Volstad—a man strongly proven to have been the very "Village Slasher" in his series of vicious killings in New York City's own Greenwich Village—taglines were already being bannered across the city's countless daily newspapers and slogged across the many at-home television sets as "crawlers" that inched across the bottom of every screen.

"Police Capture Infamous Killer in Massive Citywide Manhunt," read one teaser headline. "New Yorkers Breathe Collective Sigh of Relief After Killer Capture," said another. "Put Him in Chains," offered a third.

New York had not seen as ruthless and arbitrary a serial killer since the "Son of Sam" shooter and the butchering "Mad Max" slayings of 2011 that had plagued so much of the city and had the entire borough of Brooklyn in a state of near-lockdown for almost three days of stark terror. But even that was scaled back and far less worse than the butchery that had been visited upon the city by this modern-day Jack the Ripper, as seen in the past weeks and months.

It would, therefore, come as no great surprise that the oversight judiciary embodied in New York City's own criminal court system would be only too satisfied to expedite a plea without a mitigating deal and a later allocution that would seek the man's assured indictment. Now, indeed, might the courts finally learn about the how and the why of all of the crimes for which the alleged killer now stood accused? And within only weeks of the man's capture and decidedly slow recovery from his wounds in the hospital, charges were already being drawn up by a clutch of aggrieved city prosecutors in preparation for what might only shape up to be the trial of the century.

Busy now were the prosecutorial teams and felony trial lawyers, all of them soon overtaxed within the well-equipped and well-respected criminal court systems even before its actual trial venue, straining resources on all levels almost to capacity. Key to its prosecutorial strategy, the state's analytical research and evidence collection teams now all worked at a fevered pace, wasting precious little time in firming up its case for a quick and uncontested conviction of the man that most held responsible for the heinous murders of which he was suspected of committing across its fair city.

The savage felon must be made to pay, most thought, and for at least the short term, the man remained only heavily guarded in cold seclusion in maximum lockdown, remanded in solitude with no bail in a small six-by-nine pacing cell that came with a cot, three hots, and a commode.

During the course of the prolonged Volstad trial, even as it unfolded with time and prosecutorial discretion, the presiding judge was asked—and indeed granted—a rare allowance for a fully impaneled jury to visit the various crime scenes at which the several attacks occurred. And thus, now indeed a panel of twelve and a small group of alternates were ushered off on a series of sanctioned field trips, the trips set to visit each and all of the known kill sites, from Commerce Street and Barrow, Grove, Washington Square Park, Minetta, Bedford, Catherine and Water streets, to even the dark MacDougal Mews. All were seen by the shocked and gape-mouthed jurists who looked on in horror as they were told how each of the crimes had unfolded and what had occurred precisely where they now stood.

And now, returning to the courtroom, the hated—and hateful—Bogdan Volstad would, soon enough, be targeted with a bucketful of staggering charges in a list that almost ran to arm's length and forever pinned the frightful moniker of "Village Ripper" to the man in perpetuity. Indeed, a careful preparation of charges against the now-unmasked killer included fully eight counts of murder in the first degree, one each proposed by trial counsel for the killing of Martin Tabor, Paul Novaks, Anton Chapel, Elon Strunk, Carlton Enders, Maxwell J. Kirwin, Cranston Bruner, and even the hapless Dr. Malcolm Dollarhyde, the ill-fated funeral director who had done little more than patch up the injured intruder Volstad at gunpoint, back at the mortuary parlor and whose reward had been nothing less than a slash of a knife across his throat.

Quickly then would other even more detailed charges find their way through the vast and cormorant legal maze and laid well at the feet of the accused. In fact, a compilation of charges would directly be leveled at him, now with two counts of attempted murder also being applied for the two shots fired at Pomeroy and Macklin at the *Alhambra* restaurant.

The state's battery of savvy, keen-eyed trial lawyers would be further compelled to slap on even two additional counts of attempted murder for the man's second attack on Broome Street. Then, as if to even cap those charges, an additional two counts of the same would be tossed on the pile for the shooting of the female police officer and Macklin in the boutique doorway on West Tenth.

Finally, as if to almost fully round up what appeared to be a cornucopia of citations now being aimed at the prisoner Volstad, the trial attorneys sought to add an even heavier burden of lesser charges as well, such that might now run from grand theft auto to menacing with a weapon. Both charges had been tied back to the east Manhattan carjacking of the SUV on Catherine Street after his injuring skirmish with the ill-fated Cranston Bruner inside old Tanahey Park just near the East River.

Finally, prosecutors would ensure that an even further endpoint charge be lodged against the accused as well, that of operating a vehicle at felony reckless speeds with public endangerment, such that would also be tacked on for the wild chase the fugitive had engaged in while trying to escape the Broome Street shootings, barreling heedlessly up the West Side Highway with Pomeroy and Macklin in hot pursuit. The hammer had fallen with full legal momentum and would find no place else to land if not squarely on the head of this same miscreant, Bogdan Volstad himself.

Now, might it be only too easy for the state-assigned prosecutors tasked with trying the case in full to tie each of the weapons back to the accused given the luxury of time? Set as a backdrop to the case, a carefully studied and airtight forensic inquiry would only too quickly show that the rather unusual nine-by-eighteen-millimeter caliber of the bullets recovered from several of the shooting scenes could all be traced back to the Makarov handgun, the same weapon that would later be found in the killer's possession.

The presiding justice of the court had been duly advised by trial attorneys that their independent team of forensic examiners could now clearly fix a solid DNA trace of the suspect's blade weapon back to its logical source—this same foul Bogdan Volstad. Further, police investigators had even been able to unmask a touch of friction prints and link those partials back to the man that had quite carelessly left them behind during the commission of his crimes, nearly intact.

And all of it—*all* of it—could only point back to the accused as the wielder of the knife, with a clean four-point match, its deadly cutting edge fully consistent with the serrated penetration wounds found on each of the victims.

In their immediate custody, they already had the Russian-made Makarov pistol, along with the killer's knife, and distinctive trace evidence that presented them all with solid and unimpeachable case-to-case DNA hits for each of the victims and each of the crimes. And even more incriminating than all the rest, residual bloodstains were found that appeared to have only come from the killer during the attack on Bruner over on Catherine Street—the same attack in which he had been so rudely injured.

Clearly, with such a wealth of evidence at hand, multiple capital indictments might at its very pinnacle be all but assured. At its least there'd still be hard time spent in stifling isolation, at its best, a slam-dunk conviction—on ALL counts—for all the murders so heinously committed. Now, might the prosecutors need only a clear motive perhaps: the very why and wherefore surrounding the several killings.

Why had he done it and what was his motivation? And why a need to target only old men, most of them revered octogenarians and proud veterans of foreign wars, such that had all been welcomed home many years ago and victoriously embraced by their constituents of war and their communities?

The questions continued to only swirl about, seemingly without end or resolution, and the frustrated state prosecutors could only turn back to the police to only further interrogate the prisoner, to vigorously press the suspect now incarcerated. Perhaps now, some might have hoped, the tight-lipped and still-defiant Volstad might finally find his tongue and talk.

"Justice delayed is justice denied," the learned jurists of old might have said, and most might certainly have upheld it as a stark truth even in our present times. Carefully sequestered in only cold comfort, the fell villain sat with anger in a small retention cell under close guard in a post-arraignment setting as he awaited trial. The sinister Village Ripper would soon spend his long days and nights in dark solitude without contact with others. No cellmates, no interactions, no social intercourse with any, save that of his attorney, the prison officials, and the odd occasional police investigator who might still seek to interrogate him to perhaps pry but a minor truth or two from his careless lips.

Now, over the slow course of time and the man's elliptical objections, it had finally come to light in his conversations with case detectives that he had had strong family ties to the Baltic states, a region of southern Europe. An area just east of the Italy boot on a map of the world, it was a region that was landlocked on its far eastern edge and hemmed in by the vast Adriatic on its other. And for most of the formative years of his life, a small coastal port city called *Pula* would have been his only home.

Slowly, then, did an even greater backstory emerge and at last take shape for the several investigators who were still each seeking their simple answers, a truth that would, soon enough, rear its ugly head with a tragic tale that could only have come on the heels of the death of both parents at an early age.

Volstad the child had been orphaned at precisely a time when he'd seen only six summers and winters of his youthful life, a child too young to be without its mother and father, and a youth too soon to be left alone by himself.

It must also, therefore, have been a sufferer's tale of woe and abandonment, a sullen time of waywardness with no direction which to even guide the young lad along his cruel, untutored path. And so, the tale had begun to unravel slowly, with apprehension and sharp defiance that could only continue to spit in the face of sanity and reason. He was a sheep of never and a child of none.

Upon his better reflection—and under a strict court order to do so—the accused would stand the pale of psychiatric evaluation and endless psychological testing, all, indeed, to find out just what made this man tick. And even sleep deprivation and hypnosis had also come into play, which had finally allowed him to remember much of his wretched past as a time in which he'd been raised by a paternal grandfather, a barbarous and abusive man named Evon Dragić.

The Volstad had even learned to live with the still-murky images of an intolerant, cruel, and hateful old man ever stalking about in his head. An angry man who saw no good in anything he observed, with a cold Midas touch that had ever run quite in reverse of any conversion of gold. And indeed, the old guardian had soon come to fully despise the taxing new responsibilities that had come with the custody of the young boy and the very weight of having such a charge. Much as he had also come to hate the willful and unruly waif that had brought that very hardship upon him, and the very agony of it would torment the old grandfather's soul thereafter.

In his prime as a young man, Dragić had been compelled to run away in the early 1940s, and as a young man, had almost, overnight, volunteered for a deployment in the military that saw him quickly pressed into service and moving off to the north, away from his native homeland in far, far *Pula*. He had himself been a transplant from some Soviet satellite state early on in his own life, then an arrogant and swaggering man of oft too many words, a barbarian drunkard and a brawler of the worst order even then. One who had ever been boastful of his conscription and glorious service during his military years in his wild forays to the north and fighting well for Mother Russia.

In fact, it had been that same service then that would later find him at the tip of the spear of the push and slow encirclement of Berlin by the Russians just at the end of World War II, as part of the Soviet dagger thrust deep into the German homeland. An emboldened Red Army had savagely battled on, grappling its way forward, town by town and street by street, into a city in ruins, soon sacking the landmark Reichstag and arriving at the gates of hell, as they saw it—Brandenburg. And the year was 1945.

So proud had he been to be a part of the fierce Second Guards Tank Army—with the good General Semyon Bogdanov as the Soviet marshal heading that very offensive—even as the dread unit advanced to only thirty miles outside the last German stronghold: Berlin. And the now-bitter old man had been there for it all. Wounded twice in battle, just at the gates of the city, the younger Dragić had nonetheless been lauded for his actions and awarded the coveted Gold Star medal as a hero of the Soviet Union, one of the highest honors his country could afford its soldier-citizens.

Only then had he returned home to a place that seemed to welcome him not, with many meeting him with only gruff fanfare and a cool, uninspiring reception. Dragić had returned to an empty house and the impoverished scratch of a day-to-day life that seemed to be taking him nowhere and always with the prospect of an only bleaker tomorrow.

Only then he'd also been saddled with the unwelcome burden of the headstrong youth, this same Bogdan Volstad that had, much against his will, been forced upon him and placed in his charge, however reluctantly and unwanted.

As he returned from his own dark years of war, Dragić's depression was quick and all-consuming, seemingly finding no real bottom, being at once deep-seated and immediate. Now with an even deeper resentment of the dire circumstance that will or nil had been thrust upon him, the man's anger had soon carefully been honed to a knife's point and a razor's edge, and much of that with only an ill intent. And so soon enough, indeed, he'd turn that same rage directly at the needy little sleeve wipe of a child who had now become the very target of his discontent.

Frustrated and turned away from job after job due to his several war injuries, the disabled veteran was compelled to only cripple by on a hardscrabble life, and so slowly came to hate the child that had brought much, if not all of it, upon him. The beatings and the psychological abuse had begun almost immediately—and had sustained and fed upon itself much thereafter—and all of it almost always targeting the poor child, chiding him as the very head and spring of all of his fretful woes. The physical cigarette burnings would continue into the lad's teen years but would leave both mental and physical scars for the rest of his life. No wonder he so despised the man, even to the present time.

Now a man of his standing in his wretched adulthood, this very reprobate—this same criminal, Bogdan Volstad—must himself have been much the worse for wear, having escaped the insanity of his formative years with Dragić and the man's ruthless, unbroken control.

In later years, now living well in the shadow of his manhood, had he become his own evil Dragić of a sort, a very demon who found himself deeply troubled with life and with love, or simply lack thereof. Slowly then had Volstad morphed into an angry and embittered man, now but an imp of fame and a cruel, a man whose own name might somehow condemn him and tie him to his very past, even to his grandfather's cobweb memories of his martial exploits with the heroic General Bogdanov, considered by many as a man of brave exploit, much at a time when the brave exploit was precisely what was needed.

Volstad had conveniently blocked out much of it from his memory—the father figure, the Great War, and Dragić's own past—but he could still also sift through the chaff and rubble and easily recall the dark hours of squalor, the years of living in abject poverty with a bitter and enfeebled old man who truly never wanted him there imprimis. There had ever only been loathing and deep hostility, never any measure of love in their relationship, only brutality and beatings instead of calm and loving correction.

And so, he'd come to hate the old man with a sharp vehemence, much in perpetuity, as all manner of hardship and abuse had been visited upon him over the course of his early life. And all of it—ALL of it without seeming relief or relent. Thus, slowly, with the dull passage of time with surety, his dislike of the brutish parental figure he'd come to so detest had become almost transferential even to others. To those that might only *remind* him of the old man, this monster of a grandfather, even to an extent that would now mandate an elimination of others in a bloody effigy of those within that same age bracket, but who could ever fully fathom why. The man had already gone insane and didn't even know it, understanding only that something must be done to remedy an already untenable situation, such as it was at the time.

And thus, even at the tender age of seventeen did he simply find solace in a sharp knife and a serrated edge, and at night cut the old man's throat from ear to ear. Then he sat down and reveled serenely in his deed as he dined on *pinca, kielbasa,* and *Istrian stew,* regretting nothing. And by first light was he already gone, long before authorities had even found the body or even stumbled heavily upon the scene.

❧❧❧

And yet, all this he remembered even now as he sat languishing poorly in a stifling hole of hell in a New York detention center that was already called "The Tombs" in lower Manhattan, still only days after his trial. In his ears still rang the sharp sting and condemning report brought on by the very laundry list of charges being read home and adjudicated by the court in full:

"Criminal Court, Part 37 is now in session. The Honorable Tyler Ambrose presiding. Will the defendant and counsel please rise?

"In the matter of, and relating to, the platform one charge for an indictment on one count of murder in the first degree with premeditation in the death of one Martin Tabor, how does the jury find?"

Then the anonymous face and frosted voice of the jury foreperson rung out across the hush of the courtroom.

"Your Honor, on the single count of murder in the first degree with premeditation, we the jury find the defendant guilty."

"On a single charge on a second count of murder in the first degree with premeditation in the death of one Paul Novaks, how do you find?"

"Your Honor, on the count two charge of murder in the first degree with premeditation, we the jury find the defendant guilty."

"On a count three charge of murder with premeditation in the death of one Anton Chapel, how does the jury find?"

"We find the defendant guilty, Your Honor."

"On a count four charge of murder with premeditation in the death of one Elon Strunk, how do you find?

"On a count five charge of murder with premeditation in the death of one Carlton Enders, how does the jury find?

"In the premeditated death of one Maxwell J. Kirwin?

"In the premeditated death of one Cranston Bruner?

"In the premeditated death of one Dr. Malcolm Dollarhyde, how does the jury find?"

"Your Honor, the jury finds the defendant guilty of all capital murder charges as specified."

Then a general hush and low murmur fell over the court, sharply accented by the staccato rapping of the adjudicator's gavel and block, which quickly seemed to bring the room back to some semblance of order.

Then the well-regarded Judge Ambrose resumed his query after a decidedly pregnant pause. This trial was still not over, and soon it was time for the court to read its roll of even lesser charges that were also being brought against the defendant by trial counsel.

"In the matter of the People versus Bogdan Volstad on a class B platform of multiple violent felony charges for attempted murder in the second degree with premeditation, as specified below:

(1) "On a charge of felony attempted murder in the second degree, in the shootings at a West Fourth Street commercial restaurant venue on a duly-appointed officer of the law in Manhattan County in the City of New York, how do you find?"

"We the impaneled jury find the defendant Bogdan Volstad guilty of a charge of felony attempted murder in the shooting on West Fourth Street, as specified and upheld by the court."

(2) "On a charge of felony attempted murder in the second degree, in the shooting attempt on an unrelated civilian at a West Fourth Street commercial restaurant venue in Manhattan County in the City of New York, how do you find?"

"We the jury find the defendant Bogdan Volstad guilty of a charge of felony attempted murder in the shooting on West Fourth Street, as specified and upheld by the court."

(3) "On a charge of felony attempted murder in the second degree, in the shooting attempt of a duly-appointed officer of the law at a residential venue on Broome Street in Manhattan County in the City of New York, how do you find?"

"We the jury find the defendant Bogdan Volstad guilty of a charge of felony attempted murder in the shooting on Broome Street, as specified and upheld by the court."

(4) "On a charge of felony attempted murder in the second degree, in the shooting attempt of an unrelated civilian at a residential venue on Broome Street in Manhattan County in the City of New York, how do you find?"

"We the jury find the defendant Bogdan Volstad guilty of a charge of felony attempted murder in the shooting on Broome Street, as specified and upheld by the court."

(5) "On a felony charge of reckless endangerment in the discharge of a weapon in a public venue at a West Fourth Street commercial restaurant venue in Manhattan County in the City of New York, how do you find?"

"We the jury find the defendant Bogdan Volstad guilty of a charge of felony reckless endangerment in the shooting on West Fourth Street, as specified and upheld by the court."

The foreperson's decided response was again equally taut and severe in tone, a condemning scowl on the speaker's face almost pointing up the very contempt most in the hushed courtroom must have had for the man who'd already been accused of so many heinous capital crimes, one after the other.

"Your Honor, after due consideration, we the impaneled jury find the defendant guilty of ALL felony charges as specified and upheld by the court."

And there an end, this even as a bevy of burly bailiffs brusquely brought the convicted man to his feet and hustled him out of the courtroom. He had never once shown a single measure of remorse for any of his heinous deeds, never once casting a backward glance over his shoulder as he was led out in shackles to his new life.

☙❧☙

And when all had cleared, the cell and left old "Zek the Prisoner" alone with only his fear and engorged anger to stand him by at the ebb of the night—much to his misery—Volstad most felt the stunting solitude and dulling the pain of isolation.

Then would come the steeped and chilling darkness only too soon upon him, then would sit his fiendish sins and vilest deeds upon his wretched soul with weight, settling now with a foul, arresting stench and gifting him only with a rambling parade of his evil workings, and all of it dancing over and over in his head, rudely showcasing a past drenched entirely in pain and curdling blood.

Now would enter the killing urges in full, the remembrances of both the deeds and the many souvenirs he'd withheld so closely for his recall and grim enjoyment. And all of it enhanced well by the sharp pictographic images he held in his mind for each of the symbolic killings and all of it with the sharpest of focus: from Novaks to Kirwin and from Bruner to Tabor and beyond, even to the prudish Dr. Dollarhyde.

Now, would the Volstad spend his nights with dormancy and damp tremor, his warped mind fluttering through his series of blood-soaked dreams, with him remembering and mirroring all—just like old Jack himself—such that had by now become so all-consuming for him. And much of it he still saw with the stunning clarity of the mind's eye in grim retrospect ... even alone and in the dark.

All this he thought as he found himself still grumbling his words of defiance almost aloud, saying, "No, they shall not have me—no—never alive. By this hand, I will not be held over for their rude judgment and contrived amusement that might surely come with their enforcing prosecution."

Darkly did the villain lowly hiss at his solitude in very darkness, not certain of his next move and perhaps not even knowing that he already knew what must be. "I see your way, I see your end: a mockery of a trial and a stern and unforgiving sentence just ahead of me, with all of it looming bleakly on the near horizon. A quick and unforgiving trial is what I see, old Zek reasoned darkly to himself, such that of its very nature can only serve as my very undoing."

With a prickly impatience did he now pace his cell in quiet reflection, unsure of what to do or when. He was a man seeking answers and a miscreant still searching for a final moment of defiance, hoping to find a trace of resolve to orchestrate his only endgame, such that would be the answer to all his woe and worry. But for now, he could only measure the cell with his very footsteps, decidedly with quiet stamina, tweaking a long handlebar mustache and clasping hands close behind his back as he ever sought his most workable answer.

He was an outcast and a felon now only seeking his best moment for the ultimate act he was poised to commit even now and seeking to somehow resolve an otherwise untenable situation. Perhaps now, he could finally put an end to all of his fears and concerns and find a way out.

But it might, in fact, already have been clear that he had none ... but yet, he regretted nothing. "I will not give them the satisfaction of my full defeat," the Volstad had said as he spat into a corner of the room and punched his fist into the palm of his other hand.

"None shall ever know my secrets and none can ever know of my secret life," he thought retributively to himself. "All the lives and all the knives I've known, but in the end, I shall win out against these fools and bunglers. And in that very winning, I shall be dead by morning."

In a small six-by-nine-by-twelve cell, therefore, with molded furniture and a cold, cold slab for a bed, the evil murderer did what he had always done best. He'd found the easy way out—the way of least resistance—finding instead refuge in a stranded bedsheet strung tightly about the neck from a metal bedpost.

His would be only the second such tortuous death by like circumstance since the dubious suicide of the highly publicized sex trafficker in the New York case of August 2019, such that would, once again, raise the eyebrows of the few and cause the many to sit up and take note.

And in the morning, indeed, when the killer was found hanged by his hand in his cell, it had only been the third week of the man's greater incarceration. Who then might not be impressed by the almost delicious irony of it all—how perhaps one of the most sinister of villains had found his circuitous means of escaping an almost-certain death penalty verdict in an otherwise no-death-penalty state. Which dark sentence might at any time have been handed down by a court that seemed to be struggling to simply understand it all, still with a mountain of evidentiary material that ran a mile?

Perhaps, it might finally help to piece it all together to understand the full depth and scope of the man's most heinous deeds—the seemingly random murder of eight unsuspecting victims. But were they all, in fact, only random hits? And precisely how many had the slasher truly killed? Might there have been others? And what, indeed, might be said of the man's very trigger point, the black impetus and prodding motive that might have started it all imprimis, and all of it only circuitously culminating in the only underlying premise to be had—WHY?

And at its most unceremonious outset, the man thought to have been the Village Ripper had escaped death by simply welcoming it into his life by his hand. And with dying breath and a certain curious trick of disobedience in his eye, he never would find a way to reconcile himself with the facts and deadly deeds of his bloody past, never revealing the whys or wherefores of any of it, other than his unreasoned hatred of his grandfather.

Odd then that in the end, he would have given them nothing, but had instead been moved to simply take all with him, all of it culminating in a sick and festering truth that he would not be taken alive, or if he were, that he would be dead by morning. The Slasher had withheld all of his murky secrets and had spoken to none, save that which was said to himself in his steep seclusion as he muttered darkly in his cell to none but himself: DEAR BOSS, *catch me if you can ...*

EPILOGUE: A DELICIOUS EVIL

11 NOVEMBER

If at all the police takedown of the nefarious Bogdan Volstad had brought about a city-wide sigh of relief and had even been a kind of cause célèbre, the people were still not collectively inclined to entirely drop their guards. The city had seemingly shrugged off its mantle of fear, and gone now were the fearful over-the-shoulder second glances to warily check your six behind one's every step. And much, indeed, had returned to normal, one would have thought, or as normal as life could be in the aftermath of the spate of brutal killings. Or so it must have seemed. It was, after all, a story they'd all seen and heard before.

And yet, a seething evil still seemed to lurk in the early evening shadows of the city. And inasmuch as the capture of the criminal himself had become a matter of some considerable backslapping and interdepartmental glad-handing for a job well done, the very air of congratulatory salute was still dampened by the killer's later unexpected suicide in the dungeon tombs of one of New York's correctional facilities.

It had been a sharp slap in the face that most had not seen coming and for which few had even prepared. The Volstad had succeeded in taking his own life and cheating the hangman of his duty and his due redress. And with a halting gait and a still-knotted stomach, an uneasy city might finally see light at the end of its darkest tunnel.

But now, only nights later and blocks north and west of that very prison cell, on yet another gloomy, ill-lit backstreet of old Greenwich Village, another old man would trudge by, steadied only by a cane and his sheer will to trudge along and get back to his own small West Village flat as he lumbered home through a mist of light rain to a cold supper in some musty prewar apartment on the far western side of Bleecker.

Approaching a now closed-down Hudson Street, the old man ambled absently past the darkened doorways of the many shuttered stores and shops along his way, still driven by his dull pangs of hunger and an even greater wish to simply get out of the rain. And in truth, he was thinking of all but truly seeing nothing.

Then a sinewy arm and a gloved hand reached out from a place of darkness and pulled the man roughly back into the blind recess of a doorway. A sharp glint of the blade and a brutal swipe across the throat—once, twice. Then the body slumped under its very own weight and fell with a muffled thump to the ground. And few would even see the cloaked and hooded figure slinking away, escaping off down the street in a scurrying haze and turning the nearest corner. And in an instant, the slasher was gone, off again on another tear and bloody hunt, preparing perhaps for his next prey in a city full of victims from which to choose and delight in.

"Dear Boss," the shadowy villain almost cackled to himself with a dark exhilaration and a delicious evil. The fools had caught the wrong man and didn't even know it yet. But soon enough perhaps they would, as yet another hooded shadow shivered its way over the dark streets and melted away down the boulevard.

So, catch me if you can...